George Mackay Brown (1921–96) was one of the twentieth century's most distinguished and original writers. His lifelong inspiration and birthplace, Stromness in Orkney, moulded his view of the world, though he studied in Edinburgh at Newbattle Abbey College, where he met Edwin Muir, and later at Moray House College of Education. In 1941 he was diagnosed with pulmonary tuberculosis and lived an increasingly reclusive life in Stromness, but he produced, in spite of his poor health, a regular stream of publications from 1954 onwards. These included *The Storm* (1954), *Loaves and Fishes* (1959), *A Calendar of Love* (1967), *A Time to Keep* (1969), *Greenvoe* (1972), *Hawkfall* (1974), *Time in a Red Coat* (1984) and, notably, the novel *Beside the Ocean of Time* (1994), which was shortlisted for the Booker Prize and won the Saltire Book of the Year.

His work is permeated by the layers of history in Scotland's past, by quirks of human nature and religious belief, and by a fascination with the world beyond the horizons of the known.

He was honoured by the Open University and by the Universities of Dundee and Glasgow. The enduringly successful St Magnus Festival of poetry, prose, music and drama, held annually in Orkney, is his lasting memorial.

TITLES BY GEORGE MACKAY BROWN
AVAILABLE FROM POLYGON

NOVELS
Greenvoe
Magnus
Time in a Red Coat
The Golden Bird
Vinland
Beside the Ocean of Time

SHORT STORIES
Simple Fire: Selected Short Stories

NON-FICTION
An Orkney Tapestry

POETRY
Carve the Runes: Selected Poems

AUTOBIOGRAPHY
For the Islands I sing

GEORGE MACKAY BROWN

Simple Fire:
Selected Short Stories

Edited by
Malachy Tallack

This selection published in Great Britain in 2021 by
Polygon, an imprint of Birlinn Ltd

Birlinn Limited
West Newington House
10 Newington Road
Edinburgh EH9 1QS

9 8 7 6 5 4 3 2 1

www.polygonbooks.co.uk

'The Story of Jorkel Hayforks', 'Five Green Waves' and 'Witch' were first published
in *A Calendar of Love* (The Hogarth Press, 1967); 'A Treading of Grapes', 'Celia',
'The Wireless Set' and 'The Eye of the Hurricane' were first published in *A Time
to Keep* (The Hogarth Press, 1969); 'Sealskin', 'The Cinquefoil' and 'The Tarn and
the Rosary' were first published in *Hawkfall* (The Hogarth Press,1974); 'A Winter
Tale' and 'The Seven Poets' were first published in *The Sun's Net* (The Hogarth
Press, 1976); 'Andrina' and 'The Day of the Ox' were first published in *Andrina*
(The Hogarth Press, 1983); 'The Masked Fisherman' and 'The Christmas Dove'
were first published in *The Masked Fisherman* (John Murray, 1989); 'Dancey'
and 'Shell Story' were first published in *Winter Tales* (John Murray, 1995)

ISBN 978 1 84697 517 2
eBook ISBN 978 1 78885 468 9

British Library Cataloguing-in-Publication Data
A catalogue record for this book is available from the British Library

Typeset by Hewer Text UK Ltd, Edinburgh
Printed and bound in Great Britain by Clays Ltd, Elcograf S.p.A.

Contents

Introduction   vii

from *A Calendar of Love* (1967)
- THE STORY OF JORKEL HAYFORKS   1
- FIVE GREEN WAVES   10
- WITCH   27

from *A Time to Keep* (1969)
- A TREADING OF GRAPES   44
- CELIA   58
- THE WIRELESS SET   95
- THE EYE OF THE HURRICANE   102

from *Hawkfall* (1974)
- SEALSKIN   129
- THE CINQUEFOIL   154
- THE TARN AND THE ROSARY   187

from *The Sun's Net* (1976)
- A WINTER TALE   227
- THE SEVEN POETS   257

from *Andrina* (1983)
- ANDRINA   268
- THE DAY OF THE OX   278

from *The Masked Fisherman* (1989)

THE MASKED FISHERMAN   283
THE CHRISTMAS DOVE   292

from *Winter Tales* (1995)

DANCEY   296
SHELL STORY   322

Introduction

In George Mackay Brown's short story 'The Eye of the Hurricane', a young writer, Mr Barclay, has travelled to Orkney to flee a love affair gone wrong, and to complete his novel about Saint Rögnvald Kolson, the twelfth-century earl of the isles. Once there, however, Barclay becomes embroiled in the tumultuous decline of his landlord, Captain Stevens, a man overcome by alcoholism and by grief. For the captain, there is no escaping from his losses. Towards the end of this story, when the storm of that decline has finally passed over, Barclay reflects on the limitations of his writing. 'Love is too deep a subject for prose,' he thinks, 'only music and poetry can build bridges between the rage of the seed in the furrow, the coupling of beasts, the passions of man and woman, the saint's prayer. Seed and beast and saint are touched with simple fire.'

Though the thoughts of a character should not be ascribed to its author, this expression of doubt about what fiction can do seems to me to illuminate something in Brown's own literary endeavours. George Mackay Brown wrote fiction with the humility and creative latitude of someone who was never completely certain that the form was up to the job. He wrote fiction that, in its rhythms, in its taut, glinting language, aspired towards poetry. He wrote fiction that, again and again, kindled that 'simple fire' on the page.

Brown's stories could not be mistaken for those of any other author. His prose is so distinctive, in style and in subject matter, that it seems as distant from the work of his late-twentieth century contemporaries as his Orkney home was distant from the literary centres of the day. Though he read widely, and maintained friendships and correspondences with many other writers, Brown saw himself less a part of any Scottish 'scene' or Anglo-American tradition, and more the descendant of one specific – and specifically *local* – book.

The *Orkneyinga Saga*, written anonymously in Iceland in the thirteenth century, recounts the history and legends of the Norse earls of Orkney and Shetland over the preceding four hundred years. Brown read this chronicle first as a teenager, and would return to it throughout his life. The story of Earl Magnus, killed on the orders of his cousin Haakon, and later sanctified, provided particular inspiration. The 'violent beauty' of that event, Brown wrote, would 'form the backdrop to much of the narrative and verse that I have written.'

What he found in the pages of the saga – in addition to the stories themselves – was a well of symbols and allusions, a sense of deep narrative time, and a terse musicality that would become the backbone of his own prose. And while that spare, straightforward style was embellished, to varying degrees, with what he called 'elaborate decoration', in their clarity and directness, in the way they welcome mystery, these stories all owe something to the sagas.

Another influence, easily detected, is the rich oral culture of the Northern Isles. But it is not just the myths and folktales of Orkney that are evident – though these do make some explicit appearances, as in 'Sealskin'. Rather, it was the language of the pub and the street corner that Brown most cherished. It was the storytelling of gossips and drunks, of sailors on leave and of friends gathered around a hearth. He knew how significant such exchanges could be, how the stories people shared were part of what held a community together, both in the present and over time.

But he understood, too, the darker side of those exchanges. Stories could be used to exclude people, to push them out. They could be their own kind of violence, and could lead, at times, to worse. This is what happens in 'Witch', from his first collection, *A Calendar of Love*. There, malicious gossip has become a death sentence.

It is striking, in fact, reading these stories, that despite Brown's insistence on Orkney as the absolute centre of his world, despite island communities serving as both the subject and setting of nearly all of his short fiction, the characters on which he focused are as often as not situated on the *fringes* of those communities. They are ministers, teachers and doctors, arrived from elsewhere; they are children, loners, alcoholics or 'tinkers'; they are as much apart from as a part.

This distance serves a narrative purpose, of course. It allows these characters certain perspectives that might not be available to those closer to the heart of the community. But it reflects also, I think, a certain outsiderness in Brown himself, a sense that – as a writer, as a Catholic convert, as the son of a mother from mainland Scotland – he was always just slightly towards the edge of the place he loved so much. Exacerbated perhaps by a lifetime of poor health, which kept him from a job and from any kind of physical exertion, Brown was an embedded observer, alert always to the tensions between community and individual.

The stories in this selection are set across a period of well over two thousand years, from a reimagining of the Nativity in 'The Christmas Dove', to a post-apocalyptic future in 'The Seven Poets'. Few writers drift so easily across the ages, and few, surely, are so conscious of the past as an ongoing presence, of the weight that what-has-been still bears on what-is-now.

Yet, while the bulk of these stories take place in the past – most of them in the century or so leading up to the time of Brown's writing – they could not accurately be labelled 'historical fiction'. That genre deals in specificity, in the evocation of a particular time, while these tales are more concerned with summoning *essence*. The past they inhabit, most often, is identifiable only approximately, as it is in legends or fables. Brown usually resists the kind of details that anchor a story precisely in a particular period; and when they do occur, these anchors can seem jarring. They can land the reader somewhere unexpected.

'Celia', for instance, from the 1969 collection *A Time to Keep*, may seem, at first, to be set in the late nineteenth century, or perhaps the early twentieth. There is a darkness to it, a lamplit gloom that belongs to a previous age. But then, in an extraordinary outpouring of anguish that comes halfway through the story, Celia situates herself not in the past at all, but as Brown's own contemporary. As she justifies her drinking and her atheism to Mr Blackie, the minister, she summons grief at her own losses, and a generalised horror at life's injustice. But she also expresses rage at what is happening elsewhere, at the war then underway across the world. 'The country folk in Viet Nam,' [sic] she shouts, 'what kind of vice is it they're gripped in, guns and lies and anger on both sides of them, a slow tightening agony? Is your God looking after them?' It is a startling moment, exceptional in Brown's fiction for a number of reasons (including, it has to be said, the fact that female characters are rarely given centre stage in this way).

Brown found the expansiveness he required through time rather than through space. Orkney, for him, was never restrictive. 'There are stories in the air here,' he wrote in his memoir, *For the Islands I Sing*. 'If I lived to be five hundred, there would still be more to write.' Reaching back as he did he found 'rhythms of land and sea' that brought 'a pattern and a harmony' to all of his work. He identified threads of continuity that held the islands together through the ages, and he wove them into his words. It was an unending attunement and fidelity to place.

For Brown, I think, that fidelity was hardly a choice at all. He felt no particular urge to travel, and indeed for much of his life seems to have been positively repelled by the idea of leaving home. But for his readers, the devotion to Orkney as inspiration offers a depth of focus rarely found in literature. The islands are revealed and reimagined, over and over. Layers of time are peeled back and lifted to the light. The effect is cumulative: the place expands, gradually, beneath his gaze. This is truly a *body* of work, a lifetime's project.

In 'The Eye of the Hurricane', the writer Mr Barclay imagines the loves of those around him, in his memory and his imagination, 'caught up in their true order, and simplified and reconciled'. To me, these stories, too, seem caught in the orbit of something bigger than themselves, some point of gravity from which their energy and order derives. They turn, each of them, and 'move about it forever like the quiet stars'.

Acknowledgements

The editor would like to thank Dr Linden Bicket for her invaluable advice during the selecting of these stories.

The Story of Jorkel Hayforks

The week before midsummer Jorkel and six others took ship at Bergen in Norway and sailed west two days with a good wind behind them. They made land at Whalsay in Shetland and were well entertained at a farm there by a man called Veig. After they had had supper one of Jorkel's men played the harp and recited some verses. The name of this poet was Finn.

As soon as Finn had sat down, Brenda, the daughter of Veig the Shetlander, came to her father and said, 'Offer Finn a horse and a piece of land, so that he will be pleased to stay here.'

Veig made the offer to Finn, but Finn said, 'We are sailing to Orkney on a certain urgent matter in the morning. I can't stay.'

Veig repeated Finn's remark to Brenda.

At midnight, when the men were drinking round the fire, Brenda rose out of bed and said to her father Veig, 'I can't get to sleep. Offer Finn a gold arm-band and a silver ring to stay here in Shetland.'

Veig called Finn aside and made this offer. Finn said, 'I am a poor man and a happy man, and gold and women would distract me from the making of verses. Besides, we have an appointment to keep in Orkney on midsummer day.'

Veig told Brenda what Finn had said.

At dawn, though the ale keg was empty, the men were still sitting at the fire. Some of them were lying under the benches drunk, but Finn was discussing metres with the Shetlanders. 'I would argue better,' said Finn, 'if I was not so dry.'

Soon after that Brenda came in and offered Finn a cup of ale.

With the froth still wet on his beard, Finn turned to Brenda and said, 'Did you brew this ale, woman?' Brenda said that she alone had made it. Then Finn said, 'On account of this ale I will stay for a while with you here in Shetland.'

Then the sun got up and the Norwegians stirred themselves and went on board their ship. But Finn was nowhere to be found, and the door of Brenda's room was barred. Jorkel was very angry about that.

They say that Finn made no more poems after that day. Brenda bore him twelve children. He died there in Shetland before there was a grey hair in his beard. He was drunk most days till his death, and he would drink from no cup but Brenda's. He was totally dependent on her always. It was thought rather a pity that such a promising poet should make such an ordinary end.

'She bewitched him, that bitch,' said Jorkel.

*

In the afternoon of the same day, Jorkel's ship reached Fair Isle. They saw some sheep on a hillside there. Flan, who was a blacksmith back in Norway, said they were fine sheep. 'And my wife,' said he, 'will be looking for a present from the west. I will bring her a fleece from Fair Isle.'

Before they could stop Flan he leapt overboard and swam ashore. The sheep were grazing at the edge of a high cliff. Flan climbed up this face, disturbing the sea birds that were there, and laid hands on the first sheep he saw. He was raising his axe to despatch the ewe when another sheep ran terrified between his legs and toppled him over the edge of the crag, so that the sea birds were wildly agitated for the second time that day.

'Flan's descent is much quicker than his going up,' said Jorkel. 'What does a blacksmith know about shepherding?'

They anchored that night under the cliffs of Fair Isle.

*

They left Fair Isle at dawn and had a rough crossing to the Orkneys. There was a strong wind from the east and the sea fell into the ship in cold grey lumps, so that they were kept busy with the bailing pans.

Then Mund who had a farm east in Sweden laid down his bailing pan.

He said, 'I have made deep furrows in the land with my plough but I did not believe there could be furrows in the world like this.'

The men went on bailing.

Later Mund said, 'When Grettir lay dying in his bed at Gothenburg last summer his face was like milk. Is my face that colour?'

Jorkel said his face was more of a green colour, and urged the men to bail all the harder, since now Mund was taking no part in the game.

At noon Mund said, 'I was always a gay man at midsummer, but I do not expect to be dancing round a Johnsmas fire this year.'

The men went on bailing, until presently the wind shifted into the north and moderated, so that they were able to cook a meal of stewed rabbit and to open a keg of ale.

But when they brought the meat and ale to Mund, they found him lying very still and cold against a thwart.

'Mund will not be needing dinner any more,' said Jorkel.

*

They reached Papa Westray soon after that. There were some decent farms in the island, and an ale-house near the shore, and a small monastery with a dozen bald-headed brothers beside a loch.

The people of the island gave them a hospitable welcome, and sold them fish and mutton, and showed them where the best wells were.

The twelve brothers trooped into the church for vespers.

After the necessary business of victualling had been transacted, the Norwegians went into the ale-house to drink.

They played draughts and sang choruses so long as there was ale in the barrel. Then, when the keeper of the ale-house was opening a new barrel, Jorkel noticed that Thord was missing.

'He will have gone after the women of Papa Westray,' said Sweyn. Thord was known to be a great lecher back home in Norway.

The church bell rang for compline.

There was some fighting in the ale-house when they were midway through the second barrel, but by that time they were too drunk to hurt each other much. When things had quietened down, Jorkel remarked that Thord was still absent.

'No doubt he is stealing eggs and cheese, so that we can vary our diet on the ship,' said Valt. Thord was a famous thief on the hills of southern Norway, when it was night and everyone was sitting round the fires inside and there was no moon.

They went on drinking till the lights of yesterday and tomorrow met in a brief twilight and their senses were reeling with ale and fatigue.

'This is a strange voyage,' said Jorkel. 'It seems we are to lose a man at every station of the way.'

They heard the bell of the church ringing. Jorkel went to the door of the ale-house. Thirteen hooded figures passed under the arch to sing matins.

Jorkel returned to the ale-barrel and said, 'It seems that Thord has repented of his drinking and whoring and thieving. Yesterday there were twelve holy men in Papa Westray. This morning I counted thirteen.'

He lay down beside his companions, and they slept late into the morning.

*

Now there were only three men on the ship, Jorkel and Sweyn and Valt.

'We will not stop until we reach Hoy,' said Jorkel. 'Every time we stop there is one kind of trouble or another.'

They were among the northern Orkneys now, sailing through a wide firth with islands all around.

It turned out that none of the three knew where exactly Hoy was.

Sweyn said, 'There is a man in that low island over there. He has a mask on and he is taking honey from his hives. I will go ashore and ask him where Hoy is.'

'Be careful,' said Jorkel. 'We will have difficulty in getting to Hoy if there are only two of us left to work the ship.'

Sweyn waded ashore and said to the bee-keeper, 'Be good enough to tell us how we can recognise the island of Hoy.'

The man took off his mask and replied courteously that they would have to sail west between the islands until they reached the open ocean, and then keeping the coast of Hrossey on the port side and sailing south they would see in the distance two blue hills rising out of the sea. These blue hills were Hoy.

Sweyn thanked him and asked if he was getting plenty of honey.

The man replied that it was a bad year for honey. The bees had been as dull as the weather.

'Still,' the bee-keeper said, 'the next comb I take from the hive will be a gift for you.'

Sweyn was deeply touched by the courtesy and kindness of the bee-keeper.

It happened that as the man was bending over the hive, a bee came on the wind and settled on his neck and stung him.

The bee-keeper gave a cry of annoyance and shook off the bee.

Sweyn was angry at the way the insects repaid with ingratitude the gentleness of the Orkney bee-keeper. He suddenly brought his axe down on the hive and clove it in two.

Jorkel and Valt were watching from the ship, and they saw Sweyn run screaming round the island with a cloud of bees after him. It was as if he was being pelted with hot sharp sonorous hail stones.

Sweyn ran down into the ebb and covered himself with seaweed.

When Jorkel and Valt reached him, he told them where Hoy was. Then his face turned blind and blue and swollen and he died.

*

Jorkel and Valt got horses at a farm called the Bu in Hoy and rode between the two hills till they came to a place called Rackwick. There was a farm there and five men were working in the hayfield. It was a warm bright day, and the faces of the labourers shone with sweat.

Jorkel asked them if a man called Arkol lived nearby.

'Arkol is the grieve at this farm,' said one of the labourers, 'but he often sleeps late.'

'We work in the daytime,' said another, 'but Arkol does most of his labouring at night.'

'Arkol is a great man for the women,' said a third, and winked.

Jorkel said he thought that would be the man they were looking for.

Presently the labourers stopped to rest and they invited Jorkel and Valt to share their bread and ale. They sat under a wall where there was shadow and Valt told all that had happened to them from the time they left Bergen. But Jorkel sat quietly and seemed preoccupied. They noticed too that he did not eat or drink much.

'Who is the owner of this farm?' said Valt when he had finished his story of the voyage.

The labourers said the farmer in Rackwick was a man called John. They spoke highly of him. He was a good master to them.

Just then a man with a dark beard crossed the field. He ordered the labourers to resume their work, and then looked suspiciously at Jorkel and Valt. They were rather scruffy and dirty after their voyage.

Jorkel asked him if his name was Arkol Dagson.

The man yawned once or twice and said that it was.

'In that case,' said Jorkel, 'I must tell you that my sister Ingirid in Bergen bore you a son at the beginning of June.'

Arkol made no answer but yawned again. Then he laughed.

'And I want to know,' said Jorkel, 'if you will pay for the fostering of the child.'

Arkol said he would not discuss so intimate a matter with two tramps. So far he had not been in the habit of paying for the fostering of any child that he had fathered, and he doubted whether it was wise to begin now, especially as Norway was so far away. Furthermore, he could hardly be expected to believe the unsupported testimony of two tramps, one of whom claimed to be Ingirid's brother. Ingirid had been a most lovely and gently reared girl, and Arkol did not think the scarecrow standing before him could really be the brother of such a delightful bedmate. Besides, he had been busy all night in another sweet bed, and now he was very tired, and he begged the two gentlemen of the roads to excuse him.

Jorkel said, 'Will you pay now for the fostering of your son?'

Arkol turned away and yawned.

Jorkel drove his dagger into Arkol's throat, so that he fell dead at once on the field.

The labourers jumped down from the haystack and ran at Jorkel and Valt with their forks.

'I wish the others were here now,' said Jorkel as he turned to face them. 'Now I would be glad to have Finn and Flan and Mund and Thord and Sweyn at my side.'

Valt was quickly pronged to death there, and though Jorkel defended himself well and was still on his feet when John of Rackwick appeared on the scene, he was so severely lacerated that he lay between life and death in the farm for more than a week.

The three farm girls looked after him well till he recovered. They hovered around him day and night with oil and sweet water and beeswax.

On the day they took the last bandages from Jorkel's arm, John of Rackwick came to him and said mildly, 'Arkol, my grieve, was in many ways an evil lecherous man, and for that he must answer to a higher lord than the Earl of Orkney or the King of Norway. But also he was a loyal servant of mine, and because of that you must pay me as compensation your ship that is anchored off Selwick. You are welcome to stay here in Hoy, Jorkel, for as long as you like. There is a small vacant croft on the side of the hill that will support a cow and an ox and a few sheep. It will be a tame life for a young man, but now you are disabled because of the hay forks, and if you till your field carefully nothing could be more pleasing to God.'

Jorkel accepted that offer. He lived there at Upland for the rest of his life. In Orkney he was nicknamed 'Hayforks'. He put by a little money each harvest so that one day he would be able to return to Norway, but the years passed and he could never get a passage.

*

The summer before his death Jorkel went to Papa Westray in a fishing boat. At the church there he inquired for Thord, and presently Thord came out to meet him. They were two old men now, bald and toothless. They embraced each other under the arch. They were like two boys laughing to each other over an immense distance, thin affectionate lost voices.

Jorkel took a purse from his belt and counted five pieces of silver into Thord's hand. 'I have been saving this money for forty years,' he said, 'so that some day I could go home to Norway. But it is too late. Who would know me in Bergen now? I should prepare, instead, for the last, longest journey. Will you arrange for Masses to be said in your church for Finn and Flan and Mund and Sweyn and Valt?'

Thord said that Masses would certainly be offered for those dead men and for Jorkel himself too. Then he embraced Jorkel and blessed him. Jorkel turned round. He was at peace. The long silver scars of the hayforks troubled his body no longer.

Half-way to the boat he turned back. He gave Thord another silver coin. 'Say a Mass for Arkol Dagson also,' he said.

They smiled at each other, crinkling their old eyes.

Five Green Waves

I

Time was lines and circles and squares.

'You will go home at once to your father,' said Miss Ingsetter, rapping her desk with a ruler, 'and tell him I sent you, because you have not prepared the mathematics lesson I told you to prepare. Now go!'

A rustle went through the classroom. The pupils looked round at me, wide-eyed. A few made little sorrowing noises with their lips. For it was a terrible punishment. My father was a magnate, a pillar of authority in the island – Justice of the Peace, Kirk Elder, Registrar, Poor Inspector, a member of the Education Committee itself. He was, in addition, the only merchant in the place and kept the shop down by the pier; even before I was born he had decided that his boy would be a credit to him – he would go to the university and become a minister, or a lawyer, or a doctor.

Now, this summer afternoon, while bluebottles like vibrant powered ink-blobs gloried in the windows and the sun came four-square through the burning panes, my stomach turned to water inside me.

'Please, Miss Ingsetter,' I said, 'I'm sorry I didn't learn the theorem. I promise it won't happen again. I would be glad if you punished me yourself.'

The bust of Shelley gazed at me with wild blank eyes.

Her spectacles glinted. Down came the ruler with a snap. 'You will go to your father, now, at once, and tell him of your conduct.'

The bright day fell in ruins about me. I crossed the floor on fluttering bare feet, and was soon outside.

'You, Willie Sinclair,' I heard her shouting through the closed door, 'stand up and give us the theorem of Pythagoras.'

A red butterfly lighted on my hand, clung there for a moment, and went loitering airily across the school garden, now here among the lupins, now there over the flowering potatoes, as if it was drunk with happiness and didn't know on what bright lip to hang next. I watched it till it collapsed over the high wall, a free wind-tipsy flower.

Inside the classroom, the formal wave gathered and broke.

'. . . is equal to the sum of the squares on the other two sides,' concluded Willie Sinclair in a sibilant rush.

'Very good, Willie,' said Miss Ingsetter.

Despised and rejected, I turned for home.

II

The croft of Myers stands beside the road, looking over the Sound, and the hill rises behind it like a swelling green wave. Sophie, a little bent woman, her grey shawl about her head, was throwing seed to the twelve hens.

She smelt me on the wind. 'Hello there,' she cried. I muttered a greeting.

She peered at me. 'And who might you be?' she said.

I told her my name.

'Mercy,' she said, 'but you've grown.'

Our voices had roused the old man inside. He was suddenly at the door, smiling. Peter's face was very red and round. He had been a sailor in his youth. The backs of his hands, and his wrists, smouldered with blue anchors, blue mermaids, blue whales. 'Come in,' he cried.

It was like entering a ship's hold, but for the smells of peat and kirn and girdle. I breathed darkness and fragrance.

They ushered me to the straw chair beside the fire. I had hardly got settled in it when Sophie put a bowl of ale between my hands. The sweet heavy fumes drifted across my nostrils.

Peter sat filling his pipe in the other straw chair. The old woman never rested for an instant. She moved between the fire and the window and the bed, putting things in order. She flicked her duster along the mantelpiece, which was full of tea-caddies and ships in bottles. The collie dog lolled and panted on the flagstones.

'And tell me,' said Peter, 'what way you aren't at school?'

'I got sent home,' I said, 'for not learning the lesson.'

'You must learn your lessons,' said Sophie, setting the fern straight in the tiny window. 'Think what way you'll be in thirty years' time if you don't, a poor ignorant fellow breaking stones in the quarry.'

I took a deep gulp of ale, till my teeth and tongue and palate were awash in a dark seething wave.

'And tell me,' said Peter, 'what will you be when you're big?'

'A sailor,' I said.

'If that wasn't a splendid answer!' cried Peter. 'A sailor. Think of that.'

'My grandfather was a gunner on the *Victory*,' said Sophie. 'He was at Trafalgar. He came home with a wooden leg.'

'That was great days at sea,' said Peter. 'Do you know the ballad of Andrew Ross?'

'No,' I said.

A hen, shaped like a galleon, entered from the road outside. She dipped and swayed round the sleeping dog, and went out again into the sunlight.

'Woman,' said Peter, 'get the squeeze-box.'

Sophie brought a black dumpy cylinder from under the bed, and blew a spurt of dust from it. Peter opened the box and took out a melodeon.

'Listen,' he said. A few preliminary notes as sharp as spray scattered out of the instrument. Then he cleared his throat and began to sing:

> *Andrew Ross an Orkney sailor*
> *Whose sufferings now I will explain*
> *While on a voyage to Barbados,*
> *On board the good ship* Martha Jane.

'That was the name of the ship,' said Sophie, 'the *Martha Jane.*'

'Shut up,' said Peter.

> *The mates and captain daily flogged him*
> *With whips and ropes, I tell you true,*
> *Then on his mangled bleeding body*
> *Water mixed with salt they threw.*

'That's what they used to do in the old days, the blackguards,' said Sophie. 'They would beat the naked backs of the sailors till they were as red as seaweed.'

'Damn it,' said Peter, 'is it you that's reciting this ballad, or is it me?'

> *The captain ordered him to swallow*
> *A thing whereof I shall not name.*
> *The sailors all grew sick with horror*
> *On board the good ship* Martha Jane.

'What was it Andrew Ross had to swallow?' I asked.

'It was too terrible to put in the song,' said Sophie.

'I'll tell you what it was,' said Peter, glaring at me. 'It was *his own dung.*'

The sickness began to work like a yeast in the region of my throat. I took a big swallow of ale to drown it.

Peter sang:

> *When nearly dead they did release him,*
> *And on the deck they did him fling.*
> *In the midst of his pain and suffering*
> *'Let us be joyful,' Ross did sing.*

'He was religious,' said Sophie, 'and the captain was an atheist. That's the way they bad-used him.'

> *The captain swore he'd make him sorry,*
> *And jagged him with an iron bar.*
> *Was not that a cruel treatment*
> *For an honoured British tar!*

The house took a long dizzy lurch to starboard, then slowly righted itself. My knuckles grew white on the edge of the chair. The good ship Myers burrowed again into the fluid hill.

'Mercy,' said Sophie, 'I doubt the boy's too young for a coarse ballad like that.'

> *Justice soon did overtake them*
> *When into Liverpool they came.*
> *They were found guilty of the murder*
> *Committed on the briny main.*

'High time too,' said Sophie. 'The vagabonds!'

Soon the fateful hour arrived
That Captain Rogers had to die,
To satisfy offended justice
And hang on yonder gallows high.

I stood erect on the heaving flagstones. 'Going be sick,' I said.

'The pail!' cried Sophie, 'where's the pail?'

But she was too late. Three strong convulsions went through me, and I spouted thrice. The flagstones were awash. The dog barked. Then the cottage slowly settled on an even keel, and I was sitting in the straw chair, my eyes wet with shame and distress. Not even Andrew Ross's sorrow was like unto my sorrow.

Old Sophie was on her knees with a wet clout and a bucket.

Peter patted me on the shoulder. 'Don't you worry,' he said. 'You're not the first sailor that's been sick on his maiden voyage.'

III

Below the kirkyard the waves stretched long blue necks shoreward. Their manes hissed in the wind, the broken thunder of their hooves volleyed along the beach and echoed far inland among cornfields and peat bogs and trout lochs, and even as far as the quiet group of standing stones at the centre of the island.

I made my way shoreward, walking painfully along a floor of round pebbles. One had to be careful; Isaac of Garth, going home drunk and singing on Saturday nights, was in the habit of smashing his empty bottles on these rocks. He had done it for so many years that the amphitheatre of pebbles above the sand was dense with broken glass – the older fragments worn by the sea to blunt opaque pebbles, the newer ones winking

dangerously in the sun. If one of the sharp pieces scored your
foot, you might easily bleed to death.

There was no one in sight along the wide curve of the
beach, or on the road above. In the kirkyard the grave digger
was up to the hips in a grave he was making for Moll
Anderson, who had died at the weekend.

Quickly and cautiously, under a red rock, I took off my
clothes – first the grey jersey with the glass button at the neck,
next the trousers made out of an old pair of my father's, and
finally the blue shirt. Then I ran down to the sea and fell through
an incoming wave. Its slow cold hammer drove the air out of
my lungs. I thrashed through the water to a rock thirty yards
out and clung to it, gasping and shivering. 'Lord,' I thought,
'suppose Miss Ingsetter or my father saw me now!' A shred of
cloud raced across the sun, and the world plunged in and out of
gloom in a second. And then, for an hour, I was lost in the cry
and tumult of the waves. Shags, dark arrows, soared past my
plunging face. Gulls cut gleaming arcs and circles against the
sky, and traversed long corridors of intense sound. Seals bobbed
up and down like bottles in the Sound, and grew still every now
and then when I whistled. For a brief eternity I was lost in the
cry, the tumult, the salt cleansing ritual of the sea.

The grave digger paused in his work and, shading his eyes
beachward, saw me stumbling out of the waves. He shook his
fist at my nakedness. The sand was as hot as new pancakes
under my feet. I ran wild and shouting up the beach and fell
gasping on my heap of clothes. I lay there for a long time.
From very far away, on the other side of the hill, a dog barked.
The rockpool shimmered in the heat. The music of the gravedigger's spade rang bright and fragile across the field.
Suddenly three words drifted from the rock above me: 'You
naked boy.' I looked up into the face of Sarah, Abraham the
tinker's daughter. She rarely came to school, but whenever

she did she sat like a wild creature under the map of Canada.
She was sprawling now on the rock with her legs dangling
over. Her bare arms and her thighs, through the red torn
dress she wore, were as brown as an Indian's.

Sarah said, 'I come here every day to watch the boats passing. When the sun goes down tonight we're moving to the
other end of the island. There's nothing there but the hill and
the hawk over it. Abraham has the lust for rabbits on him.'

The tinkers have curious voices – angular outcast flashing
accents like the cries of seagulls.

She jumped down from the rock and crouched in front of
me. I had never seen her face so close. Her hair lay about it in
two blue-black whorls, like mussel shells. Her eyes were as restless as tadpoles, and her small nose shone as if it had been oiled.

'Sarah,' I said, 'you haven't been to school all week.'

'May God keep me from that place forever,' she said.

With quick curious fingers she began to pick bits of
seaweed out of my hair.

'What will you do,' she said, 'when you're a tall man? You
won't live long, I can tell that. You'll never wear a gold chain
across your belly. You're white like a mushroom.' She laid two
dirty fingers against my shoulder.

'I'm going to be a sailor,' I said, 'or maybe an explorer.'

She shook her head slowly. 'You couldn't sleep with ice in
your hair,' she said.

'I'll take to the roads with a pack then,' I said, 'for I swear
to God I don't want to be a minister or a doctor. I'll be a
tinker like you.'

She shook her head again. 'Your feet would get broken,
tramping the roads we go,' she said.

Her red dress fell open at the shoulder where the button
had come out of it. Her shoulder shone in the wind as if it
had been rubbed with sweet oils.

She stretched herself like an animal and lay down on the sand with her eyes closed.

I turned away from her and traced slow triangles and circles in the sand. I turned a grey stone over; a hundred forky-tails seethed from under it like thoughts out of an evil mind. From across the field came the last chink of the grave-digger's spade – the grave was dug now; the spade leaned, miry and glittering, against the kirkyard wall. Two butter-flies, red and white over the rockpool, circled each other in silent ecstasy, borne on the stream of air. They touched for a second, then fell apart, flickering in the wind, and the tall grass hid them. I turned quickly and whispered in Sarah's ear.

Her first blow took me full in the mouth. She struck me again on the throat as I tried to get to my feet. Then her long nails were in my shoulder and her wild hair fell across my face. She thrust me back until my shoulder-blades were in the burning sand and my eyes wincing in the full glare of the sun. She dug sharp knees into my ribs until I screamed. Then she ravelled her fingers through my hair and beat my head thrice on the hard sand. Through my shut lids the sun was a big shaking gout of blood.

At last she let me go. 'Next time I come to the school,' she said, looking down at me with dark smiling eyes, 'I'll sit at your desk, under the yellow head of the poet.' She bent over quickly and held her mouth against my throat for as long as it takes a wave to gather and break. Her hair smelt of ditch-water and grass fires. Then she was gone.

I put on the rest of my clothes, muttering through stiff lips, 'You bitch! O you bloody bully, I'll have the attendance officer after you in ten minutes, just see if I don't!'

As I left the beach, walking slowly, I could see her swim-ming far out in the Sound.

She waved and shouted, but I turned my face obstinately towards the white road that wound between the kirkyard and the cornfield. The salt taste of blood was in my mouth.

IV

The grave digger had finished making Moll Anderson's grave. He was sitting on the shaft of his barrow, smoking a clay pipe. As I turned in at the gate he wagged his beard at me, for he did not associate this shy decently clad boy with the naked insolence he had seen running out of the sea half an hour before. I wandered away from him among the branching avenues of tombstones – the tall urns and frozen angels of modern times; the fiery pillars with the names of grandfathers on them; the scythe-and-hourglass slates of the eighteenth century; and the lichened leprous tombs of a still earlier age. This small field was honeycombed with the dead of generations – farmers with stony faces; young girls rose-cheeked with consumption; infants who had sighed once or twice and turned back to the darkness; stern Greek-loving ministers; spinsters with nipped breasts and pursed mouths. I stood on the path, terrified for a moment at the starkness and universality of shrouds; at the infinite dead of the island, their heads pointing westward in a dense shoal, adrift on the slow tide that sets towards eternity.

My dreaming feet brought me to a low tombstone set in the east wall:

HERE LIES BURIED
A FOREIGN SEAMAN,
OF UNKNOWN NAME AND NATIONALITY
WHOM THE SEA CAST UP ON THIS ISLAND,
JUNE THE SIXTH, 1856

*'Though I take the wings of
the morning, and flee to the
uttermost places of the sea.'*

I closed my eyes and saw a little Basque town between the
bay and the mountains.

The feast of Our Lady of the Sea was over. The nets and the
oars had been blessed. The candles were still burning in their
niches among the rocks.

Now the young people are dancing in a square that lies
white and black under the moon.

The musician slouches, as if he were drunk or half asleep,
against the fountain. Only his hand is alive, hovering over the
strings like a vibrant bird.

The young people are dancing now in long straight lines. The
partners clap their hands and bow to each other. They shout; the
dark faces are lit up with a flash of teeth. They move round each
other with momentarily linked arms. They incline towards each
other, their hands on their knees, and stamp their feet. It is all
precision, disciplined fluency, a stylised masque of coupling.

Older men and women sit gossiping on the doorsteps.
Occasionally they sip from tall glasses. One, a fat man with a
yellow beard, looks often through a gap in the houses, at a
ship anchored in the harbour.

An old shawled woman stands alone, in the shadow of the
church. No one speaks to her; the seal of separation is on her.
She is the guardian of the gates of birth and death. In this
village she comes to deliver every wailing child, she goes to
shroud every quiet corpse. Her eyes are in the dust, from
which all this vanity has come, and to which it must return.

The hand over the guitar moves into a new swirling
rhythm. Now the square is all one coloured wheel, a great
wavering orange blossom.

Suddenly there is an interruption. A tall bearded sailor appears at an alley-opening and walks slowly across the square. The guitar falters. The dance is frozen. The old dark woman raises her head. The officer points to one of the dancers and crooks his finger: he must come, immediately, the ship is sailing tonight.

The seaman – he is only a boy – turns once and looks back. A girl has raised her apron to her face. The yellow-bearded man rises from his doorstep and makes a gesture of blessing: 'Lady of Waters, guard him this day and all days till the sail returns to the headland.'

Above the village a cross stands among the stars. Through a long silence comes the sound of the sea. The last votive candle gutters and goes out among the rocks.

The little town of moonlight and music will never see that sail again. Her voyage has ended on a northern rock. All her sailors have vanished down the path of gull and lobster, scattered in a wild Atlantic storm. One broken shape only was lifted out of the seaweed. Curious hands have carried the nameless thing in procession across the fields. They have clipped the rags from it and combed its hair, and covered the crab-eaten face. And though there was no priest to sing Latin over it, a Calvinist minister said, 'All flesh is grass, and the glory of flesh is as the flower thereof' – the orange blossom of Spain and the little blue Orkney primula, whose circles of beauty are full and radiant for a short time only; and then, drifting winterward, or broken with June tempest, lay separate shining arcs in the dust . . .

My slow circuitous walk had brought me to the new gaping hole in the earth. The grave digger was still sitting on his barrow. He bored a sidelong glance into me and said: 'There's only one way of coming into the world, but ah, God, there's two or three ways of going out.'

'That's a fact,' I said.

'Would you like,' he said, 'to see what a man *truly* is?'

Not understanding, I gave a quick nod. He groped with his hand into the small hill of clay beside the open grave, and brought out a skull. Carefully he wiped it on his moleskin trousers. 'That's you,' he said, 'and me, and the laird, and Frank the idiot. Just that.'

He laughed. 'There's nothing here to make your face so white. It's as harmless as can be, this bone. It's at peace, and not before time. When it lived it had little rest, with its randy eyes and clattering tongue. This skull belonged to Billy Anderson, Moll's grandfather. He was twice in jail and fathered three illegitimate bairns. O, he was a thieving, drunken, fighting character, and it was a good day for him when we threw him in here. Wasn't it, Billy?' he said to the skull, blowing smoke into its eye-hollows. 'Wasn't it, boy?' . . . The skull grinned back at him.

From the other side of the loch the school bell rang the dismissal.

Over the hill from the village, like a procession of beetles, came the mourners.

V

After I had finished my lessons that evening, I was summoned into the shop.

My father was sitting at the counter between a barrel of paraffin oil and a great dark coil of tobacco. There was a jar of sweets at his elbow. Over his head hung jerseys and scarves and stockings, with price tickets on them. The lamp swung from the hook in the ceiling, smoking a little. There was always a good smell in the shop.

'It's thee, John,' he said, raising his head from the ledger for a moment. 'Sit down, boy.' He counted the sticks of toffee in a glass jar and then said, 'How did thu get on at the school today?'

'Fine,' I said.

'I've been thinking about thee,' he said, 'what to make o' thee, once thee school days are over.'

He gathered up a handful of coins, and rang them one by one back into the till. Then he marked the ledger on his desk with a pencil.

'There's no future in this shop, I can tell thee that,' he said. 'The profits are getting smaller every year. The reason is, the folk are leaving the island. They're going to the cities and the colonies. Not a month passes but another family leaves.

'And then they send to the mail-order places in the south for their clothes and their ironmongery. A great lot of them do that. They forget that we depend on each other for our livelihood in a small island like this.

'And there's debts too,' he said. 'For instance, Mistress Anderson who was buried this afternoon died owing more than six pounds. So it'll be a poor inheritance for thee, this shop,' he said.

He licked his pencil and wrote more figures in the ledger. His hair glittered fraily in the lamplight.

'I had a word with Miss Ingsetter this afternoon about thee,' he went on. 'She called at the shop after school for some fly-papers. She seemed surprised thu weren't home yet . . . I made a point of asking her about thee. She says thu're an able boy, good beyond the general run at reading and writing and history. Not so bright at the mathematics. Sometimes thu're inclined to be inattentive and dreamy, she says. At times, only at times. But there's no harm in the boy, she said, and he's by no means stupid. And it's my opinion, she said, he ought to go to the grammar school in Kirkwall for a secondary education, once he turns twelve.'

'I want to be a sailor,' I said.

'The dreaminess,' he said, 'you take from your mother . . .
After the school comes the university. That'll cost money, a
power of money. Still, I'm not barehanded, I haven't neglected
to provide for things like that. With a degree in thee pocket,
thu could enter *the professions*. Think of that.'

'It's the sea I have a hankering for,' I said. 'Uncle Ben said
he could get me into the Saint Line, any time I wanted.'

'The ministry is an honourable profession,' he said. 'There
isn't a lot of money in it, but you get a free manse, and I can
tell you old MacFarland doesn't spend a fortune on food. He
gets a hen here and a pound of butter there and a sack of
tatties from the other place. On his rounds, you understand,
his visitations. Cheese at the Bu, and fish from Quoys, and a
fleece for spinning from Westburn, all for nothing. And
nobody can say the work is strenuous.'

'Supper is ready,' my mother sang out from the kitchen.

'Now doctoring is strenuous, there's no doubt about that.
They haven't a moment to call their own. They can't even be
sure of a night's sleep. There's always somebody thundering
at Doctor Leslie's door after midnight with the toothache, or
a pain in the guts, or a hook's got stuck in their hand. It's no
wonder he's taken to the drink lately. But, putting all that
aside, medicine is a fine calling. Plenty of money in it too, if
you can get them to pay their bills.'

'I spoke to Mother,' I said. 'She would like fine for me to be
a deep-sea captain. She's going to write to Ben.'

'The law,' he said, 'is a different thing. Not that there's
anything wrong with it, if you understand, but there's a shady
side to it, there's a certain amount of trickery about it that
makes the ordinary honest man wonder sometimes. You can
hardly open a newspaper without seeing some lawyer or
other in trouble for embezzling his client's money, and

carrying on. You'll hear a couple of them arguing a case like mad in the courts, and then, half an hour later, there they'll be walking down the street together cheek by jowl . . . John,' he said, 'never go to law if you can possibly help it. Not but what there aren't honest lawyers too.'

He unscrewed the lid from a bottle of black-striped balls. He took out a couple between his fingers and handed them across the counter.

'If there's one place I have a longing to see,' I said, 'it's Japan.'

He suddenly withdrew his hand and dropped the black-striped balls back into the jar.

'Not before your food,' he said, licking his fingers. 'I forgot . . . Then there's teaching—'

'Are you coming for your supper,' chanted my mother impatiently, 'or are you not?'

Outside the dog began to bark. There was a clattering of hooves and wheels over the cobbles. The poultry squawked like mad in the yard. 'Mercy,' said my father, running to the door, 'it's the tinkers. *The hens!*'

I followed him out, into the moonlight. The tinker's cart was opposite the door now. Abraham sat on the shaft. He cracked his whip and cried to the grey pony. In the cart sat Mary his wife with an infant slung behind her in a tartan shawl. Sarah walked alongside with her arms full of wild lupins.

They were going to the other end of the island where the rabbits were thick, to camp there.

'Giddap!' cried Abraham and cracked his whip. 'That's a fine dog you have there, Mister Sigurdson,' he shouted to my father. 'I'll take a half pound of bogey roll, and I'll pay you when I come back along next week.'

'No,' said my father sternly, 'you'll pay now, for you owe me sixteen and six already.'

'Hello, Sarah,' I said. She stood on the road and looked at me through the dark blue congregated spires of lupins.

'Are you seeking a tin pail, mistress?' yelled Abraham to my mother, who had come out and was standing at the corner of the house guarding the hens.

'Yes,' she said, 'I'll need one when you come back by next week.'

Suddenly my father was furious. 'We need no tin pails!' he shouted. 'There's plenty of tin pails in the shop!'

'Next weekend, mistress,' cried Abraham. He stood between the shafts and cracked his whip. 'Giddap!' he yelled. The wheels rolled in crazy circles over the cobbles and stars streamed from the pony's hooves. There was a sudden wild *cluck-cluck-clucking* from inside the cart as it moved off. Sarah stood looking at us, smiling through her screen of lupins.

My father went back into the shop, muttering. My mother stood at the corner of the house and watched them out of sight. 'One of the hens is missing,' she said. 'I darena tell thee father. He would have the police at them for sure.'

A wave of purple blossom rose in front of the moon and showered over me.

Soon the racket died away at the far end of the village. Sarah's mockery sounded from a distance of three fields. I turned back into the house. My face was wet with dew and petals, and the moon raged above the mission hall wilder than ever.

'The very idea!' cried my father from inside the shop. 'A sailor! A tin pail! *The thieves!*'

Time was skulls and butterflies and guitars.

Witch

And at the farm of Howe, she being in service there, we spoke directly to the woman Marian Isbister, and after laid bonds on her. She lay that night in the laird's house, in a narrow place under the roof.

In the morning, therefore, she not yet having broken fast, the laird comes to her.

LAIRD: Tell us thy name.

MARIAN: Thou knowest my name well. Was I not with thy lady at her confinement in winter?

LAIRD: Answer to the point, and with respect. Thy name.

MARIAN: I was called Marian Isbister in Christian baptism.

STEPHEN BUTTQUOY (who was likewise present and is a factor of the Earl of Orkney): And what name does thy dark master call thee?

LAIRD: What is thy age?

MARIAN: I was eighteen on Johnsmas Eve.

LAIRD: Art thou a witch?

At this, she raised her fists to her head and made no further answer.

That same day, in the afternoon, she was convoyed to Kirkwall on horseback, to the palace of the earl there. All that road she spoke not a word. There in Kirkwall a chain was hung between her arm and the stone.

Next morning came to her Andrew Monteith, chaplain to the earl.

MONTEITH: Thou needest not fear me. I am a man in holy orders.

MARIAN: I fear thee and everyone. My father should be here.

MONTEITH: Thou hast a scunner at me for that I am a man of God and thou art a servant of the devil.

MARIAN: How can I answer thee well? They keep food from me.

MONTEITH: I will speak for food to be given thee.

MARIAN: I thank thee then.

MONTEITH: Wilt thou not be plain with me?

MARIAN: All would say then, this was the cunning of the evil one, to make me speak plain. I do speak plain, for I am no witch, but a plain country girl.

MONTEITH: Thou art as miserable a wretch as ever sat against that wall.

MARIAN: I am indeed.

MONTEITH: Thy guilt is plain in thy face.

MARIAN: John St Clair should be here.

MONTEITH: What man is that?

MARIAN: The shepherd on Greenay Hill. He would not suffer thee to say such ill words against me.

MONTEITH: Is he thy sweetheart?

MARIAN: Often enough he called himself that.

That day, at noon, they gave her milk and fish and a barley cake, the which she ate properly, thanking God beforehand. They likewise provided her a vessel for the relief of nature. It was not thought well to give her a lamp at night.

So seven days passed, a total week. On the Sabbath she prayed much. She ate little that day, but prayed and wept.

On the Tuesday came to her cell William Bourtree, Simon Leslie, John Glaitness, and John Beaton, together with the chaplain, and two clerks (myself being one) to make due note of her utterances.

MONTEITH: Stand up, witch. Thou must suffer the witch's test on thy body.

MARIAN: I think shame to be seen naked before strange men. This will be a hard thing to endure. A woman should be near me.

They bring Janet, wife to William Bourtree.

JANET: I think none of you would have your wives and daughters, no nor the beast in your field, dealt with thus.

She kissed Marian, and then unlaced her, she making now no objection.

Then the probe was put into the said Marian's body, in order to prove an area of insensitivity, the devil always honouring his servants in that style. These parts were probed: the breast, buttocks, shoulders, arms, thighs. Marian displayed signs of much suffering, as moaning, sweating, shivering, but uttered no words. On the seventh probe she lost her awareness and fell to the ground. They moved then to revive her with water.

JANET: She suffers much, at every stab of that thin knife, and yet I think she suffers more from your eyes and your hands – all that would be matter of laughter to a true witch.

Yet they still made three further trials of the probe at that session, Marian Isbister discovering much anguish of body at each insertion.

Then they leave her.

That night she slept little, nor did she eat and drink on the day following, and only a little water on the day following that. She asked much for Janet Bourtree, but Janet Bourtree was denied access to her.

On the eleventh day of her confinement a new face appeared to her, namely Master Peter Atholl, minister of the parish, a man of comely figure and gentle in his language. He, sitting companionably at the side of Marian Isbister, taketh her hand into his.

ATHOLL: Thou art in miserable estate truly.

MARIAN: I am and may God help me.

ATHOLL: I am sent to thee by my masters.

MARIAN: I have told everything about myself. What more do they want me to say?

ATHOLL: They accuse thee to be guilty of corn-blighting, of intercourse with fairies, of incendiarism, the souring of ale, making butterless the milk of good kye, and much forby.

MARIAN: No witch's mark was found on me.

ATHOLL: The point of a pin is but a small thing, and thy body a large area. Here are no cunning witch-finders who would infallibly know the spot where the finger of the devil touched thee with his dark blessing.

Whereupon, Marian Isbister answering nothing, and a sign being given by Master Atholl, three men entered the prison, of whom the first unlocked the chain at her wrist, the second brought wine in a flask, and the third a lamp which he hung at the wall.

ATHOLL: This is in celebration of thy enlargement. Thou art free. Be glad now, and drink.

Then began Marian to weep for joy and to clap her hands.

MARIAN: I have never drunk wine, sir.

ATHOLL: This is from the earl himself. I will drink a little with thee.

Then they drink the wine together.

MARIAN: And am I at liberty to walk home tonight, a blameless woman?

ATHOLL: First thou shalt put thy mark to this paper.

MARIAN: I cannot read the writing on it.

ATHOLL: That matters nothing.

But Marian withdrew her hand from the parchment and let the quill fall from her fingers.

MARIAN: I fear you are little better than the other priest, and deceive me.

ATHOLL: You deceive yourself. Sign this paper, and all that will happen to thee is that thou shalt be tied to a cart and whipped through the street of Kirkwall, a small thing, and Piers the hangman is a good fellow who uses the scourge gently. But if thou art obdurate, that same Piers has strong hands to strangle thee, and a red fire to burn thee with, and a terrible eternity to dispatch thee into.

MARIAN: I wish I had never drunk thy wine. Take thy paper away.

Then was the chain put back on Marian Isbister's wrist, and the lamp darkened on the wall, and Master Peter Atholl left her, a silent man to her from that day to the day of her death.

John Glaitness cometh to her the next morning, who telleth her she must stand her trial before the King's Sheriff in the hall of Newark of the Yards, that is to say, the earl's palace, on the Monday following.

MARIAN: I am content.

And she occupied herself much in the interval with apparent prayer, and the repetition of psalms, wherein she showed sharp memory for an unlettered girl.

Howbeit, she ate and drank now with relish, as one who had little more to fear or to hope for. In the days before her trial, for food she had brose, and potage, and a little fish, and milk, ale, and water for her drink, without stint.

*

Two days before the commencement of her trial, there came to Earl Patrick Stewart where he was hunting in Birsay, a deputation of men from her parish, among them a few who were mentioned in the indictment as having been damaged by her machinations, namely, George Taing whose butter-kirn she had enchanted, Robert Folster whose young son she had carried to the fairies on the hill, Adam Adamson whose boat she had overturned whereby two of his three sons were drowned, these and others came to the earl at the shore of Birsay, protesting that they had never at any time laid information against Marian Isbister as having harmed them or theirs, but they knew on the contrary the charge was a devised thing by Stephen Buttquoy, a factor of the earl, for that his lustful advances to the girl Marian Isbister in the byre at Howe (Stephen Buttquoy riding round the parish at that time for the collection of his lordship's rents) had gotten no encouragement. Nor had there wanted women in the parish, and a few men also, to infect the bruised pride of Stephen Buttquoy with dark suggestions concerning the girl, out of malice and envy.

This deputation the earl heard fairly and openly, and he promised to investigate their words and allegations – 'and yet,' says he, 'Master Buttquoy is my good and faithful servant, and I will not easily believe him to be guilty of such an essayed wrenching of justice. And, furthermore, the woman is in the hands of the law, whose end is equity and peace, and doubtless if she is innocent not a hair of her head will suffer.'

*

The day before her trial she sat long in the afternoon with Janet Bourtree.

MARIAN: It is the common thing to be first a child, and then a maiden, and then a wife, and then perhaps a widow and an old patient woman before death. But that way is not for me.

JANET: There is much grief at every milestone. A young girl cries for a lost bird. An old woman stands among six graves or seven in the kirkyard. It is best not to tarry overlong on the road.

MARIAN: Yet with John the shepherd I might have been content for a summer or two.

JANET: Yea, and I thought that with my barbarian.

Now they bring her to trial in the great hall of the palace. There sat in judgment upon her the Sheriff, Master Malachi Lorimer. The procurator was Master James Muir. Merchants and craftsmen of the town of Kirkwall, fifteen in number, sat at the jurors' table.

The officers had much ado to keep out a noisy swarm of the vulgar, as carters, ale-house keepers, ploughmen, seamen, indigents, who demanded admittance, using much violent and uproarious language in the yard outside. And though it was the earl's desire that only the more respectable sort be admitted, yet many of those others forced a way in also. (That year was much popular disorder in the islands, on account of the earl's recent decree concerning impressed labour, and the adjustment of weights and measures, whereby certain of the commonalty claimed to be much abused in their ancient rights and freedoms.)

Marian Isbister appeared and answered 'Not guilty' to the charge in a low voice. Then began Master James Muir to list against her a heavy indictment, as burning, cursing net and plough, intercourse with devil and trow, enchanting men, cows, pigs, horses, manipulation of winds in order to extract tribute from storm-bound seamen, and he declared he would bring witnesses in proof of all.

Jean Scollite, widow in Waness, witness, said Marian Isbister walked round her house three times against the sun the night before the Lammas Market, whereby her dog fell sick and died.

Oliver Spens, farmer in Congesquoy, witness, said he was on the vessel *Maribel* crossing from Hoy to Cairston, which vessel was much tossed by storm all the way, whereby all except Marian Isbister were sick and in much fear of drowning. But the said Marian Isbister said they would all doubtless come safe to the shore.

John Lyking, farmer in Clowster, witness, said his black cow would not take the bull two years. The bull was from the farm of Howe, where Marian Isbister was in service. Yet his cow at once took the bull from the farm of Redland on the far side of the hill.

Maud Sinclair, servant lass in Howe, witness, said she had a child by Robert the ploughman there, that dwined with sickness from the age of three months, and was like to die. But as soon as Marian Isbister was taken from Howe by the earl's officers, the child began to recover.

THE SHERIFF: And is thy child well now?

MAUD SINCLAIR: It is buried these six days, and never a penny did I have from Robert the ploughman, either for the lawless pleasure he had of me, nor for the bairn's nurse-fee, nor for the laying-out and burial of the body. And but that I am told to say what I do, I have no complaint against Marian Isbister, who was ever a sweet friend to me and loving to the child.

THE SHERIFF: This is idle nonsense. Step down.

Andrew Caithness, farmer in Helyatoun, witness, said he had a fire in his haystack the very day that Marian Isbister passed that way with her black shawl coming home from the kirk. None other had passed that way that day.

MARIAN: Yet I never did thee harm, Andrew, and never till today hast thou complained of me. And did not thy leaky lantern set fire to the heather on Orphir Hill that same spring?

ANDREW: It did that, Marian.

Ann St Clair, in Deepdale, witness, said she got no butter from her churn the day she reproved Marian Isbister for kissing lewdly at the end of the peatstock her son John who was shepherd at Greenay in Birsay.

William St Clair, spouse to the above, farmer in Deepdale, witness, said he was ill at ease whenever the prisoner came about the house, which lately was more than he could abide. He had lost three sheep, and his son was held from his lawful work, and one day, all his household being in the oatfield cutting, a thick rain fell upon his field that fell nowhere else in the parish, and with the rain a wind, so that his oats were much damaged. And one day when he reproved Marian Isbister for coming so much about the place after his son, he that same night and for a week following suffered much pain in the shoulder, that kept him from work and sleep.

John St Clair, son to the above, shepherd in Greenay, witness, stated that he was a man of normal lustihood, who before he met with Marian Isbister had fathered three children on different women in the parish. Yet after he met Marian Isbister, he was unable through her enchantment to have fleshly dealings with her, though he felt deeper affection for her than for any other woman. And this he attributed to her bewitching of his members.

Margaret Gray, spinster in Blotchnie, witness, said she had known Marian Isbister to be a witch for seven years, ever since she made extracts from the juice of flowers for reddening the cheeks, eye brighteners, and sweetening of the breath.

SHERIFF: All country girls do this, do they not?

MARGARET GRAY: Yea, but Marian hath a particular art in it, and a proper skill to know the gathering-time of herbs and their true admixture.

Now the court was dismissed for eating and refreshment, and upon its reassembly The Sheriff asked Master Muir whether he had many more witnesses to call.

PROCURATOR: Upwards of a score.

SHERIFF: There is already a superfluity of that kind of evidence.

Then he asks Marian Isbister whether she wishes to speak in her defence.

MARIAN: I wished to speak, and I had much to say, but the words of John St Clair have silenced my mouth.

JANET BOURTREE: A curse on him and all the liars that have infested this court this day!

On this Janet Bourtree was removed from the court by officers.

The Sheriff then made his charge to the jury.

SHERIFF: Gentlemen, I would have you to distinguish between witchcraft and other crimes that are brought before me in this court, and God knows I am fitter to try those other crimes than the supernatural crime we are dealing with here today, for they in a sense are crimes in the natural order – that is, they have some sensible material end in view – but witchcraft involves seduction of souls and entanglements of nature, so that I would rather, as in the old days, some doctor of divinity and not I were sitting solemnly on this bench. And furthermore this devil's work displays itself under an aspect of infernal roguishness, on the mean level of jugglers and conjurers, so that the dignity of this court is sorely strained dealing with it. Yet try the case we must.

Gentlemen, I have said that straightforward crime is an ordinary enough matter. What befalls a man who steals a sheep from his neighbour? A rope is put about his neck and he is hanged; and rightly so, for by such stealing the whole economy and social harmony of the countryside is endangered. As men of property, you appreciate that.

And what becomes of a man who murders his neighbour, by knife or gun? For him also the rope is twisted and tied, and a tree of shame prepared. And rightly so, for an assassin's blade tears the whole fabric of the community. As men who uphold the sanctities of life and property, you appreciate that.

There are worse crimes still. How do we treat the man who denies the authority of his lord and seeks to overthrow it, either by cunning or by overt force? I speak not only of treason against the sovereign. There are not wanting nearer home men who murmur against the sweet person and governance of Patrick Stewart our earl.

A VOICE: When will sweet Patrick restore our ruined weights and measures? When will he leave our women alone? Sweet Patrick be damned!

At this point was taken into custody by the court officers a smallholder, Thomas Harra, who later suffered public whipping for his insolence; though many present swore that the said Thomas Harra had not once opened his mouth.

SHERIFF: You know, gentlemen, that under God we men live according to a changeless social order. Immediately under God is the King; then the lords temporal and spiritual; then knights; then craftsmen, merchants, officers, lawyers, clergymen; then at the base (though no whit less worthy in God's sight) the great multitude of fishermen, ploughmen, labourers, hewers of wood and drawers of water. Thus society appears as an organism, a harmony, with each man performing his pre-ordained task to the glory of God and the health of the whole community. He who sets himself against that harmony is worthy of a red and wretched end indeed. As loyal citizens, you appreciate that.

Such deaths we reserve for the thief, the murderer, the rebel. Yet these criminals, though indeed they do the devil's work, are in a sense claimants on our pity, for they think, though perversely, that they are doing good. Your sheep-stealer thinks that perchance his ram could breed thick wool and fat mutton out of that grey fleece on his neighbour's hill. Your murderer undoubtedly thinks the world would be a quieter place for himself if his victim's tombstone were prematurely raised. Your rebel (God help him) hears in his mind, through pride and arrogance, a nobler social harmony than that which obtains, for example, under our God-appointed Patrick – a sweeter concourse of pipes and lutes.

A VOICE: A piper like Patrick would have his arse kicked black and blue from every ale-house in Orkney!

On this, three more men were ejected from the court room.

SHERIFF: Today we are dealing with another kind of crime altogether, namely witchcraft.

Gentlemen, you see standing before you what appears to be an innocent and chaste girl. She has a calm honest demeanour, has she not? She could be your daughter, or mine, and we would not be ashamed of her, would we? Are not your hearts moved to pity by what you see? You would hasten to succour any woman in such parlous danger of death and the fire as she is in, and yet here, in this young person, we observe a special sweetness, a unique openness of countenance, a right winning modesty.

Gentlemen, we will not allow ourselves to be led astray by appearances.

Further, you might say, 'What is this she is accused of – changing the wind, drying the dugs of an old cow, causing a lascivious youth to be chaste? Nay (you might say) these are light derisory things, and not weighty at all in the normal scale of crime.'

Yet see this thing for what it truly is.

The souls of thief, murderer, rebel are yet in the hand of God until their last breath, but the soul of a witch is forfeit irrevocably because of the pact she has made with the Adversary.

We say this of a witch, that she is a thousand times worse than those others. She is pure evil, utter and absolute darkness, an assigned agent of hell. Of her Scripture says, *Thou shalt not suffer a witch to live.*

Regarding the apparent lightness of her misdemeanours, marvel not at that. The Prince of Darkness is not always a roaring lion, an augustitude, a harrower of the souls of men; but frequently he seeks to lure and destroy with ridiculous playful actions, like the clown or the fool at a country fair; and then, when we are convulsed with that folly, off comes the disguise, and the horn, the tail, the cloven goat hoof, the unspeakable reek of damnation, are thrust into our faces.

So, in seeming simplicity and innocence, a girl lives in her native parish. Events strange, unnatural, ridiculous, accumulate round her, too insignificant one might think to take account of. These are the first shoots of a boundless harvest of evil.

Know that evil makes slow growth in the soil of a God-ordained society. But it is well to choke the black shoots early. For if we neglect them, then in the fullness of time must we eat bitter dark bread indeed – blasphemy, adultery, fratricide, tempest, flood, war, anarchy, famine.

As men of God I ask you to consider these things, and to reach now an honest verdict in the secrecy of your chamber.

It was no long time when the jury came back with the one word *Guilty*. Then rose from his place the dempster.

DEMPSTER: Marian Isbister, for this thy crime of witchcraft proven against thee in this court, thou shalt be taken tomorrow to Gallowsha, and at the stake there strangled till no breath remains in thee, and afterwards thy body shall be burnt to ashes and scattered to the winds, and this is pronounced for doom. May the Lord have mercy on thy soul.

CHAPLAIN: Amen.

Then was Marian Isbister taken down to her prison. And at once came to her William Bourtree, Simon Leslie, John Glaitness and John Beaton, with shears, razors, and pincers, who cut off her hair and afterwards shaved her skull clean, denuding her even of her eyebrows. Then one by one with the pincers John Glaitness drew out her finger-nails and toe-nails; and this operation caused her much pain.

Then they give her water but her bleeding fingers will not hold the cup.

They put their heaviest chain upon her and left her.

That night was with her Master Andrew Monteith the chaplain, and Master Peter Atholl the parish minister, from before midnight till dawn.

MONTEITH: This is thy last night on earth.

MARIAN: I thank God for it.

Then they sought with mild comforting words to prepare her for her end. By full confession of her fault it might be God would yet have mercy on her. Yet she answered only with sighs and shakings of her head.

ATHOLL: Only say, art thou guilty of witchcraft, yea or nay.

MARIAN: It needs must be.

MONTEITH: I think the devil would not love thee now, with thy skull bare as an egg.

MARIAN: I have much pain and much sorrow.

Then they read to her from the beginning of the Book, God's marvellous creation, the happiness of Adam in the Garden, Eve's temptation by the Serpent, the eating of the fruit, the angel with the flaming sword, Abel's good sacrifice and the red hand of Cain.

To these holy words she listened with much meekness.

Then said she: 'Tell my father the sheep Peggy knows the path down to the cliff, and he is to keep watch on her to keep her from that dangerous place. And tell him there is a sleeve still to sew in his winter shirt, but Isabel his neighbour will see to that.'

Then they read to her the ending of the Book, Revelation. And having prayed, soon after dawn they left her.

In the morning, at eight o'clock, when they came for her, she was asleep. They had to rouse her with shakings and loud callings of her name.

MARIAN: It is cold.

SIMON LESLIE: Thou will soon be warm enough.

MARIAN: Yea, and there are longer fires than the brief flame at Gallowsha.

Because her toes were blue and swollen after the extraction of the cuticles, she could not walk but with much difficulty. Therefore they bound her arms and carried her out onto the street. There was much laughter and shouting at sight of her naked head. Every ale-house in town had been open since midnight, the earl having decreed a public holiday. All night people had come into the town from the parishes and islands. There was much drunkenness and dancing along the road to Gallowsha.

As she hobbled through the Laverock with her fingers like a tangle of red roots at the end of her long white arms, and her head like an egg, some had pity for her but the voices of others fell on her in a confusion of cursing and ribaldry and mockery, so that the holy words of Master Andrew Monteith could scarcely be heard.

They came to Gallowsha by a steep ascent. There beside the stake waited Piers with a new rope in his hand. With courtesy and kind words he received Marian Isbister from her jailers, and led her to the stake.

PIERS: My hands are quick at their work. Thou hast had enough of pain. Only forgive me for what I have to do.

Marian Isbister kissed him on the hands.

At this, some of the crowd shouted, 'The witch's kiss, the witch's kiss!' But Piers answered, 'I do not fear that.'

It is usual on such occasions for the sentence to be read out first, and thereafter ceremonially executed on the body of the criminal. But the clerk had not uttered three words when Piers secretly put the rope about the neck of Marian Isbister and made a quick end. Those standing near saw her give a quick shrug, and then a long shiver through her entire body. She was dead before the clerk had finished reading from the parchment. Most of that great crowd saw nothing of the strangling.

An ale booth had been erected near the stake. Men crowded in there till the walls bulged. Many were too drunk to get near the fire. To that burning came Neil the Juggler with his two dancing dogs, Firth with his fiddle and new ballad entitled 'The Just and Dreadful End of Marian Isbister for Sorcery', Richan the hell-fire preacher, the long-haired dwarf Mans with medicine to cure consumption, palsy, the seven poxes, toothache, women's moustaches, the squinnying eye – all of whom made great uproar at Gallowsha until the time of the gathering of the ashes into a brass box, and their secret removal to the summit of the hill Wideford.

*

That same day, in the palace of Holy Rood, Edinburgh, King James the Sixth of Scotland, acting on private information, set his seal to a paper ordering due inquiry to be instituted into alleged defalcations, extortions, oppressions, and tortures practised by his cousin Earl Patrick Stewart on the groaning inhabitants of Orkney, whereby the whole realm was put in jeopardy and the providence of God affronted.

At midnight, in the town of Kirkwall, the dancing was still going on.

A Treading of Grapes

The parish church of St Peter's stands at one end of a sandy bay on the west coast of Orkney. It is a small square stone utilitarian structure built in the year 1826 by the freely-given labour of all the parishioners; women are said to have carried the stones from the quarry three miles away on their backs, a slow, holy, winter-long procession. But there were churches there before the present church was erected. The inscribed tombs in the churchyard go back to the seventeenth century, and there are older anonymous stones. The minister of St Peter's in the year 1795 was the Rev. Dr Thomas Fotheringhame. He was the author of two volumes of sermons published in Edinburgh. He complained in a written account of the parish that 'the Kirk roof is full of leakings and dribblings in the winter time, and of draughts at all seasons of the year, whereby the parishioners are like to catch their death of cold, and often my discourses are broken by reason of their hoastings and coughings. The masonry is much delapidated.' ... It was soon after this that plans were drawn up by the laird for the building of the present church on the same site. But there were other churches there even before Dr Fotheringhame's wet and draughty edifice. Among the clustering tombstones is a piece of a wall with a weathered hole in it that looks as though it might have been an arched window, and slightly to one side an abrupt squat arrangement of dressed stones that suggests an altar. The Rev. Dr

Fortheringhame says curtly, 'There is in the vicinity of the
Kirk remnants of a popish chapel, where the ignorant yet
resort in time of sickness and dearth to leave offerings, in the
vain hope that such superstition will alleviate their sufferings; the which Romish embers I have exerted myself to
stamp out with all severity during the period of my ministry.'
. . . Of this older church nothing is known, except that the
priest here at the time of the Reformation was called Master
John Halcrow. A fragment of a sermon – for the second
Sunday after Epiphany in the year 1548 – was recently discovered in a folder of old documents in the laird's cellar. Script
and parchment are in the style of the early sixteenth century,
and it is possible that Father Halcrow was the preacher.

The source of Father Halcrow's sermon is the gospel
account of the wedding feast at Cana in Galilee. Since we also
have sermons on the same text by Dr Fortheringhame
(August 1788) and by the present incumbent, Rev. Garry
Watters, B.D. (Edin.) – the latter sermon preached earlier
this year and reproduced by courtesy of the editor of the
parish magazine – it might be of interest, as showing the
changing style of the Scottish sermon through the centuries,
to set them out, one after the other, beginning with that of
Mr Watters.

*   *   *

(1)
Rev. Garry Watters

'I wonder what you were thinking of, when you listened to
this New Testament lesson? I'm sure some of you were thinking of the last wedding you were at, perhaps a month ago, or
a year ago, or even ten years ago. You were thinking, of
course, of the church, and the young couple standing there

together in the empty choir, and the minister in solemn tones performing the marriage ceremony. Yes, but I suppose that you were thinking particularly of the reception afterwards in the hotel, for this piece of scripture, strangely enough, has nothing to say about the marriage ceremony at all; it's all about the reception. I'm sure you're seeing again in your mind's eye all the cars standing in the hotel car park, and the long tables covered with flowers and food, and guests being introduced to one another, and then – a crowning moment – when the happy young couple entered to take their places, with confetti in the bride's veil and on the shoulders of the bridegroom's new suit. Then the meal, to the accompaniment of lighthearted conversation, and the toasts and the speeches – some wittier than others, I suppose – and the reading of the many telegrams, and the furtive moment when the young newly-weds slip away to their secret honeymoon destination. Perhaps there will have been a talented singer or two among the guests. Certainly there was music and dancing. This never-to-be-forgotten day ended with the singing of Auld Lang Syne.

'Yes, you remember it all vividly. What you will have forgotten, in the sheer enjoyment of it all, is how smoothly everything happened. Everything went to schedule. But – and now I'm coming to the important thing – you would certainly have remembered this wedding, with some pain and embarrassment, if, for example, the organist had played Wagner instead of Mendelssohn for the entry of the bride, or if the wedding cake had not been delivered from the baker's in time, or if the toast order had got all mixed up, or if the taximan had driven the bride's parents to the wrong hotel.

'Now this is exactly what happened in the gospel story – somebody blundered. The refreshments ran done. The whole wedding reception was threatened with disaster. A thing like that is remembered for a long time in a small place. In the little town of Cana they would have gossiped about this badly-organised wedding for many a day, would they not?

'Fortunately, Jesus was a guest at the wedding, and he very quickly put things to right, at once, no nonsense about it; smoothly and efficiently he took over, and everything was straightened out. Not only that, but the wedding went with a greater swing than before.

'We read about miracles, but – ask yourselves this – what exactly is a miracle? It is not some kind of superior conjuring trick – it is rather, I'm inclined to think myself, the exercise of a supreme common sense, a looking at every conceivable eventuality with absolute clear-sightedness and understanding, so that the remedy is clear even before the difficulty arises. Turning water into wine is merely a graphic shorthand for the way in which the foresight of Jesus more than compensated for the steward's blundering. He made sure beforehand that the neglected supplies were to hand.

'He is the best organiser, the best planner who ever lived. You may be sure we can trust him with our smallest everyday affairs. He won't ever let us down.

'Think, in the wider sphere, what a brilliant business executive, what a wise ambassador, what a competent minister of state he would have made! In his hands we can safely leave the troubles and frictions that distract the world we live in. Amen.

'There's just one thing I must mention before the final hymn. Up to now, in this church, on the four occasions each year that we celebrate the Sacrament of the Lord's Supper, a wine has been used that contained a certain small percentage of alcohol. Of recent years there has been, in this congregation and indeed all over Scotland, a large and growing demand for unfermented wine to be used in the sacrament, as being more seemly. Consequently, next Sunday, after the morning service, a ballot will be taken of all the members of the congregation present, as to whether you want fermented wine at future sacraments, or an unfermented substitute more in keeping, it may be, with the seemliness of our devotions.'

(2)
Dr Thomas Fortheringhame

'Brethren, some of you might be thinking that the piece of gospel I read out just this minute anent the Lord Christ's turning of water into wine at Cana of Galilee is divine permission to you to make drunken beasts of yourselves at every wedding that takes place within the bounds of this parish this coming winter; ay, and not only at every wedding but at every christening forby and every funeral and harvest supper. It is the devil of hell that has put such a thought into your minds. It never says in holy writ that any wedding guest was drunk at Cana of Galilee.

'Magnus Learmonth, you in the second pew from the back, at the wedding you made for your third lass Deborah at Skolness at the back end of Lammas, all the guests lay at the ale-kirn like piglets about the teats of a sow till morning, to the neglect even of dancing; and two women in this same district came to themselves next morning in the ditch of Graygyres. Bella Simison, you do well to hang your head there at the back of the Kirk – it argues a small peck of grace. Andrina of Breck, you were the other defaulter – don't look at me like that, woman! – you have a brazen outstaring impudence commensurate with your debauchery. Well I know you and your runnings back and fore between Breck and the ale-house with your bit flask under your shawl. Things are told privily into my lug.

'What this text argues, brethren, is that the host at the wedding, the bridegroom's good father, was a careful and a prudent man with his bawbees. No doubt this provident man said to himself the day the marriage bids were sent about the countryside with a hired horseman, "If I order too few pigs of drink, they'll say I keep the purse-strings drawn over tight, and if I order too muckle they'll say I'm a spendthrift. And so I find myself between devil and deep. What is the right quantity of drink for a celebration such as this?" ... Being a prudent man, I say, he ordered too few pigs of drink (only it wasn't pigs of usquebaugh, whisky, in that foreign place, nor yet ale; it was jars of wine). The which when the Lord came he corrected, he set to right, as he will beyond a doubt set to right all our exaggerations and our deficiencies, since only he kens what is stinted and what is overblown in the nature of every man born. He adds and he takes from. The stringent economy of the host drew no rebuke from him. He accomplished the miracle. Then there was dancing, then there was fiddling, then no doubt near midnight bride and groom were carried into the ben room with roughness and sly jokes and a fiddle and five lanterns.

'Nor was this the end of meat and drink as far as the Lord was concerned. You ken all about the multiplication of the five bannocks and the two cod-fish, concerning which I preached to you for an hour and more last Sabbath. There came a night at the supper board when he suddenly took an oatcake and broke it and raised his jug of drink and leaned across and said to them who were no doubt wanting to fill their bellies without any palaver, "This is my body," he said, and then, "This is my blood" – a most strange and mystifying comparison indeed, that the papists would have us believe to be a literal and real and wholly breathtaking change of substance effected by a form of words. Whatever it means, brethren – and our General

Assembly has not and doubtless will not bind you to any infallible conclusions as to the significance of these utterances – whatever it means, it teaches us a terrible reverence for the things we put in our mouths to nourish us, whether it is the laird's grouse and claret or the limpets that Sam of the Shore eats with cold water out of the well in the lean days of March.

'You will not go home, therefore, and hog down your brose like swine in a sty or like cuddies at a trough. The common things you put in your mouths are holy mysteries indeed, beyond the taste and the texture. Therefore, brethren, with reverence you will make them a part of your body and your life.

'Prudence, my brethren, a proper proportioning of our goods, estimation, forethought – so much to the King, so much to the laird, so much to the Kirk, so much for the maintainance of ourselves and them that belong to us, so much to the poor – that is doubtless the meaning of this text; and for the things we lack, that we should ask the Lord to supply them, and so rest content in our estate.

'John Sweynson, I observe that you bought a new shawl to your wife's head at the Kirkwall Market, with what looks to be silken lacing round the edge of it, a thing of vanity, and new black lace gloves to her hands. She will not darken this kirk door again, no nor you either, with these Babylonish things on her body.

'Samuel Firth, of the operations of your farm, Dale in the district of Kirkbister, naturally I ken nothing, nor does it concern me. But you have seven black cows on the hill if you have one, and fifty sheep forby, and a hundred geese. Is it a proper and a godly thing, think you, that your three small bairns sit in the front pew there under the precentor blue and channering with the cold, they having no right sarks to their backs nor boots to their feet? Have a care of this, look to it, as you call yourself a Christian. Amen.

'Concluding, I have two announcements to make. John Omand, on account of the bastard child he fathered on Maria Riddoch at Michaelmas, appeared before the Kirk session on Wednesday and being duly constrained answered *Yea* to the accusation, wherefore he will suffer public rebuke three sequent Sabbaths in this Kirk on the stool of penitence, beginning next Sabbath.

'I hear that the French brig *Merle*, Monsieur Claude Devereux, master, discharged some cargo at the Bay of Ostray in the darkness of Friday night. The gentlemen of the excise were at Kirkwall, playing at cartes. Will you, therefore, James Drever, deliver as usual a keg of best brandy at the Manse tomorrow morning, when Mistress Skea my serving woman will see that you are recompensed for your pains.'

(3)
FATHER HALCROW

The Vine 'Cometh the full grape cluster upon the vine. The rain falleth. Clusters thicken, purple they are as bruises, as thunder, yet each grape containeth within itself a measure of joy and dancing, the quick merry blood of the earth.

Grape Harvest 'Cometh at last the hour of full ripeness. Labourers toil all day, they cram the baskets, their arms are red. The master of the vineyard, he goeth about the streets in the last of the sun, bargaining with such as sit idle against the wall and them that throw dice in the dust. For the grape harvest must be ingathered.

The Treading of Grapes 'And he that presseth the hoarded grapes, look, his breast and his thighs are red, as though he had endured a terrible battle, himself scatheless. And still more and more grapes are brought to the press where he laboureth, this hero.

Wine   'Now it standeth long, the vat, in a cellar under earth, as it were in a cold grave. Yet this is in no wise a station of death. Put thy ear against the vat, thou hearest a ceaseless murmur, a slow full suspiration. The juice is clothing itself in sound, in song, in psalmody.

The Wine Shop   'Now see the vintner in his shop, bottles, barrels, wineskins all about him. There cometh a steward that is preparing a wedding, a feast of note, his master's daughter will be married. This feast is not to be any mouse-in-the-cupboard affair, no, it will be a costly ceremony with harps and tapestries and bits of silver thrown to the children in the street outside. What does the vintner think – will seven jars of wine be enough? Or twelve? Or three? It is hard to say how much the guests will drink. Many strangers are bidden. They might sip with small burgess mouths or they might have throats like salt mines. He cannot tell.

The Six Jars   'In the end they agreed together upon so many jars of wine, six let us say, after much calculation according to the wisdom of this world.

The Guests   'Under the first star they travel, the wedding guests, such a crowd as you would see on any Orkney feast day – ploughman and mason and laird and labourer and grieve and notary and beachcomber, and a horde of women, besides one or two persons unbidden – in holy-day coats they crowd to one house with lights and music in it. There they will celebrate the sacrificial feast of a maidenhead.

The Word   'And presently in the door stands the carpenter of Nazareth, and his mother and twelve more forby that have a smell of fish and seaweed and limpets on them from their trade, all known faces. Yet none guessed that here was the Incarnate Word (had they not bargained with him for cradles and chairs and roofbeams?). None knew that here was Mary, Queen of Angels, Mystical Rose, Gate of Heaven, Holy Mother of God (had she not washed her linen a many a time with the other women at the burn?).

Rose of Love   'A bell strikes silence upon their babble. From this door and that door bridegroom and bride issue, separately they come forth. They stand together at last. They wait for all their random lusts, longings, desires, burnings to be gathered up into the one rose of human love. Cometh a priest and blesseth them. Then all the harps break out in one concert of joy.

The Empty Jars   'The steward maketh a sign. Now is the time for all those guests – rich and poor, young and old, farmer and fisherman, widow and maiden, to mingle together – so that this chamber seemeth to be in little the whole world and its tumultuous folk. The first jar is emptied into a hundred cups. The bridegroom, where is he? Secretly twelve hand-maidens light lamps. The bridegroom has gone into his chamber. The hand-maidens carry the bride through a door. The harps play. The steward is busy between the music and the wine. The cups go round and round. A handful of silver sklinters like rain among the children in the dark close outside. Sand runs in the hourglass, candles dwindle, the night passeth. And then one cometh, a serving man, and saith to the steward *The wine is all finished* while as yet the first flush is not upon the faces of musicians and dancers.

The Water   'Consider what a common thing is water. We set small value upon it except when the well is nothing but a few burning stones. When there is abundance of water we turn up the collars of our coats and we curse the rain. I tell you the guests at that marriage feast in Cana thought but poorly of it when the empty wine jars were filled to the brim with water at the behest of this carpenter from Nazareth. And the steward was distraught and the host's brow dark with vexation; he was like to be held in disgrace a many a day for his improvidence. And yet the woman reassureth the entire company, *Quodcumque dixerit vobis, facite* – 'Do whatsoever he telleth you to do.' So sweetly she urgeth that the serving men run to obey. Now the as-yet-unmiracled Word standeth among the water jars.

The Miracle 'The souls and creatures of that house – in particular the element of water – become utterly subject unto the Word, as all creation was in the six days of its becoming. The devious stations by which water becometh wine – the tap-root, grafting, pruning, sun, blossoming, wind, fruition, harvest, press, leaven, vat, vintry – all that long vexation was here cancelled. The Word spanned all creation, as it did in the paradise of Eden before Adam delved and Eve span. And a serving man poureth a jar of this new water. At once their cups brim with red circles. The trembling lips of the steward approve the mystery. Then all their mouths break out in celebration, like angels and holy souls that praise God forever with their *Sanctus* and their *Gloria*.

*   *   *

'Dear children, this I have spoken of is a most famous marriage. We are poor people, fisherman and crofters, and we think it is not likely in these the days of our vanity that we will be bidden to such a feast. We are poor people, Olaf the fisherman and Jock the crofter and Merran the hen-wife, we are pleased enough with oatcakes and ale at our weddings, we were born to hunger and meikle hardship, and there will be a single candle burning beside us the night they come to straik us and to shroud us.

'No, but this is not true. Let me tell you a secret. Christ the King, he hath uplifted our fallen nature as miraculously as he clothed water in the red merry robes of wine. Very rich and powerful you are, princes, potentates, heirs and viceroys of a Kingdom. So opulent and puissant are you, dear ones, for that each one of you has in his keeping an immortal soul, a rich jewel indeed, more precious than all the world beside. So then, princes (for I will call you Olaf the fisherman and Jock the crofter no longer but I will call you by the name the Creator will call you in the last day) princes, I say, I have good news for you, you are bidden every one to a wedding. Get ready your gifts, get ready your shoes to the journey. *What wedding?* you ask, *we know of no wedding.* I answer, *The marriage of Christ with His Church. And where will this marriage be?* you ask. *Everywhere,* I answer, *but in particular, lords and princes, in this small kirk beside the sea where you sit. And when is it to be, this wedding?* you ask me. *Always,* I answer, *but in particular within this hour, now, at the very moment when I bow over this bread of your offering, the food, princes and lords, that you have won with such hard toil from the furrows, at once when I utter upon it five words* HIC EST ENIM CORPUS MEUM. Then is Christ the King come once again to his people, as truly as he was present at the marriage in Cana, and the Church his bride abides his coming, and this altar with the few hosts on it and the cup is a rich repast indeed, a mingling of the treasures of earth and heaven, and the joy of them in Cana is nothing to the continual merriment of the children of God. *Sanctus sanctus sanctus*, they cry forever and ever, *Benedictus qui venit in nomine Domini*.

'Dance ye then, princes and ladies, in your homespun, there is no end to this marriage, it goes on at every altar of the world, world without end. This Bread that I will raise above your kneeling, It is entire Christ – Annunciation, Nativity, Transfiguration, Passion, Death, Resurrection, Ascension, Majesty, gathered up into one perfect offering, the Divine Love itself, whereof you are witnesses.

'And not only you, princes, all creation rejoices in the marriage of Christ and His Church, animals, fish, plants, yea, the water, the wind, the earth, the fire, stars, the very smallest grains of dust that blow about your cornfields and your kirkyards.'

'In Nomine Patris et Filii et Spiritus Sancti. Amen.'

*   *   *

I walked along the road past St Peter's Church this morning.

On the beach a few fishing boats were hauled out of reach of the waves. Behind the church lay the farms and crofts of the parish, tilth and pasture, the mill, the school, the smithy, the shop. In the field next to the church a tractor moved jerkily, trailing an airy drove of gulls; it is the time of ploughing. The young man in the tractor seat suddenly stood up and shouted, he swung his arm in wide circles. A girl throwing oats to a white agitation of hens at the end of a byre two fields away acknowledged his summons with a mere movement of her hand, a suggestion of greeting. Then she went quickly indoors (so that the neighbours wouldn't be getting any ideas for gossip). But the January air, I thought, was sweeter for that small promise of replenishment; and perhaps Mr Watters will soon have another wedding sermon to preach.

The sea shattered and shattered on the beach.

The wind from the sea soughed under the eaves of the Kirk, and among tombstones with texts and names newly chiselled on them, and those with withered half-obliterated lettering, and those that have lost their meanings and secrets to very ancient rain.

Celia

The Norwegian whaler *Erika* tied up at the pier in the middle of Monday afternoon, and when the pubs opened at five o'clock all six of the crew went into the Hamnavoe Bar. Per Bjorling the skipper was with them, but about seven o'clock he bought a full bottle of vodka and left them drinking their whiskies and lagers and went outside. It was getting dark. He walked along the street till he came to an opening that descended step by step to a small pier with a house on it. From inside the house came the thwack of a hammer driving nails into leather. One room of the house had a lamp burning in the window but the other room next to the sea was dark. Per Bjorling was about to knock at the door when it was opened from inside. He smiled and raised his sailor's cap and went in.

'What kind of a man is it this time?' shouted a voice from the lighted room. 'Is it that bloody foreigner? . . .' All the people in the neighbouring houses could hear what was being said. Maisie Ness came to the end of her pier and stood listening, her head cocked to one side.

The hammer smacked on leather, a rapid tattoo.

The seaward room remained dark; or rather, the window flushed a little as if a poker had suddenly woken flames from the coal.

'Yes,' yelled the shoemaker, 'a bloody drunken foreign sailor.'

Then silence returned to the piers and one by one the lights went on in all the houses round about.

2

The *Erika* and three other Norwegian whalers caught the morning tide on Tuesday and it was quiet again in the harbour. In the house on the small pier the shoe-repairing began early, the leisurely smack of the hammer on the moulded leather in between periods of quiet stitching. At ten o'clock Maisie Ness from the next close came with a pair of shoes to be soled. She walked straight in through the open door and turned into the room on the left next to the street. The shoemaker sat on his stool, his mouth full of tacks. Maisie laid her shoes on the bench, soles upward.

'Celia isn't up yet, surely. I don't hear her,' she said.

'Celia's a good girl,' said the shoemaker.

'I don't believe you've had your breakfast,' cried Maisie Ness, 'and it's past ten o'clock. You need your food, or you'll be ill same as you were in the wintertime.'

'I'll get my breakfast,' said the shoemaker. 'Just leave the shoes on the bench. All they need is rubber soles and a protector or two in the right heel to keep it level. You're an impudent woman. Ignorant too. Could you read the deep books that Celia reads? I don't believe you can sign your name. I'll get my breakfast all right. Celia's a good girl. Just keep your tongue off her.'

Maisie Ness went up the steps of the pier shaking her head. She managed to look pleased and outraged at the same time.

'Celia,' the shoemaker called out, 'I'll make you a cup of tea. Just you lie in bed for an hour or two yet.'

3

It was early spring. Darkness was still long but the light was slowly encroaching and the days grew colder. The last of the snow still scarred the Orphir hills. One sensed a latent fertility; under the hard earth the seeds were awake and astir; their long journey to blossom and ripeness was beginning. But in Hamnavoe, the fishermen's town, the lamps still had to be lit early.

On Tuesday night every week Mr Spence the jeweller paid his visit. He would hesitate at the head of the close, look swiftly right and left along the street, then quickly descend the steps.

The shoemaker heard his precise footsteps on the flagstones outside and immediately took down from the shelf the draught board and the set of draughtsmen. He had the pieces arranged on the board before Mr Spence was at the threshold.

'Come in, Mr Spence,' he shouted, 'come in. I heard your feet.'

And Mr Spence, without a single glance at the dark seaward window, went straight into the workroom on the left, bending his head under the lintel and smiling in the lamplight. 'Well, Thomas,' he said.

They always played for about an hour, best of three games. Mr Spence generally lost. Perhaps he was a poor player; perhaps he was nervous (he shuffled and blinked and cleared his throat a good deal); perhaps he genuinely liked to give the shoemaker the pleasure of winning; perhaps he was anxious to get this empty ritual over with. They played this night without speaking, the old man in his leather apron and the middle-aged bachelor in his smart serge tailor-made suit. The shoemaker won two games right away, inside half an hour, so that there was no need that night to play a decider.

'You put up a very poor show tonight,' said the shoemaker.

'I'm not in the same class as you, Thomas,' said Mr Spence.

He went over to his coat hanging on a peg and brought a half bottle of whisky out of the pocket. 'Perhaps, Thomas,' he said, 'you'd care for a drink.'

'You know fine,' said the shoemaker, 'I never drink that filthy trash. The poison!'

'Then,' said Mr Spence, 'perhaps I'll go and see if Miss Celia would care to have a little drink. A toddy, seeing it's a cold night.'

'No,' said the shoemaker anxiously, 'I don't think you should do that. Or if you do, only a very small drop.'

But Mr Spence was already tiptoeing along the lobby towards the dark room, carrying the half bottle in his hand. He tapped on the door, and opened it gently. The girl was bending over the black range, stabbing the coal with a poker. At once the ribs were thronged with red and yellow flames, and the shadow of the girl leapt over him before she herself turned slowly to the voice in the doorway.

'My dear,' said Mr Spence.

4

'How are you, Thomas?' said Dr Wilson on the Wednesday morning, sitting down on the bench among bits and scrapings of leather.

'I'm fine,' said the shoemaker.

'The chest all right?'

'I still get a bit of a wheeze when the wind's easterly,' said the shoemaker, 'but I'm not complaining.'

There was silence in the room for a half-minute.

'And Celia?' said Dr Wilson.

'Celia's fine,' said the shoemaker. 'I wish she would eat more and get more exercise. I'm a nuisance to her, I keep her tied to the house. But she keeps her health. She's fine.'

'I'm glad to hear it,' said Dr Wilson.

'Celia's a good girl,' said the shoemaker.

'I know she's a good girl,' said Dr Wilson. Then his voice dropped a tone. 'Thomas,' he said, 'I don't want to worry you, but there are complaints in the town.'

'She's a good girl,' said the old man, 'a very good girl to me.'

'Complaints,' said Dr Wilson quietly, 'that this is a house of bad repute. I'm not saying it, for I know you're both good people, you and Celia. But the scandal-mongers are saying it along the street. You know the way it is. I've heard it twenty times this past week if I've heard it once. That all kinds of men come here, at all hours of the night, and there's drinking and carrying on. I don't want to annoy you, Thomas, but I think it's right you should know what they're saying in the public, Maisie Ness and the other women. All this worry is not good for your lungs.'

'*I* don't drink,' said the shoemaker. 'How do I know who comes and goes in the night? That Maisie Ness should have her tongue cut out. Celia has a sweetheart, Ronald Leask of Clett, and she's applied to be a member of the Kirk. The minister's coming to see her Friday evening. She's a good girl.'

'Perhaps I could see Celia for a minute?' said Dr Wilson and got to his feet.

'No,' said the shoemaker, 'she's sleeping. She needs her rest. She's sleeping late. Celia is a very good girl to me. If it wasn't for Celia I know I'd have died in the wintertime.'

'Good morning, Thomas,' said Dr Wilson. 'I'll be back next Wednesday. You have plenty of tablets to be getting on with. Tell Celia I'm asking for her. Send for me if you need me, any time.'

5

'Go away,' said the shoemaker to Mr William Snoddy the builder's clerk. 'Just you go away from this house and never come back, never so much as darken the door again. I know what you're after. I'm not a fool exactly.'

'I want you to make me a pair of light shoes for the summer,' said Mr Snoddy. 'That's all I want.'

'Is it?' said the shoemaker. 'Then you can go some other place, for I have no intention of doing the job for you.'

They were standing at the door of the house on the pier. It was Wednesday evening and the lamp was burning in the workroom but the room next to the sea was in darkness.

'Last Saturday,' said Mr Snoddy, 'at the pier head, you promised to make me a pair of light shoes for the summer.'

'I didn't know then,' said the shoemaker, 'what I know now. You and your fancy-women. Think shame of yourself. You have a wife and three bairns waiting for you in your house at the South End. And all you can do is run after other women here, there and everywhere. I'm making no shoes for whore-mastering expeditions. You can take that for sure and certain.'

'You've been listening,' said Mr Snoddy, 'to cruel ground-less gossip.'

'And I believe the gossip,' said the shoemaker. 'I don't usually believe gossip but I believe this particular piece of gossip. You're an immoral man.'

'There's such a thing as a court of law,' said Mr Snoddy, 'and if ever I hear of these slanders being repeated again, I'll take steps to silence the slanderers.'

'You'll have your work cut out,' said the shoemaker, 'because you've been seen going to this house and that house when the men have been away at the fishing. I've seen you with my own two eyes. And if you want names I'll supply them to you with pleasure.'

'Let's go inside,' said Mr Snoddy in a suddenly pleasant voice, 'and we'll talk about something else. We'll have a game of draughts.'

The shoemaker stretched out foot and arm and blocked the door.

'Stay where you are,' he said. 'Just bide where you are. What's that you've got in the inside pocket of your coat, eh?'

'It's my wallet,' said Mr Snoddy, touching the bulge at his chest.

'It's drink,' said the shoemaker, 'it's spirits. I'm not exactly so blind or so stupid that I can't recognise the shape of a half bottle of whisky. I allow no drink into this house. Understand that.'

'Please, Thomas,' said Mr Snoddy. 'It's a cold night.'

'Forby being a whore-master,' said the shoemaker, 'you're a drunkard. Never a day passed that you aren't three or four times in the pub. Just look in the mirror when you get home and see how red your nose is getting. I'm sorry for your wife and children.'

'I mind my own business.' said Mr Snoddy.

'That's fine,' said the shoemaker. 'That's very good. Just mind your own business and don't come bothering this house. There's one thing I have to tell you before you go.'

'What's that?' said Mr Snoddy.

'Celia is not at home,' shouted the old man. He suddenly stepped back into the lobby and slammed the door shut. Mr Snoddy stood alone in the darkness, his mouth twitching. Then he turned and began to walk up the pier slowly.

From inside the house came the sound of steel protectors being hammered violently into shoes.

Mr Snoddy's foot was on the first step leading up to the street when a hand tugged at his sleeve. He turned round. It was Celia. She had a gray shawl over her head and her hair was tucked into it. Her face in the darkness was an oval oblique shadow.

'Celia,' said Mr Snoddy in a shaking voice.

'Where are you off to so soon, Billy boy?' said Celia. 'Won't you stop and speak for a minute to a poor lonely girl?'

Mr Snoddy put his hands round her shoulders. She pushed him away gently.

'Billy,' she said, 'If you have a little drink on you I could be doing with it.'

The loud hammering went on inside the house.

Mr Snoddy took the flask from his inside pocket. 'I think, dear,' he said, 'where we're standing we're a bit in the public eye. People passing in the street. Maybe if we move into that corner . . .'

Together they moved to the wall of the watchmaker's house, into a segment of deeper darkness.

'Dear Celia,' muttered Mr Snoddy.

'Just one little mouthful,' said Celia. 'I believe it's gin you've gone and bought.'

6

Ronald Leask closed the door of the tractor shed. The whole field on the south side of the hill was ploughed now, a good day's work. He looked round him, stretched his aching arms, and walked slowly a hundred yards down to the beach. The boat was secure. There had been south-westerly winds and high seas for two days, but during that afternoon the wind had veered further west and dropped. He thought he would be able to set his lobster creels the next morning, Friday, under the Hoy crags. The *Celia* rocked gently at the pier like a furled sea bird.

Ronald went back towards his house. He filled a bucket with water from the rain barrel at the corner. He stripped off his soiled jersey and shirt and vest and washed quickly, shuddering and gasping as the cold water slapped into his shoulders and chest. He carried the pail inside and kicked off his boots and trousers and finished his washing. Then he dried himself at the dead hearth and put on his best clothes – the white shirt and tartan tie, the dark Sunday suit, the pigskin shoes. He combed his wet fair hair till it clung to both sides of his head like bronze wings. His face looked back at him from the square tarnished mirror on the mantelpiece, red and complacent and healthy. He put on his beret and pulled it a little to one side.

Ronald wheeled his bicycle out of the lobby onto the road, mounted, and cycled towards Hamnavoe.

He passed three cars and a county council lorry and a young couple out walking. It was too dark to see their faces. As he freewheeled down into the town there were lights here and there in the houses. It would be a dark night, with no moon.

Ronald Leask left his bicycle at the head of the shoemaker's close and walked down the steps to the house. The lamp was lit in the old man's window but Celia's room, as usual, was dark. He knocked at the outer door. The clob-clob-clobbering of hammer against leather stopped. 'Who's that?' cried the old man sharply.

'It's me, Ronald.'

'Ronald,' said the shoemaker. 'Come in, Ronald.' He appeared at the door. 'I'm glad to see thee, Ronald.' He took Ronald's arm and guided him into the workroom. 'Come in, boy, and sit down.'

'How are you keeping, Thomas?' said Ronald.

'I'm fine, Ronald,' said the shoemaker, and coughed.

'And Celia?' said Ronald.

'Celia's fine,' said the shoemaker. 'She's wanting to see thee, I know that. It's not much of a life for a girl, looking after a poor old thing like me. She'll be glad of your company.'

'Last time I came, last Thursday, I didn't get much of a reception,' said Ronald.

'Celia wasn't well that day,' said the shoemaker. 'She likes thee more than anybody, I can assure thee for that.' He went over to the door and opened it and shouted across the lobby, 'Celia, Ronald's here.'

There was no answer from the other room.

'She's maybe sleeping,' said the shoemaker. 'Poor Celia, she works too hard, looking after me. What she needs is a long holiday. We'll go and see her.'

The old man crossed the lobby on tiptoe and opened the door of Celia's room gently. 'Celia,' he said, 'are you all right?'

'Yes,' said Celia's voice from inside.

'Ronald's here,' said the shoemaker.

'I know,' said Celia. 'I heard him.'

'Well,' said the shoemaker sharply, 'he wants to speak to you. And I'm taking him in now, whether you want it or not. And I'm coming in too for a minute.'

The two men went into the room. They could just make out the girl's outline against the banked-up glow of the fire. They groped towards chairs and sat down.

'Celia,' said the shoemaker, 'light your lamp.'

'No,' said Celia, 'I like it best this way, in the darkness. Besides, I have no money for paraffin. I don't get many shillings from you to keep the house going, and bread and coal and paraffin cost dear.'

'Speak to her, Ronald,' said the shoemaker.

'I can't be bothered to listen to him,' said Celia. 'I'm not well.'

'What ails you?' said the shoemaker.

'I don't know,' said Celia. 'I'm just not well.'

'Celia,' said Ronald earnestly, 'there's an understanding between us. You know it and I know it and the whole of Hamnavoe knows it. Why are you behaving this way to me?'

'That's true,' said the shoemaker. 'You're betrothed to one another.'

'Not this again,' said Celia, 'when I'm sick.' Then she said in a low voice, 'I need something to drink.'

'Drink!' said the old man angrily. 'That's all your mind runs on, drink. Just you listen to Ronald when he's speaking to you.'

'Celia,' said Ronald, 'it's a year come April since I buried my mother and the croft of Clett has stood there vacant ever since, except for me and the dog.'

'And a fine croft it is,' said the shoemaker. 'Good sandy soil and a tractor in the shed and a first-rate boat in the bay.'

'I'm not listening,' said Celia.

'It needs a woman about the place,' said Ronald. 'I can manage the farm work and the fishing. But inside the house things are going to wrack and ruin. That's the truth. Celia, you promised six months ago to come to Clett.'

'So that's all you want, is it?' said Celia. 'A housekeeper.'

'No,' said Ronald, 'I want you for my wife. I love you.'

'He does love you,' said the shoemaker. 'And he's a good man. And he has money put by. And he works well at the farming and the fishing. He's a fellow any girl would be proud to have for a man.'

'I'm not well tonight,' said Celia. 'I would be the better of a glass of brandy.'

'And what's more,' said the shoemaker, 'you love him, because you told me with your own lips not a fortnight ago.'

'I do not,' said Celia.

Ronald turned to the shoemaker and whispered to him and put something in his hand. The shoemaker rose up at once and went out. He banged the outer door shut behind him.

'Celia,' said Ronald.

'Leave me alone,' said Celia.

They sat in the growing darkness. The only light in the room was the dull glow from the range. Ronald could see the dark outline of the girl beside the fire. For ten minutes they neither moved nor spoke.

At last the door opened again and the old man came back. He groped his way to the table and put a bottle down on it. 'That's it,' he said to Ronald and laid down some loose coins beside the bottle. 'And that's the change.'

'Celia,' said Ronald, 'I'm sorry to hear you aren't well. I've got something here that'll maybe help you. A little brandy.'

'That's kind of you,' said Celia.

She picked up the poker and drove it into the black coal on top of the range. The room flared wildly with lights and shadows. The three dark figures were suddenly sitting in a warm rosy flickering world.

Celia took two cups from the cupboard and set them on the table and poured brandy into them.

'That's enough for me,' said Ronald, and put his hand over the cup next to him.

Celia filled the other cup to the top. Then she lifted it to her mouth with both hands and gulped it like water.

'Good health,' said the shoemaker. 'I'm saying that and I mean it though I'm not a drinking man myself. The very best of luck to you both.'

Ronald raised his cup and drank meagrely from it and put it down again on the table. 'Cheers,' he said.

Celia took another mouthful and set down her empty cup beside the bottle.

'Are you feeling better now, Celia?' said the shoemaker.

'A wee bit,' said Celia. She filled up her cup again. 'I'm very glad to see you,' she said to Ronald.

'That's better,' said the shoemaker, 'that's the way to speak.'

Celia took a drink and said, 'Ronald, supposing I come to live at Clett what's going to become of Thomas?'

'I'll be all right,' said the shoemaker, 'don't worry about me. I'll manage fine.'

'He'll come and live with us,' said Ronald. 'There's plenty of room.'

'No,' said Celia, 'but who's going to walk a mile and more to Clett to get their boots mended? We must think of that. He'll lose trade.'

'Don't drink so fast,' said the shoemaker.

'And besides that,' said Celia, 'he'll miss his friends, all the ones that come and visit him here and play draughts with him. What would he do without his game of draughts? Clett's a long distance away. I'm very pleased, Ronald, that you've come to see me.'

'I'm pleased to be here,' said Ronald.

'Light the lamp,' said the shoemaker happily.

'I love you both very much,' said Celia. 'You're the two people that I love most in the whole world.'

Celia filled up her cup again. This time half the brandy spilled over the table.

'I don't know whether I'll come to Clett or not,' said Celia. 'I'll have to think about it. I have responsibilities here. That's what makes me feel ill, being torn this way and that. I can't be in two places, can I? I love you both very much. I want you to know that, whatever happens.'

She suddenly started to cry. She put her hands over her face and her whole body shook with grief. She sat down in her chair beside the fire and sobbed long and bitterly.

The two men looked at each other, awed and awkward.

'I'll put a match to the lamp,' said the shoemaker. 'Then we'll see what's what.'

Celia stopped crying for a moment and said, 'Leave the bloody lamp alone.' Then she started to sob again, louder than ever.

Ronald got to his feet and went over to Celia. He put his arm across her shoulder. 'Poor Celia,' he said, 'tell me what way I can help thee?'

Celia rose to her feet and screamed at him. 'You go away from here, you bastard,' she shouted. 'Just go away! I want never to see you again! Clear off!'

'Celia,' pleaded the old man.

'If that's what you want, Celia,' said Ronald. He picked up his beret from the chair and stood with his back to the cupboard. 'Good night, Thomas,' he said.

'Come back, Ronald,' said the shoemaker. 'Celia isn't herself tonight. She doesn't mean a word of what she says.'

The flames were dying down in the range. Celia and Ronald and the shoemaker moved about in the room, three unquiet shadows.

'Good night, Celia,' said Ronald from the door.

'I hate you, you bastard,' she shrieked at him.

The last flame died. In the seething darkness the girl and the old man heard the bang of the outer door closing. Celia sat down in her chair and began to cry again, a slow gentle wailing.

Halfway up the steps of the close the shoemaker caught up with Ronald. 'This is the worst she's ever been,' he said. 'You know the way it is with her – she drinks heavily for a week or so, anything she can get, and then for a month or six weeks after that she's as peaceable as a dove. But this is the worst she's ever been. God knows what will come of her.'

'God knows,' said Ronald.

'It started on Monday night,' said the shoemaker. 'That Norsky was here with foreign hooch.'

'Don't worry, Thomas,' said Ronald. 'It'll turn out all right, like you say.'

'She'll be fine next time you come back,' said the shoemaker. 'Just you wait and see.'

Ronald got onto his bicycle at the head of the close.

The shoemaker went back slowly into the house. As he opened the door Celia's low voice came out of the darkness. 'God forgive me,' she was saying gently and hopelessly, 'O God forgive me.'

7

'No,' said Celia to the minister, 'I don't believe in your God. It's no good. You're wasting your time. What the Hamnavoe folk are saying is true, I'm a bad woman. I drink. Men come about the place all hours of the night. It isn't that I want them fumbling at me with their mouths and their hands. That sickens me. I put up with it for the drink they have in their pockets. I must drink.

'You're not a drinking man, Mr Blackie. I know that. I *had* to buy this bottle of wine from the licensed grocer's. It gives me courage to speak to you. Try to understand that. And we're sitting here in the half darkness because I can speak to you better in this secrecy. Faces tell lies to one another. You know the way it is. The truth gets buried under smiles.

'I drink because I'm frightened. I'm so desperately involved with all the weak things, lonely things, suffering things I see about me. I can't bear the pity I feel for them, not being able to help them at all. There's blood everywhere. The world's a torture chamber, just a sewer of pain. That frightens me.

'Yesterday it was a gull and a water rat. They met at the end of this pier. I was pinning washing to the line when I saw it. The gull came down on the rat and swallowed it whole the way it would gulp a crust of bread, then with one flap of its wing it was out over the sea again. I could see the shape of the rat in the blackback's throat, a kind of fierce twist and thrust. The bird broke up in the air. It screamed. Blood and feathers showered out of it. The dead gull and the living rat made separate splashes in the water.

'It seems most folk can live with that kind of thing. Not me – I get all caught up in it . . .'

Stars slowly thickened and brightened in the window that looked over the harbour. The rising tide began to lap against the gable ends of the houses.

'Mr Blackie,' said Celia, 'an earthquake ruined a town in Serbia last week. The ground just opened and swallowed half the folk. Did your God in his mercy think up that too? The country folk in Viet Nam, what kind of vice is it they're gripped in, guns and lies and anger on both sides of them, a slowly tightening agony? Is your God looking after them? They never harmed anybody, but the water in the rice fields is red now all the time. Black men and white men hate each other in Chicago and Cape Town. God rules everything. He knew what was going to happen before the world was made. So we're told. If that's goodness, I have another name for it. Not the worst human being that ever lived would do the things God does. Tell me this, was God in the Warsaw ghetto too? I just want to know. I was reading about it last week in a book I got out of the Library.

'I know you don't like this darkness and the sound of wine being poured in the glass. It's the only way I can speak to you and be honest. . . .

'I remember my mother and my father. They were like two rocks in the sea. Life might be smooth or rough for me – there was hunger every now and then when the fishing was poor – but the two rocks were always there. I knew every ledge and cranny. I flew between them like a young bird.

'We were poor, but closer together because of that. We gave each other small gifts. I would take shells and seapinks into the house for them. My father always had a special fish for me when he came in from the west, a codling or a flounder as small as my hand. Then my mother would bake a small bannock for me to eat with it at tea-time, when I was home from school.

'I was twelve years old. One morning when I got up for school my mother was standing in the door looking out over the harbour. The fire was dead. She told me in a flat voice I wasn't to go to school that day, I was to go back to my room and draw the curtain and stay there till she called me. An hour later I heard feet on the pier. I looked through the edge of the curtain. Four fishermen were carrying something from the boat into the house. The thing was covered with a piece of sail and there was a trail of drops behind it. My father was in from his creels for the last time.

'We knew what real poverty was after that. My mother was too proud to take anything from the Poor Fund. "Of course not," she said, "my grandfather was schoolmaster in Hoy." . . . But in the middle of February she swallowed her pride and went to the Poor Inspector. One night I woke up and heard voices and came downstairs and I saw Thomas Linklater the shoemaker having supper beside the fire. A month after that my mother married him in the registry office. He came and sat in my father's chair and slept in my father's bed. He carried a new smell into our house, leather and rosin, like an animal of a different species.

'I hated him. Of course I smiled and spoke. But in my room, in the darkness, I hated the stranger.

'Three years went past. Then it was my mother's turn. I watched her changing slowly. I didn't know what the change was, nor why Dr Wilson should trouble to come so often. Then I heard Maisie Ness saying "cancer" to the watchmaker's wife at the end of the close. My mother was a good-looking woman. She was a bit vain and she'd often look long in the mirror, putting her hair to rights and smiling to her reflection. The change went on in her all that summer. She looked in the mirror less and less. Every day though she did her housework. The room had to be swept and the dishes put away before Dr Wilson called. Half a ghost, she knelt at the unlit fire and struck a match. That last morning she laid three bowls of porridge on the table. She looked at her withered face in the mirror. Then she groped for her chair and sank into it. She was dead before I could put down my spoon. The shoemaker hurried away to find Dr Wilson. The body slowly turned cold in the deep straw chair.

'I heard the shoemaker crying in his room the day before the funeral.

' "Blessed are the dead which die in the Lord" – that's what you said at the graveside. It was a poor way to die. It was ugly and degrading and unblessed, if anything ever was.

'We were alone in the house together then, a girl and an old cobbler. It was the beginning of winter. We spoke to each other only when it was needful. He gave me the housekeeping money every Friday and it was never enough. "There'll be more soon," he would say, "It's hard times, a depression all over the country. So-and-so owes five pounds for two pairs of shoes and I had a bill from the wholesale leather merchant for twenty pounds odds." . . . I wanted cakes on the table at the weekend but there was never anything but the usual bread and oatcakes and margarine.

'Christmas came. I wanted a few decorations about the house, a tree, paper bells, some tinsel, a dozen cards to send to my special friends – you know the way it is with young girls. "We can't afford nonsense like that," the shoemaker said. "We should be thankful to God for a roof over our heads." . . . And so the walls remained bare.

'That Christmas I hated him worse than ever.

'"Celia," he said at Hogmanay, just before it struck midnight, "I'm not a drinking man. But it's bad luck not to drink a health to the house at this time of year. We'll take one small dram together."

'He brought a half bottle of whisky out of the cupboard.

'The clock struck twelve. We touched glasses. I shuddered as the whisky went down. It burned my mouth and my stomach and it took tears to my eyes. "He's doing this deliberately to hurt me," I thought. My eyes were still wet when the door opened and Mr Spence the jeweller came in. He had a bottle of whisky in his hand to wish us a good New Year. He poured three glasses and we toasted each other. The cobbler merely wet his lips. I drank my whisky down quickly to get it over with.

'It's hard to explain what happened next. I knew who I was before I took that drink – a poor girl in an ordinary house on a fisherman's pier. I stood there holding an empty glass in my hand. A door was opening deep inside me and I looked through it into another country. I stood between the two places, confused and happy and excited. I still wore Celia's clothes but the clothes were all a disguise, bits of fancy dress, a masquerade. You know the ballad about the Scottish King who went out in the streets of Edinburgh in bonnet and tradesman's apron? I wore the clothes of a poor girl but I was wise, rich, great, gentle, good.

> *Then doon he let his duddies fa',*
> *And doon he let them fa'*
> *And he glittered a' in gold*
> *Far abune them a'.*

'The world was all mine and I longed to share it with everybody. Celia was a princess in her little house on the pier. She pretended to be poor but she had endless treasures in her keeping, and it was all a secret, nobody knew about it but Celia. A wild happiness filled the house.

'I bent down and kissed the old shoemaker.

'Mr Spence, I remember, was pouring another whisky into my glass. The confusion and the happiness increased. I felt very tired then, I remember. I went to bed wrapped in silks and swan's feathers.

'It was Celia the poor girl who woke up next morning. There was a hard grey blanket up at her face. She had a mouth like ashes. The wireless when she switched it on downstairs told of people dying of hunger in the streets of Calcutta, drifting about like wraiths and lying down on the burning pavements. And a plane had fallen from the sky in Kansas and forty people were dead on a hillside.

'She cried, the poor princess, beside the dead fire.

'The next Friday out of the housekeeping money I bought a bottle of cheap wine.

'That's all there is to tell, really. You've heard the confession of an alcoholic, or part of it, for the bad fairy tale isn't over yet.

'Once a month, maybe every six weeks, the fisher girl craves for news of the lost country, the real world, what she calls her kingdom. For a week or more I enchant myself away from the town and the pier and the sound of cobbling. When I have no more money left I encourage men to come here with drink. I'm shameless about it now. Everybody who has a bottle is welcome, even Mr Snoddy. At the end of every bout I'm in deeper exile than the time before. Every debauch kills a piece of Celia – I almost said, kills a part of her soul, but of course I don't believe in that kind of thing any more.

'And so the bad fairy tale goes on and the fisher girl who thinks that somehow she's a princess is slowly fitted with the cold blood and leathery skin and the terrible glittering eye of a toad.

'This kingdom I've had a glimpse of, though – what about that? It *seemed* real and precious. It seemed like an inheritance we're all born for, something that belongs to us by right.

'If that's true, it should be as much *there* as this pier is in the first light of morning. Why do we have to struggle towards it through fogs of drink? What's the good of all this mystery? The vision should be like a loaf or a fish, simple and real, something given to nourish the whole world.

'I blame God for that too.'

There was no sound for a while but the lapping of harbour water against stone as the tide rose slowly among the piers and slipways. The huge chaotic ordered wheel of stars tilted a little westward on its axis.

'The bottle's nearly empty,' said Celia, 'and I haven't said what I meant to say at all. I wonder if the licensed grocer would sell me another bottle? No, it's too late. And besides, I don't think I have enough money in my purse. And besides, you don't want to listen to much more of this bad talk.

'All the same, you can see now why I could never be a member of your church. All I could bring to it is this guilt,

shame, grief for things that happen, a little pity, a sure knowledge of exile.

'Will Christ accept that?'

There was another longer silence in the room.

'Celia,' said the Reverend Andrew Blackie, a little hopelessly, 'you must try to have faith.'

The girl's window was full of stars. The sky was so bright
that the outlines of bed and chair and cupboard could be
dimly seen, and the shapes of an empty bottle and a glass on
the table.

'I want to have faith,' said Celia. 'I want that more than
anything in the world.'

8

Ronald Leask worked his creels with Jock Henryson all that
Saturday afternoon along the west coast. They hauled eighty
creels under Marwick Head and Yesnaby. In the late afternoon
the wind shifted round to the northwest and strengthened and
brought occasional squalls of rain. They decided to leave their
remaining score of creels under the Black Crag till morning
and make for home before it got dark. They had a box of
lobsters and half a basket of crabs, a fair day's work. As Ronald
turned the *Celia* into Hoy Sound he saw three Norwegian
whalers racing for the shelter of Hamnavoe on the last of the
flood tide. Another squall of rain hit them. Ronald put on his
sou'wester and buttoned his black oilskin up to the chin. Jock
Henryson was at the wheel now, in the shelter of the cabin.

'It's going to be a dirty night,' said Jock.

They delivered their lobsters and crabs at the Fishermen's
Society pier. Then Jock said he must go home for his supper.
'You come too,' he said to Ronald. 'The wife'll have something
in the pot.'

'No,' said Ronald, 'I think I'll go along for a drink.'

It was raining all the time now. The flagstones of the street shone. Ronald stopped for a few seconds at the head of the shoemaker's close, then he walked on more quickly until he came to the lighted window of the Hamnavoe Bar. He pushed open the door. Bill MacIsaac the boatbuilder was at the bar drinking beer with Thorfinn Vik the farmer from Helliar. Sammy Flett the drunk was in too – he was half stewed and he was pestering the barman to give him a pint, and Drew the barman was refusing him patiently but firmly. A half-empty bottle of cheap wine stuck out of Sammy Flett's pocket.

'Here's Ronald Leask, a good man,' said Sammy Flett, going up to Ronald unsteadily. 'Ronald, you're a good friend of mine and I ask you to accept a cigarette out of my packet, and I'm very glad of your offer to furnish me with a glass of beer for old time's sake.'

'A glass of whisky,' said Ronald to Drew the barman.

'Absolutely delighted, old friend,' said Sammy Flett.

'It's not for you,' said Drew the barman to Sammy Flett. 'You're getting nothing, not a drop. The police sergeant was here this morning and your father with him and I know all about the trouble you're causing at home, smashing the chairs and nearly setting fire to the bed at the weekend. This place is out of bounds to you, sonny boy. I promised the sergeant and your old man. You can push off any time you like.'

'That's all lies,' said Sammy Flett. 'Just give me one pint of ordinary beer. That's not much for a man to ask.'

'No,' said Drew the barman.

'I demand to see the manager,' said Sammy Flett.

Ronald Leask drank his whisky at one go and put down his empty glass and nodded to Drew. The barman filled it up again.

'No water?' said Bill MacIsaac the boatbuilder, smiling across at Ronald.

'No,' said Ronald, 'no water.'

'Men in love,' said Thorfinn Vik of Helliar, 'don't need water in their drink.' Vik was in one of his dangerous insulting moods.

Sammy Flett went into the toilet. They heard the glug-glug of wine being drunk, then a long sigh.

The door opened and Mr William Snoddy the builder's clerk came in out of the rain. He looked round the bar nervously. 'A small whisky,' he said to Drew the barman, 'and put a little soda in it, not too much, and a bottle of export, if you please.' . . . He wiped his spectacles with his handkerchief and owled the bar with bulging naked eyes and put his spectacles on again. Then he recognised the man he was standing beside.

'Why, Ronald,' he said. 'It isn't often we see you in the bar. It's a poor night, isn't it?'

Ronald stared straight ahead at the rank of bottles under the bar clock. He put back his head and drank the remains of his second glass of whisky.

'Ronald, have a glass of whisky with me,' said Mr Snoddy, taking his wallet out of his inside pocket. 'It'll be a pleasure.'

'Same again,' said Ronald to the barman. 'And I'll pay for my own drink with my own money.'

Mr Snoddy flushed till his brow was almost as pink as his nose. Then he put his wallet back in his inside pocket.

Sammy Flett emerged from the toilet, smiling.

Bill MacIsaac and Thorfinn Vik began to play darts at the lower end of the bar.

'Oh well,' said Mr Snoddy, 'I don't suppose you can force a person to speak to you if he doesn't want to.' He drank his whisky down quickly and took a sip of beer.

Suddenly Sammy Flett came up behind Mr Snoddy and threw his arm round his neck. 'If it isn't my dear friend Mr Snoddy,' said Sammy Flett. 'Mr Snoddy, accept a cigarette, with my compliments.'

'Go away,' cried Mr Snoddy. 'Go away. Just leave me alone.'

'Mr Snoddy,' said Sammy Flett, 'I'll take the whisky that Mr Leask refused to accept for reasons best known to himself.'

'I come in here for a quiet drink,' said Mr Snoddy to the barman, trying to disengage his neck from Sammy Flett's arm.

'And you shall have it, dear Mr Snoddy,' said Sammy Flett. 'Accompany me to the gentleman's toilet. We shall have a drink of wine together. Mr Snoddy is always welcome to have a drink from Sammy.'

'Leave Mr Snoddy alone,' said Drew the barman.

The door opened and six Norwegian fishermen came in. 'Six double scotches, six Danish lagers,' Per Bjorling said to the barman. The Norwegians shook the rain from their coats and leaned against the bar counter. A row of six blond heads shone with wetness under the lamps.

'I know what they're saying about you, Mr Snoddy,' said Sammy Flett. 'They say you're going with other women. They say you're unfaithful to Mrs Snoddy. It's an evil world and they'll say anything but their prayers. But I don't believe that, Mr Snoddy. You and me, we're old friends, and I wouldn't believe such a thing about you. Not Sammy. Never.'

Mr Snoddy looked about him, angry and confused. He left his half-empty glass standing on the counter and went out quickly, clashing the door behind him.

'Mr Snoddy is a very fine man,' said Sammy Flett to the Norwegians.

'Is so?' said one of the Norwegians, smiling.

'Yes,' said Sammy Flett, 'and he's a very clever man too.'

'Interesting,' said another Norwegian.

'I'm no fool myself,' said Sammy Flett. 'I didn't sail up Hoy Sound yesterday in a banana skin. Sammy knows a thing or two.'

Dod Isbister the plumber came in and Jimmy Gold the postman and Andrew Thomson the crofter from Knowe. They went to the upper end of the bar and ordered beer. They emptied a box of dominoes on the counter and began to play.

The dart players finished their game and stuck their darts in the cork rim of the board. Thorfinn Vik was a bit drunk. He came over and stood beside Ronald Leask and began to sing:

> *I was dancing with my darling at the Tennessee waltz*
> *When an old friend I happened to see,*
> *Introduced him to my sweetheart and while they were*
> *   dancing*
> *My friend stole my sweetheart from me.*

'No singing,' said Drew the barman sternly. 'No singing in this bar. There's guests in the lounge upstairs.'

Thorfinn Vik turned to Ronald Leask. 'That's a song that you'll appreciate, Mr Leask,' he said. 'I sang it specially for you. A song about disappointed love.'

'Same again,' said Ronald Leask to the barman.

'A beautiful song,' said Sammy Flett from the middle of the Norwegian group. He had a glass of whisky in one hand and a glass of lager in the other that one of the whalers had bought for him. 'Very delightfully sung. Have you got songs in Norway as good as that? I daresay you have. Silence now for a Norwegian love song.'

'No singing,' said Drew.

'We sing only on our boat,' said Per Bjorling. 'We respect your rules. Please to give us seven double scotches and seven

Danish lagers.' . . . To Sammy Flett he said, 'There will be
singings later on the *Erika* – how you say? – a sing-song.'

'You are the true descendants of Vikings,' said Sammy
Flett.

'No,' said a young Norwegian, 'they were cruel men. It is
best to forget such people, no? We are peaceable fishermen.'

'Such is truthfully what we are,' said another Norwegian.

The door opened quietly and Mr Spence the jeweller
tiptoed in. He shook his umbrella close and went up to the
bar. 'One half bottle of the best whisky, to carry out,' he
murmured to Drew the barman. He laid two pound notes
discreetly on the counter.

'Mr Spence,' cried Sammy Flett from the centre of the
Norwegian group. 'My dear friend.'

'Leave Mr Spence alone,' said Drew. 'He doesn't want
anything about you.'

'I am content where I am,' said Sammy Flett, 'in the midst
of our Scandinavian cousins. But there's nothing wrong in
greeting my old friend Mr Spence.'

Mr Spence smiled and picked up his change and slid the
half bottle into his coat pocket.

'I think I know where you're off to with that,' said Sammy
Flett, wagging a finger at him.

Mr Spence smiled again and went out as quietly and
quickly as he had come in.

'Yes,' said Thorfinn Vik of Helliar, 'we all know where he's
going. . . .' He winked across at the domino players. 'Mr Leask
knows too.'

'I want no trouble in here,' said Drew the barman.

'Same again,' said Ronald Leask and pushed his empty
glass at the barman. His face was very red.

'Is clock right?' said Per Bjorling.

'Five minutes fast,' said Drew. 'It's twenty minutes to ten.'

Sammy Flett drank first his whisky and then his lager very quickly. The huge Adam's apple above his dirty collar wobbled two or three times. He sighed and said, 'Sammy is happy now. Sammy asks nothing from life but a wee drink now and then.'

'I am happy for you,' said the Norwegian boy. 'I will now buy you other drink.'

'No,' said Sammy Flett, 'not unless you all promise to partake of a little wine with me later in the gentlemen's toilet. At closing time Sammy will show you the pleasures of Hamnavoe. Sammy knows all the places.'

'Here is pleasures enough,' said the oldest Norwegian, 'in the pub.'

'No,' said Sammy, 'but I will take you to girls.'

'Girls,' said the old man. 'Oh no no. I am grandfather.'

'I have little sweetheart outside of Hammerfest,' said the boy. 'Gerd. She is milking the cattles and makes butter, also cheese from goats.'

'Also I am married,' said another Norwegian, 'and also is Paal and Magnus and Henrik. No girls. All are committed among us but Per.'

'Is true,' said Per Bjorling gravely.

'Per is liberty to find a girl where he likes,' said the old man. 'Per is goodlooking, is handsome, there is no trouble that Per our skipper will find a beautiful girl.'

The other Norwegians laughed.

'He's like a film star,' said Sammy Flett. 'Thank you most kindly, I'll have a glass of whisky and a bottle of beer. No offence. Per has a profile like a Greek hero.'

'Has found a beautiful girl already,' said the boy, smiling, 'in Hamnavoe.'

'One bottle of vodka,' said Per Bjorling to Drew, 'for outside drinking.'

Drew the barman took down a bottle of vodka from the shelf and called out, 'Last orders, gentlemen.'

'Double whisky,' said Ronald Leask.

Sammy Flett said to Per Bjorling, 'Are you going to visit this young lady now with your bottle of vodka?'

'A gift to her,' said Per Bjorling. 'Is a good girl. Is kind. Is understanding, intelligent. I like her very much.'

'What is the name of this fortunate young lady, if I might make so bold as to ask?' said Sammy Flett. 'Listen, Ronald. Per Bjorling is just going to tell us the name of his Hamnavoe sweetheart.'

Per Bjorling said, 'Celia.'

For about five seconds there was no sound in the bar but the click of dominoes on the counter.

Then Ronald Leask turned and hit Per Bjorling with his fist on the side of the head. The lager glass fell from Per Bjorling's hand and smashed on the floor. The force of the blow sent him back against the wall, his hands up at his face. He turned to Ronald Leask and said, 'Is not my wish to cause offence to any man present.'

'Cut it out,' cried Drew the barman. 'That's enough now.'

Ronald Leask stepped forward and hit Per Bjorling again, on the mouth. A little blood ran down Per Bjorling's jaw and his cap fell on the floor. He turned and hit Ronald Leask in the stomach and Ronald Leask flapped against the counter like a shiny black puppet. A score of glasses fell and smashed and a rapid pool of whisky and beer formed on the floor. Ronald Leask and Per Bjorling splintered and splashed through it, wrestling with each other. Ronald Leask clubbed down his fist on Per Bjorling's eye and Per Bjorling thrashed him across the jaw with the back of his hand. Ronald Leask went down on all fours among the beer and the broken glass.

'I am sorry for this,' said Per Bjorling and held out his hand.

Ronald Leask got slowly to his feet. His trouser knees were sopping wet and the palms of his hands cut and bleeding. A small bubble of blood grew and burst at his right nostril.

'Get out of here,' said Drew the barman, taking Ronald Leask by the sleeve of his oilskin, 'and never come back again. That applies to you too,' he said to Per Bjorling.

'So this is your Scotch hospitality,' said the Norwegian called Paal, 'to strike a man without reason. This we will not forget.'

'Remember this too,' said Thorfinn Vik, and struck Paal on the ear. 'This is our bar where we come to enjoy ourselves and this is our town and our women live in it.'

Drew picked up the telephone and his forefinger juggled in the dial.

'This is cowardice,' said the Norwegian boy. He stepped forward and took Thorfinn Vik by the throat. They lurched violently, locked together, between the seats and the bar counter. Half a dozen more glasses went over and smashed. Bill MacIsaac the boatbuilder tried to prise Thorfinn Vik and the young Norwegian apart. Andrew Thomson of Knowe put down his dominoes and began to take off his jacket slowly. 'I don't like fighting,' he said, 'but I'll fight if there's fighting to be done.'

'Gentlemen, gentlemen,' piped Sammy Flett from the fringe of the fight. Then he noticed an unattended glass of whisky on the bar counter and made for it. He was hidden behind a welter of heaving backs.

'You are bad man,' said the old Norwegian to Ronald Leask and slapped him magisterially across the face.

'Enough,' cried Per Bjorling.

Two policemen stood in the door.

Dod Isbister with a bottle in his hand and the Norwegian called Magnus with a glass in his hand were circling each other at the top end of the bar. Ronald Leask lashed out at Paal with his foot and missed and kicked Henrik on the elbow. Thorfinn Vik and the young Norwegian went over on the floor with a thud that made the bottles reel and rattle and clink. Dod Isbister threw the bottle he was holding and it missed Magnus's head and smashed into the lamp bulb. The light went out. The pub was a twilight full of grunting, breathing, slithering, cursing shadows.

'All right, gentlemen,' said the voice of Drew the barman, 'you can break it up. The law is here.'

The two policemen beamed their torches slowly over the wreckage. The fighters disengaged themselves. One by one they got to their feet.

'So this is the way it is,' said the sergeant. 'You'll have to come along to the station. We have accommodation for gentry like you. You haven't heard the last of this, I'm afraid. The sheriff will be wanting to see you all next Tuesday.'

'Not me, sergeant,' said Sammy Flett. 'Sammy never laid a finger on anybody.'

'You too,' said the sergeant. 'I wouldn't be surprised if you weren't at the bottom of this, Flett.'

Later, in the Black Maria going to the police station, Sammy Flett said, 'That was the best fight since the Kirkwall men threw Clarence Shaw into the harbour last carnival week.'

'Shut up, drunkard,' said Thorfinn Vik sleepily from the corner of the van.

'No, Thorfinn,' said Sammy Flett, 'but I want to reassure everyone, especially our Norwegian guests. The beds in the lock-up are very comfortable. The sergeant's wife will give us a cup of tea and toast in the morning. I know, because I've had bed and breakfast at Her Majesty's expense on twenty-two occasions – no, this makes it twenty-three. Everybody is very nice.'

'The little Gerd,' said the young Norwegian miserably. 'I am thinking of her so very much.'

The Black Maria jolted to a stop. They had arrived.

9

In the shoemaker's room the lamp was turned down low. It threw a feeble pool of light in one corner. The shoemaker was in his iron bed; he leaned back on three pillows and struggled for breath. Every inhalation was hard-won and shallow; the slack strings of his throat grew taut to force a passage for it, and his whole torso laboured to expel it again. His breathing slowly thickened and roughened, came in a quick spasm, and then he turned over on the pillows in a storm of feeble importunate coughing.

Celia came quickly through from the other room. She sat down on the edge of the bed and took the shoemaker's damp hand in both hers. 'You'll be all right,' she said. 'Just take it easy.'

The coughing stopped and the old man lay back on his pillows with his mouth open. Celia wiped his face with her apron. Then she lifted a small brown bottle from the table and shook a tablet out and poured some water in a cup. 'You've to take a tablet every four hours, Dr Wilson says,' she said. 'It stops the coughing.' She put the tablet in his mouth and raised his head and gave him a sip of water.

'If only I could sleep,' whispered the shoemaker. He lay back on the pillows with his eyes shut. 'I'm a very poor old sick man.'

'I won't leave you,' said Celia.

'Tell me one thing,' said the shoemaker, 'then maybe I can get to sleep. Is there any man or drink in the room next door?'

'No,' said Celia.

'Tell me the truth,' he whispered sternly. 'The truth, mind. I heard someone at the door.'

'Snoddy came at half-past eight,' said Celia. 'I sent him away. I told him you were ill. What's more, I told him I didn't want his drink.'

'Till the next time,' said the shoemaker.

'I suppose so,' said Celia.

The shoemaker's breath slowly roughened as new threads of phlegm spun themselves into a thick cord in his chest. Then suddenly he was possessed by spasm after spasm of futile coughing. He drew himself up in the bed and Celia put her arms round his thin body and held him close to her until the tough cord of phlegm broke and the coughing stopped. She took a bowl from the bedside chair and he managed to spit into it. The effort exhausted him. Celia laid him back on his pillows. Then she wiped his face in her apron.

'If only I could sleep,' said the shoemaker. 'I was dropping off to sleep an hour and more ago and then I was wakened first by Snoddy and then by a terrible noise along the street.'

'There was fighting in the Hamnavoe Bar,' said Celia. 'So Snoddy said. That's what you heard. Drew had to get the police.'

'It sounded like an earthquake,' said the shoemaker.

Celia stroked his chest outside his grey flannel shirt. 'Try to sleep now,' she said. 'I'll stay beside you till you go to sleep.' ... After a time she felt his chest grow quiet under her hand. His eyes were shut and his breath came deep and even through slightly parted lips. Celia knew that he wasn't asleep, but he was pretending to sleep so that she could get back to her bed.

Outside the rain slanted darkly. A sudden gust of wind caught the downpour and threw it against the window till all

the panes surged and throbbed. Through the onset Celia
heard a discreet tapping at the outside door.

'Don't let him in,' said the shoemaker, opening his eyes.

It was Mr Spence the jeweller. 'Celia,' he said.

'The old man isn't well,' said Celia in a low voice. 'The
doctor was here in the afternoon. I'll have to be up with him
all night.'

'Perhaps if I could just come in,' said Mr Spence.

'No,' said Celia.

'I'm very wet, my dear,' said Mr Spence.

'Please go home,' said Celia, 'Please.'

Mr Spence took the flask of whisky from his coat pocket.
'We will just have one little toddy,' he said. 'Thomas won't
mind me being in the house. He tells me I can come whenever I like. You know that. A little dram for a damp night,
eh?'

'Not tonight,' said Celia, 'I'm sorry.'

The rain slanted all about Mr Spence, a diagonal bright-
dark nagging susurration on the flagstones of the pier. The
gutters bubbled. Celia could smell the wetness from his
clothes.

'Celia,' said Mr Spence in a hurt voice, 'I am a very lonely
man.'

'Everyone is lonely,' said Celia gently. 'We're all prisoners.
We must try to find out a way to be pardoned.'

She shut the door and drew the bar across it. She was just
about to turn into her own seaward room when she heard the
shoemaker speaking aloud to himself in the room with the
dim light and the noise of rain in it. She stood in the lobby
and listened.

'And so it'll be all right once we're settled in Clett. Ronald
has a small room I can bide in. It doesn't matter about me, I
won't live that long. But Celia, she'll be happy at last. She'll

soon learn to look after the cow and the few hens, yes, he'll get a pot of soup when he comes in cold from the fishing. She'll be a good wife to Ronald. And I tell you this, Ronald won't allow all them bottles in his cupboard, no, and no bloody foreigners'll get within in a stone's throw of the place, and as for Snoddy, the dog of Clett'll tear the arse off the likes of him. Mr Spence, he can come as usual twice a week for a game of draughts, I'm sure Ronald won't object to that. We'll be fine once we're settled in Clett. Not that Ronald Leask's conferring any favour on Celia, not a bit of it, he's a lucky chap to be getting the likes of Celia for a wife. She can cook and sew and wash as well as any woman in Hamnavoe. I'll maybe be a burden to them for a winter or two, but Ronald said I could come, and by that time they'll likely have another burden, a bairn in the cradle, but a sweet burden, not an old done man. Once Celia's settled in Clett she'll have a new life entirely, there'll be no more drink and no more poverty and no more stray men in the night. An end to this darkness.'

Celia went softly into the room. The shoemaker closed his eyes quickly and pretended to be asleep. But another rope of phlegm was beginning to rasp in his chest. There was a smell too, all about the bed. Celia sat beside him and wiped his face with her apron. He opened his eyes and said, 'I'm sorry. I think I've messed the bed up.' He was ashamed and his eyes were wet.

'I know,' said Celia. 'Don't worry. I'll get you cleaned up before anything else. There's a kettle of hot water on the range. Plenty of clean sheets in the cupboard.'

She opened the window to let the smell out. Rain and wind swirled in and the shoemaker began to cough. She closed the window again quickly.

For the next twenty minutes Celia washed the old man and dried him and put a clean shirt on him and stripped the bed and put clean sheets on it and set the soiled stinking sheets in a tub of disinfected water in the lobby.

'You'll feel better now,' said Celia. 'I'm going to make a cup of tea for the two of us.'

The shoemaker was racked with a violent spasm of coughing. She held him till the tough cord of phlegm shore in his throat and he spat it out. She laid him back exhausted on the pillows.

'Fighting along the street a while ago,' said the shoemaker wearily. 'It's always them foreigners.'

'It's all quiet now,' said Celia. 'Time you had another tablet though.'

She took a yellow tablet out of the bottle onto her hand and put it on his tongue. She laid her arm round his shoulders and raised him and put the cup of water to his mouth.

'They don't seem to help me, them tablets,' said the shoemaker.

'They will,' said Celia. 'Give them time. Dr Wilson's tablets always work, you know that.'

'Maybe I'll get a sleep now,' said the shoemaker.

'Try,' said Celia.

But the hoarseness was in his chest again. He coughed and spat out thick phlegm. But as always when this sickness was on him, he had hardly torn the purulent fungus from his bronchial tree when a new growth rose about it, blocking and strangling his breath.

'I'm a terrible nuisance to you,' he said, 'a silly awkward old man.'

'You're not,' said Celia, 'and you'll be better tomorrow. And there's a fine shed at Clett where you can mend boots. I'll ask Ronald to put a stove in it.'

The shoemaker was suddenly asleep, the way sleep comes to the very young and the very old. His cheeks flushed like two withered apples. He breathed as quietly as a child.

'Thank God,' said Celia.

She drew the blankets up to his chin and kissed him on the forehead.

The window paled with the end of the night.

The rain had stopped, as it often does before dawn. Celia closed the door of the shoemaker's room softly and unbarred the outer door and went out onto the pier. The first seagulls were screaming along the street, scavenging in the bins. She breathed the clean air of early morning. She stood at the pier wall and watched the sea moving darkly against the weeded steps and slipways. A rat in the seaweed squinnied at her and twitched its whiskers and went into the water with a soft plop. The sun had not yet risen, but light was assembling in broken colours over the Orphir hills. The first blackbird in the fuchsia bush under the watchmaker's wall faltered into song and then was silent again. Celia could see the boats in the harbour now and at the farm across the harbour black ploughed squares among green grass and brown heather. It would be a beautiful morning.

Then the sun rose clear of the Orphir hills and folded the girl in the light of a new day.

The Wireless Set

The first wireless ever to come to the valley of Tronvik in Orkney was brought by Howie Eunson, son of Hugh the fisherman and Betsy.

Howie had been at the whaling in the Antarctic all winter, and he arrived back in Britain in April with a stuffed wallet and jingling pockets. Passing through Glasgow on his way home he bought presents for everyone in Tronvik – fiddle-strings for Sam down at the shore, a bottle of malt whisky for Mansie of the hill, a secondhand volume of Spurgeon's sermons for Mr Sinclair the missionary, sweeties for all the bairns, a meerschaum pipe for his father Hugh and a portable wireless set for his mother Betsy.

There was great excitement the night Howie arrived home in Tronvik. Everyone in the valley – men, women, children, dogs, cats – crowded into the but-end of the croft, as Howie unwrapped and distributed his gifts.

'And have you been a good boy all the time you've been away?' said Betsy anxiously. 'Have you prayed every night, and not sworn?'

'This is thine, mother,' said Howie, and out of a big cardboard box he lifted the portable wireless and set it on the table.

For a full two minutes nobody said a word. They all stood staring at it, making small round noises of wonderment, like pigeons.

'And mercy,' said Betsy at last, 'what is it at all?'

'It's a wireless set,' said Howie proudly. 'Listen.'

He turned a little black knob and a posh voice came out of the box saying that it would be a fine day tomorrow over England, and over Scotland south of the Forth–Clyde valley, but that in the Highlands and in Orkney and Shetland there would be rain and moderate westerly winds.

'If it's a man that's speaking,' said old Hugh doubtfully, 'where is he standing just now?'

'In London,' said Howie.

'Well now,' said Betsy, 'if that isn't a marvel! But I'm not sure, all the same, but what it isn't against the scriptures. Maybe, Howie, we'd better not keep it.'

'Everybody in the big cities has a wireless,' said Howie. 'Even in Kirkwall and Hamnavoe every house has one. But now Tronvik has a wireless as well, and maybe we're not such clodhoppers as they think.'

They all stayed late, listening to the wireless. Howie kept twirling a second little knob, and sometimes they would hear music and sometimes they would hear a kind of loud half-witted voice urging them to use a particular brand of toothpaste.

At half past eleven the wireless was switched off and everybody went home. Hugh and Betsy and Howie were left alone.

'Men speak,' said Betsy, 'but it's hard to know sometimes whether what they say is truth or lies.'

'This wireless speaks the truth,' said Howie.

Old Hugh shook his head. 'Indeed,' he said, 'it doesn't do that. For the man said there would be rain here and a westerly wind. But I assure you it'll be a fine day, and a southerly wind, and if the Lord spares me I'll get to the lobsters.'

Old Hugh was right. Next day was fine, and he and Howie took twenty lobsters from the creels he had under the Gray Head.

*   *   *

It was in the spring of the year 1939 that the first wireless set came to Tronvik. In September that same year war broke out, and Howie and three other lads from the valley joined the minesweepers.

That winter the wireless standing on Betsy's table became the centre of Tronvik. Every evening folk came from the crofts to listen to the nine o'clock news. Hitherto the wireless had been a plaything which discoursed Scottish reels and constipation advertisements and unreliable weather forecasts. But now the whole world was embattled and Tronvik listened appreciatively to enthusiastic commentators telling them that General Gamelin was the greatest soldier of the century, and he had only to say the word for the German Siegfried Line to crumble like sand. In the summer of 1940 the western front flared into life, and then suddenly no more was heard of General Gamelin. First it was General Weygand who was called the heir of Napoleon, and then a few days later Marshal Pétain.

France fell all the same, and old Hugh turned to the others and said, 'What did I tell you? You can't believe a word it says.'

One morning they saw a huge grey shape looming along the horizon, making for Scapa Flow. 'Do you ken the name of that warship?' said Mansie of the hill. 'She's the *Ark Royal*, an aircraft carrier.'

That same evening Betsy twiddled the knob of the wireless and suddenly an impudent voice came drawling out. The voice was saying that German dive bombers had sunk the *Ark Royal* in the Mediterranean. 'Where is the *Ark Royal*?' went the voice in an evil refrain. 'Where is the *Ark Royal*? Where is the *Ark Royal*?'

'That man,' said Betsy, 'must be the Father of Lies.'

Wasn't the *Ark Royal* safely anchored in calm water on the other side of the hill?

Thereafter the voice of Lord Haw-Haw cast a spell on the inhabitants of Tronvik. The people would rather listen to him than to anyone, he was such a great liar. He had a kind of bestial joviality about him that at once repelled and fascinated them; just as, for opposite reasons, they had been repelled and fascinated to begin with by the rapturous ferocity of Mr Sinclair's Sunday afternoon sermons, but had grown quite pleased with them in time.

They never grew pleased with William Joyce, Lord Haw-Haw. Yet every evening found them clustered round the portable radio, like awed children round a hectoring schoolmaster.

'Do you know,' said Sam of the shore one night, 'I think that man will come to a bad end?'

Betsy was frying bloody-puddings over a primus stove, and the evil voice went on and on against a background of hissing, sputtering, roaring and a medley of rich succulent smells.

Everyone in the valley was there that night. Betsy had made some new ale and the first bottles were being opened. It was good stuff, right enough; everybody agreed about that.

Now the disembodied voice paused, and turned casually to a new theme, the growing starvation of the people of Britain. The food ships were being sunk one after the other by the heroic U-boats. Nothing was getting through, nothing, nor a cornstalk from Saskatchewan nor a tin of pork from Chicago. Britain was starving. The war would soon be over. Then there would be certain pressing accounts to meet. The ships were going down. Last week the Merchant Navy was poorer by a half million gross registered tons. Britain was starving . . .

At this point Betsy, who enjoyed her own ale more than anyone else, thrust the hissing frying pan under the nose – so to speak – of the wireless, so that its gleam was dimmed for a moment or two by a rich blue tangle of bloody-pudding fumes.

'Smell that, you brute,' cried Betsy fiercely, 'smell that!'

The voice went on, calm and vindictive.

'Do you ken,' said Hugh, 'he canna hear a word you're saying.'

'Can he not?' said Sandy Omand, turning his taurine head from one to the other. 'He canna hear?'

Sandy was a bit simple.

'No,' said Hugh, 'nor smell either.'

After that they switched off the wireless, and ate the bloody-puddings along with buttered bannocks, and drank more ale, and told stories that had nothing to do with war, till two o'clock in the morning.

*   *   *

One afternoon in the late summer of that year the island postman cycled over the hill road to Tronvik with a yellow corner of telegram sticking out of his pocket.

He passed the shop and the manse and the schoolhouse, and went in a wavering line up the track to Hugh's croft. The wireless was playing music inside, Joe Loss and his orchestra.

Betsy had seen him coming and was standing in the door.

'Is there anybody with you?' said the postman.

'What way would there be?' said Betsy. 'Hugh's at the lobsters.'

'There should be somebody with you,' said the postman.

'Give me the telegram,' said Betsy, and held out her hand. He gave it to her as if he was a miser parting with a twenty-pound note.

She went inside, put on her spectacles, and ripped open the envelope with brisk fingers. Her lips moved a little, silently reading the words.

Then she turned to the dog and said, 'Howie's dead.' She went to the door. The postman was disappearing on his bike round the corner of the shop and the missionary was hurrying towards her up the path.

She said to him, 'It's time the peats were carted.'

'This is a great affliction, you poor soul,' said Mr Sinclair the missionary. 'This is bad news indeed. Yet he died for his country. He made the great sacrifice. So that we could all live in peace, you understand.'

Betsy shook her head. 'That isn't it at all,' she said. 'Howie's sunk with torpedoes. That's all I know.'

They saw old Hugh walking up from the shore with a pile of creels on his back and a lobster in each hand. When he came to the croft he looked at Betsy and the missionary standing together in the door. He went into the outhouse and set down the creels and picked up an axe he kept for chopping wood.

Betsy said to him, 'How many lobsters did you get?'

He moved past her and the missionary without speaking into the house. Then from inside he said, 'I got two lobsters.'

'I'll break the news to him,' said Mr Sinclair.

From inside came the noise of shattering wood and metal.

'He knows already,' said Betsy to the missionary. 'Hugh knows the truth of a thing generally before a word is uttered.'

Hugh moved past them with the axe in his hand.

'I got six crabs forby,' he said to Betsy, 'but I left them in the boat.'

He set the axe down carefully inside the door of the outhouse. Then he leaned against the wall and looked out to sea for a long while.

'I got thirteen eggs,' said Betsy. 'One more than yesterday. That old Rhode Islander's laying like mad.'

The missionary was slowly shaking his head in the doorway. He touched Hugh on the shoulder and said, 'My poor man—'

Hugh turned and said to him, 'It's time the last peats were down from the hill. I'll go in the morning first thing. You'll be needing a cart-load for the Manse.'

The missionary, awed by such callousness, walked down the path between the cabbages and potatoes. Betsy went into the house. The wireless stood, a tangled wreck, on the dresser. She brought from the cupboard a bottle of whisky and glasses. She set the kettle on the hook over the fire and broke the peats into red and yellow flame with a poker. Through the window she could see people moving towards the croft from all over the valley. The news had got round. The mourners were gathering.

Old Hugh stood in the door and looked up at the drift of clouds above the cliff. 'Yes,' he said, 'I'm glad I set the creels where I did, off Yesnaby. They'll be sheltered there once the wind gets up.'

'That white hen,' said Betsy, 'has stopped laying. It's time she was in the pot, if you ask me.'

The Eye of the Hurricane

When first I went to live in the ground floor flat of Captain Stevens's house on the hill behind Hamnavoe, three months ago, he would ask me every Friday afternoon to bring him from the licensed grocer's in the town a half bottle of rum. He had a young woman, Miriam, who cleaned his room for him every morning and did his errands – a plain hard-working pleasant girl – but he never asked her to bring his weekend drink; possibly because Miriam's parents, and Miriam herself, were members of the Salvation Army, and might have conscientious objections.

It was no trouble for me to get his half bottle of rum; Friday was the day I ordered my half-dozen cans of export beer, a modest quantity of drink that lasted me all week. I drank one can every evening between tea-time and supper-time.

The first Friday of February this year Captain Stevens came downstairs, knocked at my door and entered brusquely. 'I know it's only Friday morning, Barclay,' he said, 'and I don't want to interrupt your work, but would it be too much to ask you to nip down to the town and get my rum as soon as it's convenient. I have a very heavy cold.'

'I'm sorry to hear that,' I said.

'A very heavy cold indeed,' he said. 'I spent too long the other day at the wreck, you know, the Danish fishing boat at the Kirk Rocks. Got my feet wet walking about her in the ebb.'

'There's where you caught your cold,' I said.

'Nowhere else,' said Captain Stevens. 'It's very good of you to go.' He laid a five-pound note on the table.

It was in fact a great nuisance for me to oblige him just then. Every morning, between breakfast and lunch-time, I work hard at my novel, and I let nothing distract me. In the afternoon I am at anybody's service; I keep that time for exercise; usually a walk along the Atlantic coast of the island, watching the movement of birds and water and clouds, or I might do some shopping in the town. Every evening I read or listen to the wireless, and drink my can of export. Very few friends call; I'm a stranger in the island; I don't find talk necessary; my writing comes before everything.

'I'm a bit busy, as you can see,' I said. The table was crowded with the paraphernalia of my trade – a writing pad crammed with the draft of a chapter, scored and interlined and transcribed in different colours of ink, a chaos unintelligible to anybody but myself; the partly-written fair copy on clean folded octavo sheets; blue and black and red biros; and the shrouded silent typewriter.

'I'm rather ill,' he insisted.

Well, I thought to myself, it will be an act of charity all the more meritorious because I don't want to do it. I am a Catholic and in the world as it is at present I find few opportunities for practising holy charity; the welfare state has abolished the poor and hidden the sick out of sight. I hope, in a vague kind of way, that writing is my work of charity, that perhaps my books bring solace and happiness to a few people that I have never seen or known. Here was one small extra opportunity to show that I was not altogether a timeserver in the kingdom of Christ.

'Thank you a lot,' said Captain Stevens as I put on my coat. 'Much obliged. Get me two full bottles of navy rum. The fiver will just cover it. I want this cold shifted by Monday – got a meeting of the Harbour Board that night.'

It struck me, as I walked down the steep road to the town, the captain doesn't look as if he had the cold, he isn't coughing or flushed or speaking thickly. There could of course be other more subtle symptoms.

I delivered the two bottles of rum in his upstairs room and finished copying the first third of Chapter Five before putting my Friday dinner to cook on the gas ring – smoked haddock simmered in milk and butter and thickened with corn flour and grated cheese.

Afterwards I walked along the coast as far as the Danish wreck, the *Dinesen*. She was poised high and dry among the rocks, masts and funnel and wheelhouse intact, not a scratch on her. It seemed a pity, but the local men said she could never be refloated. She was lost as irretrievably as if the mid-ocean maelstrom had sucked her down. 'And,' said Dan Fraser the coastguard, leaning against the kirk-yard wall smoking his pipe, 'there was no fog or gale to put her there. She went ashore last Wednesday, a bright mild afternoon if you remember. And there's her crew drinking and carrying on every night in the town, not caring one damn. If you ask me,' he said, 'they missed their drink and women and so they just deliberately piled her up where she is.'

That evening I was listening to an Ionescu play when I heard a couple of thumps on the ceiling over my head; it was Captain Stevens knocking. The wireless is on too loud, I thought, and lowered the volume. The knocking went on. Then I remembered he was unwell. When I entered his room he was in bed, and now he certainly had all the symptoms.

His cheeks flared, he had watery eyes, the breath hurled in his chest, and he spoke thickly and inconsequentially.

'A terrible thing, Barclay,' he said. 'I dropped one of my bottles of rum, smashed it. Never do at all. I need the hot grog. If you open that drawer, Barclay, very kind of you, you'll see a wallet, there's a wad of notes in it, fivers. Take one of them. Got it? I don't mind your wireless being on at all, play it as loud as you like. Well, look, would you just nip down to Wilson's like a good chap and get me another bottle, no, better make it two while we're at it. Thanks a lot, you're very kind.'

Wilson was the licensed grocer.

As I walked down the road I couldn't help wondering about the broken bottle. While I was in Captain Stevens's room I had noticed the two rum bottles. One was three-quarters full and was standing on his bedside table (beside the framed photograph of a beautiful young woman) and the bottle on the mantelpiece was empty but unbroken.

As it happened, Wilson's was closed when I got there. I had to go along the street to the Hamnavoe Bar. The half-dozen fishermen from the *Dinesen* were inside, drinking lager beside the fire. They seemed to me to be inoffensive enough fellows.

* * *

Chapter Five of the novel went well next morning. I got up passing eight o'clock, had breakfast of tea and toast and a boiled egg, washed and shaved, said my prayers and began to write where I had left off yesterday. I stopped work in full flush at eleven o'clock to make some bovril. This flight that I had made from city to island was working out well. I had almost forgotten Sandra; all that remained of that summer affair was a criss-cross of scars in the spirit. Lovers with their new-sharpened senses set about chiselling a form of ideal desire, an Eros, that they can worship together till death; in the end, disillusioned, the finely-honed edges inflict ignorant vindictive surgery on one another. It was all over now, the long earnest discussions on sex and freedom and God, the Bartok and Monteverdi records, the Saturday afternoon strolls through the Botanic Gardens, the love-making in her flat after brandy and coffee (two fevered statues tumbled one on the other), the recriminations, confessions, resolutions. A phrase in Sandra's last letter sticks in my mind, 'We got out of our depths, you and I.' . . . It reminds me of a summer holiday by the sea when I was about seven. Another boy called Kim and myself played day after day on a rubber raft, navigating cautiously between the beach-balls and the white legs of old gentlemen paddling. One day we drifted further out. I looked down into undulating seaweed, a vast enchanted forest. Fish glinted from rock to rock like a silent torrent of knives. Kim and I laughed uncertainly to one another. Far out in the bay a steamer passed, and in her wake the raft bobbed and rocked and tumbled. Suddenly the bathing sheds and the donkeys seemed so far away that we could never return to that secure place – we were lost forever in this beautiful alien cruel element. We looked at each other with trembling lips, and Kim began to cry. An old fisherman rowed past from his lobster pots and towed us to the shore. For the rest of that holiday Kim and I avoided each other, we never exchanged so much as a single word. . . . That was the kind of way Sandra and I 'got out of our depths'.

I had come to live, then, among simple uncomplicated people. I worked to the easy regular rhythm of fishermen and crofters. My imagination nourished itself at primitive wholesome sources, the sea and the land. It seemed to me my writing had a depth and clarity I had never achieved before. (And of course I was working in the place where my novel was rooted. That was the reason, apart from Sandra, that I had come to live in the islands.)

There was a gentle tap at the door, and Miriam came in. 'I'm sorry to trouble you, Mr Barclay,' she said, 'but it's the Captain.'

'Is his cold worse?' I said.

She looked with fleeting horror at the crucifix on my wall and the porcelain Virgin-and-child on the dresser. Then she said, 'He hasn't got a cold, and I'm more than surprised at you, Mr Barclay, bringing drink to an old man who was at death's door twice last year with rum.'

'I'm sorry,' I said. 'I didn't know.'

'You know now,' she said. 'Never take a drop of drink to him, especially when he's on one of his bouts. He nearly died twice last year. He's getting old, he can't stand it so much now as he used to. You see, he's been having bouts ever since I can mind, three or four times a year. He spends a fortune. And he won't eat a bite so long as there's drink in his room. I tell you what it is, he only began to drink after Mrs Stevens died ten years ago. She was a beautiful person. They were only married a year. Then God took her.'

'I'm sorry,' I said.

'Please,' Miriam said, 'you must help me. The best thing you can do is say No when he asks you to get him more rum from the town. Just say No. He won't be pleased at the time, but after it's over he'll thank you. Promise.'

'All right,' I said. 'I promise.'

'Thank you,' said Miriam. 'Thank you very much indeed.'

'How long do they last, his bouts?' I said.

'About a week,' said Miriam.

I did no more work on Chapter Five that morning. I could hear upstairs the broken music of their dialogue – though no distinct words came through the ceiling – the curt voice of Captain Stevens and the gentle pleadings of the girl; then a loaded silence.

I put away my writing things.

I spent the afternoon at the shops, buying fish and meat and groceries for the weekend, and arranging for a taxi to take me the fifteen miles to Mass in Kirkwall next morning.

Now that Miriam had prepared me for some days of tension in the house, I wasn't surprised when a summons came early in the evening, three loud irregular thumps on the ceiling.

He was sitting beside the fire in an old dressing-gown. He hadn't washed his face, an unusual thing, for he was a neat spruce little man. There was no sight of bottles or glasses anywhere, but I breathed thick sweet treacly air. The rum ritual was being observed in secrecy.

'Come in, Barclay,' he said. 'Pleased to see you. Sit down over there.'

'How's the cold?' I said.

'So-so,' he said. 'We'll talk about that in a minute. The writing going along fine?'

'Moderately,' I said.

'That's no life for a man, writing,' said the captain. 'Do some real work, get a croft or a fishing boat, that's the thing. You should have a woman. I wish I was young, I wish I had my time over again. I'd show them. I would do a lot of things different.'

'I think you've made a real success of your life,' I said. 'Commodore of the shipping line. The O.B.E. County councillor. Chairman of the Harbour Board.'

'Salt and ashes,' he said. 'Now, Barclay, about this cold of mine.'

'Miriam says you haven't got a cold at all,' I said.

'The little bitch,' he said. 'Did she go into your room? She had no right to be disturbing you. I'll speak to her about that. I expect she told you also that I have drinking bouts.'

'She did,' I said.

'Well,' he said, 'everybody knows. Can't do a thing about it, Barclay. It's a natural thing, like a storm, you just have to let it blow itself out, keep the ship headed into it. Do you understand that, Barclay?'

'I know nothing about it,' I said.

'I thought writers are supposed to understand things,' he said, 'the quirks of human nature. That's what they're for. Don't take hard what I say, Barclay. I like you. I'm very glad you're living in this house. I'm just explaining the situation to you, setting the course through the storm, so that you can take your turn at navigating if the need arises. The best way you can help the voyage, Barclay, is just do what I say. I'm the skipper of this ship. And the first thing I want you to do is open that drawer and you'll see a wallet.'

'No,' I said, and got to my feet.

'There should be four five-pound notes in it. Take one of them out.'

'No,' I said.

'Two bottles of navy rum from Wilson's, as quick as you can.'

Charity is no hard-minted currency to be distributed according to whim, a shilling here and a sovereign there – it is the oil and wine that drop uncertainly through the fingers upon the wounds of the world, wherever the roads of pity and suffering cross. It might help this old man, as he said, if I stood close beside him on the bridge till this particular hurricane blew itself out. But I trusted the older wisdom of women. I had made a promise to Miriam.

'No,' I said.

'Very well, Mr Barclay,' he said after a pause. 'Let me see. At the moment you are paying me a rent of two pounds a week, I think. As from Monday next you will pay me four pounds a week. In fact, I think you should make arrangements to leave this house before the end of the month. I find you an unsatisfactory tenant. Now get out.'

All night, till I fell into a drowse around three o'clock in the morning, I heard him pacing back and fore, back and fore in his room, an ancient mariner in a ship of dark enchantment.

*   *   *

Chapter Five got wedged in some deep rut of my mind. I sat most of a morning with my black biro poised over the writing pad. The phrases and sentences that presented themselves were dull, flaccid, affected. I looked blankly at the crucifix on the wall, but the Word that spanned all history with meaning was only a tortured image. The words I offered to the Word were added insults, a few more random thorns for the crown. I scored out everything I had written since breakfast-time.

It flatters us writers to think of ourselves as explorers, probing into seas that have never been mapped, or charted with only a few broken lines. But the spacious days of 'Here be Whales', cherubs puffing gales from the four quarters, mid-ocean mermaids, are gone forever. There is nothing new to find; every headland has been rounded, every smallest ocean current observed, the deepest seas plumbed. Chaucer, Cervantes, Tolstoy, Proust charted human nature so well that really little is left for a novelist like myself to do. For the most part we voyage along old trade routes, in rusty bottoms; and though we carry cargoes of small interest to anyone – coal or wheat – we should be glad that hungry cupboards here and there are stored with bread and there are fires burning in cold snow villages of the north.

Miriam came in without knocking. 'The captain's had a terrible night, the poor man,' she said. 'There's six broken cups in the sideboard. The rug's saturated. He was trying to make himself a pot of tea, and his hands all spasms. He never so much as closed an eye.' She had her coat on to go home for, as I said, she only works in the house mornings.

'He wanted me to get him more rum,' I said, 'two bottles, but I wouldn't do it.'

'You were right,' said Miriam.

'He's going to put me out on the road,' I said.

'Don't worry about that,' said Miriam. 'That was the devil talking, not the poor captain at all. Once he's better he won't know a thing he's said this past day or two.'

'I'm glad,' I said, 'because I like it here.'

'It must be lonely for you,' said Miriam. 'You should come to our Joy Hour some Thursday evening. There's choruses and readings from the Good Book, and O, everybody's so happy!' Her eyes drifted uneasily over the crucifix and the Virgin.

I said nothing.

'I'm pleased with you,' said Miriam, 'for saying No to him. He'll suffer, but his bout'll be over all the sooner. Tomorrow, or the day after, he'll be his old self again.'

There came a violent double thump on the ceiling. 'Get off, you bitch!' roared Captain Stevens. 'What are you talking to that pansy for? This is my house. Away home with you!'

Miriam lowered her voice. 'Be firm for one day more,' she whispered. 'He'll try to wheedle you in the afternoon for sure. I know him. Just keep saying No.'

'I will,' I said.

'If only Robert Jansen and Stony Hackland keep away,' whispered Miriam. 'You mustn't let them in. If they come to the door just send them packing. Be very firm.'

'Who are they?' I said.

'Seamen who used to sail in his ships,' she whispered. 'They carry the drink in to him whenever he has a bout.'

'They won't get in,' I said.

When she smiled her plain little face shone for a moment like one of Botticelli's angels.

If she had been born in a Breton village, I thought, she would be a devout Catholic girl, and rosary and image and candle – that she shied away from with such horror – would be the gateway to her dearest treasures and delights. As it was, she merely touched the hem of Christ's garment in passing.

The weather continued mild. But the *Dinesen* showed a deterioration when I walked beyond the kirkyard on Monday afternoon. The sea lay high and bright about the wreck – one thought of water on such a day as the gentlest of the elements – yet sometime during the weekend it had lifted the boat and set her down at a slightly different angle, against a rock, so that she looked now for the first time like some utterly help-less thing, and the mast sagged from the deck like a broken limb.

I was cooking my bacon and eggs on the gas ring at five o'clock, glancing occasionally through the window over the road and the town and harbour. A very old man was strug-gling up the road, carrying a loaded hold-all, and stopping every now and again to get his breath. It was a painful climb for such a frail creature. Then he turned in at our gate, and I saw that it was Captain Stevens. The door opened; I heard his quick harsh breathing in the lobby; he climbed the stair to his room. He was home, under his own steam, with another cargo of rum.

I settled down for an evening of reading, Alain-Fournier's *Le Grand Meaulnes*, an exquisite rural idyll, as far removed as could be from salt and rum; but I wasn't surprised when, soon after eight o'clock in the evening, the interruption came.

'Barclay!' roared Captain Stevens from the stair-head, 'I want to see you, double quick, no hunkersliding, at once!'

I went upstairs.

He was standing at the table, supporting himself with his fists. There was a half-empty bottle on the table and a full bottle on top of his television set and three with various quantities of rum in them ranged along the mantleshelf. He was very drunk and angry. 'Barclay,' he said, 'you understand this is a matter for the police. As soon as we dock I will report you.'

'What for?' I said.

'Don't come the holy simpleton with me,' said Captain Stevens. 'You and your fancy-women! Do you think I'm going about this ship deaf, blind, and stupid! Is that what you think? Barclay, I know this for a fact, last night you had Merran Muir and Thora Romanski and Celia Thomson in your cabin. Did you or did you not? A straight answer now.'

'I did not,' I said.

'You're a liar, Barclay. I won't have this ship turned into a whore-house. I intend to report you to the police. Meantime I confine you to your cabin.'

I turned to go. My hand was on the door-knob when he spoke again. 'I have reason to believe,' he said in a low even voice, 'that you're trying to seduce little Miriam. You will not speak to her in future. You will not so much as look at her. For if you do, by God, old man as I am, I'll thrash you within an inch of your life. Now get out.'

The bitter sea had invaded the wheatfields and lakes of *Le Grand Meaulnes*; the delicate masque was drenched, dragged under, drowned. I tried to read a few more pages, but it was no good. I went to bed and lay sleepless for hours. Near midnight he shouted from the stair-head, 'I once had a black woman.'

Later there were some bursts of laughter from his room, and once I thought he was crying, and once a cup went over on the floor with a small crash.

Then all sounds guttered into silence.

*   *   *

My novel is about the holy voyage of Rögnvald Kolson, Earl of Orkney, who sailed from Norway to Palestine (Guthaland, 'God's country' the Norsemen called it) in 1150–51. With Earl Rögnvald in fifteen ships sailed the Bishop of Orkney, a group of brilliant Icelandic poets, and the greatest captains of the north – Thorbjorn Black, John Peterson, Erling Ormson, Solmund Fishhook, Eindred Young. The voyage was rooted in pure intention; it was to be a pilgrimage, a penance, a God-faring, to redeem the time, to delete from history the Viking hawkfall. 'We must wash a great quantity of crusted blood from our hands,' said Earl Rögnvald. Christianity had been crudely grafted onto Scandinavia a century and a half earlier. 'But you do not make saints out of savages overnight,' said Bishop William of Orkney. 'The leaven needs time to work.' The pilgrims who took the dove's path to Jerusalem were in fact not radically different from their fathers who had torn harp and tapestry and fleur-de-lys all over the west less than a century before. Events took place during this holy voyage – the landfall and banqueting in Narbonne, the siege of the Spanish castle, the attack on the Saracen ship – which Earl Rögnvald chose to regard as flowers of Christian chivalry; but the roots went deep into the dark history that was to be sanctified. 'See how well they change their praying hands back into claws,' said the Bishop. 'We had better say a Mass on the deck *every* morning.'

I had made a satisfactory start with the ordering of the great ships in Norway, the craft of the shipwright, the recruitment of seamen, the Orkney wintering, a great storm in the Bay of Biscay and the passage through the Strait of Gibraltar, in the first four chapters. This was straightforward stuff, boisterous, epic, gay. The fifth chapter required altogether different treatment. At the seaport of Narbonne in France, Earl Rögnvald, paying a courtesy call, met the countess of the palace, a young widow called Ermengarde. That evening, among the wine cups and the lutes, they looked at each other, their eyes faltered, their lips fell silent. There is a small delicious silence in the saga also; but after a winter in Narbonne the Iceland skalds, and Earl Rögnvald himself, made rapturous lyrics about their French hostess as the sails flew eastward. The common seamen had got their satisfaction and their poxes in the stews of Narbonne. In the palace had been enacted a romance of the rose, passionate and chaste. In this Chapter Five I had somehow to communicate to the twentieth-century common reader, accustomed to the last hectic boring obscenities of romantic love, its sacred ceremonial root. Eight hundred years ago in southern Europe men turned from phallus-and-rut, child getting, family alliances, marriage settlements. The scales dropped from their eyes. The love lyric was born between fountain and first nightingales. Where did it come from, this dawning wonder at the mystery of Woman? Devotion to the Virgin, 'mystical rose', was one source. Also a new profane skill intrigued men at this time: the cultivation of gardens. Lovers became initiates of multifoliate mysteries, penetrating stage by stage beyond the stone masks of sickness, age, impotence, that hold the garden bewintered. Enchanted with promise of April, they seek the rosebush; and pluck often, not heart's-desire, but a cluster of wounds.

'Come and help me at once, please,' cried Miriam from the door. Her face was white and blank as a mushroom. I followed her up the stair. Captain Stevens was lying on his back on the floor, his feet under the table and his head in the fireplace. His eyes were open and he seemed to be conscious of what was happening, but he was absolutely paralytic. Miriam took his feet and I took his shoulders and we heaved him into bed, boots and all. Miriam covered him with a blanket and a coat. 'Much obliged,' he muttered. 'Thank you. A rough night, shipmates.'

There were empty rum bottles everywhere; one in the fireplace, one on the mantleshelf, one on the table beside the photograph of Mrs Stevens. There was a full bottle on the sideboard and another two-thirds empty on the small television table – Miriam emptied them both down the sink. 'Well,' she said, 'he won't get to any licensed grocer today, that's one thing sure. He's too helpless.'

'Miriam,' came the mumble from the bed, 'don't leave me.'

'I've a good mind to leave you for good,' she said sharply, 'but I won't, because then there'd be only the devil and yourself.'

'How's the old ship standing up, eh, to this battering?'

'Go to sleep,' said Miriam. 'Get that nonsense about ships out of your head. You're in a house on dry land and you're half dead with rum, and you've got friends trying to help you.'

At the foot of the stairs I said to Miriam, 'He's going to put the law on me. He says I'm taking prostitutes into the house. He says I have bad intentions towards you.'

'Pray for him,' she said gently, and went back upstairs.

I arranged the rough draft of Chapter Five on the table and took up my biro. Nothing happened. In the rose garden of Narbonne a small white hand lay in a hand rough as barnacles. A communication, something between lust and sanctity, trembled in that green place, an unspoken dialogue. Somewhere, hidden in leaves, a bird began to sing . . .

The weather continued mild. The sea rose gently round the *Dinesen* and broke the wreck into trembling reflections. But, silently and inexorably, it was tearing the boat apart. And today the local men were taking a hand in the game. They were carrying pots, lamps, spars, drums of oil out of the boat when I rounded the corner of the kirkyard. 'There'll be trouble about this,' Dan Fraser assured me, squirting brown tobacco juice at the kirkyard wall. 'Nobody gave them permission to do that. I warned them. Next thing you see, the police'll be here.'

I wandered into the graveyard. This was the first tombstone I stopped to read:

ELIZABETH STEVENS
1930–1956
MICHAEL STEVENS
BORN AND DIED
JUNE 1956

When I got back to the house passing three o'clock Miriam was buttoning up her coat in the lobby.

'I'm very glad you're back,' she said. 'I cleaned him up as best I could. I must go now. . . .' She opened the front door. 'Please stay in the house. He's asleep. He won't be able to take one step for drink this day, thank God. I'm feared all the same the horrors come on him, like they did that time last summer when he saw the Irishmen and the clocks everywhere.'

'I wouldn't know what to do,' I said.

'Just send for me,' she said. And then she did a most sweet and unexpected and trustful thing – she stood on tiptoe in the open door and leaned quickly forward and put her mouth to my mouth – a kiss small and chaste as a snowflake. She was gone before I could say a word.

The house was silent as prayer all the rest of the afternoon. I was about to light my paraffin lamp (there is an electric bulb in the ceiling but I much prefer the soft diffused radiance of oil) when I thought I heard the captain stirring above. I tiptoed upstairs and lifted the flap of his letterbox and listened. Everything was quiet.

I felt very tired, not having slept properly for nights. I sat down in the stair, midway between the captain's room and my own, and put my head in my hands. And all at once, quite involuntarily, a scheme of seduction arranged itself in my mind, and unfolded sombrely and inevitably. It concerned Miriam and myself. We moved together from station to station of lust – initial coldness, then conspiracy, shared stratagems, gratitude, a single kiss in a doorway, an offered flower, the sacrifice of a maidenhead. I saw with piercing clarity Miriam lying, white and broken and satiated, in the large double bed in my room, under the paraffin lamp, the ship's wheel, the crucifix.

So in the dark stairway of Captain Stevens's house I arranged the absurd antique ballet. The white hart stirred behind the trees; the quiver was loaded; the dogs of lust raised near and far their broken music . . .

The front door slammed open violently, feet thumped and voices called in the lobby downstairs. 'Be quiet there!' I whispered sharply over the bannister. I could see nothing. I came down and stood on the first step. Two huge men loomed in front of me. One of them had a canvas ships-bag on his back and it clanked with loaded glass. The other man – I recognised him, he was the simple-minded sailor Robert Jansen who wandered the streets every Saturday night looking for his drowned friend Walls – had two unmistakable bottle shapes under his reefer jacket. 'Hello, Mr Barclay,' he said gently. 'This is my friend Stony Hackland. We're just going up to see the skipper.'

'You can't see him,' I said. 'It's impossible. Captain Stevens is very ill.' I put my foot against the bannister so that they couldn't get past.

'Off the gangplank, shipmate,' said Stony Hackland. His enormous hand closed on the lapels of my jacket. He swung me about and pressed me as flat as a gate against the wall. The two seamen went on upstairs past me.

'You see, Mr Barclay,' said Robert Jansen, 'the captain said Stony and me were to come tonight for sure.'

Stony Hackland flung open the door of Captain Stevens's room. 'It's us, skipper, Hackland and Jansen reporting.' A shape stirred and queried in the interior darkness. Robert Jansen quietly shut the door. I was excluded.

Back in my own room I opened a can of export and sipped the cold beer and wondered what to do. I would have gone for Miriam at once, but mortification over the masque of rape I had entangled her in, held me back. Besides, what could a girl like her do against two hulking brutes like Hackland and Jansen? The old man is saturated as a sponge, I thought, he can't hold any more rum. Maybe the company of seamen is just what he needs at this moment? Then bottles began to clank in the room above. I thought of the doctor and the police.

There was suddenly such a terrific crash above that the mugs shivered and clinked in my cupboard. I leapt up the stairs and opened the door. The table had gone over, the floor was a chaos of glass, seeping rum, cups, tulip bulbs, earth, pieces of porcelain and crystal.

Captain Stevens was standing between bed and rocking chair in his dressing gown. Stony Hackland and Robert

Jansen stood in front of him, their caps in their hands. Captain Stevens eyed me coldly. He gestured and pointed. I went over and stood beside the sailors.

'Gentlemen,' he said in a quiet grave voice, 'I want you to know exactly what the position is. You are naturally wondering about Captain Falquist, you haven't seen him on the bridge all day. I must tell you that Captain Falquist died last night in his cabin, suddenly. He was a very good man, a very pleasant man. We have lost a friend. I am now in command of this ship, at least until such time as we arrive back in port. You will take your orders from me without question.

'This has been an unlucky voyage, I don't need to impress that on you. Trouble right from the start with the seamen, if you can call them seamen, most of them are better acquainted with the inside of a prison cell. I don't intend to be soft with them like Captain Falquist, God rest him. The hurricane *seems* to be over. But don't delude yourselves, gentlemen. We are only passing through the quiet centre of it. We must prepare ourselves for more tempest, more trouble of all kinds, I'm afraid. The cargo is loose in the hold for one thing. It constitutes a danger to the ship and the lives of the crew. Do I make myself clear?'

'Yes sir,' said Stony Hackland and Robert Jansen together.

Captain Stevens turned to the mantleshelf and with a steady hand poured out three glasses of rum and handed one to Jansen and one to Hackland and one to me. 'I'm not a drinking man myself,' he said, 'never have been. So I won't join you. But for the remainder of this unfortunate trip I wish you all luck and courage.'

'Cheers, captain,' said Stony Hackland.

'Courage,' said Captain Stevens, 'by God we need courage more than we need money or clothes or sleep. We need it all the time. Cradle and coffin, they're both shaped like ships

– you'll have noticed that – and it's a desperate and a dangerous voyage we all have to make, from birth into death and beyond it. Even the pen-pusher who sits at a desk all day with papers and ink. We all need courage.'

He paused for a minute, then said quietly, 'There is only one thing more important than courage – love.' He suddenly glared at Stony Hackland. 'Take that smirk off your face, Hackland,' he shouted.

'Sorry, sir,' said Stony Hackland.

'The love of women,' said Captain Stevens, 'a very precious jewel. I have known men lucky enough to possess it. They had a completeness in their lives, these lovers, everything they did seemed to be well done, faithfully done, even when it wasn't. I think of them now and I envy them bitterly, because, personally speaking, this gift of love has passed me by. I'm an old man now, I can never know what it is. (Spasms of lust, I've had them all right, but that's quite another thing.) I'm not complaining, mind you. I suppose I must thank God for the one crude gift he's given me, courage. I think I may need it before this trip's over.'

'Courage,' muttered Robert Jansen, and raised his glass. We all drank, except the captain.

'At least you can depend on courage,' said Captain Stevens. 'There's no substitute for courage when the time comes. But love – what counterfeits, what frauds and imitations it's given rise to! Poor Falquist – the fly-by-night he tied himself to, by God, though she was five hundred miles away at the time, she and no other held the gun to his head and pulled the trigger. And I've known worse than her, many, much worse.' He turned to me. 'You,' he said, 'what's your name again, I forget?'

'Barclay, sir,' I said.

'Are you married, Barclay?' he said.

'No, sir.' I said.

'Get yourself a good wife, Barclay,' he said. 'We're going through the shining eye of the hurricane. It'll only last two hours, three at the most, don't delude yourselves . . . I want you, Barclay, to go down and have a look at the cargo and come back here and report. It'll soon start blowing again and then you won't be able to go.'

He swayed and fell against the television set as if he had been axed at the knees. The box shuddered and slid to the floor and seemed to explode; valves and coils were flung all over the room. My hand was scratched by a bit of flying glass.

Stony Hackland bent over Captain Stevens and raised him by the shoulders. 'Wind's getting up,' he said.

I went straight from the house into the cold starlight and down to the small house on the pier where Miriam lived with her parents.

All the way back she only spoke once. 'You promised to look after him,' she said.

When Miriam and I arrived Robert Jansen and Stony Hackland had got the old man back into his bed, but only, it seemed, after a struggle. The room was a worse shambles than ever; the curtain was half ripped from the pelmet and a black star had exploded across the mirror; the only thing left standing was the photograph of Elizabeth Stevens on the bedside table. Captain Stevens didn't seem to recognise Miriam at first. She bent over him and put his lead-blue hands back under the blanket. 'No women on this ship,' he mumbled. 'Be put ashore first port.'

'Yes,' said Miriam, 'and it won't be long till we're there. The storm's blowing done.'

Stony Hackland and Robert Jansen sat in the fireplace drinking the last of the rum out of cups. 'He's the decentest skipper ever I sailed with,' said Stony Hackland. 'Strict, but very fair in his dealings.'

'A straight shooter,' said Robert Jansen.

Miriam's lips moved soundlessly over the stiffening face on the pillow. He opened his eyes once and looked at her. 'Elizabeth,' he said.

Then blindness, silence, cold.

Miriam turned towards the two drunk men in the fireplace. 'You'll be pleased to know,' she said, 'that you've killed Captain Stevens.'

Robert Jansen began to cry.

To me she said coldly, 'Get Dr Wilson.'

*   *   *

On the three mornings before the funeral I did no work on Chapter Five. I made myself a bite to eat, took an abrupt walk among the fields before returning to the shrouded house, read beside the fire till it was dark. The night before the funeral I read the penitential psalms and the prayers for the dead over and over again till their austerities were only a confusion of dark syllables and I dropped off to sleep in the armchair. It was no empty piety; I was concerned that the soul of that brave heartbroken man should have secure anchorage at last, somewhere.

Miriam came to the house every morning as usual. She was a whole day clearing up the debris of the final rum tempest, a formidable task, and she had to be there to receive visitors – the provost, the minister, county councillors, members of the Harbour Board, the captain's relatives (three old people who arrived from the island of Quoylay the night before the funeral, and had to be accommodated) and some of those stray flower-bearers who are always attracted by the paraphernalia of death. The undertaker came twice or thrice a day.

Miriam paid no attention to me. She left me among my sacred and profane images. I knew she considered that I had betrayed her; and so I had, but after another fashion, with my lascivious imagination.

It was a fine afternoon when they buried Captain Stevens beside his wife and son. A cluster of mourners stood among the tombstones with bared heads. The huge back of Robert Jansen shook with grief. The minister prayed. Eight seamen lowered the coffin into the grave. I stood beside the broken wall of the pre-Reformation church. *Requiem aeternam dona ei, Domine.*

The minister closed his book and the knot of mourners broke apart. The gravedigger got busy with his shovel. Another cell in this honeycomb of death was being sealed.

Beyond the churchyard wall, on its reef, the *Dinesen* had completely disintegrated. Nothing remained but her hull, a hollow cave for the sea, and the next storm would strew the beach with boards and leave only a skeleton among the rocks. Dan Fraser still stood on guard over her, smoking his pipe.

The kirkyard of Hamnavoe is two miles from the town, and so the mourners are transported there and back by bus. I happened to find myself beside Stony Hackland in the front seat.

'Tell me,' I said, 'about Captain Falquist.'

He wrinkled his brows at me. 'That was the *Orlando*,' he said. 'Fancy you knowing about that.' . . . It was obvious that Stony remembered nothing about the bacchanal on the night of Captain Stevens's death.

'Is it true,' I said, 'that Captain Falquist committed suicide?'

'Shot himself,' said Stony. 'Officially it was accidental death. We buried him at sea, off Bermuda. "Misadventure while cleaning his gun," Captain Stevens reported when we got back, and that's what appeared in the newspaper reports and,

I suppose, on his death certificate. We all knew he shot himself, all the same. He was too kind a man for skipper of a rough ship like the *Orlando*. It was a very unlucky trip. The crew, they were bad for a start, a lot of them newly out of Walton jail in Liverpool. Captain Stevens was first officer that trip. He knew how to handle them. If it hadn't been for him there'd have been murder and mutiny, sure as hell, in the first few days. As it was, they nearly killed the cook. Two days out of Boston we ran into this hurricane. Worst I ever seen. I swear I said my prayers six times a day, a thing I never did before or since. There was old Falquist up on the bridge with his long kind sad face, and Mr Stevens the first officer beside him with a face like a hunk of granite. And that night the cargo shifted, American clocks and other machinery, very delicate, very valuable – a hundred enormous containers lumbering about in the hold like elephants. And there was them bloody jail-birds down below, scared as rats, and all the more vicious because they were frightened. It wasn't a piece of cake for any skipper.

'Some kind of a personal message came through early next morning for Captain Falquist – God knows what it was – they say he was married to one of *them* kind of women, you know, that keep their treasure between their thighs and trade in any market, very pretty but treacherous as hell – God knows – be that as it may, old Falquist takes the sheet of paper from the radio officer and reads it and walks straight to his cabin and a minute after that there was this sound of one shot. And all this time, remember, the ship's wallowing about in great bloody chasms of sea, and her innards all loose. . . . We never knew about it till the hurricane was over. All we knew was, that kind good face was missing from the bridge and in its place that chunk of granite. It scared us and it put heart in us.

'That same summer Captain Stevens met his wife, a Birsay woman, Elizabeth Halcrow, very young and pretty, and in no time at all he was married to her.

'Next voyage he was given his own ship. Not before time either – the directors didn't like him because he spoke hard and direct, he never was one of your arse-lickers – that delayed his promotion. All the same, he was commodore of the line before he retired.'

The bus halted at the pier head. Stony Hackland got off with the other seamen and they all went into the Hamnavoe Bar.

Alone in the empty house that night, I turned the knob of my radio through sudden frenzies of jazz, staccato morse, a welter of foreign voices, till it came to rest in a temple of solemn sound.

It was the last movement of a quartet – possibly Beethoven; I know little about music.

The viola, a sybil, surged with deep subtle questionings, and the violins, innocent creatures of April, were pierced with the pain and loveliness of desire, and the cello said over and over again, *Lamb of God, Have mercy on us, Grant us peace*.

The pang of the violins was taken by the viola and turned into wise sad proverbs: *Beauty passes, Joy is a dream, Love uncertain*. The cello reassured, *Have no fear, Apple and dove, Thy Kingdom come*.

The violins trysted and parted and came together again, young tormented lovers. *No*, said the viola, *Misery is everywhere, Love is a shadow, Make your hearts marble*. And the cello seemed to contradict its former piety with a long sorrowful utterance, *Death is sure, Dust unto dust, All is vanity*.

There was a brief silence.

Then all the instruments consented in a final dance, Love and Wisdom and Holiness crowned one another with garlands.

The violins fled away. The viola covered their going with wise greenery. The cello, alone on the steps of the temple, brimmed with benediction: *God is good, All is well, Rest in peace.*

*   *   *

Three weeks have passed since the death of Captain Stevens.

I have completed Chapter Six of *The Holy Voyage* (The Siege of the Spanish Castle) and Chapter Seven (The Attack on the Saracen Ship) writing a thousand fluent words every morning between breakfast and lunch. Everything has gone well. I have taken deep pleasure in the work; in the cold hawkflight of the Viking pilgrims I have got release from the sorrow and confusion that engulfed this house so suddenly.

Chapter Five remains unfinished. I shall return to it later, when a great deal that is confused and uncertain now clarifies in my mind. Love is too deep a subject for prose – only music and poetry can build bridges between the rage of the seed in the furrow, the coupling of beasts, the passion of man and woman, the saint's prayer. Seed and beast and saint are touched with simple fire. The loves of Thorkeld Stevens and Elizabeth, of Earl Rögnvald and the Lady Ermengarde, of Robert Jansen and Walls, of Captain Falquist and his fly-by-night, of myself and Sandra, seem to be nothing but chaos, loss, heartbreak. I know, though I cannot celebrate it, that all these loves are caught up in their true order, and simplified, and reconciled, in the wheel of being whose centre is Incarnation; they move about it forever like the quiet stars.

I do not know how much longer I can stay here. I met the lawyer in the street one day last week. He told me that the house is to be advertised for sale as soon as possible.

I must begin to look for another place.

*

On Saturday evening, after a week of hard pleasurable work, I walked down to the town. The Hamnavoe Bar was crowded with crofters and fishermen and sailors. The crew of the *Dinesen* were there; they were all happy because now there was no chance at all that their boat could be refloated, and the order for their recall had come. They were due to fly home from Kirkwall on Monday morning. Once Robert Jansen came in looking for his drowned friend Walls and went out again. A young Dane with a curled golden beard bought drinks for everyone in the bar. Stony Hackland was very drunk. He had his arms round the shoulders of two Danes and as they swayed together above the fire he was telling them that Scandinavians were the best seamen in the world, always had been since the first ships were built. 'The boat you wrecked on the Kirk Rocks,' said Stony, 'just bloody bad luck, shipmates, could happen to anybody, not to worry, seaman myself.' The young bearded skipper ordered another double whisky for Stony Hackland.

I left the pub and walked along the dark street. Round the fountain at the pierhead the twelve Salvationists stood in a ring, and a few drunks lay against the Custom House wall listening to the holy ragtime.

'*Will your anchor hold in the storms of life?*' the songsters chanted. Miriam rattled her tambourine among the shining trumpets. The big drum thudded at her side. Her face was radiant under the street lamps.

Sealskin

(I)

A sealskin, lying on the rocks – well, he could make use of that all right. Somebody must have dropped it. Simon didn't intend to ask too particularly: put a notice in the window of the general store, for example, or hire the beadle to ring his bell round the parish. Simon rubbed the pelt with his finger. It was a good skin. It might make a waistcoat for his father, he thought, walking back to the croft. His mother might want it for a rug for the best room. He rolled up the skin. He opened the door of the barn. He threw the skin among the low dark rafters.

His mother had the broth poured out. Three of them sat at the table – his father, his mother, himself. His father could work no more because of rheumatism; the trouble had grown much worse this past winter; it was as if his body was newly released from a rack. His mother's only concern was Simon, to see that he was kept warm and well-fed, so that he wouldn't think of taking another woman into the house – at least, not until she herself was dead in the kirkyard. If ever Simon looked at a woman – on the road to the kirk on Sabbath, for example, or when the tinker lasses came to the door with laces and mirrors – a great silent anger came on her. For the rest of that day the old woman spoke to no one, not even to the dog or the cow. No other woman would share her spinning-wheel and her ale-kirn.

Thank the Lord, she thought, Simon is an ugly boy. That kept some of the parish Jezebels away. Even more important, Simon seemed not to be interested in the lasses at all. That was a great comfort to her.

There had been another son, Matthew, much older than Simon. One spring he had gone to the whaling in the north-west and never returned. That was ten years ago.

Eventually, she supposed, Simon would have to marry. Well, let him, but only after she was dead.

The old man raised his twisted hand and blessed the meal. They lifted their horn spoons and silently dipped them in the soup bowls.

(II)

In the afternoon Simon went down to the rocks for limpet bait. He did a little fishing now and then. He struck the limpets from the face of the rock into his wooden bucket with a long blue stone. The bucket was half full when he heard the first delicate mournful cry, a weeping from the waters. He looked across the bay. A girl was kneeling among the waves. She was naked.

Simon left the limpets. He stumbled up the rocks and loose clashing stones. He ran across the links to the croft. The old ones on either side of the fire gaped at him. He took his mother's coat from the nail in the lobby, and ran and slithered down the foreshore to where he had seen the girl. The sea was rising about her. She seemed to be quite exhausted. She didn't even cry out when Simon dragged her by the hair onto a rock. He threw the coat over her. Then he carried her in his arms up to the croft and the fire and the pot of broth.

'What's this?' cried the old woman. 'Where does she come from? Not a stitch on her! A strange naked woman.

She doesn't bide here. Out she goes, once she's had a bite to eat.'

The old man nodded, half asleep over the embers.

Once the girl was fed a shiver and flush went over the cold marble of her flesh. She slept for a while in Simon's bed. The old woman, grumbling, looked for woollen garments in her clothes chest. 'That's my Sabbath coat you put about her,' she said. In the late evening the girl awoke and sat beside the fire. She was not a girl from any farm in the island. Simon had never clapped eyes on her at the Hamnavoe market. They spoke to her. They asked her questions. She looked at them and shook her head. She uttered one or two sounds. She pointed through the window at the sea.

She is a very bonny lass, thought the old woman bitterly. She doesn't look at Simon with any kindness at all, so far. But there would be days and nights to come.

'Well,' said the old man, 'I think she's a foreign lass. She doesn't make anything of the English I speak, anyway. I haven't heard of any wrecks from Hoy to Westray this past week, though.'

'She can't bide here,' said the old woman, swilling out the pots with cold water near the open door.

'We're supposed to be Christians,' said the old man, and began to fill his pipe beside the fire.

Simon said he thought they would have to keep the girl for a night or two at least. She could sleep in his bed. There was plenty of warm straw in the barn where he could lie down.

The girl looked timorously at the faces in the firelight – the hostile face of the old woman, the blank face of Simon, the kind suffering face of the old man.

'You'll stay, my dear,' said the old man.

The girl smiled.

The old woman set the iron pot down on the flagstone. It clanged like a passionate bell.

(III)

The old woman was dead. Her life had dwindled away all summer and autumn like a candle-end. She lay now in her plain cloth-covered coffin with her hands folded over her breast. The old man sat in his chair at the fire. His withered eyes grew brilliant and brimming from time to time; then he would dab at them with a huge red handkerchief. Simon arranged plates of bread and cheese and fowl round the whisky flagon that stood in the centre of the table.

A face looked in at the window and presently James Scott their neighbour from Voe came in. There was a shy knock at the door – more a kind of powerful hand-flutter – and Walter Anderson the blacksmith came in. Presently there was the sound of many random feet on the cobble stones outside – one by one men from every croft in the parish entered the house.

Simon poured whisky into a small pewter goblet for each mourner as he entered.

Everybody spoke in praise of the dead woman: her thrift, her cleanliness, her decency, the golden butter and the black ale she had made.

A horse's hooves clattered outside. A tall man in blackcloth entered, carrying a black book. The room went silent as he entered.

Simon poured whisky for the minister.

'Later,' said the Reverend Jabez Grant. He opened his Bible and cleared his throat.

The old man, after two attempts, heaved himself up from his chair to hear the holy words. He hung awkwardly over two sticks.

The minister began to read above the shut waxen face in the coffin.

Through the window Simon could see Mara down at the beach, turning over swathe after swathe of seaweed, probing behind every rock. What was she looking for? Some days she came up with a lobster in her fingers, and once a trout flashed in her hands like living bronze.

'Amen,' said the minister.

(IV)

'I delivered the bairn,' said Martha Gross, 'one night in March. It was a very hard birth. Simon came for me near midnight.'

'Just answer the questions,' said the session clerk, Mr Finlay Groat (who was the general merchant down in the village).

'So back I goes with Simon,' said Martha Gross. 'When we got to the gap in the hills, I could hear the screaming of her. It was such a cold high frightening sound. "Hurry up for God's sake," says Simon.'

'Thank you,' said Rev. Jabez Grant. 'That's all, Martha.'

'It was the hardest birth I was ever at,' said Martha Gross. 'A right bonny bairn when he did come, all the same. Lawful or lawless, that's not for me to say. I do declare he was as bonny a boy as ever I saw.'

The beadle plucked Martha Gross by the sleeve.

'Call Simon Olafson,' said Mr Finlay Groat.

Simon entered the vestry as nervous as a colt in a market ring. He agreed with every proposition they put to him, almost before the words were out, so eager he was to be out of this place of high authority.

Yes, his father Ezekiel Olafson of Corse employed the woman Mara Smith as a servant-lass. Yes, he had carnal knowledge of the said Mara in the barn of Corse, also in the seaward room of Corse, on sundry occasions; once in a cave under the crags. No, he was not married. The said Mara was not married either, to the best of his knowledge. Yes, he was aware that he had offended seriously against God and the kirk. Yes, he was willing to thole any public penance the kirk session might see fit to lay on him.

Simon left the table, dabbing his quicksilver face with the sleeve of his best Sabbath suit.

The girl entered, led by William Taylor the beadle. She put a cold shy look on one after the other of the session. She seemed to have no awareness of the purport of the proceedings at all. She answered the opening questions with a startled askance look, like a seabird on a cliff ledge when men with guns are on the rocks below.

'Look here, woman,' said Mr Finlay Groat at last, 'do you know why you're here?'

She frowned at him.

Their hard questions hung in the air unanswered. Incomprehension grew. The men turned in their chairs, they frowned at each other, they tapped their teeth. A great gulf was fixed between this girl and the kirk session of the parish of Norday in conclave gathered.

They turned away from the girl. They discussed the matter among themselves, in veiled voices. Her origins. Found on the shore. Possibly from a shipwreck. What shipwreck? No shipwreck that winter. Or forcibly got rid of out of some Baltic ship, put ashore in a small boat. Ignorant of the language. Ay, but the holy signs and symbols – the Bible, the christening stone, the black ministerial bands – all Christendom should recognise them. She didn't seem to. A heavy mystery indeed. What then? . . .

'She is said to be a seal woman,' said Walter Anderson (who was the blacksmith and rather fond of the bottle when he was not a member of this holy court).

'Mr Anderson,' said the minister coldly, 'I think we will not adulterate our proceedings with pagan lore.'

Walter Anderson, chidden, muttered into his beard.

'A thing should be said in favour of Simon Olafson,' said Saul Renton the joiner. 'It was a hard thing for Simon to stand here this day. Simon is a good lad. Simon of his charity took this woman, whatever she is, into Corse, and fed her and warmed her. It is more than likely that Simon saved her life. I think – apart from the fornication – it was a good and godly thing that Simon did.'

'Let her step down, I think,' said Mr Finlay Groat. 'We can make nothing of her.'

'Yes,' said the minister. 'I agree.'

There was a concurrence of heads round the table.

The beadle tapped Mara on the shoulder.

Mr Finlay Groat stated that he had a letter from Ezekiel Olafson of Corse. *Reverend elders*, the session clerk read, *I am sore afflicted with rheumatics in haunch and knee, and so unable to obey your summons this day. Simon must thole his punishment. He is in general a dutiful son. He labours hard on the land. There are worse fishermen. His lechery has been towards this one woman alone who has no speech or name. The bairn Magnus is a joy, he greets but seldom and that for a gripe or for a soreness in his gums, like all bairns. Simon has offended and so must be punished. They wish before harvest to be married in the manse if it so be the minister's good will.*

'A righteous letter,' said Walter Anderson.

'The usual thing, I think,' said Mr Finlay Groat. 'Three Sabbaths on the stool of penitence, before all the congregation, to suffer rebuke.'

Another sagacity of heads round the table.

The beadle was sent to bid Simon Olafson and Mara Smith return into the court, to hear judgment.

(v)

Simon and Mara were married in the manse of Norday at Michaelmas that year. The wedding feast was held in the barn of Corse. Guests came from all over the island to it.

The girl refused to sit at the supper board. She stayed in the house beside the child, though other women had offered to feed him and rock him to sleep. But when the fiddles struck up and the feet began to beat round in ordered violent circles Mara put on her shawl and crossed the barn yard. The dancers saw the white figure standing in the door, half in shadow. The fiddle sang like some wild bird from the world's farthest shore. Mara lingered in the door. Simon caught a glimpse of her through the whirling circles of the dance. He refused the whisky that was going round just then. He was vexed that he had had to sit alone at the bridal table. The hot whisky had made him arrogant and masterful. At least Mara must walk with him in the bridal march. No wedding was complete without the grand bridal march, led by the bridegroom and bride. He would compel her.

But when Simon reached the barn door, through all those stampings and yells, his wife was not there.

He crossed the yard to the house. The old man was in bed already. He did not hold with whisky and fiddles. For him the wedding was over with the giving of the ring and the minister's sacred pronouncement. He moaned softly in the darkness. He was having bad pain that winter in both his legs.

Simon opened the door of the seaward room. The lamp burned on top of the clothes chest, and flung a little wayward light on the darkness. Mara was bent over the cradle, singing in a low voice to the child.

I am a man upon the land,
I am a selkie in the sea,
And when I'm far from any strand
My home it is in Suleskerry.

The child lay asleep in his crib, quiet as an apple.

From another world came broken fragments of laughter, voices, clattering plates. The fiddle screamed suddenly, once. The barn fell silent again. A voice commanded. The fiddle moved into a sequence of urgent cadences, and the feet of the men moved over the barn floor to where the line of women sat at the wall with veiled expectant eyes.

'Mara,' said Simon, 'they want us in the barn. It'll soon be time for the bridal march. You must come.'

She knelt over the crib, her head enfolded in the soft sweet breathings of her child.

The old man sighed in the darkness next door.

A slow anger kindled in Simon's belly. It would be a disgrace to Corse for generations if the things that must be done at every wedding were not done.

'I am your man,' Simon said. 'You will come now.'

In the barn the dance whirled in ever-quicker circles to the last frenzied circle when the fiddler's elbow twitches like ague and the girls are almost thrown off their feet.

Mara took off her bride-gown and hung it at the hook in the wall. From her nakedness, gently laved by the flame of the lamp, came an intense white bitter coldness: the moon in the heart of an iceberg. Simon in his thick Sabbath suit trembled. His wife climbed into the bed and covered herself with the patchwork quilt.

The taking of the maidenhead had been accomplished twenty months previously. There would be no need for that ceremony again. She breathed softly and regularly on her pillow.

The light and the darkness wavered and interfolded and
gestured on the walls of the bedroom like two ancient creatures in a silent dialogue.

Simon took his uncertain shadow away. He went on tiptoe
through his father's room. The old man was muttering what
seemed to be a fragment of scripture.

Sick at heart, Simon returned to the barn. The reel was
over. The barn was full of smoke and sweat and red faces. It
was time for more refreshment. A brimming whisky-vessel
was thrust into Simon's hands.

'Where's your wife, man?' said Frank the boatman, mockingly.

(VI)

It was strange how the soul of old Ezekiel clung to his ruined
body. He had always been a truly religious man. He loved his
nightly readings of the Bible. Even in the days of his strength
the words of Ecclesiastes had comforted him:

> I returned, and saw under the sun, that the race is not to
> the swift, nor the battle to the strong, neither yet bread
> to the wise, nor yet riches to men of understanding, nor
> yet favour to men of skill; but time and chance happeneth
> to them all. For man also knoweth not his time: as the
> fishes that are taken in an evil net, and as the birds that
> are caught in the snare; so are the sons of men snared in
> an evil time, when it falleth suddenly upon them.

It was good that a young man should know how in the end all
was bitterness and emptiness. He had never had any fear of
death – indeed for the last six or seven winters he would have
welcomed death heartily, like a friend. But death was still
reluctant to knock on his door.

He waited upon the Lord, he said.

An unexpected sweetness had fallen upon his latter days: his grandson. Surely the goodness of the Lord was never-ending. The delight was perhaps all the greater because the marriage of Simon and Mara had quickly gone sour. They moved about the croft and did their appointed tasks in the due season, but they no longer took any comfort from one another. They broke the family bread with cold hands. They listened to the scripture reading with cold faces.

His own marriage had gone cold like this in the end; but first he had had a dozen joyous lusty years with old Annie who was lying now in the kirkyard at the shore. A year, and Simon and Mara spoke only when it was needful.

It was a great sadness to him. He thought about it one summer morning. The sun shone. He was sitting in front of the cottage in the deep straw chair.

Mara was baking bread inside.

Simon was bringing a cow out of the quarry field. He had to take that one, and Bluebell, to the pier in the village before the boat sailed. They were to be sold at the mart in Kirkwall.

Old Ezekiel heard distant shouts from the hill. It was Mansie and the neighbouring boy from Voe. The shouts dwindled. When they came again they had a new thinness and clarity. The boys were playing along the shore, where sea and sky are the twin valves of one cosmic echoing shell.

The sun went behind a cloud.

And yet he should not complain. Simon was a respectful son to him. And the girl, the stranger, did everything for him that was necessary. It was not the loving ways of a daughter, of course. Still, he should not complain. He knew he must be a great nuisance to them both.

If only the dark courteous guest would knock soon on his door.

The shouts came from the end of the house. A solitary small boy danced round the corner. The lap of his grey jersey was full of shells and buttercups and stones from the beach. Mansie showered this treasure over his grandfather. Then he leapt into the old man's lap and flung his arms about his neck.

'Ah!' cried the old man in agony, for now the rheumatism was in his shoulders too.

'Get down!' cried Simon, leading the black cow in. 'Go back to the shore!' Young flesh disentangled from writhen flesh. The boy ran behind the peat-stack. They heard soon the flutter of his bare feet on the grass of the links.

The old man's face was still twisted with agony.

'You should be inside,' said Simon. 'The wind's freshening. You should be sitting inby at the ingle.'

'Mara is baking,' said the old man. 'I would only be in her way.'

'You should have on your coat then,' said Simon. 'It'll get colder.'

'My coat's on the scarecrow,' said the old man, and smiled a little to think that his next coat would be a coat of heavenly yarn.

Simon fingered his chin, considering.

A freshet of wind blew in from the sea and brought with it a little shrill fragment of song. The boy was communing with the seals on the rock. Another sleek head broke the water, and another. The seals were coming close in to listen.

Mansie, thought the old man, always liked best to play by himself. He never played for long at a time with the other boys of the district. He was lonely as a gull.

'Wait a minute,' said Simon. He went into the barn.

The blue hot reek of baking drifted from the open door.

Verily I should be very thankful, thought the old man drowsily. The wind on my face. Mansie down at the shore.

Seals, sunbursts, singing. The hillside tossing with green oats. The good smell of bread from the hearth inside . . . His head nodded on his chest.

Simon came out of the barn carrying the sealskin that he had found on the beach seven years before and had almost forgotten. He shook husks and stour out of it; the wind was grey for a moment. His father was asleep in the chair now. Simon draped the skin gently over the old man's shoulders.

Mansie, having lured the seals with his singing, began to throw stones at them. Stones splashed in the sea. There was the gentler splash of departing seals.

Simon lifted the rope from the dyke and led the black cow across the field to the road. 'Bluebell,' he called, 'Bluebell!' A red-and-white heifer that had been munching grass in the ditch ambled towards him. The two cows were seeing their last of Corse.

The old man slept peacefully in his chair.

The boy was running on the hill now, and creating panic among the sheep. He barked like a dog among them.

The wind blew colder from the sea. The sun was lost behind a huge cloud mass.

After a time Mara came and stood in the doorway. She was white to the elbows with meal.

'Leave them alone, the sheep!' she called in her strange bell-like voice. 'Come back. Come here.'

The boy stopped. The sheep were huddled in a grey agitated mass in one corner of the field. He turned. He ran across the shoulder of the hill towards the peat-cuttings.

He would only come home now when he was hungry.

The old man slept in his chair. Mara looked at him. Salt still encrusted the veins that had been nourished too long with corn and milk. She touched the sealskin that covered the shoulders of the old man.

(VII)

'So,' said the stone mason, 'what you want is one gravestone of Aberdeen granite to be erected in the churchyard of Norday.'

'That's right,' said Simon.

They were standing in the stone mason's yard in Kirkwall, among hewn polished half-inscribed stones. Simon and Mansie his son had come in that morning from the island on the weekly boat. It was no idle excursion. Simon had business to do, at the auction mart, in the lawyer's office, with the seed merchant and the ironmonger, and now last with the maker of gravestones.

Mansie was not there. He had gone off to buy something with the few pounds his grandfather had left him – he refused to say what, until the thing was actually in his possession.

'The stone is for my father and mother,' said Simon.

The stone mason wrote the names down in his notebook: Ezekiel Olafson and Annie Olafson. The chiselling of the names would cost sixpence a letter, he told Simon.

Simon had been meaning all winter, since the old man died, to erect a memorial over his parents. It looked so mean, them lying in a nameless piece of earth in the midst of the blazoned dead of Norday. Forgetfulness had caused the delay – a willed forgetfulness, in a way, for to tell the truth Simon found it unwholesome, all this tearful lauding of the dead that had lately become the fashion; and the stark bones hidden under a heap of wax flowers. The laird's wife even had a stone angel weeping over her.

'It is usual nowadays,' said the stone mason, 'to have something like this, *In Loving Memory*. And then, at the base of the stone, some text from scripture, such as *Not Lost But Gone Before* or *Asleep in Jesus*.'

'Nothing like that,' said Simon. 'Just the names and the dates of birth and death.'

The stone mason licked his blunt stub of pencil and wrote the dates in his notebook under the names, 1793–1869 and 1797–1860.

A thick-set fair boy entered the yard from the street, bearing a shape wrapped in sheets of newspaper.

The stone mason looked up from his notebook. 'I think you are a widower, Mr Olafson?' he said.

'Yes,' said Simon, 'I am.'

'Then,' said the stone mason, lowering his voice a little, 'should there not be another name on the stone?'

Mansie began to tear the paper from the parcel.

'No,' said Simon. He shook his head. 'She came out of silence and she went back into silence. I don't even know her right name. Whatever it was, it shouldn't be on a Christian stone.'

'I see,' said the stone mason.

It was a fiddle that Mansie held up. The strange exotic shape shone among the blank and the half-inscribed tombstones that were strewn about the yard.

'I saw it advertised for sale in *The Orkney Herald*,' said Mansie to his father. 'It was made in 1695 in Gothenburg by Rolf Gruning. He was a very good fiddle maker.'

'A waste of money,' said Simon.

Mansie plucked a string. The fiddle shivered and cried.

(VIII)

This story is really about a man and his music.

At the turn of the century there was a stirring in the two Orkney grammar schools of Kirkwall and Hamnavoe. Suddenly, within a few years – as if in complete vindication of the Education Act of 1872 – they produced a crop of boys of outstanding intellect. These young men went on to one or other of the universities of Scotland, afterwards perhaps to Oxford or Cambridge. Most of them made brilliant careers for themselves, mainly in the Dominions (for they still kept some drops of Viking blood; their bodies too were restless). All these clever Orcadians were men of science – medicine, botany, theology – and this practicality too was a Viking inheritance: even the old sagamen kept to the factual truth in their marvellous stories, and were suspicious of the imagination and all its works.

The sole exception in that feast of scientific intellect was a young man from the island of Norday called Magnus John Olafson.

After tasting the disciplines and delights of two universities, and being uncertain for a while about his ultimate career – for he showed, in common with his peers, considerable aptitude in mathematics and physics – he turned finally to music.

He achieved a certain measure of fame while he was still in his twenties. Edinburgh, London, Prague heard his music, and approved.

His compositions are out of favour, with most things Victorian and Edwardian, nowadays; one occasionally hears on the Third Programme his Symphony, his tone poem *Eynhallow*, his elegy for piano *The Blue Boat*, his settings of the twelfth-century lyrics of Earl Rögnvald Kolson, his ballet *The Seal Women*, and most of all perhaps his Violin Concerto with its few spare lovely melodies among all that austerity, like flowers in an Arctic field.

Magnus enjoyed his fame as composer and conductor for a decade and more; then gradually it lost its savour. With fame had come a modest amount of wealth. He did not know what to do with it. One summer he went back to the islands; first to the little town with the red cathedral at the heart of it; then, the following day, on the weekly steamer to Norday.

He did not want acknowledgment of his gifts here, and he did not get it. On the steamer he was the sole passenger, except for a boxed-in horse and a few cows complaining in the hold. He signed in at the hotel at the pier. The bar fell silent when he walked casually in. (They had spoken familiarly enough with him there ten years previously.) One by one the farmers slipped away. He was left with his lonely dram in his hand.

This was their way. They were shy and independent.

All these years he had carried Norday with him wherever he went, but his memory had made it a transfigured place, more like a piece of tapestry than an album of photographs. The great farmhouses and the small crofts had appeared, in retrospect, 'sunk in time'. The people, viewed from Paris, moved like figures in an ancient fable, simple and secure and predestined, and death rounded all. He knew of course that there was poverty, and such sins as lust and avarice and pride. He had smiled often, for example, to think of the devious lecheries of Walter the blacksmith; and how Willie Taylor, up in the hill in the springtime to cut peats, took his bowel-fruit home in the cart to enrich no land but his own; and how the mouth of Finlay Groat the merchant shone with unction even when it totted up the prices of sugar and tea and tobacco in his shop at the pier.

It was in a fable that these people seemed to move; and Magnus thought that if each man's seventy years could be compressed into a short time, his laborious feet, however plastered with dung and clay, would move in a joyous reel of fruition.

He was to be bitterly hurt and disillusioned as his holiday went on; for the people were changed indeed, but in an altogether different way.

They avoided him as if he was the factor or the exciseman. When the farm women saw him coming on the road they moved shyly out of the fields into barn or byre.

Even the boys who had sat beside him at the school desk, Willie Scott of Voe and Tom Anderson who had followed his father at the forge, spoke only when he spoke to them, and then in a painfully shy embarrassed way; and they were obviously glad when there was nothing more to say and the stranger had passed on.

A coldness gathered about his heart.

A revealing incident happened during his two-week stay in the island. A boy was drowned off the East Head – his fishing boat had been swamped in a sudden squall. Magnus was there with the other islanders at the village pier when the body was taken ashore. It was what the local newspapers called 'a tragedy', and the reporters went on to describe the 'affecting scenes' and 'the stricken island' . . . Magnus saw the women standing along the pier with their dabbling handkerchiefs, and the men gulping and turning their faces away as the shrouded stretcher was borne slowly up the road to the church hall.

He himself felt nothing – only a little irritation at the sloppiness of their mourning.

He stood utterly outside this festival of grief. He shook hands with the boy's father (with whom he had been at school) and murmured words of sympathy; but he was quite cold and unmoved.

Standing on that pier, the scales fell from his eyes – the change was not in the islanders but in himself. An artist must pay dearly, in terms of human tenderness, for the fragments of beauty that lie about his workshop. (Later that year, in London, he wrote *The Blue Boat*, an impressionistic piece for piano. It was a time of much give-and-take in the arts – poets had their preludes, composers their ballades and landscapes, painters their nocturnes and symphonies . . . Olafson's *The Blue Boat* is what music perhaps should never aim at – it is a description of a passing storm at sea. When at last the wind has swept away the thunder and the rain-clouds there is a brief silence, the dove broods upon the water; and then the piece is brought to a close with a last brief phrase. This is indeed a mystery of art, that a few musical notes, in a certain pattern and tempo, should suggest the fall of a wave on an Atlantic shore; since even in impressionistic music there is no similarity in the sound the piano makes to the actual sound made by salt water spending itself on pebbles, sand, rocks, seaweed. The music nevertheless subtly suggests the phenomenon. And why, more mysteriously still, should the same pattern of notes impress the listener with sorrow, with a grief that belongs to the sea alone, with youth gathered untimely into the salt and the silence? The end of *The Blue Boat* is all heartbreak; as if the tears shed at Norday pier that summer day had been gathered and given over to the limbecks of art for an irreducible quintessence.)

The day before he left Norday that summer he visited the kirkyard at the shore. Fifty years before a new ugly kirk had been built near the centre of the island, but the islanders still laid their dead in the earth about an ancient roofless (probably Catholic) chapel. Magnus remembered well where the family grave was. A new name had been cut in the stone.

Simon Olafson
(1837–1884)

He remembered his father and grandfather with sudden deep affection. He wandered from tombstone to tombstone, pausing to read familiar names: Walter Anderson, Martha Gross, Rev. Jabez Grant.

Surrounded by these dead, he felt human and accepted for the first time since he had returned to Norday. He murmured the names on the stones with gratitude.

A dark comforting power rose from the vanished generations.

His wanderings had brought him back to the place where he had started. There was room at the foot of the Olafson stone for another name to be carved. It struck Magnus with a sudden chill that the islanders he loved might not want his dust to be mingled with theirs.

Next day he left Norday. Nobody said farewell to him at the pier. The old ferryman – a friend of his father's – accepted his generous tip and covered up his embarrassment with dense drifts of smoke from his clay pipe. Magnus wandered for an hour in a stone web, the piers and closes of Hamnavoe. A steamer received him; he was borne across the disordered surges of the Pentland Firth. The islands dwindled. At Thurso the train bore him south to new orchestras, to brilliant friends, to the new compositions that were already shaping themselves in his imagination.

These were not paltry delights that Magnus Olafson went back to.

He had many good friends in the cities of Europe: musicians, dancers, students, writers, art lovers. They received him back into their circles with pleasure. He went with them on their summer picnics in the forests and mountains. They experienced together the new poetry of Rilke and Blok, and discussed it late into the night; and experienced the new music of Mahler, and analysed it till the rising sun quenched their lamps. Magnus Olafson was well enough liked by his cultured friends; his clumsiness with their languages endeared him; and how he whose early life had been shaped by the starkness of sea and earth was at a loss with railway timetables, cheque books, wine lists.

He often felt, in moods of depression, that he was caught up in some meaningless charade in which everyone, himself included, was compelled to wear a mask. He would take part in their passionate midnight arguments about socialism, the ballet, anthropology, psychology, and he would put forward – as well as his clumsiness with German or French allowed him – a well-ordered logical argument. But deep down he was untouched. It didn't seem to matter in the slightest. It was all a game, to keep sharp the wits of people who had not to contend with the primitive terrors of sea and land. So he thought, while the eyes flashed and the tongues sought for felicitousness and clarity all around him. He was glad when the maskers had departed and he was alone again, among the cigarette ends and the apple cores. Occasionally, out of the staleness, would emerge a thread of melody; he would note it down on the back of an envelope and, too tired to work that night, begin to loose his boot straps. (In the morning, after breakfast, he would fall on the music paper with controlled lust.)

And his guests would say, going home in a late-night tram-car, 'Is he not charming, this Magnus? And how shy! And underneath, such talent!' What they were describing was the mask; few of them had seen the cold dangerous Orphean face underneath.

And they would say, lingering on pavements in the lamp-light, 'He is so gentle and sensitive, this man from the north.' ... But Magnus Olafson had long given up the idea that artists are the sensitive antennae of society – art is, rather, the

ruthless cutting edge that records and celebrates and proph-
esies on the stone tablets of time. A too-refined sensibility
could not do that stern work.

He had a friend, a painter, who used to argue that art was
no separate sovereign mystery, with its own laws and modes
and manners, answerable only to itself; 'art for art's sake'. 'No,'
said this friend, 'in this way art will wither from the earth.'
. . . Art, he argued, must become once more the handmaid of
religion, as it had been in Greece and in the Europe of the
Middle Ages. Magnus remembered the harshness of the
Presbyterian services in Norday, when he was a boy, and
shook his head. He went with his friend one Christmas Eve
to a midnight Mass in Notre Dame. The endless liturgy bored
him, but he was moved a little by the homeliest thing in the
huge church – the crib with the Infant in the straw, the Man
and the Woman, the Beasts and the Star and the Angels. It
reminded him of the byre at Corse, and how there had
seemed to be always a kind of sacred bond between the
animals and the farm-folk who were born and died under
the same thatched roof . . . He left the church before the
Elevation.

So Magnus Olafson had many pleasant friends, but found
himself lonely among the rugs and poems and wine-cups.
There is a deeper intensity, love – surely he found release
there . . . He had the thick peasant body that rises in a slow
fruitful surge of earth to the sun, and falls away again. It
cannot be denied that this woman and that came to Magnus
Olafson's bed – modern memoirs are frank and explicit – but
none of these intelligent and attractive girls remained his
mistress for long. The spring was choked, and in what loins
did the stone of impotence lie, when most of these women
afterwards became adequate wives and mothers? His seed, it
seemed, had the coldness and barrenness of salt.

So he wandered among the cities of Europe, increasingly celebrated and lonely, and found no place (the gates of his Eden being shut against him) to establish his house.

Lately a new problem had begun to nag at him a good deal – the use of art. In this too he had a peasant's practical outlook. Everything about a croft is there for some specific purpose: the plough, the oar, the quernstones, the horse-shoe, the flail. Each implement symbolised a whole segment of labour in the strict cycle of the year, so that the end might be fruition, and bread and fish lie at last on a poor table. But this fiddle, the symbol of his art – he had squandered all his skill on it, and in return it had drained him of much human warmth and kindliness – what was the use of it after all but to titillate a few rows and boxes of cultured people on a winter evening?

If he allowed himself to brood too much on this, a desolation would come over his mind.

One autumn, after a year in which he had done little work, he thought of writing music – a tone poem, perhaps, or even an opera – with Celtic themes. In the library of Trinity College, Dublin, he was shown an ancient Gaelic manuscript. In the margin, in faded exquisite script, some student had scratched out a translation.

Thou hast heard how Jupiter changed himself into the likenesse of a Swan or a Bull. Many a country spell hath turned a Princesse into a Paddock. Girls have put on leaves and branches and become very Trees. Such Metamorphoses happen now never, or seldom, for it was the curse of the Angel in the Garden, that each creature should seek out its own isolation and build a wall about itself. Then Man (the prime sinner) took after a season a foolish pride in his separateness, for, said Adam with the Apple seed yet between his teeth, We have

graces not given unto Plants and Stones and Beasts.
Cannot I measure Stars and atoms of Dust with the span
of my fingers, and utter subtleties with my Tongue, and
lord it over the Ox and the fish? This was a false and a
foolish thought, that came nigh to tear asunder that
most intricate Web of Nature that God Himself spun on
the Six Dayes of Creation. If Chaos be not come in
againe, the reason is, that the delicate thin spunne Web
I have spoken of still holds, though grievously riven in
sundry partes. There be rocky places yet in the West and
North where young men, finding shy cold creatures of
no tongue or lineage, have led the same home to their
mothers' Doors, and begotten Children on them; they
have laboured and grown bent and grey together, and at
last lain twined in the one Grave. This is to say, Man
hath taken a deep primitive draught, and gotten drunk,
and so pledged himself anew to the Elements. Likewise
this is said, that many a country Maid, taking the shore
road home from Mass or Market, hath vanished out of
mortal ken, but she hath been fleetingly glimpsed thereafter lying upon a Rock in a great company of seales, or
(it may be) lingering alone in a little bay and looking
with large sorrowful eyes upon the Bell and Arch at the
shore where she hath learned in her childhood to say
her *Credo* and her *Ave Marias*.

Magnus Olafson was entranced, in a complex way, by the
crude paragraph. He who had never shed a tear for the
vanishing of his mother or the death of his father felt a swelling in his throat as he read. At the same time his eyes and lips
smiled at the quaintness and innocence of it all. The homily
– it was from an old Irish sermon – seemed to treat of the
question that had troubled him all that winter.

He thought of the men who had thrown off all restraint and were beginning now to raven in the most secret and delicate and precious places of nature. They were the new priesthood; the world went down on its knees before every tawdry miracle – the phonograph, the motor car, the machine-gun, the wireless – that they held up in triumph. And the spoliation had hardly begun.

Was this then the task of the artist: to keep in repair the sacred web of creation – that cosmic harmony of god and beast and man and star and plant – in the name of humanity, against those who in the name of humanity are mindlessly and systematically destroying it?

If so, what had been taken from him was a necessary sacrifice.

The Cinquefoil

UNPOPULAR FISHERMAN

There are a few men in the island I don't speak to, one especially: Fred Houton that I used to fish with in our boat the
Thistle until the day two or three years ago when he struck a
savage unexpected blow at my pride.

If he had taken a five-pound note out of my wallet I would
have forgiven him, or whisky from my cupboard; or even if
he had not turned up for the fishing one morning. For Fred
Houton and I understood each other, there was a grudging
muted friendship.

He lived with his mother in a croft in the hills, a poor place
called Ingarth.

I was pleased enough to see him most evenings. He would
throw open the door of my hut without knocking and say,
'Come on, then, boy, we're going for a pint.' Or, if we had no
money, we would sit silent and play draughts and smoke till
after midnight.

After I got to know Rosie, all that changed. It's true, I had
known Rosie all my life – all the islanders are acquainted
with one another. And a plain little thing I thought her. She
stood all day at the counter of her father's shop above the pier
and served the island with groceries, bread, knitwear,
confectionery, tobacco. She was just one among the hundred
faces, old and young and ageing, that drifted about the island.

She came to the hut one day with a copy of the *Fishing News* that I hadn't collected for a week. She came dripping with rain; my window was a gray throbbing blur. I asked her in while I rummaged in the cupboard for coppers. She said, 'Your floor could do with a wash.' She said, trembling – the four pennies in her fist – 'That's a poor fire you have.' . . . She stayed for a bite of supper. She was pretty enough with the rain-washed apples in her cheeks. She promised, at the end of the house under the stars, to come back the next night.

Soon it was a strange night that didn't bring Rosie to my hut, with a few fresh-baked scones, or a pot of jam, or a book.

I never really got to like her. I never thought her long freckled face beautiful. She brought a disturbance into my days. I enjoyed fishing more, and breathing, and drinking, because of Rosie.

'If you think I'm going to marry you,' I said, 'you're mistaken. I don't believe in that nonsense. I won't go to the kirk with you on Sunday mornings either.' (I knew she sang in the church choir.)

She said that that was all right as far as she was concerned. But maybe I would change my mind after a time.

There was a certain amount of difficulty with Fred Houton. He would come crashing through the door – as he always did – upon our silence. 'Are you here again?' he would say to Rosie. And to me: 'Come on, come on. They're wanting us to play darts in the pub.'

I told him in the boat one morning when we were setting creels that I would appreciate it if he didn't come so much about my place in future. I let him know – surely the man must have guessed – that there was an understanding between Rosie and me. Then seeing the hurt look on his face, I said, 'Well, say one night a week. Friday – that's always a good night in the pub. We'll have a drink every Friday. Rosie can bide home on Friday and do her knitting. But mind you knock at the door in future.'

One day that winter Fred Houton said to me, 'Look, Gurness, I won't be able to fish with you after Christmas. We'd better come to some arrangement about the boat.'

It turned out that his mother had had a bad twelve-month of it with rheumatism, and the work of the croft, though it was small, was too much for her now. So, Fred had to give up the fishing and resume the work of barn and byre and peat-hill.

I was vexed at the prospect of losing him. He was a good worker (and a luckier fisherman than me, I admit that). But we do not show our feelings in the island. I said, 'That's all right.'

At the new year, I gave him a hundred pounds for his share in the *Thistle*.

That seemed to be the final severance; after that he never stood noisily in my door, even on a Friday evening when my throat was dry. I drank alone on Friday in the window seat of the pub. I am not good company – I have never had any friends in the island, and I haven't needed them.

I was not even friendly with Rosie. We quarrelled often, that winter, about such things as whether I should get a new suit, for example, or a wireless to hear the weather forecast for inshore fishermen. She would say straight out that I was mean. She would say, ruffling my hair, that really I must try to be more pleasant to people. Some of the answers I gave her made her mouth tremble.

I had a young boy in the boat with me that winter, Jerome Scabra of Anscarth. He learned, slowly, the craft of fishing. I paid him three pounds a week, and he got a few fish home with him at the weekend (if there were any fish).

One Monday evening in March Rosie did not come to the hut. Nor did she come on Tuesday, Wednesday, Thursday.

I ought to have called at the shop. But I know that James Wasdale her father doesn't like me. That wouldn't keep me back, of course – it's all one to me whether they like me or dislike me or have no feelings about me at all. But I don't like the idea that any woman should think me put out on her account. It occurred to me that she might be ill. There was flu in the island, I had heard.

On Friday afternoon I sent Jerome Scabra along to the shop for a tin of tobacco and cigarette papers.

He was back in ten minutes, cutting the air with his shrill mouth.

'Well,' I said, 'are they busy in the shop? Stop that whistling. Old Wasdale fleeces the islanders right and left on a Friday.'

Jerome said there was no customer in the shop when he went in but old Jake Sandside scrounging for this and that.

'This is not the kind of tobacco I use,' I said. 'Who served you? Was it the old man?'

'No,' said Jerome. 'It was Rosie.'

I told the boy to be at the shore at seven o'clock prompt next morning.

Rosie never came back to my hut, except once.

That summer, before harvest, she married Fred Houton in the kirk. I read about it in the local newspaper. I think it is better for a woman to be thirled to a man who makes his living from the land. It is a surer steadier happier life for a girl. The sea is too dangerous.

I hear they have a bairn now. It'll be no beauty. Neither the father nor the mother have much to commend them in the way of looks.

I wish them no harm, all three of them up there at Ingarth.

But I never speak to them. I go past them in the village as if they didn't exist.

Last night a knock came to my door. It was the woman of Ingarth.

'Gurness,' she said, 'Fred and I, we would like . . . please . . . we would like it very much if you would . . . you know, Gurness, we both like you . . . come to dinner with us on –'

I threw the door shut. The door-frame rattled. My hands trembled the way they do when there is a halibut on the hook.

Something makes me happy this winter, out west. The *Thistle* is catching a lot of fish. Young Scabra is – I know it now – a lucky fisherman.

THE MINISTER AND THE GIRL

'For love we were born indeed, and so that we might under-stand truly what love is we exist for a few years on the earth, and then after our death our dust – if we have understood a little the meaning of love – lies richer in the earth than the dust of those who have devoted themselves entirely to 'late and soon, getting and spending' . . .

'When we are enjoined to love our neighbours, it is surely a difficult thing to do sometimes. For some of the people we meet in the course of our lives are not attractive to us in any way. How can we love this person whose every word on every subject under the sun offends us; even the way he speaks may set our teeth on edge. You, and I, and everybody, has met such a person. We generally avoid his company. Yet the divine injunction is plain – "Love your neighbour" – we are bound as Christians. What does it mean? It does not mean, I think, that we should go about the world with holy long-suffering

smiles on our faces for this one and that, high and low, good
and bad. By no means; one of the qualities of love is honesty,
sincerity. I think it may mean this – we are bound to enter
upon any relationship, however fleeting, with a deep respect
for the other person. You may say, "Instinctively I do not like
this person!" and closer acquaintance may not by any means
sweeten your opinion of him. Yet we must think of ourselves
as limited people – even the saints are limited – and we simply
do not understand. The distasteful person was created by
God, he is one of God's children, when we are introduced to
him we are in the presence of a marvellous mystery. Before
that mystery we must school ourselves to be patient, long-
suffering, modest, understanding. This may not be "love" as St
Paul meant it in his great meditation on love in the Epistle to
the Corinthians, but it is to stand perhaps on the threshold of
love, hoping – if we stay there long enough – that the door
may be opened to us.

'Thus it is possible to feel dislike for a person, and yet to be
in a state of charity towards him . . .'

The minister of Selskay was interrupted at this point in the
writing of his sermon. There was a knock at the door. He put
down his pen and called, 'Come in.' No one answered. Finally
he went to the door and opened it. Tilly Scabra stood there.
She muttered something that John Gillespie could not quite
catch, but he did hear the words 'trouble' and 'help'.

The Scabras were a family that lived at the other end of the
island. Even among the crofters and fishermen, who are
never snobs, they were poorly regarded. Arthur Scabra, the
minister had heard, was not really a bad man, and in fact he
had liked him the once or twice they had met and chatted on
the road. But this Arthur had come home from doing his
National Service taking with him a trollop of a girl from
Leith or Granton, and whether they were married or not

nobody knew, but anyway they took up residence with Arthur's old mother. Old Mrs Scabra did not live to see her granchildren, but she can't have ended her days in tranquillity; for Angela, Arthur's woman, was not long in showing her mettle. Debts and drink and quarrelling – among such squalid unknown things the old woman took ill, and turned her face to the wall, and breathed her last. Arthur and Angela, after the funeral, found the 'kist' under the bed with the mother's savings in it: a bundle of notes, a few sovereigns, a gold brooch. Then for a month or so Anscarth was the gayest house in the island, with parties two or three nights a week (to which all the young men went, of course); and Angela had new flashy clothes, and new ornaments of appalling ugliness littered the mantelpiece and sideboard. Of course the money gave out, and then the parties stopped, except for the weekend half bottle and the home-brew; and at Anscarth it was back to the old cycle of debts, drink and quarrelling.

The good folk of Selskay held up their hands at the stories of the ongoings at Anscarth, which up to then had been an austere respectable place. Between one lurid story and another, Angela gave birth to her first-born, a boy.

The sad thing was, she had dragged Arthur down with her. Before going away to his calling-up, Arthur Scabra had been a quiet hardworking boy. He came back after three years utterly changed, and this Jezebel from the street corners with him. From that day on Arthur had never put a hand to plough or oar. The creature wasn't ill, that was obvious – he could forage all day among the seaweed for whelks or driftwood, in rain or sun – it was just that he had lost the taste for work. 'Arthur Scabra doesn't incline to work,' said an old crofter to the minister, and spat, and laughed.

They managed to live, all the same. Hardly a winter passed without another little Scabra filling the cradle in the corner of the house. The dreariness, the drink, the fighting went on monotonously, among periods of tranquillity. If things got too oppressive indoors, Arthur would wander along the shore for an hour or two, probing in this pool and that swathe of seaweed. Then after a time one of the little ones would appear on the banks above and shout across the sand, 'Dad, come on, your dinner's ready.' . . . Then Arthur would come slowly back, and gather the bairn into his arms, and kiss it. And together they would stoop under the chattering wailing laughing soup-smelling lintel of Anscarth.

One winter little Tilly appeared on earth, and opened her eyes, and wailed. It was the minister's predecessor who had, out of charity, gone to the croft and baptised her; for the Scabras never went to the kirk.

Now here she stood, some sixteen years later, on the doorstep of the manse, muttering something about 'fighting' and 'blood'.

'You'd better come in,' said Rev. John Gillespie.

Extracts from the Diary of a Minister

I knew it would come, sooner or later. They are trying to marry me off. It is the youngest daughter of Fiord who has been chosen. At least, her old madam of a mother has chosen her to be the lady of the manse. Three times this month a note has come from Fiord – through the post, if you please: 'We would be very happy,' said the first note, 'if you could find time to come to tea on Friday afternoon. There will be no other guests. Bet has been baking a cake with cherries in it. We know you like that' . . . I couldn't go – I had this presbytery meeting in the town. The second invitation, a week later, I accepted. A drearier afternoon I have rarely put in. There we sat round the table in the parlour, eating the cherry-cake and sipping tea: Mrs Dale the hostess, and Mrs Hunda the doctor's wife, and Bet. Pressed, I said the cake was very good (so it was). The conversation was mostly about the wickedness of strikers, the scandalous things that were shown on TV, Arthur Scabra's laziness . . . Almost before I knew it the ladies had withdrawn and I found myself alone with Bet Dale. The poor girl had been instructed to put on an impressive show – it was all chatter, giggles, blushes, long silences. I couldn't stand much of that. 'My respects to your mother,' I said. 'The cake was marvellous. Thank you.' . . . She gave me a last hurt look. Then I went.

What she told old madam I do not know. All was not yet lost. Another billet-doux a few days later through the letterbox: 'We *did* enjoy your company that afternoon last week, especially Bet. She hasn't stopped talking about it since. Bet, I know, is intelligent, and she is starved of serious conversation in this island. So *please* come to tea on Friday afternoon, 4 p.m.' . . . Starved of conversation! Bet's destiny, I'm sure, lies in a farmhouse, with children and cheese-making and the growing of roses. She would be deadly miserable in a house like this. I wrote this morning: 'Dear Mrs Dale, Thank you for your invitation. Unfortunately I am not able to accept. I find that afternoon tea is bad for my digestion.' . . .

I think I have made at least two more enemies in Selskay; and one of them quite powerful.

Now it is Mr James Wasdale the merchant having a go, on behalf of his daughter Rosemary who sings in the choir.

Rosie is a more interesting girl than Bet Dale, though much plainer. I sense depths in her. She might suddenly do something unexpected – goodness knows what. She has a high true sweet soprano.

What did I find on my doorstep a few weeks ago but a bottle of Beaujolais, well wrapped against the eyes of passers-by. No note to say who the donor was. The mystery was explained that same evening when I went to the shop for my tobacco: 'O, Mr Gillespie, and did you get the wine all right? . . . Well, I thought you might like it. Rosie called with it, but you were out. No, no, of course not, you mustn't pay – it's a gift. A pleasure, Mr Gillespie.' . . . A few days more, and the second cannon in the campaign was fired – Rosie at the door with a parcel: beautiful crisp brown paper, virgin string. She held it out to me. 'For you, Mr Gillespie,' she said . . . 'But what is it? Who is it from?' . . . 'It's a fair-isle jersey. I knitted it. I'm a good knitter. I didn't knit it for you. My father said I was to take it here, to you, as a present. So here it is.' . . . I said I had plenty of jerseys. I thanked her. But really, if it was for giving away, somebody else who needed it should have it – Jake Sandside, for example, or Arthur Scabra. 'I think so too,' she said. 'But please, you take it, and give it to one of them. Then I can tell my father I handed it over at the manse door.' She is a strange honest girl. I like her, and I think she respects me, but her affections are elsewhere . . . I gave the jersey to Jake Sandside who has no shirt under his jacket.

The last dying shot in the campaign was fired today. Mr Wasdale the merchant comes to me, very troubled, after closing time. 'It's about Rosie, you see, Mr Gillespie. I'm worried about her. Perhaps if you spoke to her. I'll tell you what the position is, as far as I can make it out.' . . . Rosie, it seems, has fallen for somebody quite unsatisfactory – none other than that great growling bear of a fisherman called Gurness who lives alone in a hut on the point. Sometimes, it seems, she isn't home all night. Mr Wasdale is very very worried – Gurness is a mean violent man. It is terrible, terrible. He never thought his Rosie, etc.

I promised to speak to Rosie about it. But what right have I to put my blundering hands upon that most delicate and subtle web, the heart's affections?

This is the saddest of all – old sweet balmy Miss Fidge, the sea-captain's daughter, who lives in the big granite house on the side of the hill, has taken a fancy to me! That it should come to this! I noticed the first onset of affection about a month ago, as she was leaving the church after the morning service. (She has been a devoted church woman all her life.) Instead of the slight formal bow to me, as she passed, she lingered, she was all smiles and crinkles, she got in the way of other worshippers who were following her. 'A dear beautiful sermon,' she said. 'O how it touched my heart!' And I trying to nod and smile goodbye to this one and that one and the other one. 'You are a gifted young preacher – greatly gifted – the hearts of everyone were so touched – I could tell – O yes, indeed.' In fact it had been a rather poor sermon, not in my usual earthy-subtle style at all; a disappointment to me at the time of writing and at the time of delivery; not one for my book of collected sermons, to be published when I am ninety years old and past caring what anybody thinks. 'A little spiritual gem!' . . . 'Well, thank you, Miss Fidge, God bless you' (eager to get back into the church and have a word with the beadle about the faulty heating). 'You are a dear good young man. I bless the day you came to Selskay. I feel that in some way you are a son to me, a spiritual offspring.' . . . It was time to bolt after that. Old Flaws the beadle must have noticed my blushes . . . And so it has gone on even unto this present: that gray austere old lady dotes on me. What she has left of tenderness is spent on me. She monopolises me after the morning services every Sunday now – the other parishioners never get a chance at all with her. It is touching – sometimes when she beams at me a vanished ghost of beauty – that must have been fifty years ago – flits across her tired face. It suddenly occurred to me yesterday that, in her present frame of mind, she might easily leave me everything in her will. That would be terrible! – she has poor cousins, I hear, in Gateshead and South Shields. God bless you, Miss Fidge. This little last blossoming of earthly affection is touched somehow, I think, by 'caritas', the divine love; which should however be centred on no single individual but should hold out arms to the whole universe: in the manner of the heroes of God.

Last night after tea one of the Scabra girls came to the manse. Her mother and father had been fighting over at Anscarth – an old story, but Tilly seemed to be frightened. I took her hand to comfort her. My heart trembled for the trembling child, with pity, yes, but – I recognise it now – with something different and new and utterly unexpected.

She sat beside me in the car.

When we got to Anscarth all was sweetness and light again. But Arthur's smiling face had a long scratch down it.

The younger children were asleep all about the slatterny place: rosy tranquil tear-stained faces.

Angela made me a cup of coffee. 'That Tilly!' she said. 'Fancy disturbing you like that, Mr Gillespie! I'll talk to her, the little bissom.' . . .

For Tilly was no longer there. She was ashamed, obviously, of raising that false alarm; she had made herself scarce.

That white face kept me from sleep all last night.

A FRIDAY OF RAIN

I might have known. I might truly have known. What a fool. I might as well have sat on my arse. I might.

She must have crossed over last night or early this morning. That's it. She must have been in Quoylay all last week, taking her stink and her whine with her from door to door.

Friday is my day. Friday's the day I do my rounds. The whole wide world knows that, including Annie. Friday, Jake Sandside's day. She, and anybody else, can have the rest of the week.

Selskay, on a Friday, belongs to me.

It is not grudged, the bite I get here, the sup I get there. It is well recognised what I did in my youth, for my country, in His Majesty's navy, twenty-one years, man and boy, four war years and more, among burnings and drownings. They know, all right. People don't forget. (Well, some do.) There's always a copper for an old sailor, a pair of boots, a plate of broth. Friday, Sailor Jake's day. Now this old bag has come poaching.

I'll speak to the laird. I will.

I'll speak to Mr Gillespie up at the manse, though he has troubles of his own. Still, a word.

What's she ever done, except frighten children, and steal eggs, and pretend she had the evil eye when a fist or a face in a doorway was hard? An old bag. A boil on a decent community.

I served my country. There's the discharge papers and the fifteen bob a week pension (that wouldn't keep a libbed cat of course, but still).

In the shop, early on, I got the first hint of something wrong. 'Nothing today,' he says, his mouth like a trap. 'Sorry. No broken biscuits. The end of the ham has been taken.' So, there was an intruder.

'Good day to you,' I said with straight sailor shoulders and a salute. I keep my courtesy in every trying circumstance.

He turned away to his desk and cash-book.

It began to look then as if the wolf in the fold was Annie. But she had never been known to come on a Friday before . . .

I stood on the road outside. It had begun to rain. Where now? If I could track the old bag down, I could – not for the first time – put the weight of my tongue on her. My English words, that I learned in the navy, always make her uncomfortable.

I did not see Orphan Annie anywhere in the village. She must be calling, I concluded, at farms in the hinterland. She would be leaving the village till evening. Good thinking – then the roadmen would be home with their wages. The baskets of fish would be on the pier.

A raindrop hit the back of my hand.

The morning village was mine, at least.

Jake, old friend, your wits are losing their edge. Mr Sandside, you are drinking too much of that wine and meth. The village had been broached before breakfast time. The great queen Annie had hardly waited for the women to get their knickers on. She was out of the village, loaded, and up among the hill farms.

It was 'Nothing today, sorry', all along the village street, like an echo. 'Nothing. Call next week.' I am always polite. Perhaps they are tired of me, after thirty years at the game. I touch my cap. 'Is there any firewood to break? Kittens to be drowned?' There was nothing.

Sure enough, there was the imprint of an ancient boot in the mud, beside the pump. Her Majesty had stopped for a drink.

Outside the doctor's that big black-and-white dog took me by the sleeve. I put a stone in his mouth.

Despised and rejected.

I had been confined to the house Monday and Tuesday with rheumatism in my leg. It wasn't better still.

Up among the crofts the evil old mouth would be whining for eggs, and a bit of butter – and saying, 'Oh, that's the sweetest ale, now, I swear to God I ever put in my mouth.' The locust is in my field. While I slept it came.

In that village, only at the hardest door did I get charity. Gurness the fisherman, he gave me a fill of my pipe and a clutch of matches.

It is very strange, Friday and fishermen. They are always kinder and gentler on a Friday. How is that? Do they still remember their patron, Peter, cursing and swearing and denying that Friday morning in the courtyard of the high priest, while inside the Man of Sorrows began to enter upon his agony? All the generations of fishermen have been sorry ever since. The Catholics have their fish on a Friday. There might be something in it. I don't know.

'Don't stuff in any more shag,' said Gurness. 'That's half an ounce you've taken. Your pipe'll break.'

'Much obliged,' I said, and touched my cap-brim. 'It's Friday.'

'What is there about me?' said Gurness. 'You're not the first this morning. That old hag – what's her name, Annie – she was here when I was having my breakfast. I gave her a piece of salt fish to get rid of her.'

I saluted again, and left Gurness pulling his sea-boots on, with a spatter of rain on his window.

It amounted to this: I might not starve at the weekend, but I would be on iron rations: a turnip, limpets, tap water.

Which road had the old trash taken? She was quick as an otter, but she couldn't cover the whole island in one morning. If I took the opposite way, there might still be a picking or two. Also, there was the chance I might meet her half way, near the crossroads. Then I would have something to say to her ladyship.

I reckoned, in this rain, she would take the fertile end of the island first, the region of the big farms. Towards nightfall she might drop among the hill crofts, for a last over-brimming to her bag. It was the poverty-road for me, then.

I was right. I got a sup of oatmeal and buttermilk here, and a dried cuithe there, and an end of cheese in the other place. Near Anscarth the kids threw clods at me. It was worth enduring that black earth-storm to discover that the ale they had put on last weekend was ready and was being broached by Arthur and Angela; and in the middle of the day too, with a teething infant yelling from a crib in the corner. They are kind and reckless, as far as their means go, at the croft of Anscarth at ale-time. So, I got my cup filled maybe half-a-dozen times . . . The climate suddenly changes, for no reason, at an ale-session. Arthur and Angela turned from singing and laughing to say, had I heard about their lass Tilly and the minister, and what folk were saying, but they didn't care, Mr Gillespie was a fine man. Arthur said that was right. His daughter too, Tilly, she was a gem of a lass. Tilly and John (fancy, to call the minister by his Christian name!) were very fond of each other. But Angela said that Tilly was a little tart . . . At that Arthur and Angela glared above their ale-mugs at each other: but only for five seething seconds. Then it was time to dip in the mugs again.

Raindrops shone and tinkled from the lintel. Outside the Anscarth children played in the downpour.

I told Arthur and Angela some of my war-time adventures in the Med and the North Atlantic and the Arctic. My only ambition, in those terrible times, had been to come home to my own folk, with my wound, and throw myself on their care, and so end my days in peace. But even that – I said – was not to be. A thief from another island, that very day, was taking the bite out of my mouth. 'O never never,' I said, and I cherished the gathering glitters in my eyes, 'give old Annie Ross, that bitch of hell, a bite.'

Angela, to comfort me, filled up my mug again.

The truth is this – I hardly remember leaving Anscarth. I didn't mind the rain on the road at all – it fell on me like wild sweet dew. They make their ale strong at Anscarth. (It's a good job old Mrs Scabra, who was president of the temperance guild in her day, isn't there to see their kirn and their mugs.) The sole of one of my boots was going flip-flap, splash-splurge, along the road and through puddles. For half-an-hour I didn't mind Annie Ross at all. Let her get what she could. We have a short time only.

I lost my joy in the doorway of Fiord. A face looked at me as if it had lain for a month in a deep-freeze. *Off with you.* And a dog growling inside. Rain bounced off the flagstones. The door quivered in its frame. A virtue went out of me.

I gave myself once more to the road and the weather. The rain had begun to search to the roots. My sinus throbbed, my left lung whistled. Drink should never be taken before the sun is under the yard-arm. Mr Sandside, when will you ever learn?

Now the weather began to concentrate on my rheumatism. It plucked at my thigh bone till the whole left leg, from haunch to knee, made mad music. On I went, hirpling and hobbling. Bubbles gathered and burst at the lace holes of my boots. I stood against a wall to add my dribble to the sky-tumults.

I edged, after a time, into the barn of Ingarth.

I took off my jacket and trousers and drawers and boots, and crept under the straw. I hung inside a yellow shaking wave. After a time I must have drowsed . . .

Words dragged me back out of a good sea-dream. *Where are you? Come on, Sailor Jake. I saw you going into the barn.*

No use hiding in the straw. I've got something here to warm you.

When a man is old and wretched, and near death, shame leaves him. I raised naked shoulders through the straw. Rosie Houton stood there with a steaming bowl between her hands.

I put my face among the fumes. That broth was well worth the lecture I got. *Been at the meth again. No use denying it. Folk are getting tired of you. Very very tired. That's a fact. Do you realise what you're doing to yourself?*

Spoonful after spoonful after spoonful of the thick golden-gray stuff I put into my mouth. I burned my tongue. Bits of crust stuck in my beard. I rose and fell in the wave of straw.

Killing yourself, that's what you're doing. Your pension – spending it all on meth and cheap wine. And wandering about in all weathers.

The spoon rasped the bottom of the bowl.

'I have not drunk any meth,' I said. 'And it's Friday. I always go out on a Friday.'

Listen to that chest of yours! – You've got severe bronchitis. It might turn into pneumonia. Half-starved you are too. How much of your pension have you got left? For goodness sake buy some bread and cheese and margarine. Let me hear of you drinking meth again, I'll report you to the authorities. They'll sort you out. They'll put you in their home.

I thanked Mrs Houton for her wonderful soup.

The good woman; while I slept she had taken my clothes indoors and dried them at her fire. They steamed gently on her arm.

'You better go home soon,' said Rosie. 'The rain's stopped. Fred's in the village. Fred doesn't like tramps in his barn.'

'I am *not* a tramp. I am a pensioned sailor of the Royal Navy,' I said with as much dignity as a naked man in straw can summon.

You would never think Rosie Houton was the daughter of that misery down at the shop. She turned round while I put my clothes on. She knelt and tied the string on my boots in the barn door. *Now remember, straight home with you. No more drink.*

'Don't give anything to Annie Ross,' I said from the end of the farm road. The sun had come out. The pools on the road were burning mirrors. The rain had crossed the Sound to Torsay. The hills of Torsay were hung with sackcloth – the Selskay air was purest crystal.

I met Fred Houton near the smithy. He stopped for a word. I didn't tell him about the barn and broth. No sense in taking the edge off their charity. (He gave me a shilling.)

I called at the big house where Miss Fidge lives alone. Miss Fidge likes sailors. Her father was skipper of a coaster. Miss Fidge gave me two slices of ginger cake in a paper poke. I enjoy Miss Fidge's ginger cake with a cup of tea.

I was done in. I was completely buggered. The Anscarth ale slumbered still in the marrow of my bones. The weight of old rain was on me. Bad thoughts too wear out the spirit.

My feet dragged homewards. The rat began to gnaw again at my haunch-bone.

I wondered whether I should call at the manse. Tilly Scabra stood outside, on tiptoe, scouring the study window. Her little fist went round and round and then another pane glittered among the salted panes. Officially she's the manse house-keeper. Things are building up to a crisis there. There's to be a meeting of the kirk session on Tuesday evening next, I hear. I decided not to intrude upon Mr Gillespie and his troubles.

I turned the corner and there was my own cottage down beside the loch.

I took the silver whistle out of my trouser pocket and blew two blasts – a signal to the whole of Selskay isle that Sailor Jake was nearing port.

The dog of Skaill barked in the distance.

I *was* tired. I fell asleep in the rocking-chair beside the dead fire, a thing I hardly ever do so early in the evening.

When I woke up it was night. My paraffin lamp was lit. A few flames tumbled in the hearth.

There had been an intruder.

The room was different. Someone had shifted a chair. The water bucket was filled to brimming. There were strange shapes on the bed.

I hirpled over to investigate. A turnip – potatoes – eggs in a stone jar – butter in a saucer – a pot of rhubarb jam – bannocks and oatcakes – a poke of tea – a poke of sugar – brown serviceable boots – a jersey with darnings at elbow and neck.

What good ghost had come through the night to visit me?

I handled each item with lust and gratitude. All was well. The weekend was saved. My pipe with its tight knot of tobacco was on the mantelpiece. If only I had a sup of wine, I wouldn't have called the queen my cousin. (My tongue, after that Anscarth ale – need I say it – was like a flap of old leather.)

A presence was standing in the door with a bottle.

'I thought you were never going to waken,' said Annie Ross, and set the wine on the table. 'I had a job getting drink out of old Wasdale at this time of night.'

I couldn't say a thing.

'I heard,' said Annie Ross, 'that you were bad with rheumatics. A man told me that on the pier at Kirkwall yesterday. *Laid up*, he said – *the sailor's in his bed not able to stir. Looks as if this might be the end of him* . . . So I thought, *Tomorrow's his day. Friday. And what'll Jake do if he can't get round the houses?* I thought, *I better see what's what.* So I got a lift in Tomison's lobster boat this morning early.'

John Sandside, you are a fool.

'There's your takings,' said Annie, 'over there, on the bed. It's a fair haul. Them boots should see you through till the spring. I got enough money for a bottle of wine. There's your change.' . . . She put a couple of coins on the dresser.

You are a slanderer, John Sandside. You have taken away the character of an angel of light.

'It's started to rain again,' said Annie. 'Can I bide to my supper?'

'Yes,' I said. 'Thank you, Annie.'

'I did it for the sake of the old times,' said Annie. 'Though you haven't got a good word to say for me a many a time, and you blacked my eye the last Hamnavoe market. I did it because we were sweethearts once.'

'Forgive me, dear,' I said.

We had a good supper of bannocks and cheese and jam, and we finished the wine.

Annie stayed the night. She got a passage across the Sound in Gurness's boat on the Saturday morning.

My rheumatics, I'm sorry to say, are none better.

SEED, DUST, STAR

A community maintains itself, ensures a continuance and an identity, through such things as the shop, the kirk, the stories told in smithy and tailor shop, the ploughing match, agricultural show, harvest home, the graveyard where all its dead are gathered. (It is the same with all communities – city or island – but the working-out of the ethos of a community is best seen in microcosm, as in the island of Selskay.) Most of all the community ensures its continuance by the coming together of man and woman. There will be a new generation to plough and fish, with the same names, the same legends, the same faces (though subtly shifted, and touched with the almost-forgotten, the hardly-realised), the same kirkyard.

The place where the community lives is important, of course, in perpetuating its identity. There is that cave under the crag with a constant drip of fresh water from its ceiling; a seaman called Charlie was thrown into the cave by a surge, miraculously, when his ship foundered one day in the year 1824, and Charlie lived for a week on the sweet cave-drops before he found courage to climb up to the crofts above. So any place is enriched with quirks of nature and of chance, that make it unique . . . That the same hill was there ten thousand years ago, and will still stand solid under the blue-and-white surge of sky in ten thousand years' time, moves even the coldest islanders to wonderment with mysteries of permanence and renewal (though the hills are shadows too). And at night, in the north-east, the same star shines here as everywhere else in the northern hemisphere; but here alone it smoulders on the shoulder of the hill Foldfea and sparkles in Susill burn, and puts a glim on the hall of the laird with its brief heraldry.

The people themselves are moulded by the earth contours and the shifting waters they live among. They are made of the same dust as the hills they cultivate. It would be sentimental to say the islanders love the island they live in. Nowadays many of them say they do, and genuinely in some cases; but their great-grandfathers had an altogether different relationship with the land and the sea. They saw no 'beauty' at all; at least, if they did, no record of it has come down to us. Men and the elements had a fierce dependence on each other, a savage thrust and grappling, that was altogether different from what we commonly think of as 'love' in these gentler times. Perhaps their attitude to their women was not so very different. They would grow old; there must be a new strong generation to bring in harvest and consider the drift of haddocks; so a wife was taken as a promising seed-vessel, not a creature of transient scents and gleamings and softnesses.

The croft children came weeping into time, one after another. So the ancestral acres remained 'real', and might not still – through barrenness or bad luck or improvidence – crumble into shadow. The love that croft parents two hundred years ago put on their children had a desperateness and depth in it that modern islanders hedged with security can hardly conceive of.

Yet who could bear to root a child in the womb, and have it cherished there and brought out into time, who stopped to consider for a moment what grief, pain, disgrace, violence, destitution, madness he was releasing into the world; if not for this immediate one, then inevitably, by natural shifts and permutations, for some or other of his descendants, even in the course of a century or two? No family tree from the beginning but has had put upon it, this generation or that, every variety of suffering. These outweigh the little compensatory joys – the boy with his lure and line, the linkings of lovers, the old man's pipe and ale.

There must be a starker more compelling summons into life than anything imagined by either the 'realists' of art and fiction or the 'romantics'.

For the Greeks, the actions of men were shadows projected by archetypes. The bread that we sow and reap is a tastelessness in comparison to that 'orient and immortal wheat'. The weave we put on our bodies, however comfortable and beautiful and well-cut – what are they to 'the heaven's embroidered cloths'? All the elements we handle fleetingly 'is diamond, is immortal diamond'. And all loves and affections become meaningful only in relation to Love itself. The love of a young man and girl in a small island is cluttered always with jealousy, lewdness, gossipings in the village store. But the mystics insist that Love itself 'moves the stars'. They say that, in spite of the terror and pain inseparable from it, 'all shall be well' – in the isolate soul, and in the island, and in the universe.

The meanest one in the community feels this occasionally; he could not suffer the awful weight of time and chance and mortality if he didn't; a sweetness and a longing are infused into him, a caring for something or someone outside his shuttered self.

Mr James Wasdale the merchant locked up his shop and rattled the door twice, to make quite sure.

On a Tuesday, twenty years previously, Paula had died. Every Tuesday therefore, when it was good weather, Mr Wasdale visited the kirkyard and stood beside Paula's tombstone for a decent time. Then he touched the stone and came away.

The sun was almost down. The chiselled gilt letters filled with shadow. Mr Wasdale turned from the dust of his wife with one cold finger.

He walked for almost a mile into a magnificent sunset. He passed Sailor Jake's hovel. He passed the empty manse whose windows brimmed with cold fire. (The new minister and his family had not yet moved in.) Down below, at the shore, the croft of Anscarth was sunk in shadow: a hand put a lamp in the window.

Mr Wasdale walked on.

Before him one gable and chimney of a croft house detached itself from a cluster of smouldering green hillocks. Rosie was there, inside, hidden – his daughter who had left him for an ignorant poor crofter. There was a child in the cradle, and another – so he had heard – in her body. He held no communication whatsoever with the people of Ingarth. They got their provisions from the Tennants' travelling shop every Monday.

Mr Wasdale took a walk most evenings, before his supper; always in the other direction though, towards the crags and the sea. Why had he come this way tonight? He hesitated. He would not go a step further. He imagined for a moment what it would be to knock at the door of Ingarth. He smiled. He would rather lose a hundred pounds than do that. But, standing between the dead and the unborn, he was moved a little; as if, after long drought, a crofter had come out of the rust of his stable and smelt rain in the wind.

Mr Wasdale turned. He walked back through the darkening island. Jake Sandside leaned, puffing a pipe, against the door-post of his hut. Mr Wasdale raised his hand. Sailor Jake looked the other way.

The kindness that he felt every Tuesday for his dead wife (in spite of repeated meannesses dealt out to her while she was alive, in the name of thrift), his possessiveness and ambition for his daughter Rosie – and they were the only people, apart from his mother, that he had ever cared for in any way – that 'love' still existed. He would not deny it. But it was different now. It had nothing whatever to do with money or prestige. Age and estrangement and death had removed the seed from his keeping; it was part now of the precarious continuing life of the island.

A star shone out at the shoulder of Foldfea. His feet stirred the dark dust.

The village was all lighted squares and darkness and sea-sounds when he came back once more among the houses.

Mr Wasdale fitted his key carefully into the lock.

WRITINGS

Anscarth, Selskay,
12 August

Dear Tony, You have read about it in all the papers, of course, so there's no point in repeating the stark fact that I am out of the kirk. A month ago I resigned – it might have been braver if I had hung on until they sacked me. But I have caused enough distress to everyone. Let's hope there'll be no more fireworks display from the newspapers. (I nearly throttled the last two reporters who called at the manse.) I'm living with Tilly's folk at a croft called Anscarth, just above the beach; but not permanently; I hope to get a place of our own soon, preferably before the baby comes. The Scabras – that's Tilly's folk – are a broody family: the house is in tumult from morning to night. It's small too – Tilly and I have to share a back room with two other infants. It's as different as can be from the silence of the manse: the situation calls for more sweetness of soul than I possess. 'Dear God', I pray a dozen times a day – seething inwardly – 'give me patience.' ... Besides which Angela (the mother – she hails from Edinburgh) is forever brewing and sampling the fruits of her labour. And the old man is forever hanging around. To put it brutally, he is lazy. But there's a gentleness and a kindness about him that puts an ex-parson like me to shame.

What am I doing, then? How do I earn a living? The answer is that I am earning not a black penny; but I hope soon to be a breadwinner, for I have made a start at learning to be a fisherman. My tutor is Tilly's brother, a pleasant 19-year-old called Jerome. (The Scabras all have grand names, to compensate maybe for their tatters and crusts.) Jerome at present is fishing with Bert Gurness, a surly chap who owns a boat called *Thistle*. Jerome intends to break with Gurness and fish on his own account, with me as his partner. (We're already bargaining for a yawl – I think I have enough saved up to buy it – J. says she's a good boat.) Jerome's difficulty at this minute is to make the actual break with Gurness. I should think there's no problem. Gurness pays him only £7 a week. But J. is so shy. However, I've screwed up his courage for him as well as I can. Today is the day of the Agricultural Show in the island. Jerome means to give notice to Gurness among the cows and the roosters and the cheap-jacks.

I shudder to think what Professor Allardyce is saying about me. But there may be more charity in the world than I think now, in my present morbid state, after my dealings with elders and (especially) reporters.

I spent this morning down at the shore, selecting stones to weight our lobster creels: we have about fifty of these in the shed outside. I seemed to be alone in the island – every Selskay able-bodied person has gone to the show in a field at the heart of the island. While I was stooping and rising at the beach, selecting stones, I could hear the sounds of the fair surging and ebbing on the wind. All the Scabras have gone. Tilly wouldn't miss the annual junketings for anything. Angela has even whipped wee Marilyn out of the crib. So I sit in a blessed silence writing to you, my dear old friend of the days of our theological studies.

If you see my mother, give her my deep and genuine love. I wrote to her and all my folk a month ago, but have had no answer. I must have hurt them bitterly.

Do not you forget me, or the world would be a sterile promontory indeed.

So, picture me now, old friend, with a speckled black-and-white fisherman's jersey on me, and trousers stiff and gray with salt, working day after day on the shore, under the immense northern sky.

I try to keep off the road as much as possible, for I am an embarrassment to certain of the island folk. Some of my erstwhile choristers, for example, swerve away onto a sheep track when they sight me on the horizon. The shopkeeper – one of my elders in the old days – serves me with tobacco as though I was a spy or a criminal. There is one sweet balmy old lady, Miss Fidge, who makes no difference. 'Your sermon last Sabbath, my dear, it was so beautiful, a masterpiece . . .' I have not preached to Miss Fidge, or anybody else, for three months . . . In time, I hope, the island will forget, and accept me for what I have become.

Even in Anscarth, to begin with, I caused much uncertainty and some embarrassment. A minister, come down in the world, because of their Tilly, and now come to live with them, among all their uninhibited noise and squalor and on-goings! The awe didn't last long. But I do believe that Angela doesn't swear quite as much as she used to.

Rev. Anthony McLean, I a poor fisherman ask for your prayers and continuing concern. I know you will not plead with me to repent and come back to the fold: that would be impossible, because in a sense I have never left the fold. Not one jot or tittle of any belief has been shaken by what has happened. And if I were to 'repent', in that vulgar sense of the word, what would become of Tilly and the child that's not yet born? I love her more now than that first evening when she stood on the manse doorstep, with tears in her eyes, mumbling something about a fight.

When I dropped in on Orkney last weekend, all my vague knowledge of these northern islands was confined to an 850-year-old cathedral, heroic lifeboatmen, some neolithic stones on a wine-dark moor. Then in my hotel in the main town, Kirkwall – it calls itself, proudly, a 'city' – I was told that I simply *must* visit one of the agricultural shows. There are, it seems, a whole cluster of shows about now. The Selskay show was to be on Tuesday. I booked on the little nine-seater plane and on Tuesday morning was set down in a field half-a-mile from where the show was.

It proved to be one of the most hectic days in my life. (I had come to Orkney expecting peace, silence, solitude.) I made a tour of the animal pens, and viewed superb bulls, handsome orange-tinted sheep, cockerels in cages giving the sun a ringing salute every minute, well-groomed ponies, new gleaming farm machinery . . . All the islanders were there in their Sunday best – and they know how to dress, believe me – and the girls' complexions and skins would break the hearts of the world's leading cosmeticians.

In an adjacent field, like old mushrooms, were the booths of itinerant showmen from the south.

I had a snack in the tea tent, presided over by a gracious lady, Mrs Dale from the farm of Fiord. A snack, did I say? In London a meal like it would have cost three pounds. There were Orkney cheese, Orkney oatcakes, Orkney crab, Orkney ham, Orkney chicken. At the end of the gastronomic treat the bill came to about fifty pence!

Later I was glad of that lining on my stomach.

How delightful to move about in a crowd and know that not a soul is there with the intention of 'doing' you or conning you in any way. There was one exception, an old ex-navy man, but he was such a delightful yarn-loaded character that I didn't mind passing a few minutes with him and parting with five bob – it was worth it. (By the way, why don't some of our writers hard up for a theme get in touch with such folk as Jack Sandside, or 'Sailor Jack', as he is affectionately known in Selskay?)

Drawn by a crowd of merry youths in the entrance flap, drinking beer out of cans, I entered the whisky tent.

Because of the press of farmers in good thick tweeds, it was quite a feat to struggle through the marquee to the counter. I was greeted from far and near as if I had lived all my life in the island. Whiskies were set before me by men I had never seen before – not your English tot either, but a brimming noggin of Orkney malt whisky. It was as if I was tasting the essence of all I had seen and experienced that day. It takes a long time to learn how to handle the elixir.

Merriment, song, reminiscence all round me; and I was made to feel at home in the midst of it all.

Only one incident marred a perfect day. Two of the locals, a fisherman and a farmer, had a fight. In the midst of the revelry they suddenly fell on each other, and began to beat the daylights out. The crowd in the marquee seemed to expect this, and even to enjoy it. The tall strong fisherman seemed to be no favourite. Shouts went up for 'Fred' to finish the b— off. It was quite violent while it lasted; but eventually the police arrived; and the two pugilists were handcuffed, still struggling and swearing, and frogmarched away . . . I feel that one might have to live in a place like this for a decade at least before understanding of the folk begins to dawn – as the doors of the Black Maria opened to receive them, Fred and the fisherman were smiling at each other, and they seemed to be trying to do a difficult thing – embrace with shackled hands . . .

I was assured that the two were old enemies. They used to fish together in the same boat, but had quarrelled two years previously, and since then were at daggers drawn. The Selskay men, smiling, pushed more nips of the island whisky in front of me . . .

When I went out into the fresh air later, the whole bucolic festival began to waver about me like a merry-go-round. It's like I said – it might take ten years to understand these folk, but it takes a whole lifetime to learn how to hold their heroic whisky.

Two Selskay men, Frederick John Houton (27), crofter, Ingarth, Selskay, and Albert Sigurd Gurness (31), fisherman, Ness Cottage, Selskay, appeared in court last Tuesday charged with committing a breach of the peace at the Selskay Agricultural Show on 12th August.

Both pleaded not guilty.

The Procurator Fiscal stated that the alleged offence took place in the beer tent in the course of the afternoon. The two accused assaulted each other with such violence that Gurness's nose was subsequently found to be broken and the lobe of Houton's ear was almost bitten through. There had, it seemed, been bad blood between Houton and Gurness since they had sundered their lobster-fishing partnership two years previously. They were apprehended with some difficulty by the police in the beer tent, and after being hand-cuffed were taken to the police station in the police van. On the way there they continued to struggle with one another. A blood test showed that both had consumed a considerable quantity of alcohol. They made no comment when charged. Their attitude continued to be so truculent that they were detained at the station overnight. Gurness asked that they be lodged in the same cell, so that 'they could have it out' – a request that had not been complied with.

Both the accused were unrepresented.

Jerome Scabra (19), fisherman, Anscarth, Selskay, stated that he had gone to the show-park about 1 o'clock on the afternoon of the 12th. He always went to the Show but on this occasion he had a particular errand: to tell the accused Gurness that he would no longer be able to help him in his lobster boat after Saturday, as he was intending to go to the fishing with his brother-in-law. He had seen Gurness at the bingo tent, and told him.

Fiscal – Was Gurness drunk at that time?

Scabra – No, sir. At least, he didn't appear to be.

Fiscal – How did Gurness take the news?

Scabra – I'm sorry, I don't follow . . .

Fiscal – I mean, that you would no longer be going lobster-fishing with him after the Saturday.

Scabra – He said there was no need to wait till Saturday. He was giving me the sack, he said, there and then. Then he told me to clear off, he couldn't hear the man shouting the bingo numbers. I asked him for my wages, seven pounds. He said as I had only worked four days that week he was only owing me four pounds. If I came to his hut that night, he said, he would pay me . . .

The witness went on to say that the next time he saw Gurness that day was in the whisky tent. Gurness was standing beside the tent pole drinking with another man. Witness approached Gurness with the intention of placating him – he did not wish them to part on bad terms, as he had a high regard for Gurness as a fisherman and as a person. But before he could reach Gurness through the crowd there was a disturbance at the counter – Fred Houton and a stranger he had never seen before were having a loud disagreement. The next he saw, Gurness had come between them and separated them. But immediately afterwards Houton and Gurness began fighting with each other. He had seen some fights in Selskay, but never any like that. They resisted all attempts on the part of the public to tear them apart. At last the police arrived, and took them both in charge.

Fiscal – Do you think now, that what you had told Gurness earlier, I mean, that you wouldn't be fishing with him any more, had perhaps upset him?

Scabra – It might have. We had both got on well together. He would have difficulty in getting somebody else to fish with him. He is not the most popular man in Selskay. It wouldn't be easy for him to fish in a boat like the *Thistle* alone – dangerous, I should say.

Houton had nothing to say in his own defence.

Gurness stated that it had been a most enoyable fight. He did not know when he had enjoyed a fight more. Everybody should have a fight like that occasionally. It would make for a better island.

The Sheriff said it was disgraceful, when people were gathered together on a festive occasion like an agricultural show, that their pleasure should be spoiled by two drunken brawlers. If they couldn't hold their drink they should leave the stuff alone. He fined them each five pounds.

'After I'm dead, everything of mine goes to Fred Houton of Ingarth, Selskay. The hut, the boat *Thistle* and all gear, the money in the post-office, the furniture such as it is, and all else whatsoever – A. S. Gurness.'

The above document was found in the table drawer of Ness Cottage, Selskay, after the death of Albert Sigurd Gurness in a storm off Borough Ness on the afternoon of 6th November that same year. The deceased was fishing alone at the time. His lobster boat *Thistle* was completely broken up. The body was taken from the sea a week later by two other Selskay fishermen, John Gillespie and Jerome Scabra.

The Tarn and the Rosary

(1)

He was cast out of unremembered dark into salt, light, shifting immensities. A woman closed him in with hills, sweet waters, biddings, bodings, thunders and dewfalls of love. He sat among three sisters and one brother at a scrubbed table. Colm: that was his name. There were small noises from a new cradle in the corner. His mother was a little removed from him then. His father was in the west since morning. The cow Flos that belonged to the croft next door bent and nuzzled buttercups. Hens screeched round a shower of oats from old Merran's fist. A gentleness of beard and eyes came in at the door at thickening light with fish and an oar: his father. Then his mother and brother and three sisters and the old one went silently to their different places. The infant, Ellen, was lifted from cradle to breast. The lamp was lit. His father wiped plate with crust. His father filled his pipe. His father spoke from the chair beside the smoke and flame. His father opened a book. There was a silence. The boy closed his eyes. Then very ancient wisdom was uttered upon the house, a gentle deliberate voice prayed from the armchair: his grandfather.

(II)

In the wide grassy playground the children whirled and chir-
ruped and slouched. A whistle shrieked: the children were
enchanted to silence. They stepped quietly past the teacher
into a huge gloom, desks and globe and blackboard. Miss
Silver said, more grave than any elder, 'A terrible thing has
happened, a sum of money has been removed from my purse
this morning. This is what must happen now. You will all
empty your pockets onto your desks, every single thing, and
then we will see who took the half-crown and the two
sixpences . . .' Guilt whitened Colm's face like chalk (though
he had done nothing). Soon the desks were strewn with bits
of string, shells, fluff, cocoa tin lids, broken blades. Miss
Silver strode among all this bruck, jerking her head back and
fore like a bird. 'Very well,' she said. 'The thief has hidden his
ill-gotten gains. It is now a matter for the police. The policeman will be taking the boat from Hamnavoe tomorrow, with
a warrant, and also handcuffs, I have no doubt.' Colm felt like
a person diseased, scabbed all over with coins, so that everyone could see he was the culprit (though he had only once
seen a half-crown, between his father's fingers, the day his
father opened his tin box to pay the rent; a white heavy rich
round thing). 'We are doing the exports and imports of
Mexico, I think,' said Miss Silver in a hurt voice, turning to
the senior class. The school was a place of chastity and awe all
that afternoon – the brand of crime was burned on it . . . 'I
wonder if Jackie Hay will be long in jail?' said Andrick
Overton on the way home from school. Torquil, Colm's
brother, asked why. A surge of joy went through the boy
because it was not being said among the pupils that he and
only he was the thief. 'Did you see Jackie's mouth when the
teacher was searching the desks?' said Andrick. 'He had slack

silver teeth.' The older boys all laughed on the road, and Colm laughed too. The Hamnavoe policeman did not come and Jackie Hay was not sent to prison. Instead he bought the big boys who were with him lucky-bags and liquorice sticks next day, Saturday, from the grocery van. He smoked a packet of woodbines himself and was sick in a ditch. Nobody was sorry for Jackie Hay. Torquil's mouth was black and sweet all that afternoon.

(III)

Colm came through the village carrying a basket of eggs and a pail of buttermilk from the farm of Wardings. 'What a kind body the wife of Wardings is,' his mother always said, her voice going gentle and wondering. It was true; he liked going to the farm for the eggs and kirned-milk on a Saturday morning. Mrs Sanderson always took him in and gave him a thick slice of the gingerbread she had baked herself. She asked him questions about the school and his family in a hearty voice. She didn't seem to mind if some golden breadcrumbs fell from his mouth onto her stone floor which was always so clean. The door into the whitewashed kitchen would open for sure, sometimes when he was eating the gingerbread, and the dog came in. He didn't like dogs. He was nervous of dogs. But Rastus, the black-and-white collie, seemed to have some share in the kindliness and benevolence of Wardings. Boy and dog, after the first unsure moment, eyed each other trustfully. He patted the neck of the dog (but still with some reserve). Rastus licked the sweet crumbs from the fingers of his other hand. 'Mrs Sanderson,' he said, 'I'll have to be going now.' ... Smiling, she stood in the door and waved goodbye to him.

It was steep, the road down through the village. One terrible morning, when he was five, he had fallen; every single egg was smashed and the buttermilk was spilt; red and gray tatters across the frosty road. He ran home yelling, empty-handed. He would not even go back to get the pail and the basket. Mary-Anne had to go and fetch them.

Today he stepped easily down the brae, holding the pail in one hand and the basket in the other. So delicate his going that the buttermilk only, at most, shivered into circles. It was pleasant, the dark rich tang of the gingerbread in his mouth. Mrs Sanderson was nice. He wouldn't mind biding at a farm like Wardings.

Huge strength and power broke the skyline. Tom Sanderson the farmer was ploughing the high field with his team. He shouted to Colm and waved his arm. Colm waved back.

It was dinnertime, surely. There was not a soul in the village street. The smell of mince and boiled cabbage came from the Eunsons' house; that made him feel hungry. The only living thing on the road was the merchant's dog, Solomon – a lion-coloured mongrel – and it lay asleep in the sun under a window with loaves and cream cookies and one iced cake in it. A bare curved knuckle-ended bone lay at the dog's unconscious head. Whose birthday was it? Colm looked through the shop window at the cake. It must be a boy or girl from one of the better-off families – from the Bu farm, maybe, or the manse, or the doctor's. From the house above the shop came the rattle of plates, a shred of vapour, a most delicious smell of frying onions. His dinner would be ready too, he must hurry. There was no candle – it was more likely to be a christening cake. With his left foot he eased the bone towards the wet black nose. The bone whispered in the dust. A name was written in pink icing on the white-iced cake: *Christopher Albert Marcusson*. That must be the minister's new baby. There would be marzipan inside, spices, sherry, raisins, threepenny bits. The tawny flank heaved once, gently. Sweetness, sweetness. Colm loved all sweet things – languors and dissolvings and raptures in the hot cave of the mouth. The road swirled. His left leg was draped in rage. Teeth and eyes flashed under him, and fell away. Two livid punctured curves converged along his left thigh; they began to leak; his knee was tattered with blood. He set the eggs down carefully on the road; the buttermilk quivered once and was still. The dog skulked across the road to the tailor shop; and it looked back at him once or twice balefully. He looked down at the lacerated leg. It was very strange, his leg wasn't sore at all. On the contrary, it felt warm and pleasant and refreshed (like when you draw it out of a cold pool and let it dry in the sun). Yet he had been bitten. The merchant's dog had bitten him. Nobody had seen it happen. His lip quivered. He picked up the basket and the pail and went slowly, limping, through the dinnertime village to the house at the shore. There was really no need to limp at all, but he limped. It was terrible – he had tried to be good to the dog, to put his bone near his mouth seeing that it was dinnertime, and this was the way the beast had repaid him. His throat worked, and he felt tears in his eyes. There was a numbness now in his thigh. He hurried on. His father was sitting on the wall smoking his after-dinner pipe. Some buttermilk slopped over, the eggs clacked gently. He sobbed. His father looked at him and said, 'You're late for your dinner,' and then saw with astonishment that something was wrong. Colm set down pail and basket on the flat quern-stone at the door and with one loud wail flung himself into the fragrant gloom of the kitchen, and the startled faces, and the warm enfolding arms of his mother. He hid the mask of tears in her bosom. He held up his wounded leg. His mother said, 'There there' and 'Poor angel', and set him down on a chair. His mother issued calm orders: kettle on fire, a bandage, lysol. His three sisters dispersed about these tasks. 'That dog of Wardings,' said his mother. 'What do they call him, Rastus, I've never trusted him. The sly way he comes up to you. It's a wonder to me Mrs Sanderson lets the thing wander about freely like that. I'll speak to her.'

It was a secret. Nobody knew but himself. He wouldn't tell her till he was safely in bed that it wasn't Rastus, it was the merchant's dog, Solomon, that had bitten him. Maybe they would have to cut off his leg. He sat erect in the chair and gave out long quivering sobs.

Mary-Anne took a small round purple bottle from the cupboard and gave it to the mother.

Grand-dad muttered from his chair beside the fire, 'That's nothing, a clean bite. There's worse things than that'll happen to him. Fuss, fuss.'

His father had come in and was leaning against the kitchen doorpost, watching him, and his pipe glowed and faded in the interior gloom.

Great jags of flame went into his thigh. He screamed and held on desperately to his mother. 'It's all right, darling,' she said. 'I'm putting a drop of lysol on. That'll make you better.'

The disinfectant flamed and flickered and guttered in his white flesh. The faces came about him again. Freda was smiling – she seemed to be pleased at his sufferings. His father's pipe glowed and faded and glowed. He was the important person in the house that day. He sobbed and sniffed in a long last luxury of self-pity. His mother cut a piece of lint with the scissors.

(IV)

Colm crouched among the tall grasses of the dune. 'Colm, where are you? You must come home . . .' It was Ellen's voice that went wandering along the sea-banks, here and there, seeking him out. He wished Ellen would go away. 'Colm, something has happened . . .' His grandfather was dead, that's what had happened. He knew without Ellen having to come and tell him. The old man had lain ill for ten days in the parlour bed. A deepening silence had gathered about him. The mother and children passed from room to room in whispers. He lay there, a lonely stricken figure. 'Colm, mam wants you home now . . .' He pretended not to hear Ellen's quavering command. He scooped up a handful of sand and let it stream through his fingers. He left the dune and slipped like a shadow down to the shore. If Ellen came that way he would hide in the cave. 'Colm, it's grand-dad. Hurry up . . .' He wished Ellen would go away and leave him alone. He did not like people spying on his feelings. He did not feel anything, anyway, in the face of this suffering and death, except a kind of blank wonderment. He dipped one foot in a rockpool. A salt vice gripped his ankle. The coldness reverberated in his belly, tingled in his earlobes and fingers. He turned. His sister was going back across the field. Colm was the only person on that mile-long sweep of beach. The sea pulsed slowly over seaweed and sand. A wave smashed the bright calm rockpool.

The boy moved across a narrowing strip of sand. It must be nearly high tide. He sat down on a rock. What was grand-dad now, an angel? He stood up and sent a flat stone leaping and skidding over the highest gleam of the sea. It was full flood. 'There'll be more fun in the house now. We'll be able to sing and shout again.' He neither liked nor disliked his grandfather. Grand-dad was just a part of the house, like the cupboard and the straw chair he sat in. Grand-dad could be very grumpy and ill-natured. Grand-dad sat at the fire all winter putting ships into bottles. People on holiday, tourists, English trout fishers, came and bought them from him. Then grand-dad would be pleased, flattening out the pound notes, folding them, stowing them carefully into his purse. The ships-in-bottles were always the same: a three-masted clipper, a rock with a lighthouse, a blue and white curling plaster sea. Grand-dad had been a sailor when he was young. Then he had come home and gone to the fishing. He was very old now. It was grand-dad's house they were living in – would they be put out of it now that he was dead? Grand-dad had almost drowned one day off Braga Rock when he was coming home from the lobsters and a sudden gale had torn the sea apart. He told the story so often that Colm knew it by heart. This past winter grand-dad had added a few new words: 'Life was sweet then. A pleasant thing it was for the eyes to behold the sun. Anyway, I got ashore. But now I would be glad to be taken . . .' He had become very remote from them all lately. He smoked his pipe still and spat into a spittoon on the floor. His mother had to clean out the spittoon, a horrible job, long slimy clinging slugs of spittle into the burn – the gushing freshness of the burn bore the old man's juices out to sea. Colm and Ellen had to look about the beach for gulls' feathers to clean the bore of his pipe; if they found good ones grand-dad would open his purse carefully and give them a ha'penny each. He stopped making ships-in-bottles soon after New Year. More and more often he would pause in the armchair, his pipe halfway to his mouth, as if he was listening for something. For two whole days his pipe had lain cold on the mantelpiece. 'I won't be a trouble to you much longer,' grand-dad had said to mother. He frowned at Ellen and Colm, as if they were strangers trespassing on his peace. The fishing-boat belonged to him too. Would they have to sell it now? What way could his dad go to the fishing if they had no boat? Maybe they would starve. Colm walked up the cart-track from the beach. He sat down on the grass and put on his sandals. The sea pulsed, a slow

diastole of ebb; it surged in still, but left shining fringes; the
forsaken sand gleamed dully. They would all have to wear
black clothes, or at least black cloth diamonds on the sleeves
of their coats and jackets. That was horrible. There would
have to be the funeral, of course. His grand-dad would be put
deep in the churchyard: frail old bones, silky beard, sunk jaws.
The wood of the coffin would begin to rot in the wet winter
earth. Then spring would come, but grand-dad would know
nothing about it. There were cornfields all about the kirkyard.
In summer the land would be athrob with ripeness, the roots
in the kirkyard too. Grand-dad would have 'given his flesh to
increase the earth's ripeness': that was Jock Skaill the tailor's
way of looking at it. That, he assured Colm, was the meaning
of death. But most of the Norday women said nobody, least of
all a child, should pay attention to an atheist like Jock Skaill.
Still, there was more in what Jock Skaill said, in Colm's opinion, than in all that talk about angels and harps and streets of
gold. His grand-dad would be lost in a heaven like that. 'My
grand-father, Andrew Sinclair the fisherman, is dead.' He
could not really believe it. Merran Wylie was flinging oats to
her hens at the end of her croft. The boy and the woman
looked at each other in passing. Merran shook her head
sorrowfully, then emptied her aluminium bowl and went
hurriedly back in through her door. When he turned the
corner there it was, down at the shore, their house with the
blinds drawn against the sweetness of day. The whole house
looked blind and bereft. The door opened and a woman who
had no right to be there shook his mother's rug and went in
again, leaving the door open: Jessie Gray from Garth. All the
village women had united to help his mother. That's what
happened whenever anybody died. Bella Simison from the
smithy came to the open door and stood looking out over the
fields, shading her eyes with her hand. They were all

wondering about him, Colm, for of course he should be in the house with the rest of the family at such an important time. He stood behind the fuchsia bush in the manse garden till Mrs Simison had gone in again. It was Saturday. He heard shouts from the end of the village: the boys were playing football in the quarry field. Their shouts sounded profane. They did not understand the gravity of what had happened. Colm felt as if he was about to enter a solemn temple. He heard voices over the high wall of Sunnybrae. 'Yes, so I hear, Andrew Sinclair the fisherman . . . About ten this morning. He's well relieved, the poor man. Two strokes in a week . . .' The minister's wife and Mrs Spence of Sunnybrae, Captain Spence's widow, were talking about the death of his grand-dad.

He ran swiftly and silently across the grass to the house of death.

He stood with fluttering breath in the open door. The kitchen was full of gray whispers and moving shadows. He exchanged, furtively, the light for the gloom of the lobby.

His mother's face was purified, as if a fire had passed through it. She sat in the straw-back chair beside the dresser. The village women fussed around her. One was making tea at the stove. One was washing the best china in preparation for (probably) the funeral meal. Jessie Gray was telling stories about Andrew Sinclair – all the memorable things he had done and said in his life: from time to time the other women shook their heads slowly and smiled. Mrs Sanderson from Wardings farm was baking bannocks on the girdle. The only grieving creatures in the house were the two younger girls. Freda and Ellen hung about with blubbered faces and large eyes in the darkest corner of the room. His father sat in the window seat; he looked uncomfortable in the company of all these priestesses of death. Freda and Ellen glanced reproachfully at Colm as he entered, silently, the kitchen.

The village women turned grave complacent faces on the newcomer.

'Colm,' said his mother in a queer artificial voice, 'your grandfather's passed away.'

'I know,' he muttered ill-naturedly.

It was not death. It was a kind of solemn game with words and gestures, a feast of flowers and false memories.

He followed Jessie Gray into the parlour.

Even when he looked down on the strange familiar cold face on the pillow it was still all a mime to give importance and dignity to a poor house. Two of the village women looked smilingly down at the corpse from the other side of the bed. Grand-dad's face was a still pool.

'Touch the brow with your hand.' It was the tranquil voice of Jessie Gray, who knew all about the trappings and ceremonies of death; she had prepared a hundred corpses for the kirkyard in her time.

Colm put two fingers, lightly, to his grandfather's forehead; they winced from an intense and bitter coldness. He could have cried out with terror. Now he knew that his grandfather was dead indeed.

He saw the cold pipe on the bedside table. He remembered the gulls' feathers and the ha'pennies. His grand-dad had been a very sweet kind old man.

The women watched him slyly. He knew these women. They were waiting for him to burst into tears. That was the pious thing for a boy to do. Then they would come about the bereaved one with their false hearty comfortings. He hated to have his feelings spied on. He would not cry to please them.

'How peaceful he looks,' said Jessie Gray.

He looked earnestly into the cold pool that was growing rigid, even while he looked and wondered, with the frost of death.

(v)

'Alice, tell them what I mean by the phrase "colours of the spectrum",' said Miss Silver.

Alice Rendall was the cleverest pupil in the Norday school. When the ten-year-olds were arranged in order of merit at the start of each week, Alice sat always at the top seat with the class medal pinned to her jersey: a heavy lead disc with *For Merit* stamped on it. The little ring on top of the medal blossomed with a ribbon.

Colm sometimes had the feeling that Alice was made of china rather than flesh, there was such fragility and coldness and cleanness about her. She did not get into trouble of any kind – did not whisper to her neighbours or pass notes – did not suck pan-drops through her handkerchief – did not leave her coat in school when the sun broke the rain-clouds – had never been known to raise her hand, untimely, with an urgent 'Please, miss, may I leave the room?' Some of the girls were not above showing the fringes of their knickers to the boys under the desk; never Alice. Her face shone each morning from much soap-and-water and a soft towel.

Alice was good at nearly everything: sums, reading, writing, spelling, history, geography. She did not have much of a singing voice, it was true. Her drawings were not as good as Willie Hume's. And she could not run and somersault as well as most of the other girls. 'Alice Rendall, you have the highest marks this week again,' said Miss Silver regularly every Friday afternoon. 'You will sit at the top of the class on Monday morning. Well done, Alice. Second, John Hay. Third, James Marcusson . . .'

Colm was not particularly good at any subject. He liked history. He was bad at drawing and geography. He did a strange perverse thing every Friday: he deliberately falsified his marks, downgraded himself, so that he could share the bottom place in class with a boy called Phil Kerston. As surely as Alice Rendall was dux each week, Philip Kerston was dunce. Phil was utterly ignorant of every subject on the school curriculum. But he could snare rabbits. He could light fires in a gale. He had taken eggs from the face of Hundhead, the highest cliff in the island.

Miss Silver gave Phil jobs to do, such as look after the school fire in winter, wipe the blackboard clean with a duster, and fill the ink-wells. In school he was good-natured and quiet.

Colm sat beside Phil Kerston whenever he could. The smell of rabbits and grass-fires attracted him. Another part of the attraction was that he was a little afraid of the strange wild ignorant boy.

One Friday afternoon Phil Kerston and Colm whispered together on the front seat while Miss Silver wrote multiplication tables on the blackboard. Tomorrow, Saturday, they were to burn heather among the hills. Colm promised to bring a box of matches. He would buy it with the penny he got every Saturday from his father.

Colm ran through the gap in the hills, breathless, after Phil Kerston and Andrik Overton. The sun was hot on the gray rocks. A bee blundered from heather-bell to heather-bell. Colm stumbled up the cart track.

He stood between the two hills, Brunafea and Torfea, and looked back. Phil and Andrik had gone on ahead, into the heart of the island. Colm had never been as far as this before. He did not like to be too far away from his mother's door. He saw the village down below, and the beach with a few boats hauled up, and small moving toy cows in the field of Wardings.

So, up here was where the farmers and crofters dug their winter fires. The long deep black lines of the peat-banks stretched across a flank of Brunafea that could not be seen from the village.

But he would have to hurry. Phil Kerston and Andrik Overton were two lost voices, thin and sweet, answering each other from the interior of the island. They would not wait for Colm, who couldn't move as fast as them on account of the asthma that bothered him sometimes in the summer. They had taken his box of matches from him and gone on up.

Colm did not like to be alone in strange places. He had got his breath back now. He ran on, between the summer hills, in the direction of the voices.

He rounded a shoulder of Torfea, a little stony outcrop, and a world he had never seen before opened out before him; the barren interior of Norday. He caught his breath, it was so lonely and beautiful. There was not a croft in sight. There was nothing but sweeps of moor and bog, and, like a jewel among the starkness, a little loch. A hidden burn sang under Colm's feet. A lark, very high up, drenched the desolation with song.

Colm ran down towards the loch that was still half-a-mile away. It was Tumilshun Loch. He had heard his father and the other men speaking about it in the smithy. He had seen the English trout fishers in summer setting out with rod and reel for the place. These men with the loud voices and thick tweeds would bide among the hills till sunset. A small shiver went over Colm's skin. He would not care to spend even an hour in such a desolate place.

Where were Phil and Andrik? He couldn't hear them any more. They might be gathering blackberries. Andrik had brought a tin can for that purpose. Colm went down a few paces more in the direction of the loch. A sprig of heather scratched his bare ankle. He put his hand to his mouth. 'Phil,' he called out, 'where are you?'

The shadow of a cloud moved across Brunafea.

It was unnerving, the sound of his voice. It was like blasphemy. It bounced off the craggy face of Brunafea. It seemed to shiver across the face of the loch. It came back to him, all eeriness and mockery, and died among the far hills. Colm listened, appalled. His heart pounded in his chest.

Why didn't Phil and Andrick answer him? He would not shout like that again.

It was then that the hinterland was drained suddenly of all its colour. The lark stopped singing. The sun had gone behind a cloud.

Tumilshun lay there below, a sheet of dead pewter. Colm remembered how his father had told him that it was a very deep loch: in his time two people had committed suicide in it. Fifty years ago a girl from the croft of Swenquoy was found floating among the reeds.

Colm faced quickly back towards the gap in the hills. He climbed like a goat, from rock to heather-clump, out of the awful landscape. He could not have uttered another cry – terror had numbed his throat. He fell and rose and fell among the clumps of heather. A flood of light came over the flank of Torfea and enveloped him. He ran on. Only when he could see a segment of ocean between the hills did he turn back: there Tumilshun lay, a dark blue gleam, far below him. And there, between the loch and the lower slope of Brunafea, was a red-gray smudge. Phil and Andrick had lit their fires, and gone on.

The lark, empty of song, eased itself down. It guttered out among the coarse grass.

With a surge of joy (but ashamed at the same time of his cowardice) Colm emerged from the sinister region and saw below him the squares of tilth and pasture, and the village:

and Tom of Wardings cutting hay in his field with a flashing scythe. Further away, between the ness and the holm, the *Godspeed* entered the bay.

'Poetry,' said Miss Silver. 'William Wordsworth. "Fidelity". Page 35 in your books.'

Colm bent his head over the page. He read, silently.

> A barking sound the shepherd hears,
> A cry as of a dog or fox.
> He halts – and searches with his eyes
> Among the scattered rocks;
> And now at distance can discern
> A stirring in a brake of fern;
> And instantly a dog is seen
> Glancing through that covert green.

'You will learn this verse for recitation tomorrow morning,' said Miss Silver to the ten-year-olds.

Poetry was hated by the whole school. The children's natural style of recitation, a chant heavily accented, was condemned by Miss Silver (who had been taught Elocution at her teachers' training college). 'No,' she said, 'You mustn't drone on monotonously like that. You must recite the poem with *expression*. Like this. Listen.

> A *barking* sound the shepherd hears,
> A cry as of a *dog* or *fox* . . .'

The only poetry the island children knew were the surrealist word-games – corn-spells, fish-spells, ancestral memories of murder and grief and illicit love made innocent and lyrical – that they played in the school playground.

> Water water wallflower
> Growing up so high
> We are all maidens
> And we must all die . . .

None of the island children could recite 'with expression';
Alice Rendall could, a little. So they disliked poetry, especially
when they were given verses to learn by rote for Tuesday afternoon, which was the time devoted to poetry and recitation.
Every Monday evening, therefore, in a dozen scattered crofts,
the same ritual took place: at the kitchen table, under the
paraffin lamp, innocent mouths moved silently and resentfully
above the school poetry book, again and again; until their own
sweet natural rhythms were crushed under the relentless stone.

> There sometimes doth a leaping fish
> Send through the tarn a lonely cheer;
> The crags repeat the raven's croak
> In symphony austere.
> Thither the rainbow comes – the cloud –
> And mists that spread the flying shroud;
> And sunbeams; and the sounding blast,
> That, if it could, would hurry past:
> But that enormous barrier holds it fast.

Colm read the verse idly, once, before bed-time. The book lay
open on the scrubbed table. *A lonely cheer*. His breath trembled on his lip. He subjected the page to a silent absorbed
scrutiny. It was a lonely experience, like death or nakedness.
His mouth moulded the words: *mists that spread the flying
shroud*. He hoarded the lines, phrase by phrase.

It was the interior of Norday that was being bodied forth
in a few words.

The lamp splashed the page with yellow light.

This poet must have seen Tumilshun too, or else some loch very like it. He had felt the same things as Colm. This was strange, that somebody else (and him a famous dead poet) felt the dread, for none of the other boys seemed to; at least, if they did, they never spoke about it. But this was even stranger: there was a joy at the heart of the desolation. Colm could not explain it. It was as if the loch had a secret existence of its own. The hills stood about the loch, silent presences; they were frightening too, when you were among them, but the boy had an obscure feeling that his flesh was made of the same dust as the hills. They bore with ageless patience the scars of the peat-cutters on their shoulders. Colm felt a kinship with that high austere landscape, a first fugitive love.

The poem had worked the change.

His lips moulded, again, the incantation.

> There sometimes doth a leaping fish
> Send through the tarn a lonely cheer . . .

'Colm, it's long past your bed-time,' said his mother. 'Your face is white as chalk. Close that book now . . .'

Colm stood at his desk next afternoon, when his turn to recite came. He uttered the magical words in a high nervous treble. He looked down sideways at Phil Kerston. Phil Kerston had taken trout out of Tumilshun with his hands; his father's croft was thatched with heather from the flank of Brunafea; Phil was bound to like the poem, far more even than he did himself. But Phil sat knotting a piece of wire under his desk, idly, making a rabbit snare. Poetry to him was just another cell in the dark prison of school.

'De-dum-de-dum-de-dum,' said Miss Silver. 'No, Colm. You have learned the words, good, but you destroy the life of the poem the way you recite it. Listen now. This is the way it should be spoken: "There sometimes doth a *leaping* fish . . ."'

One day that same term Miss Silver said to the ten-year-olds, 'We have all learned at last to read, fairly fluently, out of our school text books, have we not? All except Philip Kerston, but Philip may learn to read in time. Don't worry Philip. There is something equally important – writing. You must learn how to express yourselves on paper. For, when you leave school, there will be letters to write. Now, won't there, Willie? You don't know? Of course there will . . . Perhaps one or two of you will be sailors far away from home, so you will want your parents to know how you are getting on, in Sydney, or Port Said, or Bombay perhaps. Even those who stay in the island will also need to know how to express themselves. For, perhaps Maisie Smith will be made secretary of the W.R.I. – no laughter, please – or Stephen Will of the Agricultural Society, and then Maisie or Stephen will be expected to make up minutes of the proceedings and also send a report to *The Orcadian* . . . Learning to write correctly is called what, Alice?'

'Composition,' said Alice Rendall.

'It is called composition,' said Miss Silver. 'We are going to write our very first composition this morning. Philip, fill the ink-pots that are empty or nearly empty. John Hay, pass round those new composition exercise books. The compositions are to be written in ink. I want your very best writing, remember. Does everyone have a blotter? Very well, then. Listen. The subject of the composition is this: "The World I see from my Door". '

A dozen pens scratched and hesitated across white pages for an hour.

Colm wrote idly to begin with, about the lupins in his mother's garden. They grew in summer between the rhubarb and the potato patch. If he stood on the low wall he could see the beach, his father's boat, the sea. Some days, after a westerly gale, Corporal Hourston would come to the shore looking for jetsam. The corporal was a beachcomber. One winter night he stood in the door and there were stars in the sky, hundreds of them, and a full moon. Snow had fallen all day. The furrows in a field at Wardings were long purple shadows. Some days he stood in the door watching for his father's boat to come back from the fishing. He was uneasy whenever *Godspeed* was late. Then everything he saw looked gray, the sea and the sky. The thoughts that went through his mind seemed to be gray too. One day he was alone in the house and he heard a knock at the door. He opened it. He saw a tinker wife standing there with a stumpy pipe in her mouth and a pack on her back . . .

Colm did not suppose he would be better at composition than he was at arithmetic or geography. He discovered that he could remember things much better writing them down than speaking them. When he had time to assemble his material the past ceased to be a confused flux; it became a sequence of images, one image growing out of another and contrasting with it, and anticipating too the inevitable exciting image that must follow. He liked making sentences. He put commas in, and full stops; in that way he could make the word sequences (which were, of course, inseparable from the image sequences) flow fast or slow; whichever seemed more suitable. He even put a semi-colon in the part about the moon and the snow, and then the sentence seemed to hang balanced like a wind-slewed gull. Writing gave Colm a small comfortable sense of power.

'Time up,' called Miss Silver. 'Blot the page carefully. Philip Kerston, gather the composition books and bring them to my desk.'

Next morning Miss Silver handed the corrected compositions back.

Alice Rendall sat, demure and erect, at the top of the class.

'You have a great deal to learn, all of you,' said Miss Silver,
'about how to write English properly. Spelling and punctua-
tion were, on the whole, dreadful. On the other hand, some
efforts were quite promising. Alice wrote a nice composition
about the hill of Torfea, with its wild birds, it muirburn, its
peat-cutters, etcetera. You can see all that from the door of
your father's farm, can't you, Alice? However, the best composition of all was written by Colm Sinclair. Well done, Colm.
Colm, I want you to come out to the floor and read your
composition to the school. Listen, everybody. It is really quite
original and good.'

He stood beside Miss Silver's desk, his composition book
in his hand, trying to control his nervous breaths. He read:
'The door of our house is made out of an oak beam that my
great-grandfather found a hundred years ago at the beach
under Hundhead . . .'

Then the school heard another new sound. A score of faces
looked round, startled. It was Alice. Her head was down on the
desk; her little fists trembled; spasm after spasm went through
her body. The girl was sobbing as if her heart would break.

(vi)

After tea one Saturday night, it rained. Colm put on his coat
and cap and went to the tailor shop at the end of the village.
Jock Skaill the tailor was his best friend in Norday, though he
was forty years older than Colm. The islanders could never
make up their minds about Jock Skaill: the women were
always gossiping about him in the store. – *Jock Skaill says
there's no God . . . He's a communist . . . They say he has bairns*

somewhere in the south . . . Him and his drink . . . They say he
was in prison for a while . . . He was the death of that wife of
his, if you ask me . . . The bitter mouths. The head-shakings.
The shuttered brows.

Colm's mother wouldn't have it. She maintained always
that Jock Skaill was a fine man. She knew him; they had
attended school together; they had been neighbours in the
village when they were children.

'Jock Skaill,' she would say, 'he's had an unfortunate life, if
you think about it. He was the cleverest boy by far in Norday
School, he could have gone on to the university and everything. But old Tom his father would have no grandiose
nonsense of that kind. When Jock left school he had to go
and sit at that tailor's bench. He hated it – you could see that
he was like a young dog tied up in a shed. So when old Tom
died he just put up the shutters and left the island without a
word to anybody. I suppose he went to sea. What if he did
have a wild year or two of it? It's a queer chap that doesn't sow
his wild oats in his twenties. There's many a good man been
in jail – John Bunyan for example, and James Maxton, and
Gandhi. Well, he came home and opened the shop again and
he married that girl from Hamnavoe, Susan Fea, and I'm sure
no couple were ever happier than them for a year or two. And
then the poor lass, she went into some kind of a decline, you
know, consumption, and she died in the sanatorium in
Kirkwall. Between one thing and another Jock Skaill's had a
stony path to tread. It hasn't soured him at all, that's the
wonder. He's the kindest cheerfulest man in this island . . .'

Thus his mother on Jock Skaill the island tailor, whenever
the subject was raised with malicious intent in her presence.

But Jessie Gray and Bella Simison would turn down their
mouths and keep on muttering about communists and athe-
ists and jailbirds . . .

Colm hung his damp coat on a nail in the door. Jock Skaill cleared bits of cloth, shears, a tiny triangle of chalk, a few books, the cat's milk saucer, from the end of the bench. He set out the draught board. He put a few peats into the stove.

They played silently that night, two dreaming faces over the bench in the lamplight. It was a leisurely dance and counter-dance of pieces across the board. Outside the rain drummed on the dingy window panes.

Jock Skaill only spoke when a game was over and he was filling his pipe, and Colm was arranging the counters on the board once more.

'Four years next Wednesday since Susan died. Susan was my wife. "There is a happy land far far away . . ." Don't you believe it, boy. She came out of the earth and we were happy for two years and three months, and then she went back to the earth. That's the way I think of her. She's a part of the rich beautiful earth . . . There's the cat scratching on the door. Let him in out of the rain.'

Colm won the first game.

'It's a grand feeling, to know you have children. Get married, boy, have children, but not too many – the world's full enough as it is. I have a child that I've never seen. Withered folk, grandparents, they came between the boy's mother and me. I had a great liking for that girl. I'm glad that somewhere in England there's a piece of me, a living body that came out of my own body. He walks in the wind and the sun. He will make a new human being when the time comes. That's the only kind of immortality there is . . . That fire needs a few peats.'

Jock Skaill won the second game.

'The gossiping old women, I don't mind them at all. They've been at it since the world was young. The Greek choruses began with the likes of Jessie Gray and Bella

Simison. What grieves me is the change that's come over the men in this island. They used to tell stories, not the old women's tittle-tattle, but the legends of the island, what their great-grandfathers said and did. That's the source of all poetry and drama. Not now – they discuss what they read in the newspapers and hear on their wireless sets, they have opinions about Free Trade and the Irish Question. I swear to God it makes me laugh to hear them going on about Ramsay Macdonald and Life on Mars, down there in the smithy. All so knowledgeable and important, and not one original idea among them. The marvellous old legends, that's beneath them now . . . I'm boring you, I expect. If you open that drawer you'll find a poke of butternuts.'

Jock won the third game also.

'Progress, that's the modern curse. This island is enchanted with the idea of Progress. Look at what we have now – reapers, wireless sets, free education, motor bikes, white bread. Times are much easier for us than for our grandfathers. So, they argue, we have better fuller richer lives. It is a God-damned lie. This worship of Progress, it will drain the life out of every island and lonely place. In three generations Norday will be empty. For, says Progress, life in a city *must* be superior to life in an island. Also, Progress says, "Here is a combine harvester, it will do the work of a score of peasants . . ." Down we go on our knees again in wonderment and gratitude . . . Will there be a few folk left in the world, when Progress is choked at last in its own too much? Yes, there will be. A few folk will return by stealth to the wind and the mist and the silences. I know it . . . Would you reach up for the tea caddy – the kettle's boiling.'

Jock won the fourth game also and so there was no need to play a decider.

They drank tea out of rather filthy mugs, after the draught-board was folded and put away. Then Jock Skaill told him about some of the old men in Norday that he remembered, and some of the shipmates he had sailed with.

Then he said, 'You better be getting home now, boy. Tomorrow's Sunday. Tell your mother I'm asking for her. Go home. They'll be saying in the store on Monday morning that I'm a corruption to you, if they aren't saying it already.'

(VII)

His mother said, 'Colm, go and see if you can find your father. He's in the shed, most likely.' Torquil and Ellen were spreading butter on their oatcakes. Supper had begun without a blessing from the head of the house.

The shed on the pier was a black unlighted cube.

Colm wandered up the shore road to the village. His father was most likely in the smithy. A few of the village men gathered in Steve Simison's smithy in the dark evenings. What would they be talking about tonight? The last time Colm had been in the smithy they had been discussing The Yellow Peril.

He entered the smithy shyly. A paraffin lamp hung from the rafters. There were a few men sitting round the anvil. Steve Simison had taken off his leather apron and washed his face and hands; he had a white pure look about him. There indeed was his father, sitting on the bench.

The black maw of the forge gave out a warmth still.

None of the men let on to notice the boy.

Colm tried to catch his father's eye but the company was deep in some discussion: grave tilted faces under the lamp, furrowed brows.

Colm listened. They were talking about the date of Easter.

'I can't understand it,' said Mr William Smith the general merchant. (He was probably the most important man in the island, now that the laird had declined into genteel poverty.

He kept the shop in the village and his merchandise comprised everything: groceries, wine, bread and cakes, footwear, butcher-meat, confectionery, fruit, flowers and wreaths, draperies. In addition he was the county councillor for the island, and vice-president of the local Liberal Party, and session clerk, and registrar, and Justice of the Peace. Everyone heard him always with the greatest respect.)

'I can't for the life of me understand it,' he was saying. 'It shifts about from year to year. *I'll be wanting the usual lilies and daffodils for Easter – would you order them please?* says Miss Siegfried in the shop a fortnight ago. So, thinks I to myself, there's plenty of time. In she comes again this morning. *I'll take the flowers now*, says she, *if they've come*. I had been meaning to write all week to the florist in Kirkwall. *I think we should wait till nearer the time*, says I. *Then they'll be fresh* . . . She looks at me like the far end of a fiddle. *Tomorrow's Good Friday*, she says. *This is Maundy Thursday. I require the flowers for the chapel on Easter morning. I'm afraid it might be too late now.'*

'Easter was a lot later indeed last year,' said Dod Sabiston, 'if I'm not mistaken.'

'*This is Maundy Thursday*,' said William Smith, imitating quite well the loud posh English accent of Miss Siegfried the laird's sister. 'Of course they're Episcopalians up at The Hall. So there I was in a fine fix, I can tell you.'

'But why should it be?' said Colm's father, Timothy Sinclair the fisherman. 'Why should Easter be one date this year and another date next year? I could never fathom that.'

Colm stood there silently, his eyes going from face to face.

'God knows,' said the blacksmith. 'Christmas now, that's the same date every year.'

There was silence for half a minute. Then Corporal Hourston cleared his throat and combed with his fingers his handsome moustache: a sign that he had something to say. Corporal Hourston was a retired soldier, and lived on a small pension at the end of the village, in a poor hovel of a place. He had gathered hundreds of bits of useless wisdom from Egypt, Hindustan, the Transvaal. The village men deferred to him, half mocking, half respectful.

'It's the Pope that decides,' said Corporal Hourston sententiously. 'The Pope decides the date of Easter every year for the whole world.'

They pondered this, gravely.

'The Pope,' said Mr Smith, offended. 'The Pope. The Pope has no authority over *us*.'

'No, we're Presbyterians,' said Timothy Sinclair. 'We threw off that yoke a long time ago.'

'The Pope indeed!' said Mr Smith. He turned to Colm's father. 'You're right, Tim,' he said. 'That was the Reformation. And it didn't happen a moment too soon, if you ask me.'

'It was Martin Luther that saved us from the Pope,' said Dod Sabiston of Dale.

'No,' said Andrew Custer the saddler, who was also a deacon in the kirk, 'it wasn't Martin Luther. The English Protestants followed Martin Luther. The Presbyterians followed John Calvin. Luther was a German.'

They nodded, sagely.

'It's very hard to credit,' said Mr Smith, 'that people could be taken in by such darkness.'

'We were all Roman Catholics once,' said Corporal Hourston. 'All our forefathers here in Orkney were Roman Catholics.'

'That was a long time ago,' said Timothy Sinclair. 'People were very ignorant in those days. There was no education. They couldn't read the Bible. They knew no better. They had to believe whatever the priests told them to believe.'

'The Pope, though, he still rules a great part of the world,' said Andrew Custer. 'France, Italy, Spain, South America.'

'And Ireland too,' said Corporal Hourston.

'The Irish people are very poor,' said Mr Smith. 'Very poor and very oppressed. You'll find, if you study the matter, that all Roman Catholic countries are very backward.'

The forge was sending out lessening circles of warmth. Colm shivered a little. He moved nearer to the wise deliberate lit mouths. He was glad that he did not live in Ireland or Spain. He was pleased too that his father had a respected word in these smithy councils. His father had thought about things and formed his own opinions. He was only a fisherman but the other men listened gravely whenever Timothy Sinclair opened his mouth. There was a stack of books in their house, in the window shelf. His father read for a long time every night in winter after the young ones were in bed. *The Rat Pit* by Patrick MacGill. *My Schools and Schoolmasters* by Hugh Miller. *People of the Abyss* by Jack London. *Now Barabbas* by Marie Corelli. *Selected Poems and Letters of Robert Burns*. These were only a few of the titles on the window shelf. His father was well respected in Norday for his earnestness and literacy. He was another one who could have 'gotten on' if poverty hadn't kept him tied to his fishing boat.

'You would hardly credit it,' said Andrew Custer, 'but they worship the Virgin Mary.'

A new face appeared from behind the forge. Mrs Bella Simison stood there. She had come no doubt on the same errand as Colm, to get the breadwinner in to his supper. But she saw the ring of contemptuous slightly shocked faces, and stood listening.

'When I have sinned,' said Mr Smith, 'I ask for God's forgiveness. We all sin, we are frail mortal clay, the best of us.

But your Catholic, he goes to a priest to be forgiven, he tells his sins to a man who is a sinner like himself.'

'That's not all, William,' said Dod Sabiston. 'He has to give the priest money to forgive him.'

Timothy Sinclair and Steve Simison shook their heads incredulously. Only Corporal Hourston seemed unmoved: he had known worse things beside the Brahmaputra – sacred hens, crocodiles, cows, widows and infants laid alive on burning pyres.

'That there should be such darkness in the human mind,' said Mr Smith. 'When I want to talk to my Maker, I pray. I tell him how things are with me. I ask for guidance. Your Roman Catholic takes out his rosary beads. He counts them over and over. He mumbles the "vain repetitions" that we are warned against in scripture.'

The Virgin Mary. Priests in black, accepting money from sinners. Rosary beads. Colm shivered with supernatural dread. The dark pool of the human mind. He moved closer in to the fading warmth of the forge.

'Then they die,' said Mr Smith. 'But they do not go like you and me to glory or the bad place, according as we have lived our mortal lives. O no, they go to Purgatory, a place that as far as I know is nowhere mentioned in scripture.'

'No, William,' said Andrew Custer, 'but money comes into that too. You pay to get your friends out of Purgatory. The more you pay, the sooner they get out. That's what they believe.'

Purgatory: another word to add to his sinister hoard.

Corporal Hourston cleared his throat. 'I fought beside Irishmen at Ladysmith,' he said. 'They were all Roman Catholics. They were very good soldiers. Lord Lovat was the commander-in-chief. If I'm not mistaken Lord Lovat was a Roman Catholic too, but of course he was a Scotsman.'

'I once went into a Roman Catholic kirk in Glasgow,' said Dod Sabiston. 'It was full of statues that they prayed to. There was this old woman lighting candles in front of a plaster saint. Graven images everywhere. And the smell of incense, I'm telling you, it was enough to make a man's stomach heave.'

Colm noticed a face that he had not seen at first when he came into the smithy. Tom Sanderson of Wardings had been sitting silent all the time in a dark corner that was studded with old rusty horseshoes. He was smiling quietly to himself. He took his pipe out of his mouth. He looked over at Colm and shook his head gently and smiled.

Bella Simison spoke up from beside the forge in her deep rapid stacatto. 'Don't tell me about Catholics, them and their carry-on, I have a book in the house, Tina Wasbister took it from Edinburgh, *Maria Monk*, that's the name on it, about nuns in a convent, O my God what a carry-on, them and the priests, supposed never to marry, and babies born every now and then, first done away with, then buried, the poor innocent things, in quick lime. Well, this Maria Monk, she was a nun too, and she tried to get out and . . .'

'That's all right,' said Steve Simison coldly to his wife. 'I'm just closing up. Then I'll be in for my supper.'

'You can't tell me anything I don't know about Roman Catholics,' cried Bella. She turned her flushed face from one to the other. 'I'll give you the book to read, anybody that wants it, a loan of.' Then she withdrew, in the darkness, to the smell of kippers that came from the open door beyond the forge.

One by one the men got to their feet. Colm's father lowered himself from the bench. Steve Simison closed the forge and put on his jacket. It was beginning to be very cold in the smithy.

'No doubt but it is a great abomination,' said Andrew Custer solemnly. 'It is The Scarlet Women spoken of in the

Bible. It is the Whore of Babylon. It is the abomination of desolation.'

Steve Simison raised the lamp glass and blew out the flame.

They moved one after the other towards the door, feeling their ways.

'I'll tell you a very strange thing,' said Mr Smith. 'When I was a boy the gravedigger was old Thomas Wylie. None of you will mind him. Well, Thomas, he was called on to dig a grave in the oldest part of the cemetery, you know, beside the ruined wall where there are no stones at all, only a shallow hump here and there. That's where the people were buried when Orkney was a Catholic place. Well, when old Thomas was digging the grave he came on a hoard of silver and gold coins. The story was told often when I was a boy. I marvelled at that and I still do – burying money with a corpse.'

They stood together on the dark road outside the smithy. Corporal Hourston clicked his heels and, grave and erect, marched off in the direction of his cottage. Steve Simison closed the smithy door and barred it from the inside. Colm put his cold hand into his father's great warm rough hand. There were squares of light here and there in the darkling village.

'What I can't understand,' said Mr Smith, 'is why they can't grow their own daffodils and lilies. They have a big enough garden. God knows, up there at The Hall, and it's all choked with weeds!' . . . He gave his imitation of Miss Siegfried's cut-glass accent, '*I assure you, Mr Smith, tomorrow is Good Friday, and I require the flowers for the chapel on Sunday, and you promised, you know, you promised.*'

Dark fragments of laughter, and 'goodnights'. Colm walked with his father to their house: to the fire, the table with its milk and oatcakes, the bed where he would soon kneel and say his one simple good Presbyterian prayer.

(VIII)

The young man, because of asthma, had hardly slept all night. His breathing was always more laboured in the city in the middle of summer. There had been three or four warm July days – hot days even, for Edinburgh. The canyon of the street where he lodged kept still, after midnight, some of its gathered warmth. It brimmed through the high dark window of his bed-sitter. He sweated under his single blanket, and longed for morning.

He must have drowsed for an hour or so; when he looked again the window was a silver-gray square. There would be dawn over the North Sea now, trying to burn its way through the early mists.

The man had done no work on his novel since the start of the golden weather. The sun from morning to night, among the city streets, even across the handsome squares and gardens, distracted him. His imagination was dislocated. Writing became a burden not to be borne. For the past two days he had taken a bus out to the village of Cramond on the Firth of Forth, thinking that the sea might help him. He had sat on the rocks, smoking, and watched the picnics, the children bathing, the sailing boats. But even here there was no release: he felt his loneliness like a pain. He envied the happy young folk with their towels and bottles of coke. Yesterday he had gone to Cramond again, but he had spent most of the day in the Inn, drinking iced lager.

He wished, this cold northern man, that the sun would stop shining, so that he could put his loneliness to some use, and get his writing done. He wished, alternatively, that he could pack his bag and settle with Mrs Doyle his landlady and take a boat north. And the longing and the loneliness ground out between them this asthma that distressed his daytime and kept him awake half the night.

The window brightened, quite suddenly. The sun, hidden by the tall tenements of Marchmont, had ruptured the sea haar. It was going to be another breathless idle day for him. He looked at his watch; it was passing five o'clock. He decided to get up and, before the day made him inert, write a letter.

'Dear Jock – I am not coming north this year. There are it's true so many things I want to see – Tumilshun and the hills, the churchyard, the school, the piers where I fished and the ditches where I burned my fingers. But there are other places that give me a pain at the heart when I think of them – the doorless houses in the village, the *Godspeed* rotting on the beach, the black forge, the mill with its great stones dusty and silent.

'I can only finish this new novel in a cold neutral unhaunted place.

'Thank you for that last letter. That you liked *The Rock Pastures* gives me more genuine pleasure than if, for example, Dr Leavis or Professor Trilling had signified their approval. "It tastes of earth and salt. The folk in cities will be none the worse of that", you say. "That is the good thing about all you write. That is your best gift to the world. Even old Tom Sanderson liked it. He told me so, between laughter and head-shakings, when he was here the other day about his new Sabbath suit . . ."

'Then all those thunderings at the end of the page, against the "idolatry" and the "supersition" that spoil everything! "I will never never understand" you write, "why you have been enchanted by that mumbo-jumbo to such an extent. Giving up old Calvin and his works, that was well done, but you have opened your door to seven devils worse than the first. When you come to Norday in August, in time for the agricultural show – if there is to be one this year, that's to say, for not a month passes but another farmer leaves the island – you must tell me what made you do it . . ."

'I will try to tell you now, in writing, for I have as you know a heavy awkward peasant tongue. You always beat me in an argument. If I *have* to argue, all I can offer is an unfolding sequence of images: stations that lead to a stone, and silence, and perhaps after that (if I'm lucky) a meaning. Where can I make a start? It isn't too easy, trying to assemble your thoughts at half past five in the morning in a cold Edinburgh bedroom, with the prospect of another day of hurt breathing.

'Who better to begin with – since you mention him – than old Tom Sanderson of Wardings in Norday?

'Tom Sanderson is a simple self-effacing man. In this evil time, indeed, he is ashamed of his coarseness and earthiness when he compared himself with such folk as grocers and clerks and insurance men. He is, after all, bound upon the same monotonous wheel year after year. There is nothing alluring about the work he does. He wrestles with mud and dung to win a few crusts and flagons from the earth.

'Yet see this peasant for what he is. He stands at the very heart of our civilization. We could conceivably do without soldiers, administrators, engineers, doctors, poets, but we cannot do without that humble earth-worker who breaks the clods each spring. He is the red son of Adam. He represents us all. He it was who left the caves and, lured on by a new vision, made a first clearing in the forest. There he began the ceremony of bread. He ploughed. He sowed seed. He brooded all the suntime upon the braird, the shoot, the ear, the full corn in the ear. He cut that ripeness. He gathered it into a barn. He put upon it flail and millstone and fire, until at last his goodwife set a loaf and an ale-cup on his table.

'He exists in a marvellous ordering of sun and dust and flesh. I can hear Mr Smith the merchant saying, "Nonsense

– it's simply that man has learned how to harness the brute blind forces of nature . . ." I can hear, among the cloth clippings and shears of Norday, a wiser explanation, "Man and nature learned at last to live kindly and helpfully with one another . . ." But that for me is simply not good enough; it leaves too much out, it doesn't take account of the terror and the exaltation that came upon the first farmer who broke the earth. It was a terrible thing he had done, to put wounds on the great dark mother. But his recklessness and impiety paid off at the end of the summer when he stood among the sheaves. Soon there were loaves on his table; he kept every tenth loaf back – the set-apart secret bread. Why? Because he sensed that there was another actor in the cosmic drama, apart from himself and the wounded earth-mother: the Wisdom that in the first place had lured him on to shrug off his brutishness – the quickener, ordainer, ripener, orderer, utterer – the peasant with his liking for simplicity called it God. Man made God a gift in exchange for the gifts of life, imagination, and food. But still the primitive guilts and terrors remained, for the fruitful generous earth would have to be wounded with the plough each spring-time.

'In the end, to reconcile the divine and the brutish in men, that Wisdom took on itself to endure all that the earth-born endure, birth and hunger and death.

'You have read and digested all those Thinker's Library books on your mantelpiece – Robertson, Ingersoll, Reade – and so you know that no such person as Jesus Christ ever walked the earth; or if indeed some carpenter at the time of Tiberius Caesar left his workbench to do some preaching in the hills, that doesn't mean that he was an incarnation of God – that was the fruit of a later conspiracy of priests and potentates, to keep the poor in thrall.

'But I believe it. I have for my share of the earth-wisdom a patch of imagination that I must cultivate to the best of my skill. And my imagination tells me that it is probably so, for the reason that the incarnation is so beautiful. For all artists beauty must be truth: that for them is the sole criterion (and Keats said it 150 years ago). God indeed wept, a child, on the breast of a woman. He spoke to the doctors of law in the temple, to a few faithful bewildered fishermen, to tax-men and soldiers and cripples and prostitutes, to Pilate, even to those who came to glut themselves on his death-pangs. With a *consummatum est* he died. I believe too that he came up out of the grave the way a cornstalk soars into wind and sun from a ruined cell. After a time he returned with his five wounds back into his kingdom. I believe that a desert and a seashore and a lake heard for a few years the sweet thrilling music of the Incarnate Word. What is intriguing is how often the god-man put agricultural images before those fishermen of his: "A sower went forth to sow ..." "First the blade, then the ear, after that the full corn in the ear ..." "The fields are white towards harvest ..." "I am the bread of life ..." No writer of genius, Dante or Shakespeare or Tolstoy, could have imagined the recorded utterances of Christ. What a lovely lyric that is about the lilies-of-the-field and Solomon's garments. I'm telling you this as a writer of stories: there's no story I know of so perfectly shaped and phrased as The Prodigal Son or The Good Samaritan. There is nothing in literature so terrible and moving as the Passion of Christ – the imagination of man doesn't reach so far – it *must* have been so. The most awesome and marvellous proof for me is the way he chose to go on nourishing his people after his ascension, in the form of bread. So the brutish life of man is continually possessed, broken, transfigured by the majesty of God.

'What is old Tom of Wardings that his labour should be seen at last to be so precious? Goldsmith and jeweller work with shadows in comparison.

'It is ceremony that makes bearable for us the terrors and ecstasies that lie deep in the earth and in our earth-nourished human nature. Only the saints can encounter those "realities". What saves us is ceremony. By means of ceremony we keep our foothold in the estate of man, and remain good citizens of the kingdom of the ear of corn. Ceremony makes everything bearable and beautiful for us. Transfigured by ceremony, the truths we could not otherwise endure come to us. We invite them to enter. We set them down at our tables. These angels bring gifts for the house of the soul . . .

'It is this saving ceremony that you call "idolatry" and "mumbo-jumbo".

'Here, in a storm of mysticism, I end my homily for today.

'I will come back to the island sometime, but this year I must bide in Edinburgh, alone and palely loitering. I promise I will come when this novel is finished. I long to walk by the shore and among the fields, under those cold surging skies. If it rains, I will come and sit on a cloth-strewn bench and listen to monologues about the essential virtue of man, wild flowers, the things that were said and done in Norday before my time. We will perhaps broach a bottle of Orkney whisky. I think I will be content with that.

'I belong to the island. It grieves me to think I should ever be an exile. My flesh is Brunafea. The water of Tumilshun flows in my veins.

'To return for one last time to "idolatry". When first the subject troubled me I read book after book, for and against, and heard great argument about it, and got myself into a worse fankle than ever. I might still be lost in those drifts if, in the end, a few random pieces of verse and song – those ceremonies of words – had not touched me to the heart's core:

> La sua voluntate e nostra pace . . .

> Withinne the cloistre blisful of thy sydis
> Took mannes shap the eterneel love and pees . . .
> I want a black boy to announce to the gold-mined
>   whites
> The arrival of the reign of the ear of corn . . .

> Thou mastering me
> God! giver of breath and bread;
> World's strand, sway of the sea;
> Lord of living and dead . . .

> You must sit down, says Love, and taste my meat.
> So I did sit and eat . . .

> Moder and maiden
> Was never non but she:
> Well may swich a lady
> Godes moder be . . .'

Seeing that it would still be another hour before Mrs Catrian Doyle shouted the length of the corridor that the ham-and-eggs was dished, Colm laid his letter to Jock Skaill in his table drawer. He splashed his face in cold water in the bathroom. He put on his jacket and descended the tenement stair.

The chimney tops on the opposite side of the street were smitten with the morning sun. It lay across the Meadows. It emptied itself, a silent golden flood, into the city that was already beginning to clang and chink with dustbins and milk bottles.

In a beautiful square a quarter of a mile from his lodgings Colm entered a church that from the outside looked like an ordinary Georgian house. Upstairs there were a few elderly women kneeling here and there. The celebrant entered. Colm had not seen this particular priest before – he looked like an Indo-Chinese. Once again, for the thousandth time, Colm watched the ancient endless beautiful ceremony, the exchange of gifts between earth and heaven, dust and spirit, man and God. The transfigured Bread shone momentarily in the saffron fingers of the celebrant. Colm did not take communion. He had a dread of receiving the Sacrament unworthily, and he considered that the envy and self-pity he had indulged in these last few sun-smitten days were blemishes he would have to be purged of.

During the Last Gospel it came to him that in fact it would be the easiest thing in the world for him to go home. There was nothing to keep him here. There were still meaningful patterns to be discerned in the decays of time. The hills of Norday were astir all summer, still, with love, birth, death, resurrection.

The shops were opening when Colm walked back through Marchmont. Awnings were going up on the bright side of the street. Mr Jack the tobacconist stood in his shop door and waved to him. Colm waved back.

'Been to Mass, is it?' said Mrs Doyle. 'Well now, if it isn't the good religious lodger I have staying with me. The bacon got burnt.'

Colm told Mrs Doyle that he would be taking the boat from Leith northwards that afternoon at five o'clock. He would be away from Edinburgh, he thought, for three weeks at least. He would try to be back for the opening of his new play at the Festival. If Mrs Doyle would be good enough to keep his room open for him . . .

Back in his room, he tore up the letter that he had written that morning. He packed a few shirts and books. His breathing was much easier, now that the decision had been made.

A Winter Tale

DOCTOR

I was appointed doctor in the island of Njalsay in the late summer of 1973. I came too late for the regatta and the agricultural show, but I was in time for the Harvest Home, and saw how well islanders enjoy themselves on a festive occasion. That night I got to know all the healthy ones, old and young, that I was unlikely to meet in the course of my duties.

In fact the community was almost the most healthy one in my experience. There were a few chronic sick – arthritics, asthmatics, melancholics – but I had a great deal of time to myself as the great darkness of winter began to close in. I began to read again the novels of Hardy. I arranged in a new album my collection of Commonwealth stamps.

I look after myself in the doctor's house on the brae. Mrs Pegal comes twice a week to clean the place, and she looks after my laundry. But I cook my own food; the island steaks and fish and potatoes are delicious. Occasionally, on a Sunday, I am invited for supper at the manse or the schoolhouse.

So my first three months in Njalsay have passed, uneventfully on the whole. I had been told that the islanders were difficult folk to get acquainted with. I did not find it that way. They are shy, certainly, and they have an exaggerated respect for 'professional people', which springs no doubt from the calvinistic attitude to education and the ethic of 'getting on in the world'. . . . It is all a nonsense, of course. Once you break down that class wall you discover a kind humorous friendly folk. (There are exceptions, of course – a bad egg here and there.) I was soon friendly with the blacksmith-engineer Tom Selwick and the farmers who gather in his workshop in the evenings, to tell stories mainly and argue politics. I don't go there every night; but I much prefer my evenings with Tom Selwick to those at the manse and schoolhouse.

I should say a word, in passing, (though I am no expert) on the social and economic set-up of the island. Njalsay is an affluent place, now in the late twentieth century, compared to the Njalsay of earlier times. No islanders go hungry or in rags; every farm and croft has its car and television; a banker comes from the town once a week to look after the island's money. But, in spite of that, Njalsay is a dying community. Every year the population dwindles. The young folk, for a generation and more, have been leaving the island to get work in the offices and shops of the town, and sometimes much further away. It could be argued that they were not needed, in any case; machines were doing more and more of the labour of men and animals. Crofts were absorbed into bigger neighbouring farms, and gradually the croft-houses fell into ruins. And in another part of the island the boundaries between two farms would be cancelled by the stroke of a lawyer's pen; and one of the farmers would retire to a big house in the town, which was twelve miles away by sea (but only seven minutes away by the planes of the new efficient inter-island air service). Then another farmer's wife and young ones would be happy to be finished forever with 'the filth and dung and brutishness of the earth'. Did they feel, perhaps, after a year or two of buying their food and clothes over shop counters, a certain lack; the dark earth-rhythms which had dominated their lives for generations still operant, but with nothing to glut themselves on, only the empty rituals of 'getting and spending', and a more refined and empty mode of social intercourse?

'They go', said old Josh Cott from his sickbed to me one day. 'They go, they drift away, they clear out. They think they're "bettering themselves". They sell their animals. They get rid of the acres that the same family has worked for generations. I'm sorry for them, doctor. I tell you one thing, I'm not leaving Klonbreck. Never. And Dod, he's promised me he'll never leave Klonbreck or sell it. I'm very glad to think there might be Cotts in Klonbreck still in a hundred years' time'. . . .

Poor old Josh Cott – it's true enough he won't be leaving his croft and island, for he is dying slowly of sclerosis, and I doubt if he'll see another seed-time. But I wouldn't attach too much importance to the sacred promises of the likes of Dod Cott, his only son. Dod is all for tinkering with mechanical things – cars and wireless sets and watches – and Dod's wife fancies herself in the short skirts and knee-high boots that she buys (mail-order) from the south; once the old man is dead I can't see her lingering overlong among the earth-smells of Klonbreck.

But a dying man cherishes impossible hopes; it would surely be wrong to take them from him. A last seed throbs in the winter earth.

Death has come to the old man up at Klonbreck sooner than I thought. Early on Sunday morning I closed his eyes. He will lie in Njalsay earth, but I think he may be the last of his race to do so.

His son covered his face with his hands. And Doreen said, 'Poor old dad', but it was only mouth-mime, a passing mask of regret.

Josh Cott's death was the first to happen since I came. It has been followed, in the course of a few days, by two others – a small feast of death in Njalsay. On Tuesday it was old Miss Tina Lethman, a spinster who lived alone in a house near the pier that her father had built at the turn of the century. This Tina had always kept herself rather aloof; she considered herself a cut above the other women of Njalsay. Hadn't her father made his money as the island's general merchant? Here again the foolish snobbery showed itself – the family whose symbols are counters, ledgers, letterheads is superior to those whose heraldry is plough and flail. . . . It was comical, in fact – Miss Luthman was so poor she had to live with the utmost meagreness, she had to count every penny. Yet she wrapped herself in this web-thin garment of social superiority. None but the minister's wife or the teacher's wife drank afternoon tea with her. Once, many years ago, at the time of a royal wedding, she had knitted with her own hands a beautiful shawl and sent it to the bride. In due course, back came a printed acknowledgment – thousands of them must have been sent out to every corner of the globe. Miss Tina framed hers; it hung above her mantelpiece; it was her proudest possession.

Poor Miss Tina – for the last five years she had been terribly crippled with arthritis. But, through all her sufferings, she clung to her gentility – that was the thing, it seemed, that kept her going for so long. But on Tuesday afternoon it was all over for her at last. When I came down the stair from her death-chamber her little gilt clock ticked away under the framed acknowledgment from royalty.

These deaths – old Josh Cott and Miss Tina Lethman – were in the course of nature. The third death shocked the whole island – it even made me blanch, who am accustomed to death's slow weatherings and sudden bolts. A young

fisherman called Ragnar Holm killed himself on Friday evening. He was twenty five, and he lived with his mother in a
small house where the burn empties itself tumultuously into
the sea. I had passed him once or twice on the island road,
and had always gotten a wave and a smile; and one evening I
even exchanged a few words with him in the smithy. That
night the men's talk had all been about politics. Most of the
island men are cautious progressives – liberalism is as far as
they will go. They keep some kind of ancestral memory of the
bad rule of the lairds, and so Toryism is out. They have nothing in common with the organised industrial workers in
cities; the notion of strikes and industrial action is foreign to
them, it is almost against nature – will the ripe corn wait till
some dispute between the farmer and his reapers is settled?
Will the sow refrain from farrowing till she gets better husks?.
. . . The rhythms of farm and factory are different things. The
only socialists in Njalsay are Peter Kringle who has been a
deep-sea sailor, and Mr Prinn the schoolmaster.

But now, I gathered that night in the smithy, Njalsay had a
third socialist, Ragnar Holm. He hadn't thought deeply about
it, that much was obvious, and he was poor at expressing
himself. But I could see, all the same, that he had a sincere
concern for the poor of the world. It was a socialism of the
heart, rather than Peter Kringle's rancorous kind, or the teacher's *New Statesman* kind.

That night in the smithy – the only time I ever spoke to
him – Ragnar was so carried away by 'the evils of South
African apartheid' that the other men gradually fell silent
around him. He became conscious of all the eyes that were
on him – he hadn't meant it to be that way at all, it was just a
small private exchange of opinions between himself and me.
He got flustered and tongue-tied; he lost the thread of his
argument; at last he burst out with, 'It's terrible, wicked, evil!'

– and blushed – and turned, and took his inarticulate passion out into the night with him.

'That Ragnar', said the farmer of Osgarth, 'he fairly gets carried away!'

The other men smiled and puffed at their pipes – they were inclined to be against displays of enthusiasm on any subject whatsoever.

'But still,' said Jake Nelson, 'he's a fine boy, Ragnar.'

'And I'll tell you another thing,' said Bill Rerwick, who was a crofter-fisherman, 'there's not a better man than Ragnar at the haddock-fishing.'

'His father was a good man before him,' said Tom Selwick. 'Ragnar'll cool down when he's a year or two older'. . . .

On Friday evening, while I was toasting bread and poaching an egg for my supper, there came a loud knocking at the door. Whoever the caller was, he didn't wait for me to answer. The door was thrust open, and a vivid face appeared. Tom Selwick was so transformed with shock and excitement that it took me a second or two to recognise him.

'Come!' he said. 'For God's sake! It's Ragnar, something's happened to him down at the boatshed – something terrible!' He wouldn't wait for me to get the car out of the garage. He was off across the fields to the boatshed half a mile away, running and leaping. Round the door of the boatshed a few other islanders were gathered. Shocked white faces made way for me. A fisherman gave me the lantern he carried.

Ragnar Holm had hanged himself with a shred of net. There was nothing I could do, except cut him down and then break the news to the mother. But she already knew – perhaps some old woman had told her, perhaps she had heard the crash of the fishbox and the creaking of rafter-and-man-and-twine; and guessed. 'Yes', she said, 'Ragnar. I thought this might happen. I expected it. It's come to this. Yes, indeed.

He's by with it, he's by with it'. . . . I had not expected such quietness and acceptance. I thought to myself, 'Life has made you ready for anything, old one'. But then she suddenly wailed and rose to her feet and flung herself across the bed. 'Ragnar, Ragnar,' she cried, 'why did you have to do it? There was a long good life before you! There was plenty of love for you, Ragnar, my boy!'. . . . I was glad that at this point three neighbouring women came in at the door. I left her to them. I was glad to get away from such desolation and pain. . . . Up at the house, the egg lay cold on sodden toast, and the teapot was cold. I poured myself a half tumbler of whisky.

Between the suicide and the funeral of the young fisherman, I have gotten one or two scraps of information, but nothing at all that could provide a likely clue as to why a young healthy hard-working lad should want to end his life. The heredity on both sides is sound – the father had died in the course of nature ten years before – nearly everyone on the mother's side specialised in longevity. He had intelligence, a natural courtesy and gentleness, a proper concern for the things that happen not only in his island but in the larger world outside. He went to dances and darts matches and concerts; he was popular with the island girls, though it seemed at the time he had no steady 'date'. His boat provided little in the way of wealth – no small fishing boat has ever done that, in the whole history of the island – but there was no real poverty, and no debt. It is an utterly baffling mystery. All we can be sure of is this – there are minds that have to endure terrors and anguishes and imaginings of which we tougher mortals know nothing, fortunately.

They buried Ragnar Holm today, on a dark mid winter afternoon.

There, when the other island men were in the churchyard, was that Peter Kringle – I saw him myself – down at the shore, minutely going over Ragnar's boat with eye and hand. No doubt he will make an offer for it; I hope not this side of Hogmanay, till the mother's pain has mended a little.

(In honesty I should mention here the much smaller pain that led me, against the drift, to seek solitude and darkness. That pain had a name given to it in the late nineteenth century by a famous ostracised writer. The 'temple of love' has many courts – in one of which it was a crime, until lately, to display trophies. From the wounds of a small defeat in that contention I have sought the cure of silence.)

The days get shorter; darkness encroaches rapidly as we near the solstice. Last Saturday I got a note through my letterbox: Mrs Grantham would be pleased if I could come to dinner the following evening, Sunday, at 7.30 p.m. (Mrs Grantham is the lady of the manse.)

I do not like getting such invitations, on the whole. I am one of those pernickety bachelors who have their day carefully mapped – so many hours for reading and listening to music; such and such a time for my stamp collection; the recharging of my pipe every two hours or so. These evenings out ruin the careful pattern. Besides, I like to eat when I'm hungry, and then what I fancy. (I am thought to be a passable cook.)

I am also something of a coward – I am all for peace in the community, at almost any cost. I phoned to Mrs Grantham after the evening surgery to say that I would be delighted to have dinner with the minister and herself. (This was the first time I have been invited to anything other than a supper-time snack.)

It proved to be one of those distasteful evenings that one swears will never be repeated as far as oneself is concerned; but of course it happens again and again. The bruised mind renews itself every morning. Cheerfulness sends its fresh springs up through the stone.

I found there were other guests than myself. Prinn the schoolmaster and his wife were there, and also a friend of the minister who had been a contemporary of his at the university, a Robert McCracken, lawyer, from Glasgow.

I must say the food was first rate; I could congratulate Meg Grantham with genuine warmth. There was even a couple of bottles of good wine – a thing I hadn't expected in a manse – and brandy afterwards. The two-mile walk in the cold air, also, had made me hungry.

It was the talk that ruined the whole evening. How dreadful it is when you can't speak easily and naturally to your fellow diners, and listen tolerantly to what he or she has to say. Here, on this night, cleverness was all. You had to keep a sharp ear open for subtle puns – you had to rummage desperately through your mind for witty things to say. And laughter – though nothing really funny was said all night, as I remember – played like summer lightning across the dining table. A hypocrite again, I did my best to add my leaven of cheerfulness to the symposium.

Prinn was in his high and scathing mood. I have heard him in that vein before. He is the knowledgeable man in a community of fools and morons (present company excepted.) He sticks in his barbs right and left, indiscriminately – his tongue wounds people who seem to me to be better than him in every respect. Worst of all is when he catalogues his pupils as 'louts' and 'objects' and 'yokels' . . . And Isobel Prinn sitting opposite with that thin smile on her face – her don of a husband, having to hide his talents in such barren soil. Prinn even spoke about 'that fisherman who hanged himself because the 'morbus orcadensis' had got into him'. . . .

For a time, while Mrs Grantham and Mrs Prinn were in the kitchen doing the washing-up, the Glasgow solicitor held the stage. His speciality – at least this night – was stories with a vein of smut in them. I hated myself for smiling at the end of every well-turned piece of filth; McCracken certainly knew how to put them across. I don't mind the earthiness of Shakespeare, Chaucer, Burns – there's a cleanness at the heart of the bawdry – but this slick modern filth is rootless and functionless, it stinks in the mind, it leaves a stain. I wished for the two women to finish their dish-washing and come back. Meantime McCracken had finished another story. Prinn roared with mirth. I screwed my face into a smile. What shocked me more than a little was the reaction of Mr Grantham; his chuckles were as false as Prinn's and my own – falser, because he had to show that being a man of the cloth didn't at all mean that he was a glumpot. By no means; he could relish a clever story in any vein, he was the complete man of the world.

The two women came back out of the kitchen; McCracken's latest story remained half-told. 'Blast you women!' shouted Prinn. 'Couldn't you have waited another two minutes!'. . . .

And now, late at night, the minister came into his own. Whether one or other of us prompted him I don't remember, but he began to explain his attitude to scripture.

'Now James', said his wife, 'no shop, please!'

'Yes, Jimmy, you carry on', said McCracken. 'It'll do me good. It'll make up for all the sermons that I've missed in the last ten years.'

Mrs Prinn said she thought one religion was as good as another – they all had something, didn't they? Basically they were the same.

It was as if the minister was determined to show us all just exactly how broadminded and modern he was. The miracles – they were demolished in no long time – they were simply vivid ways of impressing primitive minds. The feeding of ten thousand people with five barley loaves and two small fishes – what educated man could accept that nowadays? It was obviously a way of getting people to share out what they had. The crowd on the hillside that day was made up of certain prudent folk who had taken parcels of food with them, and others who had simply rushed off to listen to the Galilean spellbinder without a thought of food or drink. The loaves and fishes in the boy's basket – once the disciples had distributed these to a hungry few, the others took the hint, and so the whole assembly had enough and to spare . . .

'But the Virgin Birth?' said Prinn. 'And the Resurrection? Surely, as a minister, you are bound to believe them?'

Mr Grantham made no answer. His forefinger stroked his cigarette. He looked round the table, from face to face, smiling, and shook his head.

I found enough courage to say that if I was a minister and couldn't accept these things, then I would resign and look for another job . . .

Mr Grantham said he was trying to be honest in the light of modern knowledge – other men of his profession thought as he did. 'We ministers are a part of the society we live in,' he went on. 'We take our colouring from it, and we contribute our own special skill. Society nowadays will have nothing to do with miracles. Miracles were very beautiful, some of them, and served their turn in their place and age. But we modern ministers, whether we like it or not, are living in an age of scepticism and pragmatism.'

'But would you say what you've just said,' I persisted, 'to your session clerk?'

Four faces frowned at me.

'That old idiot!' said Prinn. 'For God's sake. Dung and mud and money in the bank – that's Smith's religion, that's the only miracle old Obadiah knows anything about!'

The minister held up his hand. 'Charity,' he said, 'charity, Philip, now. . . .' He turned to me and said, 'No, I wouldn't say what I've said to that good old man, because he isn't ready to receive it. He never will be, this side of the grave – he's a fundamentalist, he was brought up in the old literal tradition. And I hope he never asks me – I would find it very difficult to begin to explain' . . .

McCracken joined in the discussion then. He, it seemed, was knowledgeable on the subject of myth and religion; at any rate, he had done some reading here and there that had some bearing. He put forward the proposition, after a time, that probably no such person as Jesus of Nazareth had walked the earth; at least, not the figure as represented in the gospels, as god-hero. The fact was that everything Jesus is reported as saying and preaching had already been uttered by earlier prophets and holy men. The huge rhythms of existence – the opposites and complements such as winter and summer, birth and death, fertility and barrenness – all religion was an attempt to come to terms with these mighty forces that domi-nate the life of the tribe. The corn king dies and rises again and nourishes his people. Oh, there might indeed have been a small-time carpenter-turned-preacher on the shores of Galilee in the first century AD – it was the merest accident, a quirk of history (who could explain it?) that the attributes of the mythical priest-king, the seasonal god, had been attached to this enigmatic figure . . .

I did expect our host to assert himself at this point, but he actually seemed to accept what McCracken had said as a fair enough basis for argument; managing to suggest at the same time, with a tolerant shake of the head, that really his friend was venturing into deeper waters than he could, as a layman, understand.

Soon after that the evening came to an end.

I said my goodbyes and took my leave first of all, declining an offer of a lift in the Prinns' car. The walk, I said, would help me to sleep. (McCracken I hoped I might never meet again – he was leaving for Glasgow in the morning, to be home for the festive season.)

It struck me, walking homewards through the first swirling snowflakes, how much kinder and sweeter the atmosphere of that house and that company might have been if only Mrs Grantham and Mrs Prinn had had children.

It struck me, then, that there hadn't been a single birth in Njalsay since I had come to the island; only, last week, that little feast of death. It seemed like a foreshadowing of the day when the only people in the island were the dead in the churchyard.

Beyond the farm of Osgarth there is a lonely stretch with no houses at all. For a quarter of a mile or so you walk in complete darkness on a moonless winter night – tonight there were no stars even, and the snow was falling thicker than ever. Just over the ridge the road turns left, and you look down on the cluster of lighted windows above the shore, and further off the sprinkled lights of the neighbouring islands.

Another track branches off to the right, into the most desolate part of the island. Once Westside was a populous enough district, with a dozen or so crofts, but within the last decade it has become completely deserted. Life must have been hard for these folk – their fields were so poor that the farmers of Njalsay hadn't thought it worth while to go on cultivating them; all that marks them now are a few crazy fencing stobs and a rusted plough or two in the shelter of a broken wall.

Very bleak the district of Westside looked, athwart those falling curtains of snow.

I reached the ridge. I was glad to see, far below, the light in the window of Riggeridge farm. I had less than a mile to walk from there.

A man I did not know was standing where the road branches. The sight of him startled me – frightened me, I admit, for a second or two. On such a night one expects all the living to be part of a firelit circle.

'Please help us,' the man said. 'I know you're a doctor. My wife is in great pain. You must come.'

'Who are you?' I said. 'Where do you live? What's wrong with her?'

He didn't answer. He gestured vaguely towards the ruined district of Westside. He turned and bent his head into the snow. His feet rose and fell. I followed him.

There was just enough light to see the ditches. The man walked fast. He knew where he was going. I followed in the wake of his black footprints. I saw, with relief, that it was not going to be a solid night of snow. To the north, over the hill, a torn patch of sky appeared with a few stars shining in it.

Then, quite suddenly, there was a lamp shining in the window of what I had always known to be a deserted croft – I even forgot its name. And now the man began to run across the field that separated road from croft. I heard voices inside, bright with welcome and anxiety and reassurance.

I made my way to the croft more slowly. When I was half-way there the man appeared at the door. 'For God's sake,' he shouted, 'hurry! She's near her time!'

I assisted at a birth that night. A short time after I entered the hovel a boy was born. The man had made such preparations as he could. He had kettles on the range. There was adequate clothing for a new-born child airing over a chair that stood back-on to the fire.

The new mother was not much more than seventeen or eighteen years old. The birth had not been easy – the man told me she had been in labour for hours. She took the child with great tenderness into her arms. The shadow of the man fell over them both.

The man and the girl were so wrapped up in the marvel of what had happened that I had a short time to take stock of the situation. The house had patches of damp on one wall. One of the roofing flagstones had shifted – you could see a triangle of sky through it, there was room for a star to shine in.

It was certainly no fit habitation for a family. Yet the man had salved things from the ruin – the kettles, for example, and the paraffin lamp that burned in the window. There were a few plates and cups without handles on the table. The single shelf in the cupboard had a loaf, a basin of potatoes, tins of this and that. A zinc bucket of water made blue tremblings in the corner.

It was over. I had done what I could. The little family was wrapped in their flame of happiness.

I had a great many questions to ask them. Who were they? Where had they come from? What did the man do for a living? Had they got permission to live in the croft? It would be impossible – surely they realised it? – to try to bring up a child in a ruin like this . . .

Instead I made a quiet exit. I walked home under the wide hemisphere of stars, and my feet crackled through pure silver all the way. I fell asleep almost at once.

'No,' said Tom Selwick. 'Nobody's lived in the croft of Wanhope for seven years now, since old Ezra Sinclair died. Why do you ask?'

'I thought I saw a light in the window late last night,' I said.

'That's impossible,' said Tom. 'It could have been a reflection of the snow or the stars.'

'I saw a lighted paraffin lamp,' I insisted.

Tom shook his head.

'Do you not have tinkers in the island?' I said. 'Wandering folk.'

'There used to be,' said Tom. 'But now the tinkers don't wander any more. The tinkers have houses and cars in the town. They're better off than me.'

I knew, of course, that they weren't tinkers, or anyone who belonged to the islands. It was very hard to say what the man's accent was – he had spoken a good plain English, the kind that anyone from Shetland to the Scillies could understand.

'There's another kind of going-about people,' I said, 'that have recently come into existence. Beatniks they're called, or some name like that. They don't like society, affluence, working to timetables, serving machines. These young folk are beginning to seek out the quietest loneliest places to live in. Sometimes they settle in communities, sometimes a young couple try to make do on their own. They live in poverty. They don't interfere with other people. Some of them seem to exist on vegetables and water. They go in for meditation a lot.'

Tom laughed. 'I've heard of them,' he said. 'In fact some folk like that have come to live in Norday and Selskay. Maybe that's the explanation, doctor. If so, we'll be seeing them soon. They'll have to come down to the store for their provisions.'

I haven't done anything in the way of finding out more about that mysterious family in Wanhope croft. I ought to have gone there this morning to see how it is with the mother and child. I will certainly go before sunset. But I would not be surprised to find myself standing in the door of a cold dripping bare ruin; and to have to turn then and say to myself, 'Clifton, you idiot, it was a snow-dream you had between the manse and the village on Sunday night'; and finally to say to Tom Selwick in the smithy, 'You're right, man, it was the light of snow and stars in the window of Wanhope, no paraffin lamp at all. I was up there this afternoon, just to make sure. I expect I had drunk too much of the minister's brandy.'

TEACHER

We were invited to the Manse on Sunday evening, for dinner. It was a marvellous occasion, as I knew it would be, with Meg the cook: some kind of delicious pheasant soup, then lobster, roast pork and trimmings, a trifle as light as birds, coffee and five-star brandy, two bottles of first-rate burgundy. How does Grantham manage it, on his stipend? The trouble is, we can't compete, even if I could afford it – Isobel is a good plain cook, nothing more. So long as they don't expect too much when we have them for dinner at New Year.

Present were, besides Grantham and his missus and ourselves, Dr Clifton and an extremely witty lawyer friend of Grantham, Robert McCracken, from Glasgow, who's going away later today, I think, if he hasn't left already. I do wish he could have stayed on to see the New Year in – we could do with a leavening of his cleverness and fun in this place.

The problem at the moment is, do we invite the doctor or no? That man is enough to put a damper on any company. There he sat on Sunday night at the manse dinner, only moving his jaw to eat, which he did to some purpose. I expect he's half starved. Why can't he get that Mrs Pegal to cook a midday meal for him? He's too mean, I expect – and him with that huge salary! 'I cook for myself. I like cooking,' he said sometime in the course of the evening; and that's about all that he contributed to the conversation, except take issue with Grantham over something or other. I do not like him. I expect we'll just have to go on inviting him occasionally to the schoolhouse for a casual supper, now that the tradition has started. But the New Year dinner – I don't know – I'll have to ask Isobel about it.

In spite of Dr Clifton, then, it was a successful evening. (I hope to God ours goes half as well.) McCracken had an anthology of some of the best stories I've heard since I was at college. The man has a deeper side to his nature, though. He has read a lot of history and anthropology, and he's thought about it. He gave old James quite a run for his money, on the subject of the gospels. Altogether a most interesting man. He says he'll come back in the summer, to fish.

The weakness in my left leg is in general much better since the school closed, thank God, for the Christmas holiday. The rest, I expect, has done it some good. But of course I know all about these improvements – they lift your heart for a day or two, then down comes the shadow again, the foot begins to drag on the floor. And what about this hand I am writing with – my taut sensitive hand? Last night, for a few seconds, it was made of snow. I haven't mentioned the hand to Isobel yet. No sense in adding to her worries.

'Nothing really wrong with you at all.' The sweetest sentence I ever heard, from that specialist in Newcastle, and me thinking that day I was teetering on the brink of the grave; and also the specialist when I went in looking more like an undertaker than a healer. 'It's mostly in your mind. You're a bit of a hypochondriac, don't you know? I can't tell that to everyone, but you're intelligent. It could be that cities are too much for you – city schools – delinquents – all the urban pressures. Would it be possible for you, now, to get some quiet country school, eh? Far from the madding crowd. Think about it seriously. Moors, streams, clouds – that's the kind of place that'll keep the power in your legs, Mr Prinn' . . .

And that was that. We sold our house and most of our furniture, and read the advertisements in the educational papers, and I wrote a letter or two, and had an interview; and here we are, in a half-dead island between the Atlantic and the North Sea.

'O true apothecarie, thy drugs are quick' . . . It was marvellous, how much my health improved. I didn't exactly leap about the island like a goat, but still I could go where I wanted to be surely and freely. That desolating feeling of no blood or substance below the knee – as if a man were beginning to be a ghost from the instep up – that had vanished. I said to Isobel one midnight, after we had made love, 'There's nothing more to worry about. My sickness – it's gone like the snow. Touch me again.' The second time was a celebration and an act of thankfulness . . . Next morning, as I was walking from the breakfast table to the classroom, my leg fluttered under me. It was a momentary spasm – but I was terrified, I can tell you. I taught for the rest of that morning seated at my desk. The country children must have wondered why their instruction that day was so disjointed, and why their teacher – usually so masterful – spoke in a chaste vacant voice.

When I got down from my desk at lunch-time the strength had returned to my leg. It had been a momentary relapse – perhaps imagined – perhaps because I was worried that morning about the news from my brother in Australia. (His shop having to close – the shutters up – could it be bankruptcy? And if so . . .)

Three and a half weeks later the desolation struck again, when I rose to turn the record of that Brahms quintet. It lasted all that night and most of the following day. More of my leg seemed to be involved. The children must have noticed my hirple. Then, again, the substance took over from the shadow, and the blood beat and flowed.

Last night, at supper, the spoon fell out of my hand. It clattered and splashed into the soup plate. 'Sorry,' I said to Isobel. She gave me a white look. Now my right hand is becoming acquainted with the shadows. That never happened before; the weakness was on the left side.

What am I going to do? What will become of me? My imagination is not so strong that it can make a ghost of parts of me. I am dying piecemeal.

I ought, of course, in the first place, to go and have a talk with Clifton; tell him the history of my trouble and the symptoms; ask for a straight diagnosis and prognosis. So that, if need be, I can put my house in order.

But I am terrified to do such a thing. (It's with me like the man in the dock when the black cap is at the judge's elbow and the foreman of the jury gets to his feet.) I won't go to see him. Not yet.

Another thing. If I'm going to die – and die lingeringly and disgustingly, if the trouble is what I think it is – I can't eke out the remainder of my days, however long is left, in a community of strangers with whom I have absolutely nothing in common. I must get back to my own kind.

Thank goodness Isobel and I agreed before we married that there would be no children, ever.

If the illness were all – but it brings such enormous problems with it. Isobel guesses what it might be, I think, but says nothing. Or next to nothing. This morning, at breakfast, she said, 'Phil, dear, you're white. I think you've got a bit of a cold. You ought to go and see Dr Clifton.'

I said I didn't have a cold, and the less I saw of Clifton the better I liked it.

I must go and see him. My hand is withering. It will be a bitterness to listen to him. He doesn't like me, I know. He has the kind of inverted snobbery that claims to prefer the company of yokels and fishermen to the likes of me and James Grantham. I've wondered sometimes if he isn't 'queer', at least by inclination: seeking out the husky silent island men in Selwick's place, after dark, to gossip and laugh among.

He might even like hurting me.

How should I take advice and sympathy from the likes of him?

I began to write the above, after Isobel had gone to bed, in order to spur myself into cheerfulness. For really, in spite of all, I did enjoy Sunday night at the manse. The memory of all that good food and talk has left a glow. I said to myself, 'I'll keep a diary for one day only. I'll write about that good time, and it'll be like a fire that I can come back to whenever I'm in the dumps'. . . . But – I might have known it – the shadow has taken over from the song, the song has become a dirge, a dark whisper . . . Like the voice of Clifton among the falling snow when I offered him a lift in the car, 'No, thanks. I like walking in the darkness – you never know what you might meet.'

MINISTER

Slow enfolding of darkness. Imagine a man standing on a headland near the north of Lapland at noon: he sees glimmers and darkenings on the sea, a grayness in the south: then night begins to enmesh him again. At midnight his whole hemisphere is sheathed in blackness, except where frost and starlight put fugitive jewellery. The boreal tide is still rising – it washes our mouths and eyes and spirits. Tomorrow is the solstice, the last reach of night and winter. Soon we will begin to feel the first tremor of spring (though usually the worst weather comes in January and February). The man who stands on that Scandinavian headland will see then, far more spectacularly than us, the upsurge of the fountain of light. He will hunt and fish in a summer of blond shadowless splendours. The sign of the sun will be on the window where he sleeps and prays and makes love.

Certainly such violent alterations of light and darkness must have some effect on the people who live far in the north. But here quietness is the keynote – 'they keep the level tenor of the way.' They are withdrawn with strangers, until friendship and sincerity are tested and proved, and then there is no end to their openness and kindness, winter and summer. Meg and I know this well; we have been in Njalsay island now for three years. I would like to think that I will end my days among them, but I expect that won't happen. Meg is turning her face more and more often to the south. She wants to be there to satisfy her hunger, before her palate is too dry and sour for relishing love.

How pleasant to be here, in my comfortable study, on a midwinter night. I came up after supper to write the short Christmas sermon that has been forced on me. I lit three coloured candles on the desk, and put a fresh peat on the fire. Outside the window it is pitch black; the sudden snow of yesterday faded almost as soon as it fell. I drew the heavy curtains. Then I put a sheet of paper on the desk and unscrewed my pen. Instead of a happy little Christmas homily, I find myself brooding on the mysteries of darkness, winter, death.

For death keeps high revelry at this time of year – at least, he did in Njalsay last week. There was the old ailing man up at Klonbreck for a start. Then, a day or two after, Miss Lethman, who I'm sure died of slow starvation at last after pinching and scraping for twenty lean years. (She would have nothing to do with the Welfare State.) And last, that poor boy who killed himself among his creels and oars. How strange, to stand over three open graves in one week, and strew earth on the coffin, and say, 'All flesh is grass . . .'

And now I must confess to this sheet of paper – for nobody else would be interested – how helpless I feel in the midst of such suffering. For I visited the houses of death, and in all three places I felt useless, a reverend irrelevance. Up at the farm the surviving Cotts seemed relieved that the good old man was dead at last, whether in consideration of his long suffering or their own advantage it would be hard to say. In Miss Lethman's house there was only her old cat – I think the vet who comes to the island every month will have to do something about the creature. Down at the shore it was awful – the dreadful wailing of the old woman, and the branded face of Ragnar's girlfriend. My duty is to administer comfort – I was confused, platitudinous, in a flush and sweat – I'm sure both these women were glad to see the back of me.

No man likes to feel that he is no good at his job, especially when his uselessness in a brutish but necessary function is flung in his face twice or thrice a month . . . Meg is singing to the piano downstairs, some modern ballad or other. It's time she was in bed; I want her to be asleep when I go up.

One of the candles – the yellow one – has just had its flame drowned in a brimming sea of wax. One of the others is smoking and leaping. I must get this weirdest of meditations finished before I'm left utterly in the dark.

It is not only with the bereaved that I feel my uselessness. I have felt increasingly since the end of summer that I'm really not needed in the island at all; or rather not wanted, for every community surely needs a lamp-bearer, a bringer of comfort.

Everything seems to point that way. The meagre scatter of faces in the pews on a Sunday morning – that is disconcerting, to say the least. This was once a religious island. Oh, I know what they say – 'depopulation' . . . 'in the old days they *had* to go to the kirk on Sabbath' . . . 'better a few sincere believers than a churchful of dumb frightened oxen' . . . What unsettles me is that the islanders who ought to be there don't come – I mean the young fishermen and the farm girls, those who are standing at the door of the future with empty purposeless hands. All I seem to minister to are the islanders who come to the church because their Sundays would seem empty if they didn't come. Do I fill a space in their lives, no more?

So, this is the darkness that has stolen, shade by unquiet shade, into the soul of the minister of Njalsay parish in this bleak midwinter. Last Yule, I remember, I was happy enough.

There is something even more dispiriting. I see souls in pain in this island that I can't do a thing for, because they won't declare their troubles to me. That's why I sometimes wish I was called Father Grantham, and had a little dark confession box full of whispers in a corner of the church. Then they might come and tell me their troubles, and I would be able to dispense supernatural comfort. Ragnar Holm, for example, would he still be alive if he had been able to unburden himself?

Phil Prinn too, the schoolmaster – what's come over him this past month or six weeks? Certainly something is troubling him – his wife knows a little, but not everything, I think. He's not even putting a brave face on it any longer. That's the trouble with these clever mass-produced minds – their foundations are in the sand. The tremendous dark earth-rooted courage of old Josh Cott, in comparison!. . . . What's wrong? What in God's name is wrong with the man that he won't tell his friends even? Several dark threads have been woven this winter into the life of Philip Prinn, B.A.

Didn't a letter come, ten days ago, from Bert McCracken in Glasgow? That did nothing to cheer me up, either. Not that he said anything outright. It was all hints, confusions, shadows of pain. Barbara left him six years ago, and took the children – I don't think that's worrying him now. It's something else, something even more ruinous. 'So, old Jim' the letter ended, 'between one thing and another, life is not too sweet at the moment. Lucky you, with your Meg and your little flock in that island – no need for you, not for many a year yet, to flee away and be at rest. . . .' I showed the letter to Meg – and she agreed, there was some veiled trouble somewhere – and she agreed further that he must be invited for Christmas. (Though Meg may have had another kind of mutual therapy in mind.) He left today, assuring us of his eternal gratitude for a wonderful holiday. But – I might have known it – I was not able to get near his pain.

Then there's Clifton, the new doctor. That man intrigues me more than a little. Why has he, a young eager practitioner, left the cities of the south to waste his talents among a few healthy islanders? He is a deeper character than either Prinn or McCracken. I admit I'm a bit envious of him. There he is, on the best of terms with everyone in the island, rich and poor, beggar and laird; whereas I ply my unwanted trade at only a few orthodox doors. Dr Clifton is well-liked in Njalsay, no doubt of that, with his easy pleasant outgoing nature – but there's a mystery about him – a sense of scars healing but not yet at peace – and this cruel winter has scratched them open again.

So, after the funeral of Ragnar the fisherman, on Friday – when I was at my lowest – I was struck by a comforting idea. Why not have a dinner – a midwinter feast – and invite all those suffering souls to sit round the one table? I mentioned it to Meg. And of course she agreed; capable creature that she is, she loves planning a dinner, or a picnic, or a concert. Bert was here already; he had arrived on the Wednesday. It only remained to order the goodies from the town, and send out cards to Messrs Prinn and Clifton. And do you know – the thing actually came off – the evening was a success! Old McCracken crackled with cleverness – he even had a go at Christianity, and made out a good case (at least from the standpoint of The Thinkers' Library), but he really of course didn't know what he was talking about. And Phil enjoyed showing how clever he was – what Swiftian insight he had into the life of Njalsay. I let them go on. At least they had put aside their sorrows for an hour or two. With Clifton it was more difficult to know. He smiled, and nodded, and put in a word occasionally. Once or twice I caught him with his mask off – then he looked bored, or contemptuous. He is, as I said, a much more subtle case than my other two guests.

I needn't say how excellent were the food and the drink. Meg can put a great deal of thwarted love into a meal.

Snow was falling when we waved goodbye to them just before midnight – Phil and Isobel in their car, Clifton preferring to walk. 'A Christmas-card Yule,' said Bert as we watched the dark sky-drift and the spectre of the rosebush in the light from the window . . . (But in fact the snow was all gone next morning.)

There's another candle gone. The third one should last another ten minutes, long enough to unburden my soul of the last winter shadow, if my wrist doesn't seize up first with this torrent of written words. This is what the Christmas sermon has come to: an ill-shaped brooding on the soul's winter, a St Lucy's lament.

There was to be no Christmas sermon, at all. It was the question of the Christmas sermon that dropped the little shadow between me and my session. This too has never happened before.

It was my own fault. I sprang it on those good people too suddenly; it must have been to them like a blow on the face. 'This coming Sunday,' I announced blithely from the pulpit, 'Christmas Sunday, there will be a special service. You will be pleased to know that there will be no sermon at all. Instead, there will be a ceremony of carols, sung by the children of the Sunday School. My wife has been organising this since Hallowe'en, in addition to organising me, the Manse, the Women's Guild, and the Lifeboat committee. There will also be something new. When you enter the church next Sunday you will see, in the choir, the Bethlehem crib – Joseph, the ox and the ass, Mary with the holy child in her arms, angels, shepherds, and kings, and of course the biggest star any of you have ever seen . . . So, we look forward to a happy festival in the church next Sunday' . . . I was not prepared, after the service, for the troubled face of Obadiah Smith, of Osgarth farm, my good gentle session clerk. 'Mr Grantham,' he said, 'a word with you. I've been speaking to one or two of the other elders. It's about this service next Sunday. We don't feel all that happy about it . . .' Other troubled faces gathered about me in the church door; Andrew Sillar looked red and angry. They left most of the speaking to Obadiah, though occasionally one of them would put in a few words in an access of feeling. The crib – that was the trouble, it seemed, at first. They did not want a crib in the church. It smelt of idolatry. Didn't they have these cribs in Catholic churches at Christmas? They would have me know that this was a Presbyterian church, and always had been, and always would be. They would be very pleased if I reconsidered the crib. The last thing they wanted was trouble . . . I gave in, as graciously as I could. I knew what Meg would say when I told her (and she having spent a month putting the tableau together, and decorating it beautifully). 'Very well,' I said, 'there will be no crib.' And smiled at them . . . They were still mulish. 'Forbye this crib thing,' said Obadiah, 'there's never been a Sabbath in this kirk that a sermon wasn't preached. Never since the kirk was built. We'd take it ill if there was no sermon.' 'If there's a sermon,' I said, 'there will be no time for the carol-singing. There can't be both' . . . I was prepared to dig in my heels on this matter. 'Very well,' said Andrew Sillar, 'let there be no carols then. Carols indeed! Carols is papish too. Our kirk is founded on the sermon, the preaching of the word.' 'The carol service will take place,' I said. They must have seen that I was quite determined about it. 'Could you not see your way,' said Obadiah, 'to preach a short sermon – it need be no more than five minutes – half way through the service?' . . . Andrew Sillar was muttering away in the background about papedom and idols. 'When I was young,' he muttered to Albert MacVicar and George Brinkie, 'we didn't even keep Christmas in this island. That's a fact. "Christ's Mass" – what could be more papish than that!' . . . 'Now, Andrew, that's enough,' said Obadiah. He turned a troubled face to me. 'Please,' he said. It is because I love this old man that I said, 'Very well, there will be a brief sermon during the service next Sunday'. . . . It was as if the entire deputation gave a sigh of relief in the winter air; they were all smiles, except Mr Sillar, who looked if anything angrier than before . . .

That little quarrel at the church door last Sunday has troubled me more than I cared to admit to myself at the time; but a white piece of paper has a way of luring the truth out. I was bitterly hurt by it. And Meg's rage, when I told her over the lunch table, did nothing to help. I am more than an inadequate husband; I am a weak pastor . . . Supposing the midwinter midnight was so wrapped in cloud that the watcher on that boreal cape could see nothing – not a star, not a glim on a passing wave, not his own hand in front of his face? I don't wish to appear more important than I am. I'm not capable of putting my lips to that chalice called by mystics 'the dark night of the soul.' But last Sunday I was more depressed than I have ever known.

In fact, in the globe of this earth, in the Mappa Mundi, there is no place so bewintered and boreal that it cannot cherish the remembered blessing of light, and hope for its certain return.

In the largest island of the Orkneys there's a magnificent stone-age burial chamber. Four thousand years ago the Orkneymen brought their great departed chiefs to this fortress of death, and entombed them in one of the three recesses, and afterwards sealed the opening with a huge cube of stone. Then the hunters and farmers re-emerged into the light.

Surely no house on earth could be as desolate as Maeshowe on a midwinter day, so dark and so drained of the sweetness of existence. But in the midst of this ultimate blackness a small miracle takes place. When the sun sets over Hoy on the afternoon of the solstice, about three o'clock, a single finger of light seeks through the long corridor that leads into the heart of the chamber and touches the opposite wall with a fugitive splash of gold. This never happens all the rest of the bright year. After a minute or two the glow fades. But it is as if a seed of promise had been sown in the womb of death itself.

Meg threw open the study door five minutes ago. 'There's a man down below,' she said. 'He wants to speak to you.' 'Who?' I asked. 'I don't know,' she said coldly – 'He's a stranger. I've never seen him before.' 'Where does he live? Did he say what he wants?' 'He said something about a baby in danger, and would you come at once please – some place in Westside.' 'Nobody lives in Westside district now – not that I know of. Tell the man – whoever he is – I'll be right down' . . .

Meg had interrupted me in the middle of my description of Maeshowe and the midwinter sun. I hastened to finish it before the glow faded; my pen fairly scurried over the paper. The man could wait for a couple of minutes.

I heard Meg calling from the stairhead, and a calm deep voice answering from below. I wrote the last few words and put the sheets of paper in the desk drawer and locked it. (I don't want my wife to read this particular manuscript.) As I did so the last red candle gulped and went out.

Meg was moving about in our bedroom. I groped my way downstairs in darkness. No more than five minutes could have passed since Meg summoned me. When I reached the open door there was nobody there. I walked down the path to the end of the garden. There was sufficient starlight to see that the road that led to the village and the desolate Westside district was empty for half a mile of its length.

'Hello, there,' I called, sure that the man must be somewhere near at hand. 'Who is it? Come on, into the house.'

I waited for a long time at the garden gate. No one answered. Then I went in again out of the darkness and silence and cold, and locked the door.

The Seven Poets

(IN MEMORIAM S G S)

Finally, after very much suffering, the earth fled from cities and machines.

Yet the war had, in its dreadful way, fused mankind together. The peoples were one, in woe and horror and destitution.

A simpler species rose out of the ruins, no less intelligent, but with their faces set against science and the ruthless exploitation of the earth and its resources. 'Progress' was a word they uttered like a curse.

On the fringes of the vast deserts of ruin left by the war, they lived in small villages of not more than 250 people. (It was forbidden to exceed that number: if a village was shaken with sudden fruitfulness one year, certain young people chosen by lot had to hive off and form a new community higher up the river, in the next valley, nearer the mountain snow.)

So the earth became an intricate delicate network of villages, each self-sufficient but aware of all the others. There was no possibility of war between neighbouring communities. The making of arms was forbidden; even a boy seen sharpening a stick was rebuked. The animals ranged unmolested in their separate kingdoms. Men kept their dominion over cattle, sheep, horses, swine, poultry, fish; because it was held that men had a very ancient relationship with these creatures, a sacred bond.

It can be said, with justice, that a great deal of excitement went out of the human story once this pastoral system was established. Men considered boredom to be a small price to pay for their new tranquillity. In fact there was little boredom. The simple village system had within itself endless variety.

There were however a few restless men here and there who could not endure the life of the villages. Allowances were made for them. They were called 'the wandering ones'. They had freedom to travel wherever they chose. If they wanted to stay in a village and help with a harvest, that was good. If they stopped till the last of the snow had gone from the mountain pass, that was good. If they passed through the village at night like a furtive shadow, and drank out of the well thanklessly, and were gone in the morning, that was good also. There was no need for them to thieve – they were welcomed and fed wherever they went. I know; I have been one of those wandering folk all my life.

I have never found the village system dull and repetitive, though I must have visited upwards of five thousand villages in my time. Always there was the cluster of houses, with the occupation carved or painted over each lintel – 'Shepherd', 'Blacksmith', 'Baker', 'Fisherman', 'Vintner', 'Weaver', 'The House of the Old Men', 'Shoemaker', 'Priest', 'The House of the Women and Children', 'Poet', and the three 'Houses of Lovers'.

A village in China is very different from a village in Greenland or Africa. The legends over the doors are in a variety of scripts; so are the offered foods, and the dances in the village square, and the faces of the people in the sun.

It happened that, wherever I went after the age of forty (being then too old for the delectable House of Lovers), I chose to stay in the House of the Poet. You may say 'a strange choice', and so it was. In almost any other house I would have been better fed and more comfortable; in the 'House of the Old Men' I would have heard more entertaining lies; in the 'House of the Vintner' my head would, night after night, have been transformed to a happy beehive. But it was the poet in every village that fascinated me; they were so various, so unlike, so unpredictable.

The main duty of the poet was to write a masque, or chorus, or group of poems, for the villagers to perform in midwinter. Those entertainments were in the main naive, and crudely performed; but the villagers entered into them with deep enjoyment, and so the poets were honoured people in the communities, and never lacked for flowers and wine.

Most of them were honest workaday craftsmen. But here and there I stayed overnight, or maybe for a full week, with an extraordinary poet. In Spain, in a village high on a mountainside, the poet read me his new work. Rehearsals were about to start on it as soon as the grape harvest was in. It was an uninspired piece, and the man knew it. He poured some of the tar-smelling wine of the hills into two cups. We drank in silence. He was one of those that wine makes morose. At last near midnight he said, 'I think often of the boundless power of words. A Word made everything in the beginning. The uttering of that Word took six days. What is this poetry that I busy myself with? A futile yearning towards a realisation of that marvellous Word. What is all poetry but a quest for the meaning and beauty and majesty of the original Word? (In most languages the poet is "the maker".) Poets all over the world since time began have been busy at the task of re-creation, each with his own little pen and parchment. We do not know the great poetry of the past – the libraries are dust. But I think that Shakespeare in his lifetime made perhaps the millionth part of a single letter of the Word. Will the complete Word ever be spoken for the second time? When it is, stranger, then the world will be perfect again, and time will have an end' . . . He looked at his manuscript. 'This is my contribution to the Word – such a sound as a speck of dust might make falling on grass – no more.' He sighed among the harsh wine fumes. He did not speak again. When the flagon was empty he went to his bed. I was glad to leave the house of that gloomy man before dawn next morning, breakfastless. From the vineyards the harvesters greeted me in the first light.

They would enjoy the masque two weeks later, whatever the only begetter thought of it.

In a Mexican village the poet had done nothing for twenty years. 'The bird inside me has stopped singing,' he said. He was quite cheerful about it. The villagers bore him no grudge. The bird had stopped singing, there was nothing more to be said. The poet in the next village had to compose two entertainments each year, one for the songless village. 'I say to them,' said the once-poet, '"I gave you many fine poems before the bird stopped singing. They still remember these poems in The House of the Old Men. Why not perform them again, with the dances and tunes to go with them?" . . . But no, they refuse to do that. There must be a new entertainment each year. It is a sign of death, they say, to repeat a masque. These endless repetitions, they say, the worship of the husks of dead art – that was one symptom of the sickness of pre-Village Man.'

I left him with the wish that the bird inside him might soon start singing again. He laughed, delighted at the possibility; but then shook his head.

In a Swedish village the poet was a great heretic. His poems and plays were all about machines: tanks, tractors, motorcars, aeroplanes, the internal combustion engine ... 'These great times will come again', said the young blond visionary. 'Next time we will know how to use them without danger to ourselves. There must come an end to this cutting of corn with scythes, and sailing out into the teeth of the fishing wind with only a patched sail! That is barbarism!' ... A hundred years ago he could not have said such a thing; he would have been ritually strangled if he had whispered a tenth part of it. Even in some villages today they would see to it that his mouth was stopped. But in all the villages in that part of Sweden the people have arrived at such a mildness of the spirit that they are tolerant of their poet. They take part in his midwinter drama, in which the heroes are made of metal and have oil for their blood, but they manage to do it in such subtle ways that the drama, far from being a noble vision of the future, is reduced to burlesque, and becomes by implication a celebration of the pastoral simplicity they have attained. 'The truth is,' said this poet to me, 'they have not sufficient talent to perform my work properly.'

Once I came to a village in an African jungle. The poet, a little old withered man, made many poems every day, sometimes as many as ten. They were all about the praying mantis, its wisdom and beauty and power. He clicked with his teeth, made deep clonking noises with his tongue against his palate. 'Praying mantis, my delight, my brother, you wise one . . .' He had never composed a poem on any other subject. I could imagine, in the darkness of that jungle, the village performers declaring all one night the joy that the universe felt for that stick of an insect.

Somewhere in Siberia, one spring, I stayed several nights in the house of the poet. This man did not compose in any language. He repeated a few poems to me – not one word was familiar; there was a syllable now and then that seemed to come out of the speech of the people. (You will have to believe me when I say that I have a fair knowledge of many languages, having been on the roads since I was a boy.) I listened to his theories late into the night. I only partially understood what he was trying to do. There was some kind of kinship, it seemed, between the speech of a people and their natural surroundings. Birds, winds, waterfalls, the coil of a river, the shape of a hill, even the hush of falling snow, moulded speech. 'That is why the speech of this village is subtly different from the way they talk in that village twelve miles back, where you stayed last night. It is a matter of the utmost fascination. Human speech cannot be left to itself – it will wither – its roots are deep in the elements, our tongues take nourishment from the splash of a salmon in the river, the black howl of blizzards, the thunders and glories of the Siberian spring. So, in my poems I am steeping speech in elemental sound. This is a powerful, mysterious, and dangerous art. It will be the death of me before long' . . . He was so absorbed in theories about his art that I was poorly fed and sheltered, day after day. As I was leaving the village, having thanked him at his door for the veiled but stimulating vistas he had opened for me, I met The Blacksmith at the end of the street. 'Tell me,' I said, 'how is it possible for his masques to be performed? People can neither speak them nor understand them.' 'That is true,' said The Blacksmith. 'I used to take part in the midwinter masque when I was young – now I stand among the audience. Always we feel that we are one with the earth. We understand the silence of stones. We reaffirm our kinship with fish and stars'. . . .

Once, when I was younger, I nearly died among ice. Why I wandered so far north I can't remember – a young man must always be tempting providence.

I had no food in that white wilderness for three days, or maybe four. I remember biting my right hand like a wolf and sucking the warm blood. ('Better you than the wolves,' I said to myself.) I expected such a grey savage death.

Instead it was a small befurred man with a face genial as the sun who found me. In a very short time I was sitting in his ice-house, among a cluster of ice-houses. There were no legends over these doors, for the villagers could not read or write.

They spoke a language I did not understand, too.

My rescuer gave me to know that I should spend the night in his house. Obstinate as ever, I shook my head. I made signs to him – striking an imaginary harp, kissing an imaginary pipe and making my fingers dance. At last he understood. His smile was broader than ever. I would rather pass the night in The House of the Poet than with him. He was not in the least put out.

A boy took me by the hand and led me through a squat white labyrinth of a village to a house exactly the same as all the others. Inside the smells of blubber and fish oil were dreadful. I discovered, to my deep surprise, that the poet could speak several languages. He had been 'a wandering one' in his youth. He had gone through Scandinavia and Central Europe; he had lingered among the isles of Greece for a while; then he had walked eastwards, through Persia and India, intending to get as far as Japan. But while he was being entertained by a village in the Himalayan foothills, word had come to him that he was wanted back home. The poet in his village on the shore of Baffin Bay had died; it was for him now to make the songs of his people. I interrupted him – how had this news come to him? The poet in the Indian village had told him, he said. All true poets all over the world have this gift of divination – an exquisite network of sensibility binds them together. (I had not known this before.)

Meantime the igloo grew more and more uncomfortable. People were crowding into it – men, women, children, even infants. The air got steadily hotter and ranker. There was no room to sit – we crowded shoulder to shoulder. Others stood in the freezing night outside. All waited patiently for the poet to begin.

The words flowered out of a long deep silence.

I did not understand it, of course. The mouth cried, whispered, sang, whistled, shouted. There were seven poems in the recital. At the end of each one the villagers showed their delight with silence and sun-looks. Nowhere had I seen happier faces.

At last the recital was over; it must have been an integrated group of lyrics. They went away as mildly as they had come, leaving only that intolerable fish-stench behind, and a silence enriched.

I said to the poet when we were alone again, 'These are happy poems, surely.' 'All poetry is gay,' he answered. 'Are they love poems?' I asked. 'One is,' he said.

The young man says, "Come into my hut."

The girl answers, "I have a bird for a lover."

The man, "I will hunt that bird. There will be red drops in the snow."

The girl answers, "No.

For the bird is to take me under his wing into the north.

His nest is on a black cliff. You will never find us."

'There is the hunting poem then.

The boy says, "Tomorrow I will hunt for the first time.

Beware, walrus. Beware, reindeer.

I am coming to play at arrows with you."

At the end of the snow

The great bear stood, who does not like the game of arrows.

'Then there is the poem of the whale.

> The whale grew tired of eating little cold fishes.
> It swallowed the sun.
> Then fell the black time, winter.
> The people said, "Must we always stumble about in
>   blackness?
> The stars are too feeble.
> We want our children to play among the beautiful
>   snow crystals."
> They hunted down that whale.
> They filled a hundred lamps from his belly.
> Just when the last lamp was empty
> The sun peeped at us over a low rim of ice.
> Dead whale, drowned hunters, devoured sun.
> Inside this circle all dances are made.

'There follows the aurora poem.

> "Come, children, into my house of crystal.
> Come, the feast is set.
> Here kings sit and eat, and heroes, and the bravest hunters."
> We are bidden, night after night,
> To feast in that house of marvellous shining.
> But we linger here sick,
> Growing old, filled with regrets, in hovels of snow.

'My own favourite is the poem of the women.

> "Go away, man.
> I will not open my door to you.
> Quench your fires in the snow.
> I will never leave the dancing children."

The witch moon kissed me as I slept.
I am her blood-servant now.
She has put a sign on my doorpost.
Now many hunters come. All are welcome.

'Did you not see how the old men smiled at the poem of childhood?

"I am a salmon."
"I am a bear cub."
"I am a reindeer."
"I am the moon."
"I am the hole in the ice where ivory is."
Stop your games.
Three hunters are coming to teach you the trade –
Winter, Age, Death.

'You understand, stranger, these translations I am making for you are poor things, withered leaves plucked from the tree of our language. (I remember groves, woods, forest.) The sequence ends with the winter poem.

I don't mind winter.
I listen to stories.
I make love.
I don't mind winter now, in my youth.
My eyes, some morning,
Will be caught like two fish in the sun's net.
Tell me, poet
The cruellest things that can happen.'

'Sombre songs,' I said. 'Yet the people tonight drank them like wine, cup after cup.'

'Wine,' said the poet, and smiled. 'I remember the raptures and rages in the house of the Vintner when I was one of the wanderers. Here in the far north is neither grape nor barley. We have only poetry. The word whispers, like a ferment, in what seems to be the futility, pain, idiocy of life. It is my duty to attend to the pure essences. And I am potter here as well as Vintner. I make cups that remain beautiful in their withering hands.'

In that latitude there is a night six months long. The arctic poet tried to give me some idea of the masque that takes place in the ultimate darkness. I could only guess at the glory of it. Since – as in the lyric – this people, though eternally invited, can never enter the house of the Aurora Borealis, the imagination of the poet builds about them a palace of unimagined beauty, their primitive words and gestures are clothed in ceremony, and there they kept a tranced revelry for one night in the year.

Now, thirty years later, I find myself for the first time among the mountains of Scotland.

Andrina

Andrina comes to see me every afternoon in winter, just before it gets dark. She lights my lamp, sets the peat fire in a blaze, sees that there is enough water in my bucket that stands on the wall niche. If I have a cold (which isn't often, I'm a tough old seaman) she fusses a little, puts an extra peat or two on the fire, fills a stone hot-water bottle, puts an old thick jersey about my shoulders.

That good Andrina – as soon as she has gone, after her occasional ministrations to keep pleurisy or pneumonia away – I throw the jersey from my shoulders and mix myself a toddy, whisky and hot water and sugar. The hot-water bottle in the bed will be cold long before I climb into it, round about midnight: having read my few chapters of Conrad.

Towards the end of February last year I did get a very bad cold, the worst for years. I woke up, shuddering, one morning, and crawled between fire and cupboard, gasping like a fish out of water, to get a breakfast ready. (Not that I had an appetite.) There was a stone lodged somewhere in my right lung, that blocked my breath.

I forced down a few tasteless mouthfuls, and drank hot ugly tea. There was nothing to do after that but get back to bed with my book. Reading was no pleasure either – my head was a block of pulsing wood.

'Well,' I thought, 'Andrina'll be here in five or six hours' time. She won't be able to do much for me. This cold, or flu, or whatever it is, will run its course. Still, it'll cheer me to see the girl.'

Andrina did not come that afternoon. I expected her with the first cluster of shadows: the slow lift of the latch, the low greeting, the 'tut-tut' of sweet disapproval at some of the things she saw as soon as the lamp was burning ... I was, though, in that strange fatalistic mood that sometimes accompanies a fever, when a man doesn't really care what happens. If the house was to go on fire, he might think, 'What's this, flames?' and try to save himself: but it wouldn't horrify or thrill him.

I accepted that afternoon, when the window was blackness at last with a first salting of stars, that for some reason or another Andrina couldn't come. I fell asleep again.

I woke up. A grey light at the window. My throat was dry – there was a fire in my face – my head was more throbbingly wooden than ever. I got up, my feet flashing with cold pain on the stone floor, drank a cup of water, and climbed back into bed. My teeth actually clacked and chattered in my head for five minutes or more – a thing I had only read about before.

I slept again, and woke up just as the winter sun was making brief stained glass of sea and sky. It was, again, Andrina's time. Today there were things she could do for me: get aspirin from the shop, surround my greyness with three or four very hot bottles, mix the strongest toddy in the world. A few words from her would be like a bell-buoy to a sailor lost in a hopeless fog. She did not come.

She did not come again on the third afternoon.

I woke, tremblingly, like a ghost in a hollow stone. It was black night. Wind soughed in the chimney. There was, from time to time, spatters of rain against the window. It was the longest night of my life. I experienced, over again, some of the dull and sordid events of my life; one certain episode was repeated again and again like an ancient gramophone record being put on time after time, and a rusty needle scuttling over worn wax. The shameful images broke and melted at last into sleep. Love had been killed but many ghosts had been awakened.

When I woke up I heard, for the first time in four days, the sound of a voice. It was Stanley the postman speaking to the dog of Bighouse. 'There now, isn't that loud big words to say so early? It's just a letter for Minnie, a drapery catalogue. There's a good boy, go and tell Minnie I have a love letter for her . . . Is that you, Minnie? I thought old Ben here was going to tear me in pieces then. Yes, Minnie, a fine morning, it is that . . .'

I have never liked that postman – a servile lickspittle to anyone he thinks is of consequence in the island – but that morning he came past my window like a messenger of light. He opened the door without knocking (I am a person of small consequence). He said, 'Letter from a long distance, skipper.' He put the letter on the chair nearest the door. I was shaping my mouth to say, 'I'm not very well. I wonder . . .' If words did come out of my mouth, they must have been whispers, a ghost appeal. He looked at the dead fire and the closed window. He said, 'Phew! It's fuggy in here, skipper. You want to get some fresh air . . .' Then he went, closing the door behind him. (He would not, as I had briefly hoped, be taking word to Andrina, or the doctor down in the village.)

I imagined, until I drowsed again, Captain Scott writing his few last words in the Antarctic tent.

In a day or two, of course, I was as right as rain; a tough old salt like me isn't killed off that easily.

But there was a sense of desolation on me. It was as if I had been betrayed – deliberately kicked when I was down. I came almost to the verge of self-pity. Why had my friend left me in my bad time?

Then good sense asserted itself. 'Torvald, you old fraud,' I said to myself. 'What claim have you got, anyway, on a winsome twenty-year-old? None at all. Look at it this way, man – you've had a whole winter of her kindness and consideration. She brought a lamp into your dark time: ever since the Harvest Home when (like a fool) you had too much whisky and she supported you home and rolled you unconscious into bed . . . Well, for some reason or another Andrina hasn't been able to come these last few days. I'll find out, today, the reason.'

It was high time for me to get to the village. There was not a crust or scraping of butter or jam in the cupboard. The shop was also the Post Office – I had to draw two weeks' pension. I promised myself a pint or two in the pub, to wash the last of that sickness out of me.

It struck me, as I trudged those two miles, that I knew nothing about Andrina at all. I had never asked, and she had said nothing. What was her father? Had she sisters and brothers? Even the district of the island where she lived had never cropped up in our talks. It was sufficient that she came every evening, soon after sunset, and performed her quiet ministrations, and lingered awhile; and left a peace behind – a sense that everything in the house was pure, as if it had stood with open doors and windows at the heart of a clean summer wind.

Yet the girl had never done, all last winter, asking me questions about myself – all the good and bad and exciting things that had happened to me. Of course I told her this and that. Old men love to make their past vivid and significant, to stand in relation to a few trivial events in as fair and bold a light as possible. To add spice to those bits of autobiography, I let on to have been a reckless wild daring lad – a known and somewhat feared figure in many a port from Hong Kong to Durban to San Francisco. I presented to her a character somewhere between Captain Cook and Captain Hook.

And the girl loved those pieces of mingled fiction and fact; turning the wick of my lamp down a little to make everything more mysterious, stirring the peats into new flowers of flame . . .

One story I did not tell her completely. It is the episode in my life that hurts me whenever I think of it (which is rarely, for that time is locked up and the key dropped deep in the Atlantic: but it haunted me – as I hinted – during my recent illness).

On her last evening at my fireside I did, I know, let drop a hint or two to Andrina – a few half-ashamed half-boastful fragments. Suddenly, before I had finished – as if she could foresee and suffer the end – she had put a white look and a cold kiss on my cheek, and gone out at the door; as it turned out, for the last time.

Hurt or no, I will mention it here and now. You who look and listen are not Andrina – to you it will seem a tale of crude country manners: a mingling of innocence and heartlessness.

In the island, fifty years ago, a young man and a young woman came together. They had known each other all their lives up to then, of course – they had sat in the school room together – but on one particular day in early summer this boy from one croft and this girl from another distant croft looked at each other with new eyes.

After the midsummer dance in the barn of the big house, they walked together across the hill through the lingering enchantment of twilight – it is never dark then – and came to the rocks and the sand and sea just as the sun was rising. For an hour and more they lingered, tranced creatures indeed, beside those bright sighings and swirlings. Far in the north-east the springs of day were beginning to surge up.

It was a tale soaked in the light of a single brief summer. The boy and the girl lived, it seemed, on each other's heartbeats. Their parents' crofts were miles apart, but they contrived to meet, as if by accident, most days; at the crossroads, in the village shop, on the side of the hill. But really these places were too earthy and open – there were too many windows – their feet drew secretly night after night to the beach with its bird-cries, its cave, its changing waters. There no one disturbed their communings – the shy touches of hand and mouth – the words that were nonsense but that became in his mouth some-times a sweet mysterious music – 'Sigrid'.

The boy – his future, once this idyll of a summer was ended, was to go to the university in Aberdeen and there study to be a man of security and position and some leisure – an estate his crofting ancestors had never known.

No such door was to open for Sigrid – she was bound to the few family acres – the digging of peat – the making of butter and cheese. But for a short time only. Her place would be beside the young man with whom she shared her breath and heartbeats, once he had gained his teacher's certificate. They walked day after day beside shining beckoning waters.

But one evening, at the cave, towards the end of that summer, when the corn was taking a first burnish, she had something urgent to tell him – a tremulous perilous secret thing. And at once the summertime spell was broken. He shook his head. He looked away. He looked at her again as if she were some slut who had insulted him. She put out her hand to him, her mouth trembling. He thrust her away. He turned. He ran up the beach and along the sand track to the road above; and the ripening fields gathered him soon and hid him from her.

And the girl was left alone at the mouth of the cave, with the burden of a greater more desolate mystery on her.

The young man did not go to any seat of higher learning. That same day he was at the emigration agents in Hamnavoe, asking for an urgent immediate passage to Canada or Australia or South Africa – anywhere.

Thereafter the tale became complicated and more cruel and pathetic still. The girl followed him as best she could to his transatlantic refuge a month or so later; only to discover that the bird had flown. He had signed on a ship bound for furthest ports, as an ordinary seaman: so she was told, and she was more utterly lost than ever.

That rootlessness, for the next half century, was to be his life: making salt circles about the globe, with no secure foot-age anywhere. To be sure, he studied his navigation manuals, he rose at last to be a ship's officer, and more. The barren years became a burden to him. There is a time, when white hairs come, to turn one's back on long and practised skills and arts, that have long since lost their savours. This the sailor did, and he set his course homeward to his island; hoping that fifty winters might have scabbed over an old wound.

And so it was, or seemed to be. A few remembered him vaguely. The name of a certain vanished woman – who must be elderly, like himself, now – he never mentioned, nor did he ever hear it uttered. Her parents' croft was a ruin, a ruckle of stones on the side of the hill. He climbed up to it one day and looked at it coldly. No sweet ghost lingered at the end of the house, waiting for a twilight summons – 'Sigrid . . .'

I got my pension cashed, and a basket full of provisions, in the village shop. Tina Stewart the postmistress knew everybody and everything; all the shifting subtle web of relationship in

the island. I tried devious approaches with her. What was new
or strange in the island? Had anyone been taken suddenly ill?
Had anybody – a young woman, for example – had to leave
the island suddenly, for whatever reason? The hawk eye of
Miss Stewart regarded me long and hard. No, said she, she
had never known the island quieter. Nobody had come or
gone. 'Only yourself, Captain Torvald, has been bedridden, I
hear. You better take good care of yourself, you all alone up
there. There's still a greyness in your face . . .' I said I was sorry
to take her time up. Somebody had mentioned a name –
Andrina – to me, in a certain connection. It was a matter of
no importance. Could Miss Stewart, however, tell me which
farm or croft this Andrina came from?

Tina looked at me a long while, then shook her head.
There was nobody of that name – woman or girl or child – in
the island; and there never had been, to her certain
knowledge.

I paid for my messages, with trembling fingers, and left.

I felt the need of a drink. At the bar counter stood Isaac
Irving the landlord. Two fishermen stood at the far end, next
the fire, drinking their pints and playing dominoes.

I said, after the third whisky, 'Look, Isaac, I suppose the
whole island knows that Andrina – that girl – has been coming
all winter up to my place, to do a bit of cleaning and washing
and cooking for me. She hasn't been for a week now and more.
Do you know if there's anything the matter with her?' (What I
dreaded to hear was that Andrina had suddenly fallen in love;
her little rockpools of charity and kindness drowned in that
huge incoming flood; and had cloistered herself against the
time of her wedding.)

Isaac looked at me as if I was out of my mind. 'A young
woman,' said he. 'A young woman up at your house? A home
help, is she? I didn't know you had a home help. How many

whiskies did you have before you came here, skipper, eh?'
And he winked at the two grinning fishermen over by the
fire.

I drank down my fourth whisky and prepared to go.

'Sorry, skipper,' Isaac Irving called after me. 'I think you
must have imagined that girl, whatever her name is, when
the fever was on you. Sometimes that happens. The only
women I saw when I had the flu were hags and witches.
You're lucky, skipper – a honey like Andrina!'

I was utterly bewildered. Isaac Irving knows the island and
its people, if anything, even better than Tina Stewart. And he
is a kindly man, not given to making fools of the lost and the
delusion-ridden.

Going home, March airs were moving over the island. The
sky, almost overnight, was taller and bluer. Daffodils trum-
peted, silently, the entry of spring from ditches here and
there. A young lamb danced, all four feet in the air at once.

I found, lying on the table, unopened, the letter that had been
delivered three mornings ago. There was an Australian post-
mark. It had been posted in late October.

'I followed your young flight from Selskay half round the
world, and at last stopped here in Tasmania, knowing that it
was useless for me to go any farther. I have kept a silence too,
because I had such regard for you that I did not want you to
suffer as I had, in many ways, over the years. We are both old,
maybe I am writing this in vain, for you might never have
returned to Selskay; or you might be dust or salt. I think, if
you are still alive and (it may be) lonely, that what I will write
might gladden you, though the end of it is sadness, like so
much of life. Of your child – our child – I do not say anything,
because you did not wish to acknowledge her. But that child

had, in her turn, a daughter, and I think I have seen such sweetness but rarely. I thank you that you, in a sense (though unwillingly), gave that light and goodness to my age. She would have been a lamp in your winter, too, for often I spoke to her about you and that long-gone summer we shared, which was, to me at least, such a wonder. I told her nothing of the end of that time, that you and some others thought to be shameful. I told her only things that came sweetly from my mouth. And she would say, often, "I wish I knew that grandfather of mine. Gran, do you think he's lonely? I think he would be glad of somebody to make him a pot of tea and see to his fire. Some day I'm going to Scotland and I'm going to knock on his door, wherever he lives, and I'll do things for him. Did you love him very much, gran? He must be a good person, that old sailor, ever to have been loved by you. I *will* see him. I'll hear the old stories from his own mouth. Most of all, of course, the love story – for you, gran, tell me nothing about that . . ." I am writing this letter, Bill, to tell you that this can never now be. Our granddaughter Andrina died last week, suddenly, in the first stirrings of spring . . .'

Later, over the fire, I thought of the brightness and burgeoning and dew that visitant had brought across the threshold of my latest winter, night after night; and of how she had always come with the first shadows and the first star; but there, where she was dust, a new time was brightening earth and sea.

The Day of the Ox

There are months and years when nothing happens. Nothing has happened here since I was a child, such as happened in the ancient stories of the coast.

There is always a time of full nets and empty nets.

There is a laden barn or an empty barn: the worm has been at the root, sun and rain have been at odds with the green shoots, the people have made a wrong dance at midsummer round the fire on the hill. Mostly, it is a barn half way between plenty and dearth.

But a life-relish has gone out of the people. Why? We have been at peace for a generation. No ships have sailed from the Minch with a sharp gleam here and there, at prow or amid-ships.

The old burnt skulls knew such disturbances. Death sometimes made itself a feast in the village – old men and children, shepherd and fisherman and ploughman, knelt and fell before the knives of the southerners. Or, some winter, a fever burned them to the skull.

Yet we have their fine songs. The poet remembers a hundred rhymes and stories out of that hard time.

For thirty years there has been no new song on this quiet coast.

One evening, just before harvest, I went with others to the chief's house. He would tell us what things were to be done in the morning – if the weather was good – into what corner the first sickle must go, which women could be spared for gleaning and the binding of sheaves. The old man pointed at me – 'You will put the sickle in first.'

Heavy with all the suns of that good summer, I must have dropped into sleep where I sat among the harvesters.

I dreamed.

A man, a stranger, came into the chief's house. He said nothing. The chief's girl took a fish from the embers and offered it to the stranger, and a piece of bread. He took the food and ate it thanklessly beside the fire. Nor did he look any man or woman in the face. The girl had blown the hearth into flames. The man took off his coat, and his arm was golden-haired, as if it was circled by a harvest wind. And then he took off his woven hat, and a torrent of hair as bright as the sun fell over his shoulders.

The girl cried out with amazement.

Having eaten and licked his fingers, the man took his coat about him and left the hut, without a word or a sign of thanks. It was as if to him we were a company of shadows.

When I woke up, the people were sitting silently round the fire in the chief's house. Usually before we go to our separate huts, the poet tells an old story. Tonight, on the eve of harvest, the Song of Bread should have been on his tongue: an old blessing, first uttered on the coast a hundred years ago. But the poet was silent. At last he said, 'I have had an evil dream. A man out of a time to come was here. He left a shadow in this house that will never go away. I am cold. I will say no more.'

The girl said, 'I have not seen a man so tall and bright and handsome. It was a dream. There are no such men in the world. I was glad to give him fish and bread in my dream.'

Some of the other villagers said that they too had fallen asleep, and dreamed of an arrogant greedy sunlike stranger.

'I dreamed the same dream,' said the chief. 'I tell you this, it was a good dream, now on the eve of harvest. Such brightness, such greed, such thanklessness. For so the elements work, in ways different from our ways. The earth takes our sweat and blood, and sometimes is generous to us, and sometimes is stingy. The sea too, it covers the shore stones with twisting silver, or else it drowns a young man in his curragh and leaves the village hungry. That's the way of the elements. As for us, in our dream we dealt courteously with the stranger, and that is how it should be, as far as we understand things. . . . That golden thankless man, I tell you, is a good augury for the harvest.'

Nothing happens along this coast. In the old days, after harvest, young men would go with knives into a boat and sail to some hidden island, where they were not known, and plunder, and come home again with pieces of silver, and blood on their daggers. But the last two generations have not known such adventure. The village has settled into a grey peace.

The dream that had come upon the village was whispered among the other villages of the coast. We suffered much mockery because of the dream. They laughed behind their hands. What kind of honey and heather ale had we drunk that night? How much extra malt had the brewing wife poured into the vat? Had there been many sore heads in our village the next morning?

'Let them mock on,' said the chief. 'The scarecrow has more understanding than them.'

It seemed that the dream was a good augury. We reaped a bigger harvest than for many years.

In the time between equinox and solstice, there was no storm or rough winds on the sea. The fishing boats came to shore day after day with torrents of living silver.

I think that that midwinter was the merriest time I had known in the village. Once or twice, the mouth of the poet trembled towards a new song, but nothing new came, only the old songs of snow and fire, darkness and drinking and beached whales.

After that solstice, the chief became very bent and grey, as if a shadow had passed into him.

But he did not die.

Winter sifted into the hut of the blacksmith, and soaked into his flesh and gnawed at his marrow; and soon Blok was a burnt skull in the cairn. A child wept for Blok at the door of the House of the Dead.

The snow of winter was at last only a streak or two on Kierfea across the Sound.

'It's time now,' said the chief in his new grey voice, 'to yoke the oxen.'

It was time to yoke the first ox and unearth the plough from the summertime debris of the barn.

The monotony of another summer was about to begin. (And why had the vanished poet, who was a charred tongueless skull in the cave, why had he made such fine songs about plough and harrow, and the dialogue of seed and the ever-brightening sun, while our poet had nothing new to say about such things, but chanted over and over again the fire-forged and hammered words of the old poet, a tarnished hoard?)

It was appointed to me, that spring, to open the door of the byre and to say to the ox, 'Come, ox, it is time for us to work together, it is time to begin the ceremony of corn.'

Then I had to loosen the ox from his chain at the wall, and to lead him forth into the light. He was so used, the ox, to the winter dark of the byre and the lantern twice a day, that his first sight of the sun put a kind of madness on him. He pranced, he smote the air with his hoof, his tail lashed, he put down his head as if he would charge at the horizon and break it! But soon, the yoke at his neck, he grew patient again, a friend to the village and the hungers of the village.

As I led the ox to the big field, followed by a crowd of villagers old and young, I saw the gulls rising from the crag in fierce broken circles. There had not been such rage and commotion among the cliff faces since the three whales had stranded there ten winters ago.

I topped the ridge, gently urging the ox (and the cries of the villagers behind were almost a match for the blizzarding gulls).

Below me, on the shore, stood the winter stranger – the man in the dream – and a dozen others with him. Each man carried an axe. A ship like a great hollow bird was anchored in the Sound.

I pointed.

The villagers turned. Their mouths were suddenly silent, as they were gathered into a dream they would not wake from. They bowed their heads.

The strangers stood unmoving on the shore, among axe-glitterings.

The ox turned his horns towards the destroyers. He knelt, offering them his services.

The Masked Fisherman

A crofter-fisherman belonging to Sumburgh in Shetland stood beside his boat that was hauled high on the beach. Sometimes he looked up at the shallow cliff and the cliff path leading from the road above down to the boulders and the sand. Sometimes he looked at the sea. The wind had whipped up the waves; white crests flew here and there. It might come to a storm – there was no telling. The sooner the lines were set the better. But the man who worked the boat with him hadn't come – he was late – very likely he had been drinking in the ale-house beyond midnight.

One thing was sure: Guthorm couldn't fish by himself, especially in such a rising wind. And if he couldn't put to sea, it would be a hungry weekend for himself and those squalling children. Gilli the tosspot: he kept a wife and three sisters and an aged toothless granny and two daughters, one dark and one fair. They never starved: drunk or sober, Gilli always managed to scrounge or steal or borrow enough to keep the sea fruit in their mouths, even if it was only a cod's head stuffed with liver and oatmeal.

Why did Guthorm share the boat with Gilli? He liked the man, for all his unreliability, for all his laziness, for all his lies. How comes there ever to be affection between one man and another – even between a good man and a sly shiftless man? Guthorm thought, *He makes me laugh, that Gilli* – all those stories about the women in his household and their ways and words with each other and with the world: yes, but whenever Gilli sat down at fire or at board, how all his women from the oldest to the youngest turned their faces against him, and soon railed at him in one wild discordant chorus! The good fisherman could not but laugh at Gilli's stories – and whether they were true or false made no difference, the laughter leavened the dullness and dutifulness of his days.

Well then: the wind was rising, the now favourable tide would soon be on the turn. Gilli had let him down again. Gilli was lying in a drunken sleep that not even the seven fierce-tongued women could break.

There was the rent to pay to the laird, taxes to the earl. Those hard men took no account of ill luck or incapacity. Their due of fish had to be laid at the heraldic door of the Hall, in foison or in famine.

Guthorm left the boat and began to walk up the beach. And there, coming down the path from the road above he saw a young man. Old Guthorm squinnied at him: he knew every man in the parish by his walk and the set of his shoulders: but this man was a stranger. As if to emphasise his anonymity, he was wearing a hood that half covered his face. He approached Guthorm with a lithe sure step: he was used to going on seaweed and on great boulders, that much was sure.

'What's wrong, old man?' he called as he approached. 'It's a good fishing day! Why have you turned your back on the sea?'

The music his mouth made, that was strange too: but it was agreeable, very pleasant, it had a lilt to it – and it seemed neither inquisitive nor over-familiar nor hectoring. It was as one honest man speaks to another.

'I should be fishing,' said Guthorm, 'and I would be fishing, but my friend who shares the boat with me, I think he isn't very well today.'

'Let me take his place,' said the stranger. 'I know a thing or two about the sea and the ways of fish.'

There was something very likeable about the young man – Ah, he would have liked such a one for a son! But his daughters were still at the age of playing 'trolls and princesses' in the little kale-yard of Quoy. And hungry they would be, and their thin washed-out mother, and himself too, if the boat wasn't launched sometime today.

'You can come and welcome,' said Guthorm.

Together they pushed the little yole out into the waves.

How Guthorm wished, before the fisherman's sun had climbed but a few golden steps up the sky, that he had kept his little boat noust-bound that day. It was a coarse-looking craft, lying under the rock – but once afloat it was a delicate dancer. For his guest, sitting at the oars, kept edging the boat in among the fiercest darkest tide-swirlings of Sumburgh. Ah, his boat – as desperately he leaned over the side and hauled in haddock after haddock – how often in the next hour he thought it would be upset, and himself and the white-cowled stranger thrown out and drowned, and their bones gathered forever into fiercest salt shuttles! Time after time, as Guthorm dragged in more fish still, he cried over his shoulder to the oarsman to have a care! To get out of these dangerous whirls and swirls into calmer water!

Either the younger man was deaf or mad; for, if anything, he set the bow further in towards the deepest vortices of the tide-race, and Guthorm was thrown back and fore among the thwarts – never however letting go of his line that still as he hauled it in, burgeoned with ever more splendid fish. But what is the good of a magnificent catch, thought Guthorm, if you drown before you can eat it? And, wedging himself against the

stern-thwart, he unhooked the strongest flashingest cod he
had seen all that summer.

Now the boat was whirling and plunging in the tide-race,
well into it, and the oarsman was standing up and laughing
as he tugged at this oar or that, guiding Guthorm's yole into
the black turbulent heart of the stream where, it seemed, the
strongest sea creatures pastured. (So Guthorm thought, but
all his sea-life he had kept prudently to the edges: where, up
to now, he had pulled in a sufficiency.)

Cod after splendid cod, and once an immense halibut! The
bottom of the boat had layers of shrugging twisting fish now,
slowly stilling and tarnishing. Guthorm thought, as he
dragged another cod from the hook: 'This is the day of my
death, for sure! How strange, the sea is giving me more treasure today than ever before. It is sad, my children and that
poor wife of mine won't know anything about it. This huge
haul of fish will sink to the bottom with me. How those little
orphans of mine will have to pick about in the ebb for whelks
and mussels! They'll never know what a rich splendid fisherman their father got to be on the day of his death! It is sad
indeed' . . . Even while Guthorm was thinking those things,
he was aware of a surge of joy rising through him. Surge after
surge, a reckless gaiety in his veins responded to the tumult
of the waters. Spindrift clung to his beard, his arms to the
elbows were blue and chilled, fish by fish he thumbed and
flung from the hooks (only a hook here and there was empty);
and Guthorm heard strange sounds issuing from his throat.
He was laughing out of deep enjoyment for the first time
since the grey and silver had come into his black beard. In the
sagas, it was chanted that this hero and that had gone to his
death, in battle or in tempest, laughing!

'They'll never believe,' he thought, 'that Guthorm, the
gloomy old crofter of Quoy, died like a hero!'

A splendid cod yelled soundlessly from its torn mouth, and was thrown (threshing) on the heap.

Who were those people standing on the shore? Guthorm flung spray from his eyes, and saw Gilli's women, the old and the young, standing at the big rock. Gilli's mother had her hands raised skyward, like a sybil. Oar and rowlock whirled up and hid them: another wave, and those women teetered in a full pellucid prism between sun and sea and stone: till another thong of spindrift cut Guthorm across the eyes.

'I think there are not quite so many fish now,' he said.

So suddenly that it startled him, the mad thing of a boat rode placid on a slow pulse of sea. Guthorm pulled in naked hooks.

'That was good fishing, old one!' said the stranger. 'Well done.'

He dipped the oars, making towards the noust and the rock and the waiting women.

'You swine!' Guthorm yelled at him. 'You scoundrel! Thief and murderer! You all but made a widow and orphans today! Fool that you are, you know nothing about the dangerous waters out there. Have you never heard of Sumburgh roost? If I was a younger man, I would settle things with you – I would – be sure of it – before this day's sun went down! What kind of a man are you, anyway, muffling up your face in that hood? Not a monk, that's for sure. An outlaw, likely, that daren't show his face like an honest man!'

The boat rattled over the tidal stones, thudded gently and whispered on the sand. The fisherman and the stranger leapt ashore. Together they shoved and hauled the yole up the noust to the sheltering rock. It was twice as heavy now with its weight of fish.

The sky between sun and sea was a madhouse of gulls: a thousand flashing intersecting screaming arcs, circles, dips, flurries.

Gilli's women came about, but not too close on account of the stranger. One had a deep straw basket. Three carried sharpened knives.

'What are you wanting here?' cried Guthorm. 'There's no fish for you, not out of this boat! Go home, tell that drunkard of yours that I – that's to say, my friend here and I – have caught the biggest haul of fish that Shetland has seen this summer. See if that news will cure Gilli's hangover. Ale and fishing don't mix – tell your hero that. My friend here and I will divide the fish between us. So, off home with you, eat limpets and kale blades – that's all I have to say.'

But already the stranger was dividing his share of the catch among Gilli's women. With shameless hands they plucked the fish from him.

Turning to go, the shore breeze took the man's cowl and blew it back. His hair streamed out, gleaming. And an incense came from it – it enchanted the women's nostrils, fleetingly! The locks had been artfully cut, the curls (wind-lifted for a moment) stirred in bright cold clusters: not at all like their men-folk's cropped greasy shocks and stubbles.

Quickly the man pulled on his cowl again, as if anonymity was necessary both to himself and them.

The stranger walked up the sand-cut path towards the road. Lithely and easily he went: again, not at all like the crofters and fishermen who, after a morning's fishing, still kept for a time the sea-and-boat lurch and stagger. (Moreover, after the age of thirty or so, they began to stoop between plough and nets, thrawn and thwart with labour.)

And there, suddenly, the stranger was, sprawled on his face, his fingers clutching at tussocks of sea-pink and dockans! He had not looked where he was going – as folk who fish regularly for a living do – and he had stepped on a tassel of wet sea-weed.

At that, Gilli's fool of a wife began to cackle with mirth. She threw back her head and the strings of her neck tautened and she laughed, skirl after skirl.

The hooded man picked himself up. He turned and waved back at the woman. His teeth shone in the sun.

'You're a lot of trulls,' said old Guthorm to the women. 'But for that man it would have been a poor hungry weekend up at Gilli's house. Get home with you. Tell Gilli, I'll be looking for another man to go fishing with after midsummer.'

That same evening when the fishing women of Sumburgh were splitting and salting the day's catch, Einar of Gulberwick, a laird, rode down to the shore. The women turned their backs on Einar: one of them spat. Einar was not well liked by the common people. He was only happy when he was among men of rank and valour: councillors or merchants from Norway and Scotland. A surprising thing it was that Einar had come now and reined in his horse beside women stinking with fish guts. That he should speak to them was a thing unknown hitherto.

'Which of you women was it?' said the laird. 'One of you women did this terrible thing. It was enough to make my cheek blanch, hearing it. Are you not afraid of justice and punishment?'

Gilli's old granny turned and faced him. 'What are you talking about?' she cried. 'Have we stolen? Have we slandered the king or the bishop? Leave us alone.'

'Where did you get all those fish?' said Einar. 'Not from Gilli – he's been sleeping all day.'

'A man gave them to us,' said Gilli's tall black-headed daughter. 'A stranger that took Gilli's place in the yole this morning.'

'So,' said Einar, 'this man gave you all that fish. And one of you – some ignorant thankless hag – laughed at the man when he slipped among sea-weed. Do you not know who he was, that man?'

'His face was hidden,' said Gilli's cripple sister. 'He didn't speak like us.'

'That man,' said Einar of Gulberwick, 'is his grace the Earl Rögnvald Kolson, Lord of Orkney and Shetland and Caithness and Sutherland. That man is the living nephew of Magnus, our saint! To sneer at such a man, the way you did, is next door to treason. Earl Rögnvald is my guest up at Gulberwick. Earl Rögnvald could, if he liked, put you out on the roads to beg! I am very displeased.'

'Tell the earl we did not know,' said Gilli's wife. 'We're sorry. Tell the earl that.'

'*I* am displeased,' said Einar. 'But the strange thing is, Earl Rögnvald has been relishing the insult all day! He is a strange man, Earl Rögnvald. He has been making a poem about the incident all day, and laughing as he sets the hard stony sounds among the stream of the vowels.'

'I never thought,' said Gilli's wife, 'that I would ever be put in a poem!'

'So it was you that laughed,' said Einar. 'Let me think. The subtleties of a poem are lost on the likes of you. The earl – my guest – has studied the art of poetry long and hard. I don't understand poetry very well myself. Still, I am honoured that a poem should have been made under my roof by such an illustrious man. But I wish he had chosen a nobler theme.'

'You're lavish with words,' said Gilli's eldest sister, a tart one. 'We'd rather be hearing the poem.'

'It goes like this,' said the horseman.

The hooded fisherman,
    down on his face he goes.
Down among sand and seaweed
    he fouls his clothes!
From an old girl in the fish-gleams,
    mockery rose.
An earl in a fisherman's coat,
    who knows, who knows?
From mingling of lord and lieges
    a good grace grows.

The women listened, wondering.

   'I like that,' said Gilli's wife, 'better than all his fish. Tell Rögnvald Kolson that.'

The Christmas Dove

The rich merchant had a house on the hill outside the town. Servants came and went in the rooms, and tended the stable and garden and wells.

The merchant's children fed a dove in a golden cage, on cake and sweetmeats.

One day the smallest child left the cage door open, and the bird was up and away into the wind and sun. A servant tried to catch it, but it flew from his fingers and the servant measured his length in the dust.

Tearfully the children trooped into their father's office, to tell him about the lost dove.

'Tut-tut,' said he. 'Go away – I'm busy. Can't you see the clerks writing in the account books – a camel train leaves for Syria tomorrow. I've told you a hundred times not to come to the office during business hours . . . Sammy, tears is it? Why are you crying? The dove flown away – is that all? I'll buy three doves at the market tomorrow. Now go and leave us to get on with our work . . . Sixty bales of wool. A hundred jars of best oil . . .'

The merchant's children came out into the yard with dark stains on their faces.

There they saw a servant who was dust from head to foot, and with scratches on his arms. (This was the servant who had tried to catch the dove.) The children pointed at him. They laughed.

The dove was frightened. It had lived its whole life in the cage, from the time of the breaking of the egg, and the yellow wind and the stone alleys and the people coming and going in the village frightened it. The town birds darted at it. One bird cried: 'What are you, fluttering stranger?' And another with dusty wings said: 'Fly away, you milksop, there's little enough bread and seeds in this town . . .' A red bird screamed: 'Look out for the hawk! He lives up there, high, in his crystal cage of wind.'

Dearly the dove would have loved to be back in his safe golden cage in the merchant's villa, with children feeding him cherries and sweet crusts. But he did not know the way.

The dove flew out of the town, with its noise, dust and hostility. He darted over the desert sand, blown into undulations by the wind, with its palm trees and oases of water, and the golden eye of the sun above. Suddenly the sun was fractured, a wavering shadow covered the dove, and when he looked up what he saw was the yellow eye of the hawk.

The dove almost fell from the air, he was so frightened! But he gathered what wits and courage he had left, and he turned and flew towards a little green hill with sheep grazing on it, and a shepherd boy with a long crook. The dove fell panting on a stone. The sheep looked at him mildly. The boy broke off a piece of his loaf and offered it to him. Then the boy went down to the stream with a cup and filled it for the lost bird. The dove had never tasted anything as delicious as the oaten crust and the broken circles in the cup of water.

When the dove looked up, he could see the hawk going in a slow dark wheel northwards, after other prey.

'What's that boy up to now?' he heard a dark grumbling voice say. 'Look, boy, we don't keep you to feed a useless bird, we keep you to see that the sheep are safe. There's a ewe over there that's put her hoof in a bunch of thistles. See to it . . .'

Three shepherds came up from the village, each with a skin of wine, and all they did was complain about the village inn and the hordes of strangers in the village, and how the innkeeper was taking advantage of the situation to put up the price of his wine again. 'The scoundrel!' . . . 'An outrage.'

The boy ran to take the prickles out of the ewe's leg. The dove, frightened by the shepherds, unfurled his grey pinions to fly away. 'A good sign, a dove,' said one of the shepherds. 'It's usually that hawk after a new lamb.'

The dove scattered grey blessings on the sheep-fold, and flew south, away from the vigilant hawk. Now the sun had moved down the sky, and as it touched the horizon a flush engulfed the desert. Through an air red as wine the dove spied, far below, three travellers with laden camels. The travellers halted. They unburdened the camels and tethered them. They lit a fire under a rock. One opened a bag and passed food – oranges and cakes – to his companions. A silver wine flask shone in the firelight, passing from hand to hand, from mouth to mouth.

This too was a scene of peace. The dove trembled in the darkening air, then faltered and fell on the rock near the little tableau of travellers and animals, fire and refreshment.

'A dove!' cried one of the men. 'When it hung up there trembling, I thought it was our sign again.'

'Welcome, bird of peace,' said a deep gentle black voice. He offered a date to the dove. The dove took it into his beak.

'Fly away, dove,' said the third man. 'The desert is a danger-ous place for you to be. Aren't you afraid of the hawk? There'll be nothing left of you after sunrise if you don't find a lodging, nothing but a few bones in the sand.'

'The whole world is a dangerous place,' said the traveller whose voice was like a golden harp. 'The meaning of history will be Death, all time will be a scattering of bones, unless we find the place soon.'

The dove flew higher and higher up among the stars. He hung there, trembling, uncertain which way to turn. Then, over the desert, he saw far away the lights of the little town. That was where he belonged. There were the children and the golden cage and the circles of cake and milk and safety.

But where, in all that hundred houses great and small, was the house he belonged to?

The dove hovered over the darkling town, with its watchman's lantern at the main gate, and the lamps burning in prosperous windows, and candles in poor men's niches.

The dove was as lost as he had been all day. (And somewhere the hawk sat furled, nourishing himself with dreams of blood and death.)

The dove, stooping lower, saw a friend! The shepherd boy, with a small lamb in his arms, had entered the town gate and now had set his face to the darkest part of the town. The dove hovered above the boy and the lamb. 'I'll come to no harm,' said the dove to himself, 'if I stay near this boy.'

The boy stooped in at a dark door, where there was only a glim of light. Shadowy animals moved about inside. It was (thought the dove) the poorest house in the town. A tall shadow, a man, bent over a kneeling shadow that held a bundle in her arms.

The shepherd boy stood in the doorway, afraid to go in.

But the dove flew onto the boy's shoulder, and paused there a moment, and flew up to a cold rafter, and furled there, under the stars.

Dancey

A boy, William Ness of the croft of Eard, was on the hillside one day, walking into the tail of a blizzard, well muffled, to see if any of his father's sheep was in trouble, when he saw someone approaching slowly, rising and falling in the drifts.

The blizzard had moved on southwards, and now the sky was clearing over the islands. William Ness saw that the stumbling lost one was a woman. He had never seen her before. He approached, cautiously.

The boy asked her who she was, and where she was going. She only shook her head.

She was wearing a grey cloak with a hood, and it was soaked, more coldly and intensely than any hour-long blizzard could have penetrated. Her coat hung so heavy on her that she could hardly stand, much less walk.

After his faltering questions had got no answer, his first impulse was to turn and run home as fast as he could. Women from the sea still moved through the old men's winter stories, and that and a hundred other images were vivid and terrifying and beautiful in the boy's mind.

The young woman turned and pointed back towards the cliff and the open sea, whose cold blue brightness was beginning to be blurred and stained by another blizzard. Then, more insistently, she pointed to the sheep shelter further up the hill. She laid her cold wet hands on the boy, and she said over and over again, urgently, a single syllable that he could not understand. Her whole body yearned towards the sheep-fold, over which the first snowflakes of the oncoming blizzard were now drifting.

William Ness shook his head. Words were useless. He pointed towards the valley below and the seven or eight crofts with smoke rising from the chimneys. There they might be able to help her. There were a few old sailormen in the valley. Perhaps they would understand her tongue.

She consented, with a weary shake of the head, to go with him. Meantime the entire sound, and the coast beyond, were blotted out by the snow cloud. Flakes swirled thickly round the woman and the boy. A lamp had been lit in the croft of Hard. It dimmed in the storm's onset. The further crofts were ghost houses.

The nearness of help and warmth seemed to give the young woman new strength. She walked alongside him. He could smell the strong salt from her clothes. Once or twice she stumbled on a rock or in a rut. The boy was familiar with the ground. He held out his hand to her. The intense coldness of her clutch put a shudder through his body that reached as far as his heart. But he held on tight and led her down a sheep path.

Near a spring where some of the higher valley crofts got their water the stranger stopped. She bent down and kissed the boy. Then her knees gave and she collapsed.

'Come on!' said William Ness, shaking her. 'We're nearly there.'

She did not stir. He touched her face. His fingers flinched away from a still more bitter coldness. He turned and ran helter-skelter through the thickening blizzard to his parents' croft.

The room was full of neighbours. It was one of the last days of Yule, when the families trooped from croft to croft with little gifts.

William brought into the house a swirl of flakes. The flame in the lamp leapt in the draught.

'Shut the door, boy,' said his father.

'You're that cold!' cried his mother. 'Come over and sit by the fire.'

The stout brisk woman from the next croft, Madge, chafed his hands till the bones ached.

A fisherman put a whisky glass to his mouth and bade him drink. A fine fire kindled in his stomach and comforted all his body. Two or three valley children came about him. They imitated this old one and that. They plucked mimicry and laughter from each other. William laughed too.

His mother carried round a board of cheese and oatcakes. His father followed with the huge crock of ale.

Billo who had been a sailor began to sing a ballad but forgot the words. They rallied him with mockery and encouragement. He tried again, twice, and faltered. At last they latched his mouth with a glass of whisky. There was much laughter.

The door opened. The laird's gardener came in. They saw that the night was thick with stars. The newcomer opened his whisky bottle . . .

One by one the children began to yawn and rub their eyes. Two of them curled up in a corner beside the uneasy dog and went to sleep.

In a lull of the conversation, William said, 'I met a strange woman on the hillside. She fell down. She's still out there. Maybe we should go out and bring her in.'

But William had such a low voice that only his mother and Madge heard him.

'I declare,' said his mother, 'that boy sees things that nobody else sees.'

'A bairn's imagination,' said Madge. 'They grow out of it.'

Then Tommy the joiner, after much pleading, put his fiddle to his chin and began to play. Pair by pair the young folk circled each other in the middle of the floor. The old man Anders stuck a red-hot poker in his mug till the ale hissed and steamed; as if he didn't have enough of a flame in his face already.

Round and round the dance went. William drowsed with his head on Madge's great stony knee.

Near midnight the door was thrown open. The newcomer was so coated in snow they did not recognise him until he had wiped the grey mask off his face. The music stopped. The dance faltered and stilled. It was Mr Spence, the general merchant from the north side of the island, five miles away. 'A good Yule to you all,' he said gravely.

'You're welcome,' said William's mother. 'We didn't expect a visitor from so far away on such a night.'

'I came to say, a ship struck on the reef of Hellyan in the snow storm this afternoon, just before sunset. The shore's covered with bodies. They've all been taken into the kirk hall. Tommy Wilson, I came specially to see you, about coffins. Thirty-two bodies so far. The minister and the schoolmaster think she might have been an emigrant ship, out of the Baltic bound for America. There were a dozen women, most of them young. There were half a dozen bairns, God help them.'

William's father poured out a large dram for the news-bearer. Some of the whisky splashed onto the table.

There would be no more music or dancing that night . . .

There was silence. Then a small pure voice repeated his story of the young foreign woman on the hill. 'She's still there,' said William Ness. 'She fell and wouldn't get up again.'

His father raged at him, 'Why didn't you tell us this?'
William hid his face in Madge's skirts.

Three young men were putting on their coats and caps. A
lantern was brought from the cupboard and lit.

'Thirty-three coffins,' said Tommy. 'I'll have to send to
Hamnavoe for wood.'

'There'll be wood in plenty from the ship,' said the factor.
'Staves and planks everywhere. They'll take their ship with
them under the earth.'

'She fell beside the spring,' whispered William.

The searchers, going out, paused. 'Beside the spring . . .'
There had been so much snow all night that if a woman were
lying near the spring she would have the whole hillside for
her shroud. They knew every contour; they must look for a
long low hump.

The pure sweet voice of the boy spoke again. 'The sheep-
fold,' William said. 'Look there, too. The woman kept pointing at the sheepfold.'

An hour later, two of the searchers brought in the body of
the young woman and laid it in the barn.

The third man returned half an hour later, carrying a child.
It was still alive. The peat basket was emptied of peats, and
blankets were laid in it and the child was set in a nest of
blankets.

A spoonful of watered whisky was tilted into the infant's
mouth. The child opened its eyes and cried once – a sound
new but older than all languages – then it drifted into sleep
beside the hearth.

What should be done with it?

'There's bairns in every croft in this valley, but mine,' said
Madge. 'I'll take it, if nobody else wants it. I'll have the blessing of a bairn without the burden of a man.'

Nobody disputed the fostering.

Well after midnight Madge Selquoy carried the ship-wrecked child to her croft across a field deep and blue-black under snow.

It looked like being a good harvest in the valley, nurtured all summer with bounteous sun and a sufficiency of rain.

A generation had passed since the shipwreck. A slow wave of time had gone over the valley, taking away some old ones (and also, as sometimes happens, a few young fishermen were scattered and lost in a quick wave of the sea). But always there was a stirring of children in this croft or that: the rise and fall of generations.

Particularly in the croft of Strom down at the shore there was rarely silence while the sun was up. The solid rooftree was shaken morning to night with cajolery, laughter, hector-ing, rage, songs. The woman of the house, Dancey, had been ten years married to Andrew Crag who had the fishing boat *Hopeful*. They also had a few acres where they kept two cows and grew potatoes and cabbages and oats, and they had a score of sheep on the hill. But most of what nourished Andrew and Dancey Crag and their six children came out of the sea.

And Dancey would help push the boat *Hopeful*, loaded with creels or lines, into the sea in the morning, up to her thighs in the cold water. And then again, in the afternoon or early evening Dancey was there when *Hopeful* returned, sometimes heavy with fish, sometimes with only a thin scat-tering along the bottom boards.

'What are you thinking about?' she would say tartly to Andrew whenever there was a poor catch. 'How am I going to feed your bairns on a few trashy haddocks like this?'

Andrew would remark mildly that he had no control over the vagrancies of fish. 'I do my best but I can't compel them.'

Plenitude or scarcity, Dancey would take the basket of fish on her back and hump it up to Strom, where several mewling cats waited for her, and gulls flashed above waiting for the gutting to begin.

Inside, the youngest child might be wailing from its crib, and two little ones playing with water or wild flowers on the doorstep; the three eldest were safely folded in the school. Many a morning, that fine summer, while Dancey made butter or stoked the hearth for the baking of bannocks, she could hear the murmurs of multiplication, poetry, geography, drifting from the small school above.

'A few poor things of mackerel,' she said to Andrew one day. 'Go up to the hill, see if the sheep are all right. I think you might be better with sheep than fish. If the weather holds, there might be a good harvest. There'd better be.'

Then she turned and gave the five-year-old boy Joe a ringing slap on the side of his head for putting his fingers in the butter. And Joe yelled as if the sky had fallen down on him. And Andrew went away up to the hill to see to the sheep.

Even in that exceptionally fine summer, there were a few anxious days in the valley when the eight fishing boats were out; after a golden morning the wind got up and the outer sea roughened like sackcloth, and the waves came crashing in over the shore stones, peal after peal.

Then there were the anxious women standing here and there on the sea-banks, alone or in small groups, shading their eyes westwards, dumbly willing their men to come back, even if they hadn't a fish to show for the venture and hazard.

Dancey was never among those watchers. 'Fools!' she said. 'The fires'll be out when their men come in cold. What can they do about it? The sea will work as it wants to.'

And the boats came in from the claws of the storm, one after the other. As they passed the croft of Strom, going on home, the women would look askance at the door. What kind of a woman was she, who seemingly had no care or keeping of her man, and was so completely acquiescent in the will of the sea, whether it was benign or murderous?

Then when Andrew came up, tired and soaked with salt, she would make room for him beside the hearth, and break the peat into yellow flames, and say, 'How many fish did you catch? Half a basket – it could be worse. You fool, could you not have seen the storm coming?' . . . Then she would heat ale in a pot, and add sugar. While he drank, the bitter incense of sea rose up slowly from his trousers and jersey and boots.

And Dancey, up to her elbows in oatmeal, bent and kissed little Willa who had nipped a finger in the jamb of the door.

In one or two of the crofts, a woman would be saying to her fisherman that she was similarly warming with hot ale and peat flames, 'What do you expect? She isn't one of us. A foreigner from God knows where. None of us will ever be able to understand her. Hard on her man and on her bairns. But she does keep them well fed and well clad, that's true . . .'

A generation, a slow ponderous wave of time, had gone over the island and the valley since the winter of the shipwreck, and it had taken away many of the older folk, including the old people of Eard, into whose end-of-Yule celebration the child of the sea had been carried with a small flicker of life in it.

Up at Eard lived William Ness, a bachelor, who farmed his few acres and had little to do with the other folk of the valley. He lived by himself, a careful secretive man. Not even a tinker was suffered over his threshold; only the missionary, and the laird's factor when he came for the twice-yearly rent. Children were sent away gruffly. Young women, going up that way with buckets to the spring, had to go through the deep heather behind the house.

William Ness looked after his few beasts and acres tolerably well. But he never went out fishing. After his father died, the boat *Swift* lay on the noust and began slowly to warp. Now she was a poor shrivelled husk beside the eight well-kept fish-seekers of the shore.

On a Sunday he would put on his dark suit and take his Bible and go to the kirk five miles away. But always alone, never one of the little groups of worshippers here and there on the road. Remote and stern, he listened to the sermon. During the prayers, he drooped his head a little. He did not open his mouth during the hymns and psalms. He would place one penny gravely in the collection plate, going in.

A strange lonely man. Yet the valley people accepted him, as the valley had accepted all kinds of people for hundreds of years since the first ox had dragged a plough through the heather. Nature in individual men and women was as unpredictable as the sea.

And the wave of time had carried away Madge Selquoy, the foster mother to the shipwrecked child, but not before the child had been reared and nurtured and instructed in all the ways needful for an island girl to know.

There had been a few initial difficulties. What name was Madge to call the child? The child was about a year old; she must have a name, but there was no means of knowing what name she had been given. The ship was so broken up that only her port of registration, Danzig, was found carved on a timber. Danzig the child was called too, when the minister came to christen her. And there was another complication, for nobody could tell whether the bairn from the sea was Catholic, Lutheran, Orthodox or Jewish. Drops of water were sprinkled on its head, and Mary Danzig cried a little, then slept.

'And mercy me,' said old Philip of Graybigging, 'once the bairn comes to the age of speaking, what way will we know what she's saying, and her with a foreign tongue in her head?'

But when Dancey was two years old or thereby – her birth-day would forever be a mystery too – she spoke the slow lilt-ing cadences of the other valley children, a language touched with a slight melancholy: Scots-English words thrown upon a loom of ancient Norn.

And Dancey mingled freely with the children of the valley, and all went well in their work and play. But always this aura of mystery clung to her.

An upsurge of time brought together the girl Dancey and Andrew Crag, the crofter-fisherman, whose father had fallen from the crag to his death going after gull eggs five years since, and whose mother was 'wearing away' in the deep chair beside the hearth fire. The old woman put bitter looks on Dancey when Andrew first brought her to Strom, in the way of courtship. She had been kind to Dancey when Dancey was a child and a young girl. But to have another woman sharing her little kingdom! It was a hurtful thing. 'That foreign slut!' she would mumble, but loud enough for the girl to hear. Once the old woman opened her eyes and there was Andrew kissing the girl goodnight in the open door, with a star out beyond them, cold and brilliant. 'Andrew Crag!' she said harshly, 'this was a decent house always. It is my house – Strom belongs to me. You leave here this very night. Go. Go and live with that creature, whoever she is . . .'

But in the morning she had no memory of what she had seen or said. She knew that her thread was fraying. She would not take to her bed – bed was the next stage to coffin and grave. She ruled the little house of Strom, grim and feeble, from her chair beside the fire.

'I can't go to the fishing and leave her,' said Andrew. 'What am I to do?'

Dancey rolled up her sleeves and came down and milked the cow of Strom and fed the few hens. Whenever she entered the house the old one muttered darkly. She would shake her fist, but feebly, for the strength was out of it.

'You'd feel better after a wash,' said Dancey.

'I'm cleaner than ever you were in your life,' said the old woman.

'I'll make a little porridge,' said Dancey. 'Then you'll feel stronger.'

'Don't touch anything in this house!' came the thin cracked voice. 'I'm not hungry. Don't put a finger on pot or plate.'

She drowsed. And when she woke, she did consent to sip a cup of warm milk. 'Thank you, Andrina,' she said. 'That's kind.' (Andrina was the name of her younger sister who had died of measles twenty years before.) Then she nodded off to sleep.

'I'll help you into bed,' said Dancey.

'I'm not ready for bed yet,' said Mrs Crag. 'I feel more comfortable in this chair.'

She drowsed, and woke in an hour. 'Where's Andrew?' she muttered. 'Where's that boy? Is he home from the school yet?'

'Andrew's out in the boat,' said Dancey. 'He'll be home at sunset.'

'He's taken money out of the chest where I was keeping it. The chest under the bed. A shilling now and half-a-sovereign again. The money I was keeping for my wedding . . .' And she wept: soft easy soundless tears, to think that her son should take her dowry, last precious thing, from her.

'Who are you?' she said to Dancey another day. 'It's kind of you to come. Yes, that's more comfortable, the way you've put the cushions. There was a woman here today – did you see her? – a tinker wife. She stole the china teapot from the sideboard, the one I got for my wedding from the missionary's wife.'

'The teapot's still there, mother,' said Dancey. 'Look!'

'Well, there was a woman here and she was trying to take something. She thought I was asleep. But I was watching her all the time.'

Dancey took the wet warm flannel to her face while she slept and dried her gently.

Mrs Crag woke when Andrew came in with a full basket of haddocks, lurching with it in a kind of slow heavy dance from door to corner. The thump of the basket on the stone floor wakened her.

'Oh Simon!' she cried. 'You never had a catch like that! Your tea's on the table. Come over to the fire and warm you first. Simon, I've built up a fine fire for you. Look!'

The golden hearth shadows were all over the interior of Strom. (Simon had been her husband's name.)

'Simon,' she said, 'I never knew we had a lass – a daughter. She's been with me all day.'

'You should be in your bed, getting a good rest,' said Andrew. 'You've never left that chair for ten days past.'

The old woman considered this for a while.

'So that's it,' she said darkly. 'Once I'm in bed I'm finished. I'm out in the ebb. You can send for Tom Stanger anytime, once you get me in bed. First bed, then coffin. Then everything's yours, the house and land and boat and the money under the bed. You're cruel. While I'm in this chair, there's nothing you can do, you jailbird!'

Exhausted by her spate of words, her head drooped again.

While she slept, Dancey heated broth for Andrew and he ate it with buttered oatcakes, and afterwards beef and tatties.

He kept glancing miserably over at the chair where his mother was ripening for death, so slowly and mysteriously.

That night Dancey did carry her over to her wooden box-bed. But when she woke at dawn she flared up, like a lamp in a draught. 'I'm not dead!' she shrilled. 'I'll live longer than any of you . . .'

And when Dancey carried her over to her chair beside the reinvigorated hearth, she said, 'I have a lot of things to do in this place before I go.'

Andrew cried a little. Dancey had never seen the glister on his cheeks before. He turned away from her, put on his seaboots and oilskin. Then he kissed his mother and went out quickly.

'Who was that man?' said the old one.

She even, that morning, took two or three spoons of thin porridge from Dancey's hand. 'That was right good,' she said. 'Did you make it? Well, I pay you well enough for anything you do. Why are you neglecting the fire? It's very cold.'

Dancey piled peat on the hearth until it could hold no more. Still the old one complained of the cold.

Outside, the first daffodils were beginning to open in the schoolhouse garden. A few new lambs cried thinly from this field and that.

'I was never so cold,' said old Mrs Crag.

Dancey put the thickest shawl about her shoulders, and broke another peat into the blaze. 'Now then,' she said, 'be good till I come back. I won't be long.'

She went out and across the fields quickly to see if her own ewes had given birth. Her hens came against her in a fierce hungry red wave. Two lambs stottered round their dam in the spring sun. The cow Sybil blew her bugle again and again, 'Milking time!'

Dancey took some honey in a cup back to Strom: honey, if she could sip it, might put some strength into Mrs Crag.

No, she didn't want honey, or anything. 'My mouth's frozen, I can't open it. I only remember one coldness like this, and that's the night they took the bodies out of the ship in the snow. I never saw coldness like that. There's a white shawl in the kist, put it on me. The dead woman in the barn of Hard! And then they brought the bairn in, out of the drifts. I was young then, not long married. I remember thinking, "Poor thing, you'd be better dead." There was life in it still. Whether it lived or died I don't know. I can't remember . . .'

She took a spoonful of brandy, though half of it ran down her whiskered chin.

'Where's that boy?' she whispered. 'What I'd like Andrew to do is, I'd like him to buy a shop in Hamnavoe with the money. He'd be happy then, and his bairns after him. This crofting and fishing's a poor life. In Hamnavoe, Andrew'll get a good respectable wife. Her hands would be clean always.'

When the sounds of the first ebb were all along the shore, the old woman said, 'I'm tired. I want to go to bed now.'

Before Dancey could get to her, she slumped sideways in her chair. She was dead when Dancey laid her out on the bed.

That evening Tom Stanger came with his tape measure and boards.

Word was sent to the gravedigger, the doctor, the registrar and the missionary.

In every croft curtains were drawn. In the rich spring light, the valley would be blind till after the funeral.

Before midsummer Andrew Crag and Mary Danzig Selquoy were married in the barn of Strom.

The wave of time went over the valley, and removed Shalder the beachcomber and the laird's shepherd and Tom Stanger the joiner-boatbuilder-undertaker. Somebody else had to make Tom's coffin.

And William Ness sat up at Eard, and worked his fields, unbeholden to anyone.

Sometimes the harvests were good enough, and sometimes they were poor, but mostly they were adequate, no more. The people drew most of their food from the sea.

And time broke upon the valley, a slow wave, and carried away the old and the fated, but brought new children, scattering them in this croft and that. In the croft of Strom, the cradle in the corner was rarely empty. After twelve years, from the furthest side of the valley could be heard the medley all weekend from inside Strom, laughter and lamentation and chastisement and encouragement.

Andrew Crag came home from the sea day after day and a wave of children broke about his knee.

'A poor catch that, on a fine fishing day! What ailed you, man? . . .' And the small boy Stephen, who was clinging too hard to his father's knee, was sent reeling away by a mild sweep from Dancey's open palm. The child in the cradle then would join its thin wail to the yells of Stephen. And the other children would laugh all about the shrill anguish.

'A fisherman needs patience,' said Andrew mildly. 'I'll tell you something else – that boat of mine won't last much longer. She's dangerous in a heavy sea. Tom would have patched her to serve for a year or two yet. What way can I buy a new boat? . . .'

Dancey set a bowl of broth before him on the bare scrubbed table.

'It'll be a fair to middling harvest,' she said. 'Nothing to speak about. It's a good thing I'm here, to see to it. Or we'd starve here at Strom.'

*

There came the summer of the golden harvest that was spoken about for a generation afterwards.

That year the elements of sun and rain and wind were so exquisitely measured and scattered upon the furrows that the little black-ploughed fields sown with barley and oats had shallow pools of green soon and then the sloping rectangles were all green, all crammed with murmurings and whisperings in the wayward wind of early summer, and jewelled after a shower; and at morning and evening the lark stood high above the ripening stalks, and the blue hemisphere rang with the rapture of its singing.

The valley folk waited anxiously; many a year such promise had been ruined by a week-long deluge of August rain. And if an easterly wind came with the rain, a whole summer of work could be all but ruined.

The weather kept faith with the crofters. The corn changed overnight, from green to bronze, not uniformly, but croft by croft would receive the blessing. Then, after the pledge and seal of the sun, it was time to put the scythes in.

It did not take the cockerel to wake them, those late summer mornings.

The crofters did not wait for their own ripening time. Whenever a field took the burnish, there they all went with their scythes, and before dark the last stook was set up.

There were a few grumbles here and again. 'That's not fair! It should be our field for cutting in the morning, not theirs!' (Mostly it was the women who complained.)

The men would sit down under a stook, smoking their pipes, and discuss the rotation mildly. The women would pour ale out of the great stone jar – and usually before they dispersed it had been agreed whose field was next for cutting.

Always they cocked their heads, hearkening for a smell or taste of rain on the wind. A few of the older men and women

knew days before whether it would rain, and they always
took into their calculation the airt of the wind and the phase
of the moon. Even the sun held portents; too clear and
intense a light portended prolonged rain, and very soon. The
best promise was a faint bloom of haar, or mist, along the
horizon at morning and evening.

Day after day of faintly diffused sunlight fell into the valley,
and flashed from the swinging scythes of the harvesters. The
swathes fell before them. The women followed after, gathering and binding. The children ran among the stooks, chasing
rabbits and birds. There was no school till harvest was over.

There among the harvesters laboured the squat strong
figure of Dancey. Only she did not stoop and gather like the
other women; she swung a scythe with the men. With keen
crisp susurrations the line of scythes went through the dense
coroneted barley.

Old Billo Spence the ex-sailor licked his finger and held it up
to the wind. His nostril flared. 'No rain for the next few days,' said
he ... The harvesters let Billo go home early, for he was crippled
with rheumatics and couldn't keep up with the other men.

A child from the croft of Svert wailed suddenly! A bee had
stung him.

All the crofters worked together, in this field and that,
except William Ness of Eard. William Ness had never been
beholden to anybody. William Ness cut his own harvest. Let
them keep to their own fields. Let the women especially keep
away from his acres, with their gossip and inquisitiveness.

Sometimes the harvesters would cast an eye up at Eard.
The oatfield there was ripe for cutting all right – in fact one
corner had been cut – but there was no sign of the solitary
harvester. He must be all right, as far as anything could be
right with the creature, for his door was standing open. But
his cow in the field above was raising a great outcry.

The day dawned clear and fresh for cutting the two fields of Strom. The harvesters arrived, singly and in groups. Dancey had porridge and boiled eggs and bannocks on the table for them, 'to give them strength' . . . Andrew she sent to the fishing – 'he would be nothing but a hindrance'. She swung her scythe for an hour or two, but she had to break off every now and again to go inside and get more food ready for the harvesters, and replenish the ale jar, and see to the infant in the cradle. The valley children had never had a day like it, leaping back from the flash and onset of the scythes, hurling themselves on the threefold stooks, chasing the rabbits that leaped and danced from their diminishing domain.

Once or twice Dancey, coming out with the cheese and oatcakes and ale jar, cast her eye up at the croft of Eard and its bellowing cow.

'There's something wrong there,' she said.

The harvesters shrugged their shoulders. He had never needed them. Let him see still to his own affairs.

Andrew Crag came up from the shore with a full basket of crabs. The children were too steeped in bronze and ripeness that afternoon to pay much attention to him. 'I think it'll come to rain,' said Andrew. 'But not for a day or two.' He held out a mug to be filled with ale. 'Get inside,' cried Dancey.

By sunset the two fields were cut. The harvesters trooped home on half a dozen different paths.

Dancey put on her coat and took the steepest path up the hill.

'Get out,' yelled William Ness from the floor. 'Nobody asked you to come here.'

He was lying on a rag mat near the dead hearth, with his right leg splayed at a wrong angle.

'Get out,' he shouted. 'I fell, that's all. I tripped on a stone out there in the field and came down. I'll get up again when I'm ready.'

'Your leg's broken,' said Dancey. 'You need the doctor.'

'I want no doctor,' said William Ness. 'The leg'll mend. I can't afford doctors.'

'I don't care about you,' said Dancey. 'You can die for all I care. That poor cow of yours, Queenie, she needs milking. Listen to her. She's in agony.'

'Milk her,' said William. 'Then go.'

'And your hens are starving,' said Dancey. 'Where do you keep your oats?'

When Dancey had milked the cow and fed the hens, she came back and rekindled the dead fire.

'How long have you been lying here?' she asked.

'A day and a night,' said the man. 'I had just begun to cut the oats when I fell over that stone. Leave the fire alone.'

Dancey plied the bellows and the fire was all roaring yellow and red rags.

'I've just told Jacob Voe,' she said. 'Jacob's gone over the hill to get the doctor.'

'This house is private property,' said the man. 'You're trespassing. The laird will hear about this.'

'You must be hungry,' said Dancey. 'Let's see what you have in your cupboard.'

'You slut,' he muttered.

'O Lord, what misery!' cried Dancey from the open cupboard. 'A few bits of salt fish. A few tatties. Some mouldy oatmeal. I knew you were mean, but I little thought it was as miserable as this. I'll go home and get some hot broth for you.'

'You'll go home and you'll never darken this door again!' cried the man on the floor.

'I'll boil an egg or two in the meantime,' said Dancey. 'I'd better be here when the doctor comes.'

She boiled three eggs and shelled them and emptied them into a bowl, after blowing the peat dust out of it. Then she set the bowl of salted eggs down beside William Ness, with a horn spoon in it. 'Eat,' she said.

He wouldn't touch the spoon. He wouldn't even look at it.

'House-breaking,' he said. 'This is a serious business. A matter for the police.'

'I'm not going to force it down your throat,' said Dancey. 'If you want to die of starvation, you can. You've had plenty of practice.'

She found a broom behind the door and set about sweeping the floor all round the stricken man. 'We can't let the doctor see a hovel like this. I expect he's seen many a poor place in his time, but never a pigsty like this . . .' Sometimes she swept a spider's web with the broom from the rafters, or a hanging curtain of smoky filth from above the hearth.

'The doctor might be able to save your leg – it's hard to say,' said Dancey. 'The eggs are cold. But eat them. You'll need all your strength.'

The man closed his eyes, as if he were sleeping. But from time to time he moaned a little.

'Sore, is it?' said Dancey. 'Just wait till Dr McCrae begins to put you together again.'

It was time to light the lamp. Dancey 'tut-tutted' while she scoured the greasy lampglass with her apron, and trimmed the wick, and shook the bowl to see how much oil there was in it. 'I don't suppose it's been lit since last winter,' she said. 'And then only for a few minutes till you read your chapter and got into bed.'

They heard the clip-clop of hooves, the rattle of wheels, from the throat of the valley a mile away.

When Dr McCrae arrived, the inside of Eard was softly irradiated.

They heaved William Ness, moaning, on to his bed. 'A good thing you found him when you did,' said Dr McCrae. 'Another night and he'd have been a gonner. Now, man, this is going to hurt you. Dancey, would you put on some water to boil? Your oat field? – it's your leg I'm worried about, man, not your oat field. You'll be lucky if you can hobble as far as the door this side of Hallowe'en. Dancey, if you open my bag you'll find a big blue bottle with tablets in it. Yes, take it over . . .'

Next morning, Dancey left the neighbour woman Angela in charge of the children of Strom. She took a can of hot broth across the burn and up the side of the hill to Eard. She pushed open the door.

'Here's some soup, man,' said Dancey. 'If I can find a bowl that's passing clean. Broth like this'll have you on your feet in no time. Tell me if you want more salt in it. Here.'

William Ness let on not to be aware of her existence. He lay in the box-bed with his eyes lightly closed. He could have been dead but for the faint flutter at his lips and the pulse in his temple.

'I'll set it on the chair then,' said Dancey. 'When you're hungry, you'll eat. I'm not going to coax you.'

The man on the bed said nothing.

'Every cornfield's cut except yours,' said Dancey. 'It's a poor thin crop, like the man that sowed it. But it's a pity to let it lie waste. The rain's coming, Andrew says.'

She took the scythe out of the barn and whetted it on a stone and set about cutting the oat-field of Eard. By mid-afternoon it was all finished – the field cut and the stooks set up. She had done it alone. It was a very small field.

When Dancey went into the house to tell William Ness that his harvest was cut, he was still lying there with his eyes closed. The bowl of broth lay cold on the chair next to the bed, with the horn spoon lying in it.

'I suppose better men have died of starvation,' said Dancey. 'Anyway, your field's cut.'

Before she went home, she took in a bucket of water from the spring. 'Tomorrow, I'll tidy you up,' she said. 'The doctor and the missionary'll be coming to see you. I'll leave the broth. Even if it's cold it's nourishing enough.'

As Dancey went in at the door of Strom, she heard the clip-clop of the doctor's gig coming on the road between the hills.

Down at the shore, Andrew was setting his basket of fish on a flat rock. The sun took silver flashings from them.

William Ness lay as quiet as a corpse, but for the flutter of a nostril, while Dancey poured water from bucket into basin, and unwrapped a piece of green soap from a flannel. 'I ought to heat the water,' she said. 'But the cold water might put a spark of life in you.'

When she wet the flannel and soaped it to wash his face, he swung at her with his fist. The blow caught Dancey off balance and she reeled against the bedpost. 'Ah!' said Dancey, 'that's what I like to see. You're mending. You're getting your strength back.'

She wound one fist through his grey-black hair and held his head down on the pillow, and with the other hand she washed his face thoroughly. Once he tried to bite her – she took the cold flannel and whipped it across his mouth. 'You've got ten good years of life in you yet,' said Dancey, 'with all that strength.' Her flannelled finger went into his ear-whorls and nose-flanges. Then she took the towel to him and rubbed so hard that he let out a soft moan. 'I've brought a comb too,' said Dancey.

He made no resistance while she combed his beard and his hair. 'You'd be a bonny enough man,' she said, 'if only you kept yourself clean and tidy. What you need is a wife. I don't suppose any lass in this island would have you. But if you were to put an advertisement in the *Orkney Herald . . .'*

When she saw tears oozing out of his closed eyes, and glittering in his eye-pouches, Dancey said she'd go out and milk his cow. 'I think what you need is a mug of warm milk and a couple of eggs.'

He would not eat or drink, still. She left the milk and the new-boiled eggs and the oatcakes on the chair beside the bed, growing cold. 'The bairns'll be home for their dinner. I'll be back in the afternoon.'

He had bitten his lower lip so fiercely that a bead of blood stood there.

When Dancey returned in the late afternoon, William Ness was asleep. He hadn't touched the milk or the food. The pure breath of sleep came from his mouth, soft and rhythmic – he looked like a boy lost in the wonderment of falling snow. Dancey kissed him on the forehead. Then softly she left the house. She milked Queenie the cow in the upper field; then she went home.

When she returned in the morning, he was awake. The mug and the plate were empty.

'Well done!' cried Dancey. 'You'll get a fresh haddock for your tea. I should change your bed today. Are there blankets in that kist?'

'I don't want your charity,' said William. 'I'll pay you for the work you've done. There's a black box at the foot of the cupboard, far back. Be good enough to bring it here to me. The key is behind that loose stone in the wall – yes, that one. Bring it, too.'

He unlocked the little black lacquered box and inside, in separate compartments, were gold coins and banknotes. The sovereigns spilled from his fingers back into the box, golden music. The notes looked like discarded mummy wrappings and had an ancient smell.

'How much do I owe you for your services, up to now?' said William Ness.

Dancey laughed. 'Lock it all away,' she said. 'You'll need it all to pay the undertaker and the gravedigger, and for the funeral whisky.'

Treasure-box and key were restored to their separate secret places.

'You're a very strange woman,' said William Ness.

The cow Queenie lowed from the field above.

When Dancey returned with the pail of milk, he said, 'My leg is not so painful today.'

He drank the warm milk so eagerly that his whiskers were festooned with white droplets.

As Dancey was leaving, he said in a low voice, 'I think I would like a piece of haddock with butter about it, and a bannock.'

Dancey met the missionary on the sheep path. 'He's getting stronger every day,' she said. 'He'll be very pleased to see you for a change.'

Before the month was out, William Ness was on his feet again; though he hirpled on a stick for the rest of the winter.

One morning Dancey said, 'You can do for yourself now, can't you? You can milk Queenie and light your fire? And take in peats and water from the spring? Then I'll be off.'

'Thank you, woman,' he said.

Dancey never crossed the threshold of Eard again.

It was plain to be seen by all in the course of the next winter that the croft reverted slowly to its former state of filth and neglect. The little windows lost the glitterings Dancey had put on them. But on a Sunday morning William Ness emerged from that withered door in his black suit with his Bible under his arm, and set out slowly on his staff to the kirk five miles away.

The accident had not put one drop of honey into his nature. He did his slow business – if he had to – with the other valley folk curtly and ungraciously. If a child wandered near his door, he would swipe at it with his stick and utter some wild meaningless syllable. On winter nights the valley boys threw stones against his door. One night of snow a stone went through his window. Two days later the policeman from Hamnavoe arrived in the valley and sharply interrogated the pupils in the school. A policeman come for them! They were grey as cinders in the face at the thought of chains and dungeons.

The boy who had broken the window was never discovered.

And Dancey: for William Ness it was, between him and her, what it had always been, as if the affair of the broken leg had never happened. If they chanced to meet, on the peat road or along the shore, he would look through her as if she was made of glass.

Dancey always had a few words for him. 'It's time you were getting a new cow, man. Queenie is done . . .' 'Have you put that advertisement in the paper yet for a bride? . . .' 'Watch yourself in this snow – it's very slippery up at the spring . . .'

Never an answer. He had ears of stone, going past her with the limp he always had now since he broke his leg.

As Dancey had predicted, William Ness lived for ten more years. Then, when no smoke was seen from his chimney for three mornings in April, the shepherd from the big house found him slumped in his chair, with a cold smile on his face, and a spider spinning a web between his dropped hand and the wall.

Only as many men as were required to carry the coffin attended the funeral. Andrew Crag was at the fishing that afternoon.

A month later the postman from the island post office five miles away walked down the valley with a letter for Andrew Crag, esquire, Strom. The address was typewritten, the flap of the envelope had a red embossed seal to it.

Andrew opened the letter with trembling fingers (a letter like this boded no good).

It was from the solicitor in Kirkwall. 'Dear Sir, I enclose a copy of the will of the late William Ness, of Eard. I should be glad if you could come to our office in Kirkwall as soon as possible, to sign the necessary forms and finalise the business. Yours faithfully . . .'

William Ness's will was short and simple. 'I leave all my worldly goods and assets to Andrew Crag of Strom in this island, to get him a new boat. Any man with a wife like he has got, with her clattering tongue and her interferences, deserves to be out of the house as often as he can, among the silences of the sea. His old boat *Hopeful* is the worse for wear. Let Andrew Crag order a new boat from the yard in Hamnavoe. Whatever monies are left over to be equally divided among his children, the poor man . . .'

Shell Story

The seagulls came to the island pier.

The old wives came out with bowls, with crusts and bits of fat in them.

They threw the scraps to the gulls.

While the food still hung in the blue air, the gulls gobbled every fragment up.

'That's Tommy Ritch, that gull, that's my Tommy,' said one old woman, pointing to a gull that was stretching his wings on the pier. 'Tommy got his death off Yesnaby thirty-one years ago come June.'

'Here you come again, Willie Anderson,' said another old wife. 'Look at him gobbling up that hen giblet. He was always hungry when he came in from the sea. My neighbour Willie, he was lost on the trawler *Nevis*, a long while ago.'

'I think that gull is my brother Drew,' said one old woman. 'But I was only two when his ship went down off Iceland. So I don't remember him. I can't tell if it is Drew or not.'

So the old wives spoke to the gulls after every dinnertime, calling them by the names of drowned fishermen and sailors that were kin or acquaintances.

One old wife, Charlotte, looked every afternoon into the gull-shrieking, gull-beating air over the village and every afternoon she shook her head. She could never see her man Jock Wylie in the white screaming gull-drift. Jock Wylie had gone down in unknown seas, the winter after they were married . . . Still Charlotte threw bits of bannock and bits of bacon to the gulls . . . And Charlotte was getting on for a hundred years old.

Still the village wives kept up their singsong.

'Here's a piece of bread for you, Bertie Ness . . .'

'You like chicken wings, don't you, Ally Flett? Take it . . .'

'I swear, Jerry Thomson, you're a greedier gull than you were a ferryman . . .'

'I bet you'd sooner have beer than this end of bacon, Dickie Folster . . .'

Old Charlotte threw her scraps to the gulls and viewed every one from her shaded eyes, and shook her head and went home.

One day there was such a storm that even the gulls kept to their crag ledges in the Black Craig.

Oh, it was a howling gale out of the east!

The fishermen and their wives and children stayed inside, behind their rattling doors.

They saw through their salt-crusted windows a woman struggling down to the pier. They thought every moment she would be blown into the white-crested waves. And, 'It's Charlotte!' they cried in croft after croft.

Then the village folk saw that a solitary bird had fallen and furled on the very edge of the stone pier.

Old Charlotte took a piece of fine cake that she had kept from the last island wedding, full of fruit and nuts, fine flour and rum, and she put it into the seabird's beak. It seemed to be a bigger bird than the usual gull.

The bird ate the bridecake, and it flew three times round Charlotte's head, and then it swung away out to the open sea.

And the wind blew salt spray over the roofs.

The old woman knocked at every door along the village street.

When the man of the house tugged the door open – so fierce the gale blew – Charlotte said in a young sweet voice, 'Jock my man, he's come back to see me at last from the wastes of ocean.'